Dedicated to those who experience homelessness.
May they be lucky enough to find friends like
the Old Maids.

NO PLACE LIKE HOME FOR MURDER

Sixth Book in the Old Maids of Mercer Island series

By Lynn Bohart

Cover Art: Dijartsy

Published by Little Dog Communications

Disclaimer: This book is a work of fiction and while some of the businesses, locations, organizations, or historical references in the book may be real, others have been created to fit the storyline. I admit I take a fair amount of liberty, while still attempting to capture the grandeur of the Pacific Northwest and other locations.

CHAPTER ONE

Fall is the perfect time for a murder. Especially in the Northwest when you're snuggled into your recliner with a hot cup of tea, holding a good British mystery novel, while the temperature outside has dropped into the low forties. That's exactly where I was on a Monday night in early November.

Since I'd lost my black and tan miniature dachshund Mickey to a grand mal seizure a few weeks earlier, I had his best friend and partner in crime, Minnie, tucked in next to me, her warm little body giving me comfort. It was almost midnight, and I was due to be in the Inn's kitchen at 7:00 the next morning to help my partner April make breakfast for our guests. And yet, I was happily nose-deep in a book I'd found at a used bookstore.

A brisk wind rattled the leaves of the big oak tree outside my window, scraping branches along the building. I shivered and settled more deeply into the fluffy robe I had wrapped around me. When the grandfather clock in the Inn's foyer finally chimed twelve, and the echoes of its rich bells rolled across the old Victorian building I called home, I thought it was the perfect backdrop to follow DI Maple into the bowels of a centuries-old church as she chased a diabolical killer.

My left hand rested on the soft, red fur of Minnie's head as the young female detective opened a creaking door and eased her way into the chapel. She'd lost her torch in the chase, so her only light was from the moon as it filtered through a broken stained-glass window, leaving fractured splashes of color on the dirty, cobblestone floor at her feet.

What a great description.

My imagination filled in the images of a crumbling Victorian stone church with its tall steeple and belfry as I reached for my tea. When DI Maple heard a soft footfall from somewhere behind her, my pulse quickened.

Just what the author wanted.

I took a sip of tea just as the young detective whipped around and tripped over a dead body, face-planting onto the dusty floor between two sanctuary pews. I almost spit out a mouthful of hot liquid as a chuckle erupted from my throat.

Probably not what the author wanted.

But since I had a habit of doing exactly the same thing at the most inopportune moments, I felt a sense of camaraderie with young DI Maple. I used a napkin to wipe my mouth and delved back into the story, my nose practically twitching at the dust motes floating in the air of that ancient church.

My cell phone rang, making me groan with irritation. I pulled my phone off the table next to me, wondering who would be calling so late. A glance at the screen told me it was my close friend and book club member Rudy Smith.

I swiped on the phone and said, "Rudy, can I call you back? I'm right in the middle of—"

"There's a dead woman on my floor!"

"I'm sorry… what?"

I had a momentary brain fart as I wondered how Rudy knew there was a dead woman on the floor of that little chapel in Britan. And then I realized she was talking about something completely different. I dropped the leg rest of my chair and sat up, pushing poor Minnie unceremoniously onto the floor.

"Rudy, what are you talking about?"

"I had a friend over for dinner, and now she's dead. I don't know what to do. There's blood everywhere," she said in a rush.

"Slow down and tell me exactly what happened."

"I don't know. I… I'm so confused," she said, taking deep, erratic breaths. "Someone knocked me out, and I woke up on the floor of my kitchen next to her. There's so much blood, and… my God, I don't know what happened. What's happening, Julia? What do I do?"

I still struggled to separate the murder mystery I held in my hand from, well, the actual murder Rudy was hyperventilating about.

"Did you call the police?"

"Of course, I did. But now what do I do?" she asked, her voice rising. "What do I say? I mean, there's a dead woman in my kitchen!" she finally screeched.

She was a heartbeat away from becoming hysterical, an emotion anathema to Rudy, so I attempted to modulate my tone.

"Well, don't touch anything," I said firmly. "The police will want to dust for fingerprints."

"It's my kitchen, Julia!" she snapped. "I've touched every. Single. Thing. In sight. Multiple times! Don't you get it?"

And… there it was. She'd lost it.

"You know what I mean, Rudy," I said as calmly as I could. "Don't accidentally step in the blood or anything."

"This is me you're talking to, Julia. I wasn't the one who sent the president of the university sailing headfirst into a pond at Carter's memorial service last month. That was you!"

I thought that was rather harsh under the circumstances, but technically correct.

"Listen, Rudy, what I mean is that you need to calm down."

"Julia, I need help!" she said with a hitch in her voice. "How did this happen?"

She was about to cry. When distant sirens in the background reminded me she'd called the police, I realized Rudy's life was about to spin out of control.

"Look. Sit tight. I'll be there as quickly as I can."

"Just meet me at the police station," she wheezed like a deflating balloon. "I'm sure I'll be in handcuffs by the time you get here."

"Why?"

"Because it's my favorite steak knife sticking out of her neck."

Although my nickname for Rudy was The Boss because she was always in control and, well, bossy, whatever had just happened had unhinged her. I'd never heard her like that. And that's despite the number of close calls our group of friends has experienced during several murder investigations over the last year and a half. Even in the most extreme circumstances, Rudy had always been the steadfast one.

I quickly got dressed, donned my warm coat, and drove up the hill to her home. She lived in a cul de sac on a crest overlooking Lake Washington and the glittering lights of Seattle across the water. Although not wealthy, Rudy lived comfortably in the house she'd retained from her divorce and the retirement she'd earned as a top-notch investigative journalist for the Seattle Times.

By the time I got there, it was approaching one o'clock in the morning and the temperature had dipped to a crisp 42 degrees, with the wind causing the tall pines surrounding her home to sway back and forth like drunken sailors. Rudy's driveway was blocked by a carousel of flashing red and blue lights from two police cars and an ambulance. I climbed out of the snug interior of my Pathfinder, cursing myself for not wearing gloves, and approached the driveway, pulling my coat tightly around me. There were no guards posted and no police tape to prevent me from gaining access to the front yard. If I were lucky, I could perhaps sneak past all the commotion and get inside the house before anyone stopped me.

I ducked down and scooted past the emergency vehicles on the far side of the driveway, heading for the front porch. Circling around a police cruiser, I took the cement walkway between the house and the garage and had almost made it to the front porch, when I stepped off the path and into a flower bed. I lost my footing and crashed through Rudy's azalea bushes, face-planting in the dirt.

Sound familiar?

I jumped to my feet and dusted myself off, grinding my teeth on dirt and leaves. After spitting those out, I was testing my ankle to make sure I hadn't sprained it when I felt a presence behind me.

"I'm sorry ma'am, but this is a crime scene."

A young officer stood with his hand out, ready to extricate me from the bushes. Although I was dating David Franks, a Mercer Island police detective, he was probably home fast asleep. I'd met David when a close friend of mine had fallen dead in her peach cobbler at my dining room table. She'd been poisoned. To be clear, it wasn't the peach cobbler that killed her, and I didn't poison her. Someone else did that. But David had been one of the detectives assigned to the case, and we began to date not long after my friends and I helped bring the culprit to justice. Since then, we've been involved in four other murder cases. But David and I hadn't seen each other for almost a week because he'd been tied up investigating a string of home invasions on the island.

I decided to play that card, anyway.

"I'd like to speak to Detective Franks," I said, puffing up my chest with the kind of authority that belied the fact I'd just taken a header into Rudy's planter.

"He's not here. I'm sorry, but you'll have to wait at the street."

Just then a familiar black SUV pulled up next to the police cruiser, and the tall and athletic Detective Sean Abrams got out. His steely blue eyes glinted when he saw me standing in the flower bed, and not in a friendly way. He was dressed in tight jeans, cowboy boots, and a dark button-down shirt under a black leather jacket.

"You didn't roll out of bed looking like that," I sniped, stepping back onto the pavement, and wiping my hands together to rid them of dirt. "How's Angela?"

He and my daughter were dating, so I thought perhaps he'd just come from her place.

"Why am I not surprised that you would beat me to my own crime scene?" he asked. "You even beat the forensic team."

The forensic team had, in fact, just pulled in behind him.

"I'm here for moral support," I replied, raising my chin an inch to emphasize my point.

"We'll see about that. First, you might want to wipe the mud off your cheek, and then this officer will guide you out of the way." He nodded to the young officer.

Detective Abrams marched inside with two forensic technicians close on his heels. I was escorted to the other side of the driveway where I would have to cool my heels, which wasn't hard given the temperature. When a brisk breeze rustled the few remaining leaves on a big maple tree next to Rudy's garage, forcing chilly air to burrow beneath my collar, I silently wished I'd worn a scarf.

After cleaning off the aforementioned mud from my cheek, I decided this news was too big to wait until morning. I pulled out my phone to call Blair and Doe, the other two members of our book club. While I waited for Doe to pick up, the front door of a home across the street opened to reveal a beer-bellied man in a thin t-shirt and boxer shorts. A Yorkie bristled at his feet, yapping at all the commotion thirty yards away. Other neighbors had also assembled at the ends of their driveways, staring at the activity. Some had their cell phones out recording the comings and goings of the police officers.

I leaned against Detective Abrams' car as I waited, enjoying the heat from the engine as it seeped through my coat. Doe finally answered the call, complaining that I'd woken her up, and that she had to get up at 5:30 the next morning. On the other hand, when Blair answered, she was at one of the casinos where she and her husband had dined with a business acquaintance and were still gambling. In the end, they both agreed to meet later that day at the Inn to figure out how to help Rudy.

After twenty minutes or so, Detective Abrams emerged through the front door with his hand on Rudy's shoulder. She seemed tiny compared to his 6-foot plus frame and looked more like his little sister than a woman in her mid-sixties. She was wrapped in a long, wool sweater over jeans and a turtleneck, and there was clearly blood on her clothes and hands. I also saw blood on her chin. Another officer followed behind them carrying a small duffle bag. I presumed it was filled with a change of clothes, since I was sure they would take the ones she had on.

"You can't be arresting her!" I snapped, lifting off the car. "This is ridiculous. She couldn't hurt a fly."

Rudy turned woeful eyes in my direction.

"We're just taking her in for questioning," Detective Abrams said. "Officer, please move Mrs. Applegate out of the way—again."

The same young officer stepped in front of me, forcing me to back up. Detective Abrams opened the rear door of a police cruiser, while the other officer threw the duffle bag into the front seat and got in. As Detective Abrams steered Rudy into the back seat, she whipped her head around to me.

"Julia! Find Ginger!"

"What?"

"Find Ginger! Try the bridge encampment," she yelled as the door slammed shut.

A moment later, the police car backed out of Rudy's driveway carrying one of my best friends away in handcuffs, while a woman lay dead in her home.

Didn't see that one coming.

CHAPTER TWO

I own the St. Claire Inn, located on the east side of Mercer Island, a small body of land in the middle of Lake Washington. The island is connected to Seattle by one of the world's longest floating bridges. My husband Graham and I had bought the old Victorian home with its octagonal turret, dormer windows, and wraparound porch the same year he divorced me for a younger woman. He then went on to campaign for and become the governor of Washington State. I'd always thought he meant the inn as my consolation prize. *Men!*

Since we were always booked this time of year, I was busy the next morning helping April make a Southwestern frittata and biscuits for the guests. April wore her favorite apron with front pockets over a colorful, long-sleeved African dyed shirt and comfortable loose-fitting muslin pants, looking right out of the Taste of Home cooking magazine. While we worked, I filled her in on the events from the night before.

"So, Rudy is sitting in jail," she said, as she folded peppers and onions into the egg mixture.

"I hope not. They took her in for questioning, though. I waited up until 3 a.m. in case she called me, but I finally had to go to sleep." I stifled a yawn as if on cue. "Anyway, I called David first thing this morning, but he didn't know any more than I did."

April eyed me as she poured the egg mixture into a baking pan. "And the evidence so far is a dead woman on her floor and blood all over Rudy?"

"Don't forget Rudy's steak knife sticking out of the woman's neck."

"Oh, I haven't forgotten that little piece of information," she said, slipping the pan into the oven. "But there had to be other evidence. I mean, to take her in for questioning."

"Not necessarily. You watch all those crime shows, don't you? The police need to get her statement immediately, and the best place to do that is at the police station. Plus, I'm sure they took her clothes as evidence and swabbed her for DNA." I heaved a big sigh, while I flipped sausages on a large griddle. "I'm worried about her, April. She was frantic on the phone last night. I've never heard her like that. And then when Sean brought her outside, she... well, she looked defeated."

"Wouldn't you be?"

A scream from the other room stopped us with looks of surprise.

"It's those girls again," April said. "I swear, it's like having a pair of demons here. You know, they like to tease Ahab, don't you?"

Ahab was the African Gray parrot I had bought at an estate sale so that a young man dressed like Marilyn Manson wouldn't buy it and subject it to a life of heavy metal music. The bird came equipped with a variety of phrases and sound effects learned from a couple of years of background TV shows his owner had watched.

"I'll take care of it."

I pushed through our swinging door as the girls chased each other around Ahab's cage. According to their parents, they had been best friends since kindergarten. One had short brown hair and big brown eyes, while the other had long curly blond hair and a pug nose. Pug Nose seemed to be the instigator. At only ten years old, they had perhaps the brattiest personalities I'd ever come across. I sell antiques on the property, and they'd already broken one of my vintage table clocks. They'd also lost pieces from one of our games and stepped on Minnie's foot making her squeal when they barreled through the hallway. And they'd only been there one day. The moment they saw me staring at them, they slid to a halt, while Ahab bounced nervously around the cage clucking to himself.

"We weren't bothering him," Pug Nose said disingenuously.

"Pay no attention to the man behind the curtain," Ahab squawked in his tinny voice. "Just the facts ma'am. Gotta call the police!"

The girls giggled.

I crossed my arms and glared at them. "We don't put up with teasing or mistreating any of the animals here," I said sternly. "You should probably go back upstairs and wait for your parents. We'll have breakfast out shortly."

With downcast faces, they marched out of the breakfast room toward the staircase, passing a fall display of antiques and pumpkins I'd assembled to the side of the entryway. As they passed the reception desk, the door blew open, scattering a pile of fake autumn leaves across the floor at their feet. The girls turned to me with wide eyes.

"We didn't do that," Brown Eyes said.

When the door slammed shut, making them spin around, they whimpered and ran up the stairs.

The Inn was haunted, and I suspected that was Chloe acting as my backup. She was only ten when she died, along with her mother and brother, in a fire on the property decades earlier. Chloe often teased guests she didn't like or who tested her patience. I suspected these girls might be in for a wild ride over the next few days.

I quickly picked up the leaves and replaced them in my display, moving them further from the door. When I returned to the kitchen, I told April what had happened,

"Maybe Chloe can keep them reined in for us," she said with a smile.

"Or scare them to death. I vote for that," I said with a wicked laugh. "Okay, what else can I do?"

She turned from the stove. "I'm finishing up the biscuits, so why don't you get the yogurt and berries out?"

I went to our large refrigerator and brought out a large container of blueberries and a carton of yogurt. As I proceeded to rinse the berries, my mind returned to Rudy.

"I know it would be normal for anyone to feel scared and defeated if they found themselves in a situation like this, but this is Rudy. Self-assured, pit-bull, super competitive Rudy, who swung off a balcony a few months ago to save a self-serving state senator from certain death. It's just so hard to think of her cowed by, well, anything."

My cell phone rang. I didn't recognize the number and so swiped it on.

"Julia, it's Rudy." Her voice sounded flat.

"Are you home?"

"I'm at Elliott's. My house is still a crime scene. And they took my phone, so I'm using his. I just got here, and I'm exhausted."

Elliott was Rudy's ex, who had been making overtures about the two of them getting back together after he'd walked out years earlier because he had to 'find himself.'

"You mean you've been at the police station since last night?"

"Yeah. I did a lot of sitting around waiting, but the questioning was grueling."

"I've been thinking about you all morning. How can I help?"

I put the phone on speaker so April could listen in. She wiped her hands and moved over close to me.

"I'm too tired to tell you everything now. I need to rest and get my head on straight."

"I understand. Blair and Doe are coming over this afternoon. Any chance you could join us? Fill us in on what's happened then?"

"I can't promise. What I need right now is an attorney. A good one. I was too fuzzy-headed last night to ask for one. And to be honest, I thought that would make me look guilty. I realize now that none of this looks good. But I don't know any attorneys who could manage a homicide case. Could you call Angela and ask her for a recommendation?"

"I'll call her right away. But, Rudy, who was the woman who was murdered? And are you in any real jeopardy?"

"I'm afraid I am. And she's a woman I met at the shelter, along with Ginger, the woman I need you to find. I'm pretty sure Ginger was at my house last night."

"Listen, April is also here. Tell us as much as you can about what happened."

"I'll have to be quick. I seriously need to sleep and recoup." Rudy heaved a deep sigh. "You remember that I have always wanted a rock fountain in my backyard. Well, I met a woman at Wings of Hope, the homeless shelter where I volunteer. She used to do landscaping, so I paid her to put one in for me. Her name is—was, Romaine. God almighty, I can't believe she's dead." She choked out a sob.

"Just take your time," I said.

We waited while she composed herself.

"Anyway," she began again, "I invited Romaine over for dinner last night because she had just finished the fountain over the weekend. After dinner, while we were enjoying dessert, my doorbell rang. I opened the door to find a woman standing there in the dark. I couldn't see her well because my front porch light was out. I even flicked the switch on and off. Anyway, I think it was this woman named Ginger. Ginger has mental health problems and is still mostly homeless, so I asked her what she was doing there. As soon as I said her name, she backed up mumbling to herself. I stepped outside my door when my world went black."

"What do you mean?"

"Someone hit me from behind because I blacked out immediately. And my neck is sore as if someone karate chopped me. The police took a picture, but there wasn't a bruise, so I'm not sure they believe me. Anyway, I woke up on the floor of my kitchen sometime later, groggy, and with a very dead Romaine next to me."

"I'm so sorry, Rudy. Did you touch her or try to revive her? I saw blood on you," I said.

"Yes, but... I also have scratches on my face, Julia. I have no idea how they got there, but according to the police, Romaine had blood and skin under her fingernails. Plus, they found hair that looked like mine clutched in her fist." She released another heavy sigh. "They think we got into a fight, and I killed her."

A deep chill settled into my chest. "I know you didn't do this, but it sounds bad," I said quietly.

"Well, that's not all. They found the residue of something in Romaine's wine glass."

"Drugs?"

"Yeah. Look, I'm positive I'm not responsible for her death. And I don't know why, but someone is setting me up."

"Rudy, it's April. Do you have any idea why someone would kill this woman or want to set you up for her murder? It just seems so extreme."

"The only thing I can think of is that Romaine had asked me to do an investigative piece on homeless people disappearing off the streets of Seattle."

"Doesn't that happen all the time?" April asked. "I mean, they just move on?"

"Yes. But in this case, she knew of at least five people who have disappeared under suspicious circumstances. And she named a guy she suspected might be the culprit. Romaine went to the police about it, but since she didn't have any evidence they couldn't do anything. That's why she came to me. I thought about this all night as Detective Abrams was hammering me with questions. I think whoever did this wanted Romaine out of the way and then set me up to take the fall so I couldn't do the story."

"It just seems like such an over-the-top way to stop you from doing a story," April said.

"It would work if I'm arrested for her murder!" Rudy snapped.

"We're going to figure this out," I said, glancing at April.

"Okay, but we really need to find Ginger," Rudy said firmly.

"Won't she be on your security cameras?" April asked.

"I heard one of the officers say my security system had also been disconnected. My porch
light and my security system. Sounds suspicious, don't you think? Those are just two of the questions that still have to be answered. Anyway, Detective Abrams said they'll focus first on things like surveillance cameras in the neighborhood, taking statements from the neighbors, and forensics. Then, if Ginger, or whoever it was, shows up on the security cameras, they can try to find her."

"Well, those things are important," I said, feeling the need to defend our Mercer Island police.

"I agree. But right now the forensics point to me. So if it were Ginger at my door, she could be my only witness to what happened."

"She wouldn't be reliable, though, would she?" April asked cautiously. "I mean, with her mental illness."

"Maybe not. But if it was her, why was she there? And how did she get there? Someone had to bring her because she doesn't drive."

"What does she look like?" I asked.

"Middle aged. Petite. With bad teeth, and a sallow complexion. She has thick, frizzy gray hair and slouches. She hangs out at the homeless encampment under the bridge down by Aubrey David Park. But she moves around a lot. She goes over to Seattle because that's where most of the resources are for free dinners and the like. If you find her, you'll have to approach her carefully, though. She's harmless but gets spooked easily. I've worked with her a couple of times when she was on her medication, helping her do a resume to get jobs at fast food places, so mention my name."

"Does Ginger have a last name?" April asked.

"Spalding. Ginger Spalding." Rudy paused and sucked up a sob. "God... we need to find her quickly, Julia. If she disappears like the other people Romaine talked about, I'm sunk."

I finished helping April make breakfast, and together we got everything onto the sideboard in the breakfast room just as guests began arriving. Pug Nose and Brown Eyes rushed down the stairs ahead of their parents but slowed to a crawl when they saw me.

"Run, Toto, run!" Ahab squawked, bouncing around his cage again.

The girls meekly tucked themselves in line behind an older couple. Once I was done setting things out, I snuck into our small office tucked under the staircase behind the registration desk to call Angela.

My daughter serves as a Deputy Prosecuting Attorney in Seattle. Even though I'd been involved in a number of murder investigations, I wasn't all that familiar with how the legal system operated. The only person I'd ever bailed out of jail was my brother Ben after he was arrested for obstructing justice during our investigation into whoever killed our childhood friend, Carter. Truth be told, when David arrested Ben, I thought it was as much to give me a message as to punish Ben. And the message was to stay out of his investigations.

But this was different. This was Rudy, and while I was confident Rudy had played no role in killing anyone, getting her exonerated might be difficult.

"Mom, she needs a criminal attorney," Angela said, when I explained the situation.

"I know. That's why I'm calling. I'm sure she didn't do this, Angie, and she asked me to see if you had any recommendations. Do you know any good criminal attorneys?"

"Of course, I do. And I'll help in any way I can. But I also have to be careful; it will probably be my office that prosecutes her if she's arrested."

"That won't happen," I said with more confidence than I felt. "They only took her in for questioning."

"Don't be too sure. They'll go where the evidence leads them. Anyway, call Brenda Valentine. She's good. Tough like Rudy with a no-nonsense attitude. They should get along great."

"Thanks. So, you haven't talked with Sean about this?" I was afraid her boyfriend might have mentioned my accident in Rudy's planter.

"I didn't see him last night. He went out with an old college roommate. Listen, I'm due in court, but I'll text Brenda to let her know you'll be calling. Give me a couple of minutes."

I waited the required few minutes and then put in a call to the Valentine Law Firm. The receptionist put me on hold, but it was only a few seconds before a throaty voice with the hint of a Southern accent came on the line.

"Mrs. Applegate, so nice to meet you. I'm a fan of your husband's, even though he's a Republican."

"Ex-husband," I said. "And I wish our meeting was under different circumstances."

"Of course. Angela said you'd be calling. I also think very highly of your daughter. In fact, I've tried to recruit her, but she insists she prefers putting the bad guys in jail rather than figuring out how to free them."

She chuckled good-naturedly, but I was in a hurry.

"So, how does this work?"

"Well, the sooner I talk with Mrs. Smith, the better."

"The police took her phone, but she's staying with her ex-husband. I'll text you his number."

"Perfect. I'll clear my appointments. And Mrs. Applegate—"

"Please, call me Julia."

"Julia. I'm aware of your penchant for getting involved in murder investigations. You need to be careful. You don't want to gum this up for your friend. Do we understand each other?"

I swallowed, feeling like a small child who had just been admonished by the school principal. Fortunately, Brenda wasn't exacting a promise from me, which to be honest, I wasn't prepared to give. Instead, I just said, "Understood."

"Good. I'll look forward to hearing from Mrs. Smith."

CHAPTER THREE

At three o'clock, Blair Wentworth and Doe Kovinsky, the other two members of our book club, were nestled in my apartment as a chilly wind blew leaves and twigs around the main parking lot outside. Doe serves as the CEO of her deceased husband's waste management company and had to leave an important meeting to join us. She was dressed in her usual black pantsuit and had her mammoth leather bag slung over one shoulder when she arrived. It carried her laptop and God knows what else but was big enough to sink a ship. After our first murder case she had bought a gun, and I envisioned it might be tucked somewhere inside that bag.

Blair came straight from a hair appointment, also dressed in her signature outfit. This meant her shapely figure was squeezed into tight leggings and a form fitting, low-cut, V-neck sweater, complete with three-inch heels. The only unique thing about Blair's look was a new blue streak foiled into one side of her shoulder length blonde hair.

"The blue matches your eyes," I said, handing her a glass of iced tea.

"I know, right? Not sure Mr. Billings will like it, but since I'm getting close to sixty-four, I'm not trying to impress anyone anymore."

Doe choked, nearly spitting out iced tea. Blair gave her a suspicious glance. I hid a smile, knowing exactly why Doe's throat had closed up at Blair's comment. Day or night, Blair dressed as if she were going out clubbing. In fact, for as long as I'd known her, I'd never seen her dressed casually. No jeans and T-shirt for her. She always dressed to make an impression, and that impression was to attract men. And her list of four husbands proved it worked.

"Hey, it's not as if you're not trying to make an impression," Blair said to Doe with an arched brow. "I mean, if I'm not mistaken, that expensive black pantsuit is by Raey."

Doe finally swallowed. "You're right. And I spent a fortune on it because every day that I walk into that office or boardroom, people expect to see my husband. Instead, they get me."

"Don't sell yourself short," I told her. "Didn't you say your quarterly earnings are up?"

"Yes. But there's always another company trying to encroach on our territory. Either that or the union is hitting us up for more money or more amenities. I need everyone to take me seriously."

Blair bumped her on the shoulder. "Doe, you're tall, elegant, and have the most formidable chest of any woman I've ever met," she said with a seductive wink. "If you want to know the truth, it's something I've always been jealous of, especially because those mamas are natural." Blair nodded towards Doe's large breasts. "Trust me, there's not a chance in hell your colleagues aren't taking you seriously."

The three of us laughed good-naturedly, but it made me think that, like Blair, Doe could also be challenged when it came to dressing casually, just in a different way. Her attire always looked as if she were about to take a shift as a department store mannequin. In other words, every crease was crisply ironed and every wrinkle removed. I sometimes wondered if she hoarded laundry starch, because regardless of the weather, the circumstances, or her state of mind, her clothes were always perfect.

"So, tell us what you know," Doe said, putting her glass down.

We were situated in my small living room with a fire going in the fireplace. I relayed everything Rudy had shared with me that morning, including what Ginger looked like.

"Sounds like our first line of attack is to find this woman named Ginger," Blair said, perching a shapely hip onto one of my bar stools.

"And she's homeless," Doe said.

"Yes. Rudy said to try the homeless camp here on the island."

"Sorry, but I won't have the time to help today," Doe said quickly. "We're in a bidding war for a big contract, and I pushed a meeting back for late this afternoon so I could be here now."

"No problem," I replied.

"But I want to help. Since we pick up the garbage at several of the Seattle homeless camps, if you can get a decent sketch of this woman, I could have my guys look for her."

"That'd be great," I said. I turned to Blair. "You have time for a little homeless reconnaissance?"

She shrugged. "For Rudy... anything."

"Okay. She said we should check out the homeless camp under the bridge. Let's just go and casually ask if anyone knows Ginger."

"It would be better if you had a story," Doe said. "Otherwise, they're likely to be suspicious."

"I suppose you're right," I said, thinking. "I've got it. Why don't we say that Ginger's aunt passed away and left her a little money. That way people might be more likely to try and help."

Doe nodded. "I like that idea."

"What about getting the sketch for Doe?" Blair asked.

"José is almost finished with his degree in graphic arts. I bet he could do it. I'll have him see Rudy and together they could produce a sketch."

"The police might even be able to use it," Doe said.

"I'll text her when we're done here," I said.

"I think it's important we don't go into the homeless camp talking about the missing people Romaine mentioned," Blair said. "After all, that's what got her killed."

"I agree. In fact, let's stick to the story about her aunt. We could print up little business cards with the name of a fake law firm."

"If we're going to do that, then I'll get a burner phone," Blair said. "I don't think we should give out our own phone numbers in case someone wants to call us."

"Also a good point." I glanced at my watch. "It's 3:30. Any chance we could be ready to go in an hour?"

"Can you get the cards by then?" Doe asked.

"I have some. We buy the kind you can put into your printer. We use them to write short thank you notes to leave on guest's pillows."

"Okay, I'll run out and get the phone and send you the phone number to put on the cards," Blair said. "Then, I'll change clothes and meet you back here."

Doe glanced down at Blair's feet. "You don't think three-inch, red patent leather heels are appropriate for a homeless camp?"

Blair arched a perfectly penciled brow. "I know how to fit in when I have to."

"Well, you might want to take Julia's Pathfinder then and leave the Porsche behind, too. Just sayin'," Doe said with a smile.

CHAPTER FOUR

It was 4:45 when Blair and I parked off SE 22nd Street just outside of downtown Mercer Island. Blair had, in fact, changed clothes but not to look more casual. She had donned a black pencil skirt and burgundy cashmere sweater, along with three-inch black heels instead of red. Over everything, she wore a black wool coat.

"I see you just opted for a less flashy version of yourself," I said.

She arched her back and raised her chin. "I figured if we're supposed to be representing a law office, I should look the part."

I smiled. "And you do."

Since my normal attire in wintry weather was jeans, a cable knit sweater, and my favorite loafers, my only change of clothing was to switch into black slacks and to lose my heavy socks.

The afternoon was chilly but dry, with dark clouds hovering on the far side of the Cascades. The camp was tucked under the bridge on the Seattle side of the island. Since we were downwind, the air was fragrant with the unmistakable smell of an outhouse carried along on the lake breeze.

"Hope this will be short," I said, wrinkling my nose.

By the time we reached the underside of the bridge, the camp had come into view.

"It's bigger than I thought," Blair said, eyeing five or six tents.

We left the sidewalk and stepped onto a large, hard packed dirt area that extended under the bridge. We walked through patches of dried grass scattered with discarded gum wrappers and soda cans, empty syringes, and dog poop. I eyed Blair as she stepped gingerly around all the trash and dog poop in her fancy shoes.

"Having second thoughts about wearing those shoes?"

"Never," she said with a flick of her head.

We reached the edge of the camp where someone had stacked old 2x4s alongside an old rake with its metal prongs facing up. The handle of the rake had been nearly buried in dog poop and rotting trash. I mentally made a note to avoid stepping on the rake prongs.

I gazed around the edges of the camp, which was lined with piles of trash, including broken electronics, a couple of bikes with their wheels missing, empty liquor bottles, and two metal trash cans charred by fire. Cartoonish gang tags had been sprayed across the cement walls of the freeway overpass, creating a colorful backdrop to the dismal environment. To one side of a tent was a child's toy scooter lying on its side, with no child in sight.

"You don't think kids stay here, do you?" I whispered to Blair.

She shrugged. "I don't know."

It made my heart ache to think of someone so young subjected to this type of chaotic existence. On the other hand, I remembered reading that families were the fastest growing segment of the homeless population.

To our right was the offending outhouse, sitting next to a large, overflowing dumpster. A dinged-up old RV sat at the far side of the camp.

Seven or eight haggard-looking people milled about, all watching us suspiciously. A couple of them disappeared into tents as if we might be from the health department. I glanced back toward the safety of my car, feeling completely out of my comfort zone here. When a dog barked, I swung around to see an older man sitting in a chair with his hand on the neck of a big, black dog. The hard look on the man's face and the intense stare from the dog seemed to send a clear message that we weren't welcome.

"C'mon," Blair said. "Let's get this done."

As we moved further into camp, the rickety door to the RV creaked open, and a burly woman with a broad nose and a five o'clock shadow came down the steps. A lull fell over the group.

My chest tightened under this woman's scrutiny. She approached us, stopping in the middle of the camp with a cigarette dangling from one side of her mouth. Her expression was one of naked hostility, and her attitude was clear—if you came to mess with us, don't.

"What can we do for you?" she asked in an unfriendly, hoarse voice.

Blair and I hadn't rehearsed this, so I spoke up first, stepping forward.

"We're here from Baker and Baker, attorneys at law," I said, holding out a card in my gloved hand.

She ignored the card I had carefully crafted with a made-up logo and continued to suck on the cigarette before blowing smoke in my direction.

"We're looking for Ginger Spalding," I continued, allowing my hand with the card to drop to my side. "We're hoping someone here might know how we can contact her."

Her eyes flicked over to three people sitting in camp chairs. Although not a word passed between them, she relayed a message of caution, nonetheless.

"Whaddya want with her?" the woman asked, bringing her attention back to us.

"We were asked to find her to let her know that her aunt passed away and left her a small inheritance. We don't have her address and would like to see that she gets it."

The woman eyed Blair, who stood quietly by my side. "Are you mute or somethin'? How come she's doing all the talkin'?"

Blair's softly arched eyebrows lifted. "Not at all. I just didn't think my input was needed in such a short exchange. The point is, do you want to help Ginger or not? The attorneys we represent could care less if she steps forward to collect the cash, but we'd like to see that she gets it."

"How much we talkin' about?" the woman asked, suddenly interested.

Blair shook her head. "That's not for us to say. Although from what Mr. Baker Sr. said, I doubt it's enough to allow her to retire in style. But it's still her money, and she can do whatever she wants with it."

I was impressed with Blair's ability to undercut the woman's suspicions, while still sounding authentic.

"She isn't here," a voice cut in from behind us.

We turned to find a disheveled man, with earnest brown eyes step forward. He was thin as a rail, with stained teeth, long stringy hair, a beard, and glasses with one cracked lens.

"We haven't seen her since yesterday," he continued. "Some guy in a blue van picked her up."

The woman from the RV spit into the dirt near Blair's toe, prompting Blair to look down at the spittle and then up at the woman. The woman was tall, but in Blair's heels she beat her by an inch or two. Knowing Blair and her inability to back down from a fight, every muscle in my body tightened. A tense moment stretched out between them as the woman's jaw hardened.

"I guess you got what you came for," she finally said. "Thanks for stopping by."

She and Blair still hadn't broken eye contact, so I turned back to the man with the glasses. "I'd appreciate it if you'd take my card and give it to Ginger if you see her."

He took the card. As he did, the sleeve of his jacket pulled up revealing needle marks on his forearm.

"Sure. But she goes to Seattle a lot. She could be anywhere."

I nodded. "I understand. Thank you."

"Don't wanna go with no one in a blue van," a voice called out from the other side of the camp. "Blue van means you ain't never seen again,"

I glanced up but could only see three people with their backs to us.

"Forget it," Blair said, grabbing my arm. "Let's go."

As she threw a final, threatening look at the woman from the RV, I backed up. When Blair relented, I finally swung around to leave, bringing my foot down onto the prongs of that damn rake. The rake swung up and slapped me in the side of the face, launching a pile of brown, smelly dog poop into the air. I cried out in pain, while Blair lifted her chin to watch the airborne stench arch over the camp, hitting the side of the RV with a loud splat.

It seemed everyone in camp was stunned into silence. Then, they burst into laughter. The burly woman with the five o'clock shadow turned to me with a storm cloud gathering across her face, as the feces slid down the side of the motorhome behind her.

Blair chuckled. "Our job is done here, Julia. Let's go."

CHAPTER FIVE

When we got back to the car, I said, "Damn, that stung."

I was looking at my face in the rearview mirror. I had a small welt on my cheek from where the rake had hit me.

"At least we know Ginger was there," Blair said. "And good job with that rake. If I didn't know better, I'd think you planned it."

"Very funny," I said, rubbing the welt. "I just wish we knew where the blue van took her." I glanced at the clock on the dashboard. "Listen, it's getting late. How 'bout we grab an early dinner at the Shore Club?"

"Great idea. Mr. Billings said he'll be home late tonight, anyway."

Fifteen minutes later, we sat at the big picture windows that overlooked the club's Olympic- sized swimming pool, sipping white wine while we waited for our food.

"What did you think about that blue van comment earlier?" Blair asked. "I thought it sounded ominous."

"I agree, but that guy might have just been mouthing off."

"I was surprised by the lack of help, though," she said, swirling the wine in her glass. "I mean, we're trying to give someone money. And yet, everyone acted like we were scam artists."

"Well, we were… sort of."

"Yes, but you'd think these people would be more accommodating when we're trying to help one of their own."

"These people?"

Blair's eyes flicked over to mine. "Sorry. I didn't mean that in a derogatory way. I just thought they'd want the best for Ginger."

"I imagine having to live on the street pretty much strips you of any trust you have in others," I said. "I'm sure we seemed like just two more people with an angle. Which, technically, we were."

Blair sat back with the corners of her pretty mouth pulled down. "We're just trying to help Rudy."

Before I could reply, my phone jingled. I pulled it from my purse and answered it.

"Ms. Applegate, it's Brenda Valentine. I just talked with Rudy and was wondering if we could meet in person. Rudy suggested I fill you in on more of the information."

"Can you come to the Mercerwood Shore Club? I'm having dinner with a friend."

"Um… is this one of the women in your group?"

"Yes. And she already knows all about what happened."

"Okay, I can be there in a few minutes."

"Can I order you something?"

"A whiskey neat."

We ordered Brenda's drink, and then a minute later Rudy called.

"Hey, has Brenda Valentine called you?"

"Yes. She's meeting us at the Shore Club."

"Good. Listen, Elliott showed me your text about doing a sketch of Ginger. But I have a picture of her from a shelter event earlier this year. I'll figure out a way to get it to you."

"Perfect. Doe said she'll give it to her guys who empty the cans at the homeless camps."

"Okay. By the way, I like Brenda. She was honest and said it appears I could be in trouble. But she also said that she believes me and agreed that it looks like someone might be setting me up."

"I'm glad," I said. "She seems competent."

"I agree. And Julia… thanks again."

"We're here for you. All the way."

We hung up, and I told Blair what Rudy had said. By the time our food arrived, a petite, middle-aged woman appeared at the entrance to the dining room. She had graying hair cut close to her head and wore a sharp black skirt and blazer with a blue silk blouse and low-heeled black shoes. I recognized her from the picture on her website and waved her over as her gaze swept the room. At my signal, she smiled and weaved through the tables with bold strides before plopping into the empty chair in front of her drink and dropping her purse on the floor. Without a word, she took a big swallow from her whiskey glass, placed it back on the table, and then leaned back in her chair with her eyes closed.

"Thanks. I needed that," she said, opening her eyes again.

I was a little surprised by her lack of social etiquette.

"I'm Julia," I said. "And this is Blair Wentworth. She's part of our book club."

"Of course," she said with a broad smile. "I know your husband," she said to Blair. "Your reputation precedes you. It's nice to meet you."

Blair's rock-solid confidence seemed to waver a moment as she stared at the attorney. Since Blair was the most noteworthy flirt I'd ever known, it was unclear what Brenda meant by Blair's 'reputation.'

"I'm sorry," Brenda said quickly, realizing her misstep. "That was rude. What I meant was that I'm familiar with how you and your friends have helped to solve several murder cases. Your fearlessness, as it were, is a bit legendary. My husband is Peter Dunne—"

Blair inhaled and said, "Dunne Motors."

"Yes. I kept my maiden name for professional purposes, but Peter knows Jack very well. In fact, they often have drinks together after a round of golf. Then, my husband comes home to share tales of your escapades with me. Jack is quite proud of your... how should I say? Bravado."

I chuckled. "More like the lack of any impulse control." I glanced at Blair. "But there is no one I'd rather be in a fight with. She is one fierce woman."

Blair's already artificially blushed cheeks turned a rosy red. "Thanks, Julia."

"Well, it's a pleasure to meet you both." Brenda gestured to our food. "Please, I'll talk while you eat."

I picked up my fork. "How's Rudy? She just called, but we didn't talk long."

"She's in shock. She told me that, and I quote, 'the horror of finding a friend murdered in my kitchen was only eclipsed by being the number one suspect for the murder.'" She smiled and shook her head before taking a sip of her drink. "I'm not sure I've ever heard anyone use the word eclipse in a conversation before."

"That's Rudy," I said with a smile. "She can also tell you how many words there are in Webster's dictionary."

Brenda smiled. "Well, I think right now she feels overwhelmed."

"I have to admit that I've never heard her so out of control," I said. "She scared me last night."

"She's clearly a strong woman. But she was at the police station until six this morning and is emotionally exhausted. Not only that, but she thinks she may have been drugged last night."

"Really?" Blair said, sitting forward.

"She remembered she had a funny taste in her mouth when she woke up and said she was a little fuzzy headed when the police arrived. At the time, she chalked it up to the shock and being knocked out. That's why, although she thinks it was Ginger at the door, she couldn't swear to it. She only remembers the outline of a woman with frizzy hair standing in the dark."

"We tried to find her today—Ginger, I mean. Rudy asked us to," I said.

"Yes, she told me. Any luck?"

I shook my head. "We visited the camp here on the island. They knew Ginger, but said someone had picked her up yesterday, and she hasn't been back."

"Well, keep trying. I recognize that she may be an unreliable witness, but she's all we've got right now."

"Did the police test Rudy's blood for drugs?" Blair asked.

"No. She didn't say anything last night. But as soon as she told me, I took her to have her blood drawn and photos taken of where she thinks she was karate chopped, just in case. It probably won't do much good. Most likely anything she was drugged with would have worked its way through her system by now, and there's only a slight bruise now on her shoulder."

"Why would someone have drugged her after they'd already knocked her out?" Blair asked.

"Probably because they didn't want her waking up in the middle of whatever it was they were doing." She took another drink. "She said she'll call you later to fill you in on everything she knows. Right now, though, she wants to rest. This has taken a toll on her. And let's face it, she feels responsible for Romaine's death."

"She wasn't, though," Blair said.

"No. But she's smack dab in the middle of it, so it's hard to see reason."

"Who was this Romaine, anyway?" I asked. "None of us knew her."

"Rudy met her at the Wings of Hope homeless shelter when she was there helping residents put resumes together. From what Rudy said, Romaine and her husband used to own a landscaping company, and she was trained as a master gardener. But her husband was diagnosed with a rare form of cancer. Even though they had insurance, his treatments and medications forced them to blow through all their savings. After he died, Romaine took over the company and realized it had been running in the red for months. In fact, her husband had taken out two large business loans that she couldn't pay back. Before long, she lost the business and her home and ended up on the street."

"She didn't have family that could help her?" Blair asked.

"Apparently not. Believe me, it happens more often than you know. What do they say? Seven out of ten people are one paycheck away from being homeless." She shook her head and took another sip of her drink. "But for the grace of God... Anyway, Romaine had landed a job at a local garden center, which also gave her a place to live. They have an apartment onsite because so much of their product is out in the open, and she worked the night shift. Romaine got the job in early October. About the same time, Rudy hired her to install a cascading waterfall in her backyard. When she finished, Rudy invited her over for dinner to celebrate."

"And someone murdered her," Blair said.

"Right," Brenda replied with a shrug.

"So, they had to know Romaine was there," Blair said.

"Right again," Brenda said.

"But why kill her?" I asked, forgetting my dinner for the moment. "And why kill her in Rudy's kitchen? It seems so absurd."

"Romaine told Rudy that she believed someone was taking homeless people off the streets. For what reason, Romaine didn't know. But she didn't think it was good, because the people just disappeared, leaving all their belongings behind. A couple of them were her friends."

"Couldn't they have just checked into some sort of rehabilitation program?" I asked.

"Romaine didn't think so. She showed Rudy a medallion left behind by one of the men who disappeared. I guess it was important to him because he'd won it for a swimming competition when he was in college, and it was the only thing he thought he had done right in his life. She said he would have never walked away without it."

"Did Romaine have any idea who was behind the disappearances?" Blair asked.

"She told Rudy about a man called Patch. She said that she'd seen him at two different camps and that he seemed to have resources."

"What does that mean?" Blair asked.

"If someone needed a sleeping bag, he could find it. If you needed a pair of gloves, he was your man. And then a few months ago, he began talking about being able to find people one-off jobs that paid well."

"That's a good thing, right?" Blair asked.

"Well, according to Romaine, he focused on people who didn't have family."

"Why would that matter?" I asked.

"Because they wouldn't have anyone to come looking for them," she said with a lift to one eyebrow.

"Wow," I said, feeling the weight of that sentence hit me.

"But how did Romaine know all this?" Blair asked.

"Patch approached her about one of those jobs before she got into the shelter. Rudy thought Romaine was very smart and had a good BS detector. And Patch rang that bell hard. Romaine thought he was smarmy and way too intrusive with his questions. He'd get all chummy with people by helping them out and then over time pepper them with questions about how they ended up on the street."

"And about their support system," Blair said.

"Right. That's what he wanted to know. If people cared enough about them to check up on them if anything happened. At least that's what Romaine thought. She told Rudy his questions extended beyond family and friends. He'd ask about social workers or even probation officers who might expect these people to report in. Romaine lied and told him she had a brother who checked up on her regularly, even though he couldn't help her financially. She also mentioned a past employer who had given her a cell phone so that she could always call him if she needed help."

"What happened?" Blair asked.

"Patch dropped her like a hot potato. That's what convinced her." Brenda finished her drink and put the glass down along with a twenty-dollar bill. "Listen, I have to prep for court tomorrow on another case. You should get together with Rudy and see if you can glean any more information from her. This isn't over."

"What do you mean?" Blair asked, alarmed.

"When the DNA comes back from the skin under Romaine's fingernails, it will likely be Rudy's. She has several deep scratches on her face that she doesn't remember getting. And they'll run tests to find out what that residue was in the glass and whether Romaine had ingested it." She shifted her glance directly at me. "Listen, I take back what I said earlier about tempering your involvement. We need you. I only have one investigator, and the case he's working on just got ugly. If Rudy is innocent, and I believe she is, we're going to need all the ammunition we can get, because my guess is that she'll be arrested by the end of the week."

CHAPTER SIX

The next afternoon, Rudy felt well enough to join us in my apartment. As I studied her from across the room, I realized how gaunt she looked, and the scratches on her face were raw and just beginning to scab over. She did, in fact, look like she'd been in a fight. She also had deep circles under her eyes and a distant and preoccupied expression on her face that gave me pause, thinking the "boss" might still be off duty.

Doe and Blair were with us, and Minnie had snuggled in next to Rudy on the sofa, as if she knew Rudy needed comforting.

I had talked with David earlier that day, but he was very circumspect in his answers, making me nervous about Rudy's prospects. And perhaps for the first time ever, the four of us sat quietly, without food or drink to bolster the mood. After what Brenda had said the night before, I felt like a doomsday clock was ticking. We needed to act fast.

Rudy was aimlessly rubbing her right hand back and forth along the top of her leg, as she stared blankly at the floor.

"You okay?" Blair asked, putting her hand on top of Rudy's to stop the rubbing.

"Yeah," she replied, sitting back. "I know I've been absent, but I just needed time to process all of this."

"No apologies necessary," Doe said.

"Any news on Ginger?" Rudy asked. She was now tapping the heel of her foot against the floor.

"We didn't find her," I said. "Although a man said that someone picked her up at the camp Monday afternoon."

A light glinted in Rudy's eyes, and she stopped the nervous movement and sat forward. "Could they identify who picked her up? What they looked like?"

Blair and I exchanged glances. "We didn't think to ask. Sorry."

"But they said it was someone in a blue van," Blair said. "And then someone added that you didn't want to get picked up by the blue van because you never came back."

"A blue van—that's something," Rudy said.

"Did you see a van at your house that night?" Doe asked.

Rudy thought for a minute and then shook her head. "I opened the door to complete darkness except for the streetlight at the end of the drive. All I saw was the shadow of the woman standing there."

"Do you think they used Ginger to get you to open the door?" I asked.

She nodded. "I do."

"And Ginger had never been to your house before?" Doe asked.

"No. I've only ever talked to her at the shelter, where she's usually on her medication and lucid. But the woman that night was mumbling when I opened the door," she said, thinking. "I suppose that's another reason I thought it was Ginger. I've seen her do that a couple of times when she hasn't taken her meds."

"And you don't know what happened to her after Romaine was killed," Blair said.

Rudy shook her head. "She was gone when I woke up."

I had an idea and sat forward in my chair. "Before you blacked out, did this woman touch anything? Like maybe the porch railing or the door?"

"Why would that be important?" Blair asked.

"If she'd never been to Rudy's house before, her fingerprints shouldn't be there. But if they were, then it would prove Rudy is right."

"Wait a minute," Rudy said, her eyes lighting up. "Ginger's OCD and touches almost anything she passes as if to ground herself. When I opened the door, the woman mumbled something and then took a big step back so that she was even with the railing on the porch. I'm sure she reached out and tapped the porcelain birdhouse a couple of times. You know, the one that sits on that small table near my front door. Man, the more I think about it, the more I'm sure it was Ginger."

"Now if we could only find her," Blair said.

"I'll let David know. Maybe they'll fingerprint the birdhouse," I said, pulling my phone from my pocket. "I'll be right back."

I slipped into my bedroom and dialed David's number.

"Hey, you," he said when he answered. "I miss you."

"I miss you, too. By the way, how's your investigation going? Have you caught the home invaders, yet?"

"We have two guys from Federal Way on our radar. But I bet you didn't call about my home invasions."

I laughed. "You know me so well. Listen, Rudy is here, and we're talking about what happened Monday night. She remembered something that might be important."

"What's that?"

"Rudy says that when she opened the door, a woman named Ginger was standing there. She knows Ginger from the homeless shelter."

"I read that in the report. But it also says Rudy wasn't sure it was Ginger."

"She's feeling more certain now. According to Rudy, Ginger is OCD and feels compelled to touch things. The woman at her door that night reached out and touched the porcelain birdhouse that sits on a table near Rudy's front step. She did that just before Rudy was hit from behind. And, David, Ginger has never been to Rudy's home. I thought you might like to fingerprint the birdhouse in case you could at least confirm that part of Rudy's story."

I stopped talking and held my breath, hoping David wouldn't dismiss the idea out of hand.

"Why didn't you just call Sean?"

"Um… because I'd rather have an excuse to talk to you," I replied quickly and then shut up again.

He chuckled. "Okay. I'll let him know. The forensics team has already dusted inside the house, but they wouldn't have dusted anything on the front porch." He paused. "Julia, do I need to worry about you?"

"What do you mean?" I asked innocently.

"You know exactly what I mean. I've been buried in these home invasions and may not be up to speed on Rudy's case, but I know you well enough to know you won't let her go through this alone."

"No, we won't. But so far we've only done what she asked us to do."

"Which is what?"

"Help her hire the best criminal attorney we could find and—"

"What else?" he prompted me.

"Try to find Ginger."

There was a long pause, and I thought maybe I'd over-stepped.

"I'm sure Sean would like to find this Ginger, too, even if it's just to rule her out. But I also know it's probably lower on his list of priorities right now, since Rudy isn't even sure it was her. So, a little extra help wouldn't hurt. Just don't get carried away," he cautioned.

I'd been holding my breath and released it. "What do you mean?"

"Like actually going after the bad guys once we know who they are."

"We're not there, yet. And to be honest, I'd prefer leaving that up to you, anyway."

"Glad to hear it. Did you find any information on this Ginger?"

"A little. Blair and I went to the homeless camp here on Mercer Island posing as representatives from an attorney's office who wanted to let her know a relative had left her some money. The people at the camp knew Ginger but said that she'd been picked up in a blue van Monday afternoon and hadn't been back."

He sighed. "Okay, I'll let Sean know that, too."

"But, David, someone also needs to find this Patch guy that Romaine talked about. He's the one she thought was luring people off the street."

"That may be getting a bit ahead of things. We don't know if he had anything to do with her death. Right now, Sean and Nick will be examining all the evidence in Romaine's murder. If Patch shows up on the radar, then—"

"Who's Nick?"

"Nick Levine. He just passed his detective's exam, so they promoted him to replace me when I retire at the end of the year. They brought him on early to bring him up to speed."

David had finally decided to pull the plug and retire after our last investigation to mitigate the two of us getting crosswise when things like this happened.

"What do you think of him?"

"He's okay. Doesn't matter what I think, though. I won't be here. Anyway, let Sean take care of Patch. You take care of Rudy."

"Okay. Can you find out how soon she can get back into her house? She's staying at her ex-husband's."

"I'll try. Listen, I gotta go. I have a call coming in. We'll talk later. Love you."

"Love you, too. And thanks."

When I returned to the living room, Doe was asking Rudy, "What else can you tell us about Romaine?"

Rudy was still tapping the heel of her right foot on the floor. "She'd been at Wings of Hope for a week or so when I met her and was teaching the staff how to re-pot plants that had become root bound. Except for her mismatched clothes, you'd never suspect she might be homeless. She was clearly smart and well educated. We got to talking, and I realized just how intelligent she was. And talented. She showed me pictures of the landscaping projects she'd done, and I'd go so far as to say she was an outdoor artist."

"How old was she?" Blair asked.

Rudy thought a moment. "Maybe fifty or thereabouts." She shook her head. "It just pisses me off that someone took her life away just as she was getting it back."

"Did she ever talk about anyone who she was afraid of or anything that would put her in danger?" I asked, coming back to sit down. "Maybe she overheard something she shouldn't have at the nursery where she worked."

Rudy shook her head. "All she talked about were the people disappearing off the street and how she wanted me to look into it. Unfortunately, I wasn't the only person she told. She'd not only gone to the police but mentioned it to others at the shelter."

"But people move around so much when they're homeless," Blair said. "It's just hard to believe someone is luring them off the street. I mean, for what purpose? They don't have money."

"Many homeless people are transient," Rudy agreed. "But a lot of them call the Puget Sound their home and tend to stay in the area they know best. And they protect the few belongings they have. Just leaving everything behind without a word to anyone is unusual."

I sat back. "It does sound like someone needs to investigate. But David just said looking into that would take second place to Romaine's murder."

"I'm positive they're related, though," Rudy replied with earnest.

I had sat down next to her on the sofa and placed my hand on her knee. I gave it a squeeze. "This will all work out, Rudy. You'll see. We're a team, after all."

"I hope you're right," she said with a sigh. "Because I'm too old to go to jail."

A loud knock at the door interrupted us, and Rudy's face blanched. Her shoulders dropped, and she turned to me with the haunted look of someone about to go to the gallows.

"I hope I didn't speak too soon," she said.

"Hold on," I said.

I got up and went to the door, wondering if I should have told Rudy to escape down the hallway and out my back door. But that wasn't like Rudy. She would face this with the same sort of courage I'd seen her display countless times before.

When I opened the door, Detective Abrams, and a man I assumed was David's replacement were standing there with grim expressions. Detective Abrams had a sheet of paper in his hand, which he held out to me.

"We're here for Mrs. Smith," he said.

CHAPTER SEVEN

After Rudy was taken into custody, there wasn't much more for us to do, so Blair and Doe left. Afterwards, I called Elliott and Brenda Valentine to let them know Rudy had been arrested. Then I called David, more than a little angry that he hadn't given me a heads up. He was in the car and pulled over to take the call.

"First of all, I didn't know they were coming to arrest her," he said. "And I left the office right after we talked to interview someone about this burglary case. Secondly, I can't do that sort of thing, Julia. I'm still a law enforcement officer. But I know this can't be easy for any of you."

"Do you know why they suddenly arrested her?" I still had a clip to my voice.

"I only know they got the toxicology report and the DNA back."

"Damn! That's what I was afraid of and exactly what Brenda predicted." I slumped down onto the sofa.

"Who's Brenda?"

"Rudy's attorney. She met Blair and me at the club last night and said it probably wouldn't look good for Rudy when those two reports came back. She's being set up, David. She didn't do this."

"Look, I like Rudy, and can't imagine a scenario where she would murder someone. But we're forced to go where the evidence takes us. I'll talk to Sean and see what else I can learn. So don't do anything crazy, you know, like try to break her out of jail."

"I would never do that," I said, my mind racing about how I might even go about it.

"Right."

"Okay," I said lightly. "I get it. But Brenda has already asked for our help. And now that Rudy has been arrested, it's all-hands-on deck. The first thing we need to do is to find Ginger. That's what we'll focus on."

He sighed. "Okay. But be careful. The moment people know you're looking for Ginger, you could become a target."

After David hung up, I decided on a simple dinner and pulled out a can of chicken noodle soup and heated it up. I ate leisurely and was just finishing the dishes when Brenda called.

"It's just as I thought," she said when I answered. "The blood Rudy had on her hands and blouse was Romaine's. And the blood and tissue under Romaine's fingernails was Rudy's. Plus, the hair in Romaine's hand was Rudy's."

"They could have gotten that from her brush."

"I know."

"What about the white powder?"

"GHB."

"The date rape drug?"

"Yes. They found it in Romaine's system as well as in the wine glass on the counter."

"Did they find any of the drug in Rudy's house?"

"Not that I know of."

"So, what now?" I asked, my stomach churning. "When will you get the results from Rudy's blood test?"

"Tomorrow, probably. And she'll be charged sometime tomorrow afternoon. Bail for a murder charge will be high, though."

"We'll help if we have to," I said.

"Then I'll be back in touch when I know more. And, Julia, we may need more fire power."

"What do you mean?"

"We not only need to find Ginger but try to substantiate what Romaine told Rudy about people disappearing off the street. The last thing I want is to put you or your friends in danger, but who do you know that might be able to help with tracking down this Patch dude to find out how he might be involved?"

It took only a split second for me to reply. "Don't worry about that. We'll be your boots on the ground."

"Good, because someone is going to have to go undercover in the camps. I'd send my investigator, but like I said, he's booked. Also, people would likely clam up if they knew he's a private investigator. Rudy gave me the names of the five people Romaine said had disappeared. One of them was staying at a veteran's camp in South Seattle. But Romaine mostly stayed in the Magnolia Park camp."

I nodded. "Well, then, I guess those are the places where we start."

"Okay," she said. "Get a pencil and paper, because I have more to tell you before you do this."

After we hung up, I made a quick decision and went into my office to search through a small box of people's business cards I kept. When I found the one I wanted, I gave the woman whose name was on the card a call. I also texted Blair and Doe and asked them to come back based on what Brenda had told me. Doe replied that her meeting would end in about fifteen minutes and said she'd come straight from there.

An hour later, we sat in front of the fire with glasses of wine, while heavy rain pounded the ground outside. I had just finished filling them in on my conversation with Brenda.

"We need to mobilize," Blair said. She was sitting on the sofa clad in thick, black leggings and a form-fitting blue turtleneck sweater with her long legs crossed at the ankles. "We have to clear Rudy, but have you noticed how she's changed?"

"What do you mean?" I asked.

"Just her demeanor. I get that she's stressed, but it just seems like there's something else going on. This afternoon, she was acting as if she was on too much caffeine."

"I think we need to cut her some slack," I said.

"I've noticed some changes in her over the last few months, though," Doe said. "She's much more on edge. I chalked it up to Elliott trying to get back with her, plus I know her knee has been bothering her again."

"Well, the circles under her eyes make me think she hasn't slept since the night before this all happened. Which is understandable," I said.

"I agree. And I'm not sure how I'd feel about someone being murdered in my own home," Doe said."

I was facing my Wizard of Oz poster on the wall across from me and murmured, "No place like home for a murder."

A long silence made me turn to my friends. They were both giving me hard stares.

"Sorry," I said.

Doe sighed. "Okay, first things first. How do we help Rudy short of going into the homeless camps?" Doe asked. "Because whoever had Romaine killed did it to cover up what they're doing out there. Do I have that right?"

"Yes," I said. "At least that's what we think."

"Look," Doe began, "I don't mean to be Debbie Downer, but do you know how many homeless camps there are around Puget Sound? My guys run across them all the time. Some are pretty well-established, while others just seem to pop up overnight."

"I know," I replied. "But Brenda said that before she got her job, Romaine had been living in a homeless camp down by the Magnolia Bridge. That's where we should start."

"How did she expect you to investigate?" Doe asked.

I paused before saying, "She thought we should go undercover."

"In a homeless camp?" Doe's eyes went wide with surprise. "That's ridiculous. It's one thing to go in and ask questions, but which one of you wants to go live there?"

"Look, Romaine had the names of five people she knows have gone missing. And she'd heard rumors of others."

"How was she so sure they disappeared under suspicious circumstances?" Doe contested. "They could be anywhere."

"Because she knew them, and it wasn't something they would normally do. Look, you don't have to do this, Doe. We'll…"

"No. You're not going to do it, either. It's too dangerous," she said, crossing her arms over her chest.

Doe stared at me in a way I thought she probably stared across the boardroom table when she was up against the wall on some weighty decision. I glanced at Blair who was being uncharacteristically quiet.

"What do you think?" I asked her.

"I'm not afraid of doing it," she said. "I'm just not sure we know how."

"What do you mean?"

"You don't fake being homeless," Doe answered.

"I have that covered. I called a woman I met at a dinner for Vision House earlier this year. She wrote a book about being homeless, and I've asked her to join us. She should be here soon."

There was a knock at my front door, interrupting the conversation.

I glanced at my watch. "Maybe that's her."

But when I answered it, I found April with a tray of chocolate chip cookies.

"I thought you guys could use a snack," she said.

"Ha," I laughed. "Having a psychic as my best friend and business partner is bad for my waistline." April had what's called a sixth sense and often knew things before I did. I opened the door wide. "Come in and join us."

April placed the tray of cookies on the kitchen counter and glanced at Blair. "These are sugar-free, Blair, so help yourself."

Blair was a diabetic and was often left out when we took advantage of April's baking prowess. But not tonight. Blair thanked April and then swung her legs off the sofa to go to the counter.

Doe got out of the chair. "You're a dream, April. I'm starving. I had to be up for a 7:30 meeting and only had a protein bar for lunch. We're about to put in a bid for North Seattle, which Emerald City Refuse has had tied up for over a decade. We really need this contract."

We converged at the kitchen counter, and I got out plates as people grabbed cookies and napkins. Meanwhile, I quickly updated April on everything we'd learned since Rudy's arrest.

"So, don't tell me," April began. "One or more of you is going to go undercover as homeless people."

"Have you been listening at the door?" I said with a mischievous smile. "It makes perfect sense, though, don't you think?"

"But you don't have much to go on. You'd be forced to do the same thing Romaine did, namely ask a bunch of questions, which is exactly what got her killed." April's dark eyes narrowed in concern.

"I have a little more information," I said. "Romaine told Rudy that she thought she saw this Patch guy once in Federal Way going into a building. He was dressed differently and wasn't wearing the eyepatch."

"That's interesting," Blair said. "So, maybe he's faking being homeless and being blind in one eye."

"Maybe," I said. "Romaine was on the bus and didn't get a good look at him. But she did see him with a woman named Evergreen outside the Salvation Army food bank the day before Evergreen disappeared. The two of them were talking to another man."

"And you think Evergreen went with these men somewhere?" April asked.

"I don't know. But according to Romaine, none of the five people who have gone missing had anyone who would come looking for them."

"I suspect a lot of the people who live on the street are separated from their families," Doe said quietly, while she nibbled on a cookie.

Blair shifted in her seat. "Yes, but it sounds like going undercover is the only way to get the information we need."

"C'mon you guys," Doe snapped. "It's too dangerous."

"I understand your concerns, Doe. But we can do this," I said, sneaking a glance at Blair.

"And Mr. Billings' nephew could make us look homeless," Blair added.

The nephew she referred to worked in the costume department at one of the local colleges. And Mr. Billings was Blair's nickname for her husband. She'd given it to him the weekend they'd met in Billings, Montana and spent the night together in a motel. They were both still married to other people at the time and thus the need for a nickname. Since learning the actual meaning behind the nickname, however, I couldn't think of him without the raunchy visual image it conjured up because it referred to a specific part of Jake's body.

Doe's dark eyes narrowed. "Looking homeless is not the same as being homeless." She stopped and gave a defeated sigh. "I guess there's no other way. But I can't go. I really do need to be at work. These negotiations are too important."

"That's okay. Blair and I will go. And April can look after the Inn," I said, turning to her. She gave me an affirmative nod.

"Romaine said this Patch guy mostly hangs out at the Magnolia Park encampment," Doe said. "I've seen that camp—calling it a dump would be a compliment."

I glanced at Blair with her perfectly coiffed hair and makeup. "You up for this? It wouldn't be for just an hour or so, but perhaps days."

"Yeah," she replied without thought. "This is Rudy's life we're protecting."

April sat forward. "By the way, did Romaine describe the second man she saw with Patch and Evergreen at the Salvation Army?"

I referred to my notes again. "Tall, skinny, and walked with a limp. There's something else, though. Evergreen agreed to take the job Patch was offering. Romaine thought the tall, skinny guy might have been the guy that would hire her."

"Why did she think that?" April asked.

"Because the day before, Evergreen told Romaine that Patch wanted her to meet the guy offering the job. The next day she saw the three of them together outside the Salvation Army."

"And Rudy told all of this to Detective Abrams?" Doe asked, a little surprised.

"I assume so, but all of this happened in Seattle. Listen, if we're going to do this, we're going to need help. It can't just be me and Blair."

"What do you mean?" Doe asked.

"One of the missing people, a guy named Jacob, was a veteran. He hung out at a veterans' camp in South Seattle. Romaine knew him because she was ex-Army and had stayed there for a while. Apparently, Patch also shows up there."

"So, you're thinking we need to be in two locations?" Blair asked. "How do we do that? We don't have anyone who could go undercover in a veterans' camp."

"I could do it," a voice said.

CHAPTER EIGHT

Four heads swiveled toward my brother Ben, who stood at the end of the hallway dressed in his familiar khaki cargo pants, loose muslin shirt, and heavy coat, holding a box. Ben was three years older than me, and a forensic anthropologist who focused on artifacts, not bodies. After almost losing his life at the hands of the people who had recently killed his best friend Carter, he'd decided to stick around for a while. In fact, he'd bought Carter's old house and had been offered a position as guest lecturer at the University of Washington. As someone who had spent the better part of his life roaming the globe hunting for ancient artifacts, I had no illusions Ben would settle in the Seattle area permanently. But it was nice to have him close by, at least for now.

"Where did you learn to move with such stealth?" I asked him.

He shrugged his broad shoulders. "The Brazilian jungle," he said with a grin. "Actually, the back door was ajar, and I didn't know if you had an intruder. I mean, it's not like that's never happened before."

Doe flinched. "Sorry. I was the last one in. I guess I didn't close the door all the way."

I waved off her apology. "No problem. So, you're volunteering your services, Ben? You don't even know what for."

"Yes, but I'm a veteran. And you said you need a vet."

"Okay, but what's that?" I asked, nodding toward the box in his hands.

He set it on the kitchen counter and pulled a stack of paper from it. "It's a manuscript I found at Carter's. Believe it or not, he was writing a story."

"Well, he was a prolific writer, wasn't he?" Doe asked.

"Yes, but always about historical stuff. This is a story about an investigation he and Julia and I conducted when we were kids."

"No way!" I said, jumping up and moving over to grab the manuscript. As I skimmed the first page, I said, "Oh, for heaven's sake. It's a short story. He's called it 'The Case of the Missing Will.'"

"Sounds like Nancy Drew or the Hardy Boys," Blair said with a chuckle.

I shook my head as a wave of sadness washed over me. "Damn, I miss him."

"Maybe you could finish the story for him," Ben said, encouraging me with a raised eyebrow.

I chuckled. "We'll see. First we need to solve the case of the dead woman in Rudy's kitchen."

"I heard about that on the news." Ben narrowed his eyes. "So much for keeping me informed about what's happening in your life. Is that why you need an undercover vet?"

"Yes. And sorry I didn't call you. But it's been a whirlwind. In fact, Rudy was arrested this afternoon for the murder. We're trying to figure out how we can help her," I said, gesturing to the others. "Want to hear what you might be volunteering for?"

"Only if I can have that last cookie," he said, nodding toward the tray.

"Help yourself," April said, pushing the plate forward.

Ben grabbed the dessert and then perched on a bar stool next to April. While he ate, we filled him in on the full story: Romaine, Patch, Ginger, and the blue van.

When we'd finished, Doe said, "I didn't know you were a veteran, Ben."

"Yep. Navy, at the tail end of the Vietnam War."

"You were a pilot?" Blair asked in surprise.

"Forward air controller," he said, wiping his mouth.

"This could be dangerous, though. Someone has already died," I said.

He nodded. "I get it. But look, you played a key role in solving Carter's murder. This is the least I can do in return. When are we going to do this? Because I have two lectures this week."

"We should also plan this out better than what we've done in the past," Doe added with a hint of reproach in her voice. "After all, it would be nice if no one was abducted, drugged, or held in an underground vault this time."

"Good point," I concurred, a flush of emotion spreading throughout my body at the memories.

"Plus, let's face it, none of you know the first thing about living on the street," April said. "My guess is that it will be way more complicated than you think."

"You have no idea," Ben said.

"You've never been homeless, have you?" Blair asked him.

"Technically, no. But I've spent weeks in the jungle wearing the same clothes with no place to shower or clean up despite the blistering heat and humidity. To say that you begin to smell ripe is an understatement."

Blair's nose wrinkled. "Oh," she said, shifting uncomfortably in her seat.

"I have that part covered," I said. I glanced at the pendulum clock on my wall. "In fact, she should be here any minute."

"Who?" Blair asked.

"A woman I met at Vision House; a transitional housing program headquartered in Renton. They had a local author speak at one of their events, and I sat next to her at the dinner. She had been homeless for a couple of years and wrote a book about how she survived and got off the streets."

"How can she help?" Ben asked.

"She has firsthand knowledge."

Doe leaned forward in her seat. "Yes, but what exactly would she do?"

"Look, you're right. None of us has any idea what to expect out there. Just mussing up our hair and putting on dirty clothes won't cut it. We need to know how people survive. Where do they go for food? How do they wash their clothes?"

"If they wash their clothes," Blair said.

It seemed the romance of going undercover had suddenly lost its luster for Blair.

"Remember that during the recession, a lot of families lost their homes, suddenly finding themselves on the street or living in their cars. I'd like to have more of a head start than they did on how to survive."

"You also need to know where the safety nets are. Just in case you get into trouble," April said. "She could probably help with that."

A knock at the door brought me out of my chair. "That must be her."

A moment later, I ushered a woman in her fifties into the room. She was dressed in loose jeans, a heavy sweater, and had her graying hair pulled back into a ponytail.

"Everyone, this is Emma Hospers. I've filled her in on everything we know so far."

We went around the room and introduced ourselves, and then I offered Emma iced tea or wine. She took the iced tea, and I offered her the wingback chair by the fire.

After we'd all settled in and Emma had greeted Minnie, I said, "In talking to Emma earlier about all of this, she told me she knew Evergreen." I turned to Emma and nodded.

"Yes, I saw her only a few months ago. She was working hard to get her life together. But I also know the name Patch."

"I thought you'd been off the street for several years," Blair said.

"I made a lot of friends out there and try to stay in touch. Every couple of weeks, I go back and check on a few of them. I bring them cigarettes or coupons for free food. And when I can, I help out at the Salvation Army's community dinners."

"And you've heard Patch's name?" Doe asked.

She nodded. "A couple of times. Rose Marie, an older woman with mental health problems, told me about him. People will often take advantage of her and steal her food or clothes, so I try to help her out. I saw her a few weeks ago, and she told me about this Patch guy and how he had given her a brand-new wool coat for the winter because all she had were a couple of sweaters she could layer. Oliver is another regular on the street who told me he doesn't trust Patch. In fact, he said this Patch guy tries to be too friendly."

"That's how he's been described to us," I said. "Apparently he offered a job to Evergreen, which she accepted. Then, she disappeared."

"How did she end up on the street?" Ben asked.

"Wow, where to begin? Evergreen was only in her mid-twenties when I met her. She'd already had a hard life. Her parents died in a car accident when she was twelve. That sent her into the foster care system, where she was abused. She ran away when she was sixteen and ended up on the street selling herself to stay alive. After all, people need to survive," Emma said with a shrug. "I try not to judge.

She drank heavily but was never really into drugs. She tried rehab but always relapsed and ended up back on the street. By the time I met her, she was still selling her body to make money. But she was sweet and funny and an exceptionally talented street artist. Her dream had always been to illustrate children's books. In fact, she's responsible for a couple of the better street murals in Ballard."

"Seems like it should have been her foster parents who were made to disappear," Blair murmured.

"I agree," Emma said with a sigh. "But listen… if you do this, you'll hear stories worse than that. You really don't know what you're getting into. I didn't mean to make it sound easy in my book if that's what you think," she said to me.

"You didn't. I remember you talking about having to dumpster dive for food and riding the bus all night just to stay safe."

"You paid attention."

"It opened my eyes," I replied. "Because you also made me realize that many of the people out there have jobs and families. They're just not able to save enough money to pay first and last month's rent to get housing."

"Seattle is an expensive place to live," she said. "And even though this is considered a liberal area, be prepared to be looked down on. I've been spit on and kicked. A man once walked sideways past me as if he thought I carried a disease. And a woman purposely spilled hot coffee on me one day and then stopped to say, 'Oh, I'm sorry. But it's not like you don't have other stains on your clothes.'"

"God, I would have kicked her butt," Blair said, staring into her wine.

"I wanted to," Emma said. "But much of the public has the attitude that homeless people are there by choice. Don't get me wrong, there is a small percentage who choose to stay out there because of the freedom they feel. But most people have no idea the range of issues these people deal with. Hell, I didn't have an addiction or mental health issues, and it still took me over two years to get my life back together. When you're knocked down like that, you carry the weight of your failures on your shoulders."

"In the book, you said you were assaulted, which sent you into a downward spiral. And that's how you ended up on the street," I said.

She sighed. "It was worse than that. But I'd rather not go into detail. Suffice it to say that for someone who grew up in a deeply religious family, my entire sense of self was destroyed. My faith.

Any trust I had in men. And frankly, any trust I had in other women."

"Why other women?"

"Because two cheerleaders watched the whole thing. I was a nerd who loved numbers more than people, you see. So, I was different." She took a deep sigh. "Anyway, I struggled for a long time but eventually got my master's degree in finance. But I'd lost any relationship I had with my family, got depressed and ended up in a psych ward, and then went to live with my grandmother. Unfortunately, she died a few months later. Suddenly, I was on the street. The only advantage I had was my grandmother's car."

"I don't know how anyone would recover from all of that," I said.

"And yet, I was lucky. I would have been the perfect target for a predator. I didn't have any family in the area to help, and I didn't have any idea what I was doing out there. I would drive around during the day trying to find work, food, or a place to sleep at night. It was exhausting."

"How did you get back on your feet?" Doe asked.

"My car needed repairs, and I was driving without insurance or a valid driver's license. I parked in a church parking lot overnight in December. Around midnight there was a tap on my window. It was the night janitor from the church. He allowed me to stay in the church basement for the night. The next day, I met with the pastor and told him my story. He let me stay there for almost a week while I did light bookkeeping for him. Then, he helped get me into a shelter."

"And that saved you?" April asked.

"Not completely. As I said, it isn't easy. I stayed at the shelter for a couple of weeks until a fire closed it, and I was back on the street. This time without my car. But, once again, Pastor Mike came to my rescue. When things got really bad, he'd allow me to stay at the church for a night or two. And he drove me to one of Seattle's big free clinics once so I could get an infected toenail treated. He would also get me clothes and toiletries when I needed them. Believe me, that's the kind of help a lot of the people on the street don't have."

"I guess you were lucky," Blair said quietly.

"Look, I think what you're proposing to do is admirable. Maybe even heroic. Especially, because people disappear off the street more often than you realize, and no one seems to care. But my purpose in writing the book was to help the public understand that many of the people who live out there have had more than their share of bad luck and just need a helping hand. I didn't include everything in the book, though."

"Like what?" I asked.

She took a deep breath before saying, "It's not uncommon for women to be physically assaulted. We're easy targets out there. Something you need to be aware of. I woke up one night with a guy on top of me. I couldn't fight him off, so he just did his thing and left. I was also beaten once when someone wanted to steal the shoes I was wearing. As a result, I ended up shoeless in the middle of January. You're going to need to be careful." She paused. "But I think someone should avenge Romaine's death, and I would definitely like to know what happened to Evergreen."

"Then, you'll help us?"

"I'll do whatever I can."

"I think we're going to need some coaching, if you're up for it."

Emma stood up and grabbed her coat. "Listen, I've got to run, but whatever you need, I'll be there. Just let me know. I'm available all day tomorrow. Just give me a call."

Everyone thanked her before she left. Then Blair said, "She's great, Julia. Good call. We should set something up for tomorrow so we can get going. But will you tell David about this? I doubt he's going to be happy about you going undercover."

"He's already told me he knows I'm going to be involved."

"But going undercover on the street is different," April said. "You'd be back on the front lines. I don't think he'd like that."

"What about Mr. Billings?" I asked Blair. "He might not be too excited about it, either."

She shrugged. "He's putty in my hands," she said. "I can convince him."

"What if this time we actually do this in an official capacity?" I suggested.

Everyone was silent. We'd spent the last year and a half running afoul of the police as we barged ahead in our investigations, even coming close to getting arrested.

"What are you thinking?" Ben asked.

"Let's work through Brenda, Rudy's attorney. She practically begged me to get the rest of you involved. And she has a private investigator on staff. Maybe she could supply us with things like recording equipment and someone stationed close by in case anything goes wrong."

"I think that's pie in the sky," Doe said. "If she asked for your help, then she's probably short on resources, which means the people in this room will have to provide the back-up you need."

"Unless…" Blair began.

"What?" I asked.

"We take José," she said with a smile.

José was my maintenance man who had grown up in the Watts area of Los Angeles and sported several gang tattoos. He was muscular enough that people didn't bother him and had a black belt in something-or-other, which gave me confidence he could protect us.

"That's a good idea. I'll talk to him tomorrow morning. Rudy will be charged sometime tomorrow afternoon. If she can meet her bail, she'll be out and can help plan all of this."

"Why wouldn't she be able to meet bail?" Blair asked.

"Brenda said it could be spendy based on a murder charge. Plus, she'll be paying Brenda's legal fees, which I'm sure aren't small."

"She won't have to worry about meeting her bail," Doe said firmly. "I can't be a working part of this, so you'll have whatever you need from me in the finance department. Let's just get her out of jail. I'll let my staff know to interrupt me if you call tomorrow."

"Thanks, Doe," I said with relief.

Everyone left, and I cleaned the kitchen feeling anxious about the next few days. We had taken great risks before to solve murders or to help people in trouble, but somehow this felt different. We would take on new identities and live in a world completely foreign to us, all of which posed threats to our personal safety. And underlying all of that was the fact we would be looking for a killer.

I was just about to get ready for bed when a framed photo of my two dogs Minnie and Mickey fell over on the side table next to the sofa.

I glanced around. The Inn had been haunted ever since a fire had destroyed most of the building back in the 1960s, killing John St. Claire's wife Elizabeth, two of her children, and their dog. When the home had been rebuilt, subsequent owners reported odd occurrences and even sightings. Since I'd owned the property, I'd had several encounters with Elizabeth, her daughter Chloe, and occasionally heard their dog Max.

I moved into the living room and lifted the frame, gazing misty-eyed at Mickey, the black and tan long-haired miniature dachshund I'd lost just a few weeks back. I didn't know if he would also haunt the building one day, but I suspected this time it was Elizabeth just reminding me to treasure those I loved.

CHAPTER NINE

After breakfast the next morning, I found José in the garage replacing the cord on a lamp we used in the library.

"Got a minute?"

He looked up. "Sure. What's up?"

It was cold in the garage, so he was layered up with a sweater under a heavy jacket. I launched into a brief explanation of the murder and our plans for Blair and me to go undercover. A smile picked up the corners of his full mouth, and his dark eyes flashed.

"I'd like to see that. I've been with you guys when your backs are to the wall, and I'd put my money on you every time."

"Well, at least Blair," I said.

"Hey, Miz Applegate, you're one tough lady."

"Thanks. I think. Well, my proposal would give you a front row seat. I was hoping you'd go with us."

His black eyebrows popped up. "Into a homeless camp?"

"Yes. We'd be in the same camp, but you would set up camp separately and pretend not to know us. I don't think I could get David fully behind this unless we had a built-in protection plan, and Ben will be in a different camp."

"So, I'm your protection plan."

"Right. Look, José, I don't want to sugar-coat this. It could be dangerous. But we could really use your help."

His dark eyes turned inward as he fiddled with the lamp plug. At five foot eight or so, he wasn't large, but I knew he worked out and had martial arts training. Besides, he was smart and seemed fearless. We'd seen that when he'd helped us in Chicago during our road trip from Hell.

"What's the goal?" he asked.

"Just to get information on this guy they call Patch and find out what may be happening to the people who go missing."

"Then we'd report back to the police," he said.

"Right."

He pulled his lower lip between his teeth for a moment, thinking. "Listen, Miz Applegate, you've done a lot for me. And I'm honored you'd even ask. So, yeah, I'm in. Just tell me when."

"First, we're going to learn as much as we can about what it takes to be homeless from someone who's been there. We don't want to inadvertently blow our cover, and we need to know how to survive out there. I'll set something up in the next day or so. Meanwhile, your hair is already long enough, but you might want to let your beard grow out a bit."

He flashed me a brilliant smile. "Will do."

When I was done talking with José, I tried valiantly to ignore the knot in my stomach. We were really going to do this—try to fit into a world completely unfamiliar to us and potentially dangerous. But I sucked up my nervousness and called Brenda to let her know about our plans.

"I'm glad you called," she said. "Rudy's arraignment has been set for 2:30 this afternoon. While the judge doesn't have to allow for bail, since Mrs. Smith has a clean record and this is her first offense, I'm very hopeful."

"You mean she might not be released on bail?" I hadn't even contemplated that Rudy wouldn't be free to defend herself.

"The evidence against her is strong, which means she'll likely be charged with first degree murder. In cases like that, the judge doesn't have to allow bail. I don't know what the prosecuting attorney's office will push for. But once again, she's an upstanding citizen with no priors, and so hopefully they won't fight to keep her locked up."

"Should I call Angela?"

"She won't be allowed to help you. It would present a conflict of interest, and you don't want to put her in a difficult position."

"Do I need to be at the arraignment?"

"No. However, if Rudy can't pay the bail, someone will need to be available to help her out. And, like I said, bail for a first-degree murder case can be upwards to a million dollars or more, depending on the flight risk."

That knocked the wind out of me. "You're kidding!"

"Not kidding. In Washington state if you can't pay the full bail amount, though, you'd go to a bail bondsman and pay ten percent of whatever the bail is. And before you ask, she doesn't want Elliott to help her. Something about not wanting to be indebted to him."

"I get it. He's angling to get her back, even though he walked out on her several years ago. Anyway, tell Rudy not to worry. Our friend Doe Kovinsky said she'd be on call for funds if Rudy needs help. I'll text you her phone number."

"Sounds good."

"By the way, did Rudy's blood test come back?"

"Yes. And it was negative for any kind of drug. I'm afraid that won't help."

We hung up, and I flopped into a chair for a moment to allow my breathing to slow. Despite all the murder cases we'd been involved in, none of us had ever been arrested. Well, except for Ben, but not the rest of us. Suddenly, this was feeling all too real and much more consequential. Once I'd caught my breath, I called Doe and explained the situation.

"I've got this," she said. "I'll call my accountant and have him ready for the call when it comes in." She gave me his name and phone number to pass along to Brenda.

"Thanks, Doe. I just…" I stopped mid-sentence to swallow. "I just never thought it would get this far. This is scary, and the odds seemed stacked against Rudy."

"I agree. But we're not going to let some despicable human being take our friend from us. At least not without a fight."

I sent the accountant's information to Brenda, and then I went to the Inn's office to make a valiant attempt at doing bookwork. A call from David interrupted me as I caught my breath at the size of our electric and gas bill.

"I just talked with Sean," he said. "He said I could let you know that they got camera footage from two of Rudy's neighbors showing the front of her house that afternoon."

I sat up straighter. "Anything useful?"

"Yeah, a dark blue van with the words 'Johnston Electronics' stenciled on the side pulled into her driveway around 9:15 that night. Two men and a woman were in it. The footage we have from the neighbors is pretty grainy, though."

"What about Rudy's security camera?"

"It must have been disabled before that. Same with her porch light."

"Damn! A blue van. Remember what that guy at the homeless camp said about a blue van picking up Ginger?"

"Yeah. That's a good piece of information now. But they didn't find any fingerprints in the house other than Rudy's and Romaine's. And, before you ask, the forensics team was booked today with two other jobs. But someone just left to pick up that birdhouse."

"Okay. Fingers crossed on that one. Do you know how long that van was at her house?"

"Under fifteen minutes. They knew exactly what they were doing."

"How about a license plate number?"

"It was linked to a car that was junked two years ago."

I slumped back in my chair. "Darn it."

"Listen, I've gotta go. You want me to stop by later?"

"Yeah. How 'bout I make something special? After all, I might be gone for a few days."

"What do you mean?"

"Let's discuss it tonight?"

We hung up, and I finished paperwork before checking in with April. By 6:00, I had homemade spaghetti sauce simmering on the stove and a bottle of red wine ready for whenever David got there. I thought an evening for just the two of us was warranted. Not only did I have to convince him that my going undercover was a good idea, but I thought I deserved some close contact of a personal nature given that soon I might be going undercover as a homeless person looking and smelling like yesterday's trash.

CHAPTER TEN

A heavy storm woke me the next morning, with pelting rain that slammed into the ground outside my window. David had left late the night before after we, well… you know. I thought I'd sleep in a few extra minutes, but an aggressive wind made the Inn's rafters groan and rattle in protest, making sure I stayed awake.

"Wow," I said to Minnie as I slid out from under the covers and pulled on my robe. "Sounds like a good day for a fire while we do some research."

Minnie scooted down a set of steps at the end of the bed and ran from the bedroom into the living room to the sliding doors that open onto a small, fenced yard. I followed her.

"Okay," I said, opening the door, "but you're not going to like it out there."

She slipped through the small opening just as a gust of wind buffeted the building and almost blew her over. She made a U turn and came back inside. I sighed.

"Okay, I guess I'm taking you out on your leash."

I checked my phone first and noticed that Rudy had texted me the night before to let me know she was out of jail and that she would call me later. I replied with several heart emojis before grabbing my robe and an umbrella. I dropped my phone into the pocket of my robe and attached the leash to Minnie's collar. A minute later, I stood by the flower beds against the building, while Minnie did her business. It was only 6:30, with little sunlight because of the clouds, and the biting cold made me shiver. The fact I was braving the storm for only one dog instead of two, though, made me momentarily sad remembering how irritated I used to get when Mickey would take forever lifting his leg to mark every plant and bush he could find. Male dogs! The jingle of my phone brought me out of my reverie, and I let Minnie go while I pulled the phone out of my pocket and thumbed it on.

"Julia? This is Emma," she said before I could even say hello.

The clip to her voice raised alarm bells. "What's wrong?"

The wind was blowing so hard that rainwater was layering the entire left side of my face, making me turn my back to the wind.

"My friend Rose Marie has been taken."

"What? Wait. Hold on." A gust of wind almost ripped the umbrella from my hand. "I'm outside with my dog. Let me get inside. I'll call you right back."

I hung up and grabbed Minnie's leash. "C'mon, Minnie! We need to get inside."

My poor puppy looked bleakly at me as she squatted next to a bush, her red fur plastered against her body. When she'd finished, we hurried inside. I let her off the leash, grabbed a towel and quickly dried her off. Then, I used another towel to dry my face and hair before stripping off my wet robe. Dressed only in my pajamas, I plopped down on my sofa and called Emma back, while Minnie did what all wet dogs do. She ran around the room, rolling on the carpet.

"Okay, tell me what happened," I said to Emma.

"After talking to you yesterday, I decided to go visit one of the shelters," she said. "I saw a woman outside I know named Ileana. She was a friend of Rose Marie's. They both suffer from mental health issues."

"And what happened?"

"Although Ileana cycles on and off her medication, she was pretty lucid and warned me to stay away from Chang's Restaurant near Magnolia Bridge. When I asked why, she said she was dumpster diving with Rose Marie there the night before last. Rose Marie left her to hunt through the dumpsters around the corner, and when she didn't come back, Ileana went looking for her. She came around the corner just as a man was pushing Rose Marie into a van. She hasn't seen Rose Marie since."

"Oh, my God," I said with an exhale. "That makes six. Listen, I'll get our group together this afternoon. You available?"

"Of course. But listen, Julia, I'm sick about Rose Marie. Her mental capabilities not only make her vulnerable; she's another one without family. No one will look for her."

"Did Ileana report this to the police?"

"No. Most of these people are afraid of the police. She didn't tell anyone. She just wanted me to be careful."

"And she didn't get a good look at the man?"

"I don't know. She said she ducked behind a dumpster so he wouldn't see her."

"Are you okay with me reporting it?"

"Will they believe you? I mean, you're hearing it third hand."

"As I said, I'm well connected in that department. What does Rose Marie look like?"

"Oh, um, she's probably in her mid-fifties, thin and shuffles her feet when she walks. Dark eyes. Her hair is thinning and kind of a salt and pepper gray." She paused a moment. "I guess that's it."

"Did Ileana say what color the van was?"

"No."

"Okay, I'll share this with the police. Unless you hear from me, come to the main entrance of the Inn this afternoon at 4:30. We need to put a plan together and get going."

When I hung up, I called David and told him what Emma had told me.

"Can you do anything about that?" I asked him.

"I'll let Seattle PD know."

"Okay, I'm organizing a group meeting here at 4:30. With this newest abduction, we really need to get going. Can you be here?"

"I really can't be anywhere near what you're doing. Besides, I'm stuck with these burglaries," he said apologetically.

"No problem. I'll report back later. And thank you, David, for trusting me."

We hung up, and I started making phone calls. The first one was to April to let her know I might be late into the kitchen to help with breakfast. I called Blair next, and she offered to call Doe. I texted José and Ben, and then called Brenda. I finally called Rudy and filled her in on our progress, noting how tired she sounded.

"You don't need to be here," I said. "Why don't you rest today?"

"I'll be there," she said. "I'm pissed as hell about this, and I'm not going down quietly."

"Okay. See you this afternoon."

By the time I finished, I felt like we were putting together an army. Not our usual modus operandi.

After helping April serve breakfast, I spent most of the day tending to Inn business, but my mind kept wandering to the meeting planned for that afternoon. At two o'clock, I moved our big whiteboard into our dining room, placing it at the end of the long table, which seated twelve. In here, we could close the pocket doors and have complete privacy.

Around noon, I staffed the front desk while Crystal, our daytime help, did laundry and cleaned rooms. I brought Minnie with me to our small office behind the reception desk. I was there when the bell rang. I came out to find a buxom young woman with dark hair pulled into a loose bun. Another dark-haired woman admired my fall display of antiques near the front door. Since I change the display throughout the year, this time I'd placed a Hepplewhite mahogany armchair in front of the side window with a standing Tiffany lamp behind it. On a long, oak library table against the wall, I'd organized an Alice in Wonderland teapot with four teacups. Then, I'd tucked fake pumpkins and colorful gourds by the feet of the chairs and finally scattered silk fall leaves across the small area carpet; the same leaves Chloe had blown around the day before.

"Can I help you?" I asked the woman at the desk.

She looked to be in her late twenties. Her brown eyes were quick and intelligent as she gave me a big smile.

"We're checking in," she said. "Last name Argus."

"Oh, yes," I said, going to the computer that sat just below the counter. I pulled out the keyboard and typed in their names, which came up as Donna and Deirdre Argus. "You're here for a meeting with Overlake Hospital."

"That's right. We've been hired to do penetration testing on their computer system."

"That sounds scandalous," I said with a big smile.

She laughed. "Okay, wrong kind of penetration. We'll be testing for security breaches." She handed me a card which read Double D IT, LLC.

"Ha," I laughed. "Double D for Donna and Deirdre. Cute."

"Well, it could also mean these," the other woman said, stepping forward. She cupped her equally large breasts with the palms of her hands and had a huge grin on her face. "We're also twins, as you can see. We just couldn't let it go."

I broke out in laughter. "I love it. It's creative… and memorable. And isn't that what marketing is supposed to be? Which one is which, though?" I asked, looking back and forth between the two of them.

"Oh, sorry," the first twin said. "I'm Donna. You can tell it's me because of this small scar on my chin." She pointed to a moon shaped scar on the right side of her face.

"And I'm Deirdre," the other one said. "And you can tell it's me because I'm the one with the big mouth." As Donna rolled her eyes, Deirdre added, "Meaning I don't have a filter and say pretty much whatever comes into my head."

I chuckled. "I usually find that admirable."

"You wouldn't if she found it necessary to make comments about every guy you dated to their face," Donna said.

I grabbed the registration book and slid it over. "Well, why don't you both sign in? Do you have a car?"

"Yes, we rented one," Donna replied.

"Okay, we'll need the license plate number, too."

A door in the hallway above us slammed open, and the two boisterous girls I had come to think of as the demon team raced down the stairs and past our new guests, yelling at each other the whole way. They nearly knocked Deirdre over as she browsed our brochure rack, and then they disappeared into the breakfast room and out the back door onto our deck.

"Sorry," I said. "Those are two of our… uh, more rowdy guests. If they disturb you, please let me know."

"Exactly why I'll never have children," Deirdre said, going back to browsing the brochures. She suddenly pulled out the brochure on the Inn. "Wow! This place is haunted. You didn't tell me that, D," she said, turning to her sister. "You don't really have ghosts, do you? I mean, it's just a marketing gimmick, right?"

As if on cue, one of the pumpkins from the display next to the front door rolled into the center of the foyer and stopped. The two young women turned and stared at it wide-eyed.

I shrugged. "No, not a marketing gimmick."

"Hell, yeah," Deirdre said turning back to me. "I totally believe in the paranormal. I swear I saw a little girl dressed in turn-of-the-century clothes standing in the window of an abandoned house one night a couple of years ago. There were no lights on, and yet she glowed."

"You'd also had a lot to drink," her sister admonished her.

"I was not drunk," Deirdre said.

"Well, the ghosts here are real but friendly," I said. "We describe them in that brochure, so feel free to take it with you."

I had just finished checking them in when Crystal returned.

"Crystal, these are the Argus sisters. Can you show them to the suite?"

"Sure," she replied, grabbing the key from my hand. "By the way," she said, leaning in close. "Chloe is in a mood today. Every time I closed the dryer door, she swung it open. I finally snapped at her to let me finish my job."

I laughed and pointed to the pumpkin in the center of the floor. "She's been active out here, too. By the way, I have a private meeting in the dining room at 4:30."

She nodded and left with our two new guests. While Crystal took the women to their room, I replaced the pumpkin and said out loud, "Be good, Chloe."

At 3:00, the Inn's guests began to assemble in the breakfast room to enjoy April's oatmeal raisin cookies, raspberry bars, and lemonade for an afternoon snack. The two bratty girls rushed in from outside to fill their plates. Minnie growled at them, so I picked her up quickly to keep her out of harm's way, and so she wouldn't take a chunk out of one of their ankles. The two girls grabbed handfuls of cookies and then rushed back up the stairs to their room.

"People come and go so quickly around here," Ahab squawked.

"That's from The Wizard of Oz," an older woman cried. "He thinks he's Dorothy."

A couple of other guests laughed.

"You have no idea," I said mostly to myself.

I put Minnie down and then joined April in the kitchen as she was finishing up the dishes.

"Do you want to join us for the meeting this afternoon?"

She looked at me sideways, her eyes narrowed into a squint. "No. I've had a headache all afternoon. When I'm done here, I think I'll go lie down for a while."

To me, April was just short of being a medium, which meant she had a sixth sense about things. She often called something out moments before it happened, like phone calls or people at the front door, and sometimes had visions of things to come.

"I didn't sleep well last night," she added.

"No dreams or visions?"

"Weird dreams. I don't remember specifics other than two men working with PVC pipe as if they were building a drain or something."

"I wonder if that means we're going to have plumbing problems. Look, just get some rest. I'll clean up the breakfast room after our meeting."

She nodded and dried her hands on a towel. "Okay. Good luck. I hope you devise a good plan. Just be careful."

"We will. There's a whole group working on this one."

She placed her hand on my shoulder. "Whatever you decide to do, for once, be the one who remains in the background. Let the others take the risk."

I pursed my lips. "April, this is Rudy. We have to help. But at least this time, we have both Ben and José involved. They're better equipped to handle whatever comes up."

"Let's hope so."

April left for the guest house, and I went into the breakfast room to mingle with the guests and to make sure the afternoon snacks and lemonade were replenished. The rain had subsided slowly over the course of the day, but the wind continued to whip up white caps on Lake Washington.

By 4:15, the dessert trays were almost empty and only a single woman remained, sitting by the window murmuring to Ahab. Wind always excites Ahab, and he bounced around in his cage next to the back door. The woman's name was Gretchen Engle, and she was in town for her daughter's wedding, a union she confided to me she didn't approve of, since her daughter was about to marry another woman. Ahab had jumped down off his perch and had come right up to the cage bars. As Gretchen murmured to him, he clicked his tongue, which was a sound he made when he was feeling content.

"Do you like birds?" I asked her, coming up to her side.

She turned to me. She was probably in her early fifties with piercing gray eyes.

"I have a menagerie of birds at home. Two parakeets, a cockatiel, a couple of finches, and a cockatoo. No parrots, though."

She turned back to Ahab. "He's a beauty. You must have paid a pretty penny for him."

"Actually, I bought him at an estate sale when I overheard a young man with tattoos and black eye makeup say that he wanted to buy him and take him home to teach him heavy metal songs." I laughed and shook my head. "I decided quickly that I couldn't condemn the poor bird to that. So, I outbid him and brought Ahab home."

"No place like home. No place like home," Ahab suddenly squawked.

"How delightful," she said, her face beaming. "He likes The Wizard of Oz."

"Yes, he can be quite charming. But not all the time," I said with a smile. "He lived with an older woman who watched a lot of cop shows. So, we never know what might come out of his mouth...uh...beak."

"Good cop. Bad cop," Ahab squawked.

She chuckled with good nature. "That must keep you on your toes."

"It does. What time do you have to be at the rehearsal dinner tonight?"

"Not until 6:30," she replied as she stood up. "I have some work to do before I go."

"Oh? What do you do?"

"I'm a freelance writer."

"That sounds interesting. For businesses?"

"Yes. But also individuals. I write letters, brochures, speeches, things like that. I'm working on a book proposal for someone right now." She stretched her back. "In fact, I'd better get to it."

"Listen, have fun tonight," I said.

She sighed. "I'll try. I love my daughter, and I only want her to be happy. I'm not old-fashioned or prejudiced. I'd just imagined a different life for her. An easier life."

"I understand. Maybe tonight you'll get a chance to see the couple together and how much they mean to each other and feel better about it."

"I hope so. Have a good evening."

She headed for the stairs just as my phone jingled. It was Ben.

"Hey, you texted earlier. What's up?"

"Any chance you could come to the Inn for a group meeting in a few minutes? Another street person has gone missing, so we need to get going."

"I'm on campus, so it will take me about thirty minutes, but I'll be there."

"Thanks."

I spent the next ten minutes stocking the dining room with bottled water and a snack tray. Rudy was first to arrive. The deep circles and sagging skin under her eyes told me she wasn't sleeping much. But the scratches had begun to heal and looked pink against the gray pallor of her skin.

"You okay?" I asked, putting my arm around her.

"I'm tired," she said, rubbing her eyes. "I've spent hours searching through years' worth of articles on the homeless population in our area. I wanted to get a sense of the politics involved, the support system, and the location of homeless camps and shelters. There are a lot of them. I created a map," she said, holding up a folded piece of paper.

Blair came through the front door at the same time as Emma. They hung their coats on the coat tree, chatting amicably, and then Emma stopped to admire my antiques.

Blair's skin-tight navy leggings and equally form-fitting green turtleneck, which was belted with a wide gold sash, was in complete contrast to Emma's loose-fitting, linen blend pants secured at the ankles with little ties and then topped off with a faded blue and green pin-tucked gauze blouse. The two women couldn't be any more different, and yet they behaved as if they'd known each other forever.

"This place is lovely," Emma said, as her gaze swept the entryway.

"Thanks. It's home."

She grinned. "Yes, it is. By the way, when we met yesterday, I remember that you wore that beautiful, beaded jacket at the dinner."

I smiled. "I don't get much occasion to wear it. But it's nice of you to remember."

She glanced around again. "Was this originally your home before it was an inn?"

"No. We bought it to turn it into a bed and breakfast. It was built in the 1940s by John St. Claire." I pointed to a black-and-white framed photo of the St. Claire family hanging on the wall behind the reception desk. Just then, the same pumpkin from my antique display rolled into the center of the floor again. "Uh, he and his wife, Elizabeth and their three children lived here," I said, picking up the pumpkin. "A fire destroyed much of the original home. Elizabeth and two of her children died in the fire along with their family dog." I replaced the pumpkin. "My husband bought it for me years later to fulfill my dream of owning a bed and breakfast. Then he divorced me," I said with a shrug. The pumpkin rolled out again.

"Oh dear," Emma said, watching the pumpkin with curiosity. "Is there a slant to the floor?"

"Nope," Blair replied, waltzing up next to her as they both stared at the pumpkin. "The Inn is haunted." Blair picked up the pumpkin and set it back where it belonged.

Emma's eyebrows lifted. "The Inn is really haunted? Is that what I'm witnessing?"

"Yes. Emma, meet Chloe," I said with a gesture to thin air. "Chloe, meet Emma. She's a friend. So, leave her alone. Anyway," I continued, ignoring Emma's look of surprise, "we'll be meeting down the hall in the dining room."

I led them the short distance down the hallway but noticed that Emma's gaze had drifted back to the foyer.

Blair leaned into her. "You'll get used to it. They're very friendly... unless you insult them."

My phone pinged. It was David.

"Hey, just wanted to give you an update. We're trying to find that blue van. We've gotten additional footage from Rudy's neighbors. All the homes up there seem to have cameras, so we're going through the footage. Anyway, we're also attempting to track the van through traffic cameras as it left the island. There are cameras at the entrance to the freeway leading to Seattle. We've tracked it on and off the floating bridge. Now they're working on where it might have gone after that. But can you ask Rudy if she remembers seeing a blue van in the neighborhood that afternoon?"

"Sure, hold on."

I gestured to Rudy to come over and asked her about the blue van.

She shook her head. "No. I was gone most of the day. Why? "Just a second."

I relayed her answer to David.

"Okay, because that same van was parked on her street earlier in the afternoon, but

no one appeared on camera. We believe that's when they disabled her alarm system and porch light."

"Oh, boy," I said, exhaling. "But won't that help her?"

"I hope so. It doesn't prove anything, but it's certainly suspicious. Anyway, I'll let you know if we find anything else."

"Thanks. I'll call you after the meeting."

Doe came in through the front door just as I hung up. She hurried down the hall to give me a hug. "I hope you have snacks. I'm starving."

"Don't you ever take a break to have lunch?" I asked her. "You are the boss, after all."

She smiled warmly. "Yes, and I have all the responsibility that goes with it. So, I rarely get a break to eat. I count on you for that." She winked, took off her coat and went to sit next to Blair.

I glanced at my watch. It was 4:35, so I stepped into the room.

"Everyone get a snack and some water. I'm expecting two more people, and then we can do introductions and fill you all in on what we know about the murder and the abductions."

CHAPTER ELEVEN

People grabbed cookies from a tray in the middle of the table and settled into their chairs. José appeared and sat next to Rudy in front of the windows. I took the chair at the end of the table by the whiteboard and leaned over to tell Rudy why David had called.

"Damn. I wonder if the people in the van knew I'd be gone," she said, referring to the van being at her house that afternoon.

When everyone was settled, we went around the room and introduced ourselves. Emma only briefly mentioned her time on the street and the book she'd written. Ben appeared just as we finished.

"Sorry to be late," he said, sneaking in.

"No problem," I assured him. "This is my brother Ben, everyone. He'll be going into the veterans' camp."

Ben sat down, and I turned to look around the room, noticing that both Ben and José had already begun to let their beards grow out.

"Okay, there are pens and paper on the table in case anyone wants to take notes. So, let me set the stage."

I spent the next ten minutes filling them in on everything we knew so far, including the man named Patch and what role Romaine had thought he played.

"I think that's an accurate recounting of the events," I said with a shrug. I turned to Rudy. "You want to add anything?"

She stood up and moved to the whiteboard. "Thanks, Julia. These are the names of the five people Romaine thought were missing," she said, pointing to the names listed. "There's Evergreen, who is a white woman in her late twenties. An older white man named Jacob who stayed in the veteran's camp. A younger trans Hispanic man that went by the name Pepper. He's the one we think left a swimming medal behind, something Romaine said he would never do." She turned back to the board. "The last two are a middle-aged Black woman called Kalisha, and a young gay man called Emmet."

"And Romaine thought this Patch guy was the one setting them up for... what?" Ben asked.

"We don't know," I replied. "But that's what we want to find out."

"And you suspect the tall, thin guy with the limp you mentioned was the one offering them jobs," Ben said. "Do we know who he worked for?"

"No," Rudy replied.

"Do we know the full names of any of these people?" José asked.

I looked at Emma. "Do you happen to know Evergreen or Rose Marie's last names?"

She leaned forward so she could see everyone. "Most people don't give out their last names on the street. I don't think Evergreen ever mentioned hers, although she told me that Evergreen was her real first name. It's an unusual name, so that may help. And I'm trying to remember what Rose Marie told me. She said once that her last name rhymed with, um..." she paused, thinking. "Oh, yeah, turd. God, how could I forget that? Her last name was Bird, although I don't know how she spelled it. Anyway, she said as a kid she got the nickname Bird Turd."

"But why abduct them?" José asked. "That's what I don't get. They don't have anything to steal."

"Well, they do if they're getting social security or disability checks from the government," Emma replied.

"Why don't you tell them about Rose Marie," I said to her.

She nodded, took a breath, and then said, "Julia came to me because she thought I could help prepare you for what you'll encounter when you go undercover. I was in this world for over two years. And I made a lot of friends. Unfortunately, I heard just this morning that a second person I know was abducted recently."

"You say abducted," Ben said. "You're sure of this?"

"As sure as I can be, given that it came to me as secondhand knowledge." She proceeded to relate how Ileana had witnessed Rose Marie being pushed into a van.

"So, that's six people," Doe whispered.

"Yes," I said. "Originally, I thought we'd have time to research and plan more, since Romaine was already dead. But we don't know what's happening to these people. They might be dead, too. Or, as Emma suggested, someone could be holding them prisoner to collect their disability checks."

"Which means, we might be able to save them," Doe said with a light in her eyes. She glanced over to the whiteboard. "Let's get everything we know onto the whiteboard."

Ever the CEO, I thought.

Over the course of the next twenty minutes, we wrote up every piece of information we had. As I watched Rudy write, I noticed her hand tremble and wondered again how useful she would be during this investigation. A couple of times, she even stopped to massage one hand with the other. Fortunately, people around the room were talking or taking notes, so I hoped no one noticed.

"Okay, now we need to plan our approach so that no one else gets killed," Blair said.

"Well, I'm going to the vets' camp," Ben said with a brief wave of his hand.

"And Blair, José, and I are going to the Magnolia camp," I said, turning to Emma. "I'm hoping you'll school all of us in everything we need to know to be believable out there. It wouldn't be good to look like we're faking it."

"Also," Doe said, "some of my drivers are out looking for Ginger. No word on that yet, though."

Rudy produced her map of the camps and makeshift sites under bridges and along alleyways. Emma tweaked it slightly with the current knowledge she had of a couple places that had been closed by the city. Afterwards, Rudy went to our office to make copies for everyone, while Emma discussed what to expect and how to act.

"Don't act too friendly," she said. "I know you need information in a hurry, but if you start getting all chummy, they'll walk away. On the other hand, if you appear too needy, they'll take advantage of you."

"We need to earn people's trust," Ben said.

"Right," she said. "It's best to stay to yourself in the beginning. Be suspicious of others. Act like you're afraid someone might try to steal something from you. And don't start asking questions right away. That'll be a sure giveaway."

"We need to fit in," Blair said.

"Yes," she agreed. "Remember, these people feel like they've been kicked around their entire lives. Most of them don't remember what happy is."

"Sounds awful," Doe murmured.

Emma glanced at her. "It's not great. You wake up each day wondering if you'll eat that day. You'll feel lucky if you find a half-eaten Subway sandwich in a trash can with flies on it."

My gut twisted a little and glanced around the table. People were silent.

"I've had to scavenge for worse things in the jungle," Ben said, breaking the silence. "In fact, I've eaten bugs when I had to." He turned to José. "You okay with that?"

My young, good-looking maintenance man studied Ben for a moment, and then said, "I grew up in the Watts area of Los Angeles in flophouses with roaches crawling on me at night. I could hear the rats chewing on garbage. I didn't starve, but I had to fight for everything I got. I can do this."

"Okay," Emma said. "The strategy is to avoid looking like you're searching for information. Don't look people directly in the eye and never ask a direct question about the investigation." She looked at Ben. "For instance, Jacob disappeared from the veterans' camp, and that's where you'll be. But don't start asking questions about Jacob. You were in the Navy, right?"

Ben nodded.

"Jacob was Air Force," she said, glancing at the white board. "So, maybe get a conversation going about fighter jets and what you thought about the war. Positive or negative. It doesn't matter. Someone will likely mention Jacob. Then you can say you'd like to meet him someday and boom! You'll find out he's no longer there. The point is to get the information in a roundabout way."

"It would seem so natural to just ask a direct question, though," Doe said.

She smiled at Doe. "You're the CEO of a big company. Being direct is second nature to you. Not to these people." She turned to José. "You could take a weapon with you. You good with a knife?" José nodded, which made me raise an eyebrow. "Okay, talk about why you carry the knife. Maybe it's because you used to live in Watts, and you are carrying the knife because a friend of yours disappeared down there. No one ever saw the guy again, and you're not going to end up like that."

"I get it," I said. "That's brilliant."

"Just common sense," Emma said. "The goal is to blend in."

"Listen, one of the things we need to find out is what all six of these victims had in common," Rudy said. "I mean, besides not having family that would come looking for them."

"Like what else?" José asked.

"Like were they all offered jobs just before they went missing? If so, where? Who else did they talk to? Was Patch their only contact? Or were they offered jobs by anyone else? We've got to try to connect the dots." She pulled out a small stack of papers and passed them around. "I took the liberty of writing out introductory questions and statements you might use to get things going. If you can, adapt them to something personal."

Everyone was reading through Rudy's list when April appeared at the doorway looking unsteady on her feet. Despite the cold temperature, there were beads of sweat on her forehead, and her eyes were wide and glassy.

"What's wrong?" I said, getting up and moving quickly around the table to her.

She stared at me like I wasn't there, her breath coming fast. "I…I…" she said, almost choking on her words.

Doe was sitting closest to April and jumped up to take her arm. "Here, sit down, April," she said, guiding April into her chair.

I crouched down next to my friend. "April, you're scaring me. What happened?"

She took several deep breaths, put her hand on her chest to calm herself, and then said, "I took a nap, like I said. I had a headache. But I saw a fire. It was intense. And… and a body was burning." Her hand went to her nose. "I could smell it. Burning flesh. It was awful." She gagged suddenly, and I thought she might throw up.

I gestured to Rudy to give me my bottle of water. I handed it to April, who took a long drink.

"Where was the fire?" I asked her.

She shook her head. "I don't know. But it was all around me. Someone else was there, too, but I couldn't see who. I was afraid for my life." She lifted her head and glanced at the people around the table.

"What is it, April?" Blair asked, leaning forward. "What's wrong?"

74

Tears formed in her eyes before she said, "I think one of you might die."

CHAPTER TWELVE

April's comment cast a pall over the room. We watched silently as Doe ushered April out of the room to take her back to the guest house to lie down again. Afterwards, I explained to Emma what April's special talents were.

"And she's for real?" Emma asked.

"Her talent is very real," Rudy said.

"In fact," Ben interjected. "She's been right about several things, not the least of which was a description of where I was being held prisoner a few weeks ago by a power-hungry secret society willing to kill me for a box I was looking for." He rubbed his ribs absent-mindedly, no doubt remembering the injuries he'd received during said abduction.

"But what April said doesn't necessarily mean someone in this room will die," I added hastily, returning to my seat. "She doesn't typically see actual events but rather images she has to interpret."

"But she said someone might die," Blair said.

"Yes, but you know as well as I do that what she saw was probably death in general, and she connected it to us."

"But let's be honest," Ben began. "She clearly saw something that scared the hell out of her."

"He's right, Julia," Rudy said. "She saw something that really upset her. We need to be on alert."

"You, too," I replied. "Someone was murdered in your kitchen."

She nodded. "I had Renfroe Security come out today to give me a quote on a new security system."

"I can stay here at the Inn," José offered. "Just to have someone on the property."

"And I can move in for a while, too, if you need me," Ben said.

"You guys forget that by tomorrow we'll all be sleeping on the street."

"Maybe not," Emma said.

Everyone paused and turned to her.

"What do you mean?" I asked.

She took a deep breath and glanced around the room before saying, "I think you may have set yourself up for failure."

"What does that mean?" Blair asked stiffly.

Emma shrugged. "Look. You may not be aware of how much homeless people move around. It's one of the reasons you're probably having trouble finding this woman named Ginger."

"Yes, but what did you mean?" Ben asked.

Emma looked over at me. "You and Blair went to the camp here on Mercer Island in a pretty public way. People there know who you are now."

"And many of them move around," Ben said flatly. "Damn."

I cringed and glanced at Blair, who sat stone-faced, staring at Emma.

Count to three.

"She's right," Ben said. "If anyone recognizes you, the jig is up."

My emotions were fighting for control inside my chest. What a fool I was.

"We blew it," I murmured, slumping back in my seat.

Doe came back and sat at the table. "Blew what?" she asked.

Blair released a defeated sigh. "We tipped our hand when we went to the Mercer Island camp looking for Ginger. So, now, Ben and José will be the only ones going undercover."

"Maybe not," Emma said gently. "I could go instead. I'm better suited for it anyway." Blair stiffened again but Emma caught herself this time. "Wait. I'm not saying you couldn't withstand the dirt and grime. The lack of privacy. The stench. Or even the physical risk."

"What, then?" Blair asked with an edge to her voice.

"What I'm saying is that you wouldn't look or act the part. Not convincingly, anyway. For instance, the desperation in a person's eyes. The physical weight of the guilt and shame you feel for having let everyone in your life down. Or the persistent fear for your safety. You can't fake that stuff. It lives within you like a virus. Also, I don't mean to sound misogynistic," she said, glancing at Ben and José. "But frankly, the men will probably do better in this situation. Men don't tend to wear their emotions on their sleeves like women do. They'll tough it out no matter what, which of course, is what homeless people do." She turned to me, her expression softening. "Evergreen was my friend. I want to know what happened to her. So, I'm happy to do this."

"But what about your job? This could take several days. Or even longer."

"And couldn't you relapse?" Blair asked. Her voice still reflected a hint of rebuke.

She smiled. "It's not like being an alcoholic. I work for myself now doing people's taxes. Let me do this. I could tell people that someone I hired stole money from me, and my business went under, and once again, I lost everything. I'm known out there. I can make this work."

"Then what role do we play?" Blair asked.

"Look, your plan was good, but you've left out a major source of information."

"What's that?" Doe asked.

"The shelters. Most of these people cycle in and out of the shelters. It would be good to get eyes and ears inside the ones closest to these two camps."

"That's a good idea," Doe said. She turned to Rudy. "I don't suppose you could go back to doing your resume clinics."

She shook her head. "No. I... I don't think I'm up for that, nor do I think Wings of Hope would want me there right now."

The room was quiet for a moment.

"If Rudy can't go back to the shelter, maybe you and Blair could," Emma said, turning to me. "You could continue to play the roles you played when you went into the camps, but this time, you're there as volunteers. That way, you might learn something. You'd have to be careful just like those in the field. Ask too many questions and people will become suspicious. But at least there, your presence won't be questioned."

"That's a good idea," I said reluctantly. I wasn't quite ready to let go of our original idea, but I also realized she was right about our having already played our hand. I turned to Rudy. "What's the name of the shelter closest to the vets' camp?"

"Everyday Miracles," she said, glancing at her map.

Emma turned to Blair. "I think that should be yours. And you can put your nails back on to do it."

Blair's blue eyes lit up in surprise. "How did you know I had my nails removed?"

For the first time, I realized that Blair had had her hands in her lap much of the time, and that she had, in fact, had her fake nails removed.

Emma grinned. "Because ever since you sat down, you've been fidgeting with your bare nails or kept them hidden under the table. Did you do that in preparation for going undercover?"

Everyone around the table was staring at Blair's hands as she rolled them into fists.

"You'd make a good detective," she said a little embarrassed.

Emma eyed Blair. "Don't be embarrassed. That was smart. But you're clearly a woman who takes care of herself. Why don't you offer to teach a class on personal hygiene or personal appearance? How to do make-up, simple hairstyles, how to dress, things like that. Just remember these women won't have the money to buy expensive clothes, or have their nails or hair done," Emma said. "You'll have to teach them to work with what they have, which is almost nothing."

Blair's eyes lit up. "I love that idea. I could pay to have my hairstylist come in to do their hair for free. I could do nails and talk about how to dress while she does their hair. And before you say anything," she said, turning to Rudy, "I can dress like the perfect nine-to-fiver if I have to."

Ben chuckled and then quickly dropped his chin when Blair turned to him.

"That's brilliant, Blair," I said, ignoring my brother.

"Julia, you could take over my resume clinics," Rudy said. "I could give you templates to work from."

I inhaled a little nervously. "Um, I could try it. I mean, I'm not a writer, like you."

"But resumes are kind of formulaic," she said. "You can do this."

"Okay, back to your general safety," Ben cut in. "Since we'll be in the field, I think it would be a good idea to have David stay here."

"I agree," Rudy said. "I could also stay here."

"Hold on," Doe said. "No way can David stay here if Rudy is here. She's out on bail."

"You're probably right." I turned to Rudy. "Okay, you come stay with me. To be honest, I'm not fond of you staying in that big house alone since you're clearly on someone's radar. Meanwhile, now that the plan has changed, we need to clarify what each of us is doing and when."

Blair got up. "I'm going to call my hairdresser right now."

She left the room, while the rest of us went back to planning. Rudy interrupted us when someone mentioned how to keep in touch with each other.

"Wait. Since I'll be here anyway, I could set up a command center at the Inn. "And Elliott bought these for us," she said, dropping prepaid cell phones on the table. "Pass them around."

"Excellent," Ben said.

Rudy pushed them across the table. She even gave one to me, saying, "You and I should be home base. We'll all share numbers so no one is using their personal numbers, just in case someone else gets their hands on one of these."

"Good call," I said. "Sorry for the pun," I said with a smile.

We took the next few minutes to share phone numbers and record them in the phones.

"And we should keep these only to report in, right?" Ben asked. "I mean, not too many people on the street have cell phones."

"Actually, a lot do," Emma said. "There are a couple of programs that give them out to people for emergencies, especially if they have health issues. But hide them and only use them when you need to. And texting would be best."

"I agree," Rudy said. "Also, put them on vibrate."

It took a couple of minutes for everyone to get settled with their phones. Then Ben said, "Since today is Friday, I can go out tonight. But I agreed to tutor a student on campus on Sunday."

"That's okay. Stay on the street tonight and tomorrow, and I can pick you up Sunday morning," I said. "Then you could go back to the camp Sunday night. Unless you have a lecture on Monday."

"I do, but I got someone to cover for me."

Blair returned with her blue eyes dancing. "My hairdresser said she'd love to help. I'll call Everyday Miracles when we're done and see if they're interested."

"That's terrific, Blair," Doe said.

"I'll call Gloria about you doing the resume clinic," Rudy said to me. "I'm sure it won't be a problem."

"Okay, then. We all have a role to play," I said, feeling my optimism rise.

"Does anyone have an old camp stove I could borrow?" Ben asked.

"There's one in the garage," José said. "Plus, a one-man tent."

"I won't need the tent. You can use it," Ben said.

"I have a beat-up sleeping bag and an old canvas tarp, and I'll carry anything else in a trash bag," José said.

"If you don't take the tent, how will you stay dry?" I asked my brother.

"An old lean-to I used in the Brazilian jungle. It's ripped in places, but it will be enough."

"That's good," Emma said. "The more you guys look like you just grabbed things off the ground somewhere, the better."

José nodded. "I'll get the camp stove for you before I leave." He glanced at Emma. "If you and I are going to the Magnolia camp, we need a signal if we want to talk."

Emma thought for a moment and then said, "If I say to you for any reason, 'stop staring at me,' that means we need to talk."

José smiled. "Good. And if I need to talk to you, I'll ask you for something."

"When do you plan to move out?" I asked Ben.

"As soon as I leave here. I've already highjacked a rickety old shopping cart and have some things packed in it. I'll grab the camp stove, and then I'm ready to go. I have everything in the back of Carter's old station wagon. Can you drop me off a mile or so from the camp?"

"Sure. José, why don't you go with us, and I'll drop you off somewhere near the Magnolia Park?"

"Okay. I can leave anytime," he said.

"Listen, Ben," Emma said. "The veterans' camp is a fairly large camp. A big guy named Swamp is the de facto boss. You'll have to get his permission to stay there."

"Really?" Blair asked. "How do they enforce that?"

"These are all ex-military, and they're used to taking orders. They'll throw someone out if they have to. Anyway, as I recall he'll ask how and where you served. And then he'll direct you to the edge of the camp. That's where all the newbies go. And remember that because some of the people there suffer from PTSD, the police are called in more often, so stay off their radar if you can."

She turned to José. "The Magnolia Park camp isn't in a park. It's just north of Magnolia Bridge in a big parking lot near the train yard. It's a more transient camp, so just set up shop wherever you can. I'm told this guy Patch hangs out there a lot. The closest bathroom you can even hope to use is a Shell station about a mile away. But Lily of the Valley Mission is in the neighborhood, and they serve one meal a day to the homeless. You can use their bathroom. Just be there by 8 a.m. or you can forget getting anything to eat." She turned back to Ben. "There isn't a charity close to your camp, so you're on your own when it comes to food. But there are some restaurants close by. Dumpster diving is common around there. But the lack of nearby facilities is one of the reasons I didn't stay there long. Saint Ignatius Church, however, is close to the stadiums. That's where I got help. If things get too bad, go ask for Father Mike."

"Do you really feel you're ready to go back, Emma? You've already done so much for us," I said.

She her gray eyes my way. "Absolutely. In fact, I was just thinking about what a force of nature you and your friends are." She glanced around the table. "Each of you are willing to risk your life to help people who have just about given up. I didn't know Romaine, but she obviously went to the right person when she talked to you, Rudy."

Rudy's gaze dropped. "I don't know about that. It might be what got her killed."

"Don't think that way," Emma said. "Perhaps she was meant to get the ball rolling so the rest of you would have a reason to come together and stop whoever is doing this."

"That's philosophical of you," Ben said with a note of appreciation.

The hint of a smile flashed across Emma's face. "Tragedy doesn't only prey on the weak and vulnerable. I met an ex-university professor several years ago whose wife had committed suicide. Her death sent him into a spiral." She looked at José. "And I've known several young people like you, who just didn't make it out of the hell they were born into."

She sat back and placed both hands on the table and stared at them for a second, while we all waited.

"I didn't know Romaine, Jacob, Pepper, or the others. But I did know Evergreen and Rose Marie. They were troubled. Sometimes manipulative. They could even be selfish and mean at times. But they've been preyed upon their entire lives. Whatever these people are intending to do with them, I guarantee they don't deserve it. And I'm pissed as hell that when they've already been kicked to the curb, someone else is there ready to do them more harm." Her head swiveled back towards me. "So, yes. I'm definitely in. I'll head out tonight as well."

CHAPTER THIRTEEN

It was after six o'clock by the time I pulled my Pathfinder around to the front of the Inn. The air was damp with moisture, but thankfully, it wasn't raining. Ben and I hauled out what few things he had from the back of Carter's old car and loaded them into my SUV. We were just finishing up when José came out of the garage with the camp stove and gave it to Ben. He jerked his head toward his little Toyota pickup truck. "I'll get my stuff."

Emma had left, but Blair and Rudy came out of the Inn, just as Doe appeared from the guest house.

"I hope April is okay," Rudy said, glancing at Doe as she strode across the driveway.

"I'm going to stop over there before we go," I said.

"I'm heading home to put together a nail kit and make some notes on how to teach these women how to dress properly for interviews," Blair said.

"And I'll go home and pack a suitcase," Rudy said. "How about we set up command in the reception hall? That'll give us complete privacy, and we can leave everything there,"

"That's a great idea. We don't have any events until the end of the month. You guys have your cell phones?"

Rudy patted the pocket of her slacks, while Blair held up her purse.

"We're all set," Blair said. "Did you call David?"

"I texted him to let him know what we're doing."

"Okay, then, I'm off." Blair gave me a hug and left.

"Do you think this will work?" Rudy asked me, watching Ben and José pack supplies into the back of my car.

"I never know if anything we do will work," I said with a sigh. "But whatever we learn might help your case, and there's at least one woman, Rose Marie, who we might be able to save. We have to try."

Rudy smiled weakly. "Emma was right. We have an amazing group of friends. I'll get my stuff and be back soon."

She squeezed my hand and left just as Doe came up to my side.

"How is April feeling?" I asked,

"I got her to take half of a sleeping pill," Doe said. "She'll rest a bit."

"Okay, I won't disturb her, then. I'll check on her when I get back. I'm taking Ben and José over to their camps."

"Look, Julia, I don't have an official role to play in all of this, but you know I'm here if you need me. I just can't abandon these negotiations. It means too much to the company. I hope you understand. But if push comes to shove… well, you know. Call me. I'll figure out a way to help."

"I know," I said, enveloping her in a hug. "Go make money. We may need it to bail someone else out of jail."

She laughed and headed for her Mercedes.

I turned to find Ben and José coming out the front door of the Inn looking like they had just stepped out of a soup kitchen. Ben had changed into tattered and badly stained cargo pants, a ratty looking sweater and old Navy peacoat, while José had donned torn jeans and layered three dirty thermal shirts under a ragged corduroy jacket. They had both dusted themselves with dirt, even going so far as to rub dirt around their fingernails. I was impressed.

"So, we ready to do this?" Ben asked.

"You look, well… you look awful. And I can smell you from here." I waved my hand in front of my face.

"Perfect," he said. "I splashed some cheap wine on my clothes, and I have this." He pulled out a dented flask. "It's filled with the most awful tasting hooch I could find."

Using Rudy's map, we pulled up across the street from the Shell station Emma had mentioned thirty minutes later. Ben got out and pulled his cart out of the back of the Pathfinder.

I got out as well. "Stay safe," I said, watching him adjust a small American flag he'd paperclipped to the end of the cart.

He wrapped his arm around my shoulders. "I'm just glad this once you're not putting yourself in harm's way."

"Yes, but you just got yourself out of harm's way."

"I can take it," he said. He kissed me on the forehead. "If Mom could only see me now."

We both laughed.

"Hey, don't forget that she's connected to you just the way she is to me. I have no doubt that she'll let me know if you're in trouble."

"I still have to get used to our dead mother calling you on your cell phone."

He gave me a short wave and pulled the cart up onto the curb.

My mother had died eighteen months earlier of emphysema and then shocked me one night by calling me on her old Hello Kitty cell phone when I was embroiled in a murder case. That phone was smashed when I was held hostage, but somehow, she'd found a way to contact me on my own phone. She now could manipulate all sorts of electronics and had helped to scare the bejesus out of a few bad guys that way. I typically didn't hear from her, however, unless either Ben or I were in trouble when, somehow, she sensed the rising danger around us.

I watched Ben amble away, shuffling a little as he pushed his cart. He hunched his shoulders like someone who was weighed down by a thousand disappointments, and it made me misty-eyed thinking of how lucky I was to have him in my life again.

When I dropped José off, I grabbed him into a tight hug. "You're more than my employee, you know? You're like my son."

When I released him, it was clear my show of affection had embarrassed him.

"I love you too, Miz Applegate. Don't worry. I'll stay safe. Besides, you know Chloe likes me. She follows me around when I'm at the Inn. Maybe she'll come and keep an eye on me."

I grinned. "I hope so. If not, I'll suggest it to her when I get back. Just be sure to check in with us once a day, okay?"

"Yes ma'am. Will do," he said with a quick salute.

He sauntered off with the black trash bag slung over his shoulder as if he did this every day, and I found myself choking up again. I felt like the mother hen watching her chicks leaving the nest to find their way on their own. Why was I so protective of the men in my life?

When I got back into the car, I remembered what José had said about Chloe. It didn't surprise me that she followed him around. She probably had a crush on him, like every other woman he met. Too bad he wasn't interested in the fairer sex.

The wind had picked up again when I returned home, and I glanced up to find that heavy rain clouds had filled the sky, making me worry about my chicks' first night on the street. After feeding Minnie and checking on the guests, I went to the kitchen to get a couple of April's chocolate chip muffins and then went to the guest house to see how she was doing. She was sitting in her small living room sipping hot tea.

"I come bearing gifts," I said, pushing the door open and holding out the muffins. "You feeling better?"

I took the muffins into the kitchen and cut one in half, bringing them back to her with a fork. She had changed into loose-fitting lounge pants and a long black tunic and had her slippers on. Her dark eyes seemed to have shrunk into her head, and her dark skin looked pale, if that could happen.

"Thank you," she said, taking the muffin. "I haven't eaten. Have you?"

"No. Rudy is coming back to stay with me, so we'll probably order pizza. I'm just worried about you."

She took a bite of the muffin, swallowed, and then sighed. "I'm relaxed. I'm not sure how good I feel, though."

"That was a bad one, wasn't it? Have you ever reacted to your visions that way before?"

She swallowed another bite of muffin and then placed the plate on the table next to her. "Only once. When I was a kid. I was visiting family in Florida and had a vision that an alligator had eaten my cousin. I was only seven, I think, and didn't understand what you call my visions. I just thought it was a bad dream. But I woke the whole house up screaming and crying that my cousin Sammy was going to die."

"What happened?" I asked quietly.

She took a deep breath. "Sammy was fine. But his father, who I'd seen slap him the day before, got his arm caught in a woodchipper a day later." Her gaze dropped to the floor. "No one put the two together except my grandmother, who had had the same gift since she was a child. She took me aside and tried to explain what I'd seen and how it was connected to Sammy's dad, and that it wasn't my fault."

"Because you thought it was?"

"Of course. Somehow, I thought I'd punished Sammy's dad for slapping Sammy. But that's how these things work sometimes.

Instead of Sammy getting eaten by the gator, like in my vision, his father's arm got eaten by the woodchipper."

"The visions aren't always a straight line."

"No. In fact, there's often no line at all," she said.

"Do you remember what you saw earlier? I mean, was it clear enough that you know for sure one of us is in mortal danger?"

"I saw the PVC pipe again. But I also flames and felt intense heat. And the smell of burning flesh was overpowering." She visibly shivered at the memory.

"Anything else?"

She raised sorrowful eyes to me. "I heard someone scream… 'Julia… gun!'"

CHAPTER FOURTEEN

Since I'd given her a key, I found Rudy hanging out in my living room when I got back to the Inn. When I slipped in the front door, she said, "Pizza should be here in five. How's April?"

I flopped down in my recliner, allowing Minnie to jump up with me. As the little dog squirmed around in my lap, licking whatever exposed skin she could find, I filled Rudy in on what April had told me about her vision.

"She didn't actually see you or anyone else get hurt or die, then?" Rudy asked.

"No. But I think the vividness of it really scared her. Especially the smell of burning flesh. But she also heard someone call my name."

My back doorbell rang, and I hurried to retrieve dinner and tip the delivery guy. Rudy and I got out plates and napkins and then sat down to eat. Fifteen minutes later, David called.

"Hey, what's up?" I asked, wiping my hands on a napkin.

"Is Rudy there?"

"Yes. Let me put the phone on speaker." I did that. "Okay, we're listening.

"Nick talked with a man who lives next door to Rudy. He was home around the time her house was broken into. But then he left for the airport and has been gone until now."

"And?" Rudy bristled with impatience.

"His office window overlooks your driveway. He had it open because he was smoking, something his wife doesn't allow in the house."

"That would be Owen," Rudy said with a grimace. "I often see him on their back patio with a cigarette."

"Well, Owen says he heard the van come up your driveway and then saw three people get out. It was dark, so he didn't see them clearly, but he's pretty sure the person in the passenger seat was a woman."

"Nothing else?" I asked.

"One potentially big piece of news. Sean interviewed the owner of the garden center where Romaine got that job, along with a couple of the employees. He was told that a tall man with a limp came in one day to shop and casually asked about security. The kid he was talking to mentioned they had someone living on the property and gestured to where Romaine's apartment was."

"Damn," Rudy said.

"The kid didn't realize what he was doing. But clearly, they now knew where Romaine lived," David said. "Because when we gained access to her apartment, someone had been there."

"What do you mean?" Rudy asked.

"The place had been trashed as if somebody was searching for something. Maybe they thought she kept notes or had photos."

"I'm surprised they didn't search my house, too." Rudy leaned forward. "You know, I was thinking, we need to find the last names of the people who went missing."

"How do you propose we do that?" I asked.

"I made a list of questions," she said, pulling a folded piece of paper out of her jacket pocket. "For instance, find out the shelters they stayed in. The shelters would have their last names. If nothing else, we could get physical descriptions from them."

"That's a good idea," David said. "But you don't necessarily want to tip your hand to the shelters in case any of their staff are involved. What else?"

"It would help to know if any of them have been arrested, received checks on a regular basis, were in rehab programs, or the hospital."

"Seattle PD would have checked the hospitals," David said.

"But what if I text the group to see what they can find out through their roundabout questioning?" she asked. "For instance, maybe Ben can find out if Jacob had ever been arrested. And didn't Emma say Evergreen had been in rehab? The only last name we have is Rose Marie's. Once we have the others, the police can begin a formal search."

"Good thinking," David said. "Because even though Seattle PD has done some digging, they don't have much to go on."

"Do you want to start setting up the command center tonight?" Rudy asked me.

"Yes, and I think you should oversee it, while I take over your writing clinic and help April with the Inn."

"Just be careful," David warned us.

"We will. And I'll be around other people when I'm at the shelter."

"Rudy, do you know if anyone overheard Romaine when she talked with you about the missing people?" David asked.

She thought a minute. "No. We were alone both times. But I'm sure she told other people."

"But everyone at the shelter knew about her new job at the garden center, right?" I asked.

"Yes. I'm sure the shelter had her new address, too."

"Are you thinking someone at the shelter is involved?" I asked David.

"It's a possibility," he replied.

"I don't think it was anyone at the shelter," Rudy said.

"Maybe not. But you never know who they might have recruited to gather information. Money is a powerful incentive. And a lot of people go in and out of a shelter," he said.

"But, if they were passing along information, they would have known about her apartment at the garden center," I said.

"The apartment isn't easy to find," Rudy interjected. "I visited her there once. The garden center is a large complex. They bring in plants from overseas and then ship them throughout the United States. Her apartment was upstairs next to the main office, and she had a separate entrance off the side of the building. If you didn't know that you'd have trouble finding it."

After we'd finished dinner, Rudy and I used the Inn's laundry cart to take the computers and printer across the back driveway and across the small parking lot in front of the reception hall. We had located the new event center where an old carriage barn from the original hotel had stood since the early 1900s. During our third murder investigation, someone on our radar burned down the old building. Fortunately, no one was hurt. In honor of its history, however, we'd designed the event center to look very much like the rustic old building we'd lost. The new building was modernized with a long, central room that had big windows and a deck overlooking the lake. A small foyer led into the main room. Plus, we had installed a catering kitchen, Wi-Fi, nice bathrooms.

We set up two tables just outside the kitchen with two laptops and the printer. The corkboard walls on either side of the kitchen would be used to pin up photos and create charts of who was connected to whom. We were in the process of organizing file folders when my burner phone pinged.

"It's a text from Ben," I said, looking at the phone. "He says the infamous Patch is at the camp. And he sent me a picture of him."

Rudy came over to look. Ben had taken the picture from about thirty feet away. The distance, and the fact that it was at night prevented us from seeing him clearly. But Patch looked to be about 5' 11", with a medium build and dark hair.

"This is good," Rudy said.

"I just wish we could see him better."

She pointed to Patch's left hand. "He's wearing a large class ring. Text Ben back and tell him to see if he can find out what it looks like up close."

I did as she asked, and twenty minutes later, we headed back to my apartment.

"You up for some tea?" I asked her.

"No. I need to see Elliott. He was gone this afternoon when I picked up my stuff to

come stay with you. He probably thinks I went back to my house, so I should go fill him in on everything."

"Okay," I said. "How do you feel about getting back together with him?"

We were just about to the door of my apartment. She sighed in response to my question.

"I don't know. He's being very attentive and contrite about leaving me. I just don't know if I can trust him."

"I understand completely," I said.

It made me think of how Graham had suddenly announced one day that he wanted a divorce. We maintained an amicable relationship, which was difficult on my part since he had quickly married a woman a good two decades younger than me and twenty pounds thinner.

"Well, you'll work out what's best for you," I said, opening the door to my apartment. "At

least he's supporting you through this."

Minnie was waiting for us and bounced around my feet when we stepped inside.

"I just can't believe this is happening," Rudy said, as we made our way down the hallway.

"Never in my lifetime did I think I'd ever get arrested, unless it was for being an activist for some cause."

"We'll get through this," I said. "We always do."

"Listen, I better get going," she said, grabbing her purse. "I've got the key, so I'll see you in the morning."

I waited until I heard her car pull away, wondering how she was going to navigate all of

this. It wasn't going to be easy. I made a cup of tea and then texted everyone to let them know we'd established the command center and to text either me or Rudy if any of them needed us. Since it was only 9:00, I decided to brush up on how to write a resume and sat down at my computer.

Around 9:30, the burner phone Blair and I had used to go looking for Ginger rang. It was the first time I realized how many phones I had. But a hushed voice said, "Is this the woman who works for the Baker Law Firm?"

I paused, my mind whirring. *Baker Law Firm?* Oh, yeah. My cover story.

"Yes," I replied. "Who is this?"

"My name's Greg. You gave me your card at the camp down by the bridge when you were looking for Ginger. I know where she is. But first, what's in it for me?"

"I, uh, um, I don't know. How about a hundred bucks?" I said without thinking.

"Cash?"

"Yeah. Sure," I replied, thinking quickly that I could grab cash from the office.

"Okay. Meet me down at the camp right away."

"How do I know you'll tell me the truth when I get there?"

"I got no reason to lie."

"You'll have a hundred reasons to lie in a few minutes," I said, regretting offering so much money.

"Look. I like Ginger. And she should get whatever money is coming to her. But you'd better hurry. Big Bertha, the woman in the motorhome, tipped off the blue van. They're on their way here to pick her up."

"I'll be there as soon as I can."

I'd had enough experience with these kinds of escapades to know I shouldn't go alone, and so I quickly called Blair to explain.

"You want me to go with you?" she asked.

"Yes but call Doe and see if she can join us. I have a feeling that a couple of older women shouldn't be down there alone at night. I'll meet you on the street where we parked the other day."

"Got it," she said.

I went to the Inn's office to get cash, called April to let her know I'd be gone for a while, and then jumped into my Pathfinder. The rain had held off, which was a blessing, but it was cold. Going to the encampment brought back bad memories about the dog feces, and I still had a small bruise on the side of my face from where the rake had hit me.

When I got to the street that led to the bridge encampment, I parked along the curb. Blair's Porsche pulled up behind me a few minutes later. Doe was with her, and the three of us got out and headed down the hill towards the camp.

"Do you expect trouble?" Doe asked. "Is that why I'm here?"

Blair barked out a laugh. "Sure. Whenever I think we might need protection from a bunch of homeless people, I think of calling you."

Doe stiffened. "Then why did you call me?"

"I just thought it would be better if there were three of us," I said.

"And it's harder to hide three bodies," Blair said with a chuckle.

Although she wore comfortable shoes, Doe still had on her business suit and a nice wool coat, with a red silk scarf tucked in around her neck, making me think she'd just gotten home from work. We turned the corner at the bottom of the hill where the camp came into sight.

"Look, if this Greg is right, Ginger will be at the camp. But he said the blue van was coming to pick her up. If that happens, we may never see her again."

"So, this is a rescue attempt," Doe said grimly.

I stopped short and shot her an irritated glance. "Do you want to help Rudy or not? Because, right now, this is the best way to do it."

"Of course, I do," she said with a resolved nod.

Once again, the smell of the encampment wafted over us as we approached. If I knew Doe, she'd have a floral hankie pressed against her nose in short order.

The black dog barked again as we stepped into camp, and I gave him the evil eye, daring him to cause trouble. People watched us curiously but didn't evaporate into the surrounding tents as they had before.

Greg came forward, pushing his glasses up. "You have the money?" he asked, rubbing his fingers together.

I kept my hand in my pocket. "Where is she?"

He chewed his lip and then jerked his head to the left. "She just walked over to the outhouse."

I glanced toward the edge of the camp. A couple of tents stood in the way, so when the door to the outhouse opened and a small woman wearing a hoodie stepped out, I couldn't see her clearly. I decided I had to go on trust and turned back to Greg, holding out five twenty-dollar bills. He snatched them from my fingers.

"I don't suppose there's any chance you'll use that for food," Blair said.

He sneered and then shifted his eyes toward Ginger. "You'd better hurry. The blue van just pulled up."

We turned back to see Big Bertha come out of the RV and throw her cigarette to the ground, before disappearing behind the tents. She reappeared and walked up to a tall, Black man wearing a stocking cap and bomber jacket standing under a streetlamp. He handed Bertha something, which she quickly thumbed through and then stuffed into her pocket. Without a word, she whirled around and headed back to her motorhome. The Black guy turned back toward the van, which was parked at the curb. Where another man was helping the woman in the hoodie into the back of the vehicle.

"Damn!"

I started toward the van, but Blair grabbed my arm. "It's too late. Let's get to the car and follow them."

"Yes, let's," Doe said in a muffled voice. She had taken off her scarf and was holding it in front of her nose.

"Okay," I said, leading them quickly away.

We nearly ran back up the hill to the cars, breathing hard by the time we got there. After all, at our age, running anywhere was an accomplishment, especially uphill. I pulled my keys out and started for the driver's side when Blair stopped me.

"I should drive," she said.

"Why?"

"You're kidding, right?" she said with a sarcastic smirk.

Truth be told, when it came to driving fast, Blair could have qualified for the Indy 500. Her first husband had been a NASCAR driver, and he'd taught her the finer points of driving at a breakneck speed. I'd been her prisoner, uh, passenger, on more than one occasion when we'd been in hot pursuit, which always felt like a life-altering experience. I wasn't thrilled at the prospect of doing it again.

"Just decide, and then let's go," Doe said, climbing into the passenger seat.

"This isn't a car chase; we're only following them."

I opened the door and got in behind the wheel. Blair shrugged and climbed into the back. I glanced in the rearview mirror and watched the van pull up the road about sixty yards behind us going the opposite direction. I started the engine and did a U turn.

"Do you think they saw us?" Doe asked, still catching her breath.

"No. We were too far away, and it's dark," Blair said.

"Should we call David?" I asked, as I sped up the street after the van.

"What could he do?" Blair asked.

"Couldn't he send out the State Patrol to follow these guys?"

The van was two blocks ahead of us and was just pulling onto the freeway on-ramp.

Blair released a scoffing laugh. "What would we say? That we paid $100 to a drug addict who was clearly going through withdrawals and said the woman coming out of the john was Ginger, although frankly it was too dark to see for sure? And this woman willingly got into a van that we're now chasing?"

"Well, when you put it like that," I said, following the van toward Seattle.

"We just want to see where they take her," Doe said. "Right? We're not going to do anything stupid."

A nervous twitch soured my gut because Blair had a propensity for engaging with the bad guys without a thought for her safety or anyone else's. In that regard, stupid could be her middle name.

"Of course not," I replied, feeling my nose grow.

Traffic was unusually heavy, helping to camouflage the fact we were following someone. We crossed over Lake Washington on I-90 and proceeded into Seattle, following them down to Alaskan Way, where we almost lost them under the Viaduct.

"I think it's time we check in with David," I said.

"I'll do it," Doe offered.

"Can you put it on speaker?" I asked.

Doe rang David and told him what we were doing.

"Do you know for sure it's Ginger?" he asked, his voice coming through the speaker.

"To be honest, we didn't get a good look at her," Doe said. "It was dark, and she had on a hoodie. Plus, she seemed to go willingly with them."

"How much do you trust the guy who called Julia?"

Doe glanced at me. "I'm not sure. He seemed strung out and was very anxious to get the money."

"Listen, I can't justify sending a patrol car after you or even calling Seattle PD. But tell Julia, under no circumstances are you to interfere with whatever they're doing. If you suspect anything, call me. Am I clear?"

Doe and I shared a glance.

"Crystal clear," she said.

"David," I said loudly. "Someone needs to check up on the woman who lives in the RV under the bridge. They call her Big Bertha. She's the one who let the blue van know Ginger would be there."

"And... she took money for it," Doe added. "We saw one of the guys in the van pay her."

"Okay. I'll put somebody on it."

When Doe hung up, Blair said, "What if they're going to kill her?"

"Then, I guess we call 911," I said.

"What good will that do? She'll be dead."

"Look, it's not like we're armed, Blair," I said, glancing at her in the rearview mirror. "We don't have any way to stop them. Let's try and not get ourselves jammed up for once."

Blair sucked in a deep breath and then released it. "Fine. When did you become the voice of reason?"

CHAPTER FIFTEEN

Blair was the most reckless of our bunch. Whether it was a deep-seated sense of confidence or just blatant lack of self-control, I wasn't sure. But she never seemed to flag in the face of danger. On the other hand, although I was no coward, I was slower to engage because at times like those, I was filled with real fear. The difference was that I had a black and white sense of right and wrong. When faced with a choice, I just couldn't seem to let wrong win. And so, while I was valiantly trying to accept the modified and safer role we'd chosen this time round, I knew if push came to shove, I'd be right beside Blair trying to save Ginger.

We passed the Magnolia homeless camp, and I glanced over, my eyes searching for signs of Emma or José. The van finally took a two-lane road up a short hill. We followed it into an alley behind a row of businesses.

"Turn off your lights," Blair said, leaning forward from the back seat.

I doused the lights, casting the alley into deep shadow. The taillights from the van glinted a pale orange near the end of the block as it turned into a driveway.

"I wonder where it's going," I murmured, slowing down.

I rolled the car forward then pulled into an empty lot behind an insurance company. The van was parked behind a building next to us with a stand of trees and bushes in between. Before the two men exited the van, I turned off the engine. A second later, Blair was out of the car.

"Dammit!" I got out and met her at the taillights. "What are you going to do?" I whispered.

"Just getting a better view," she whispered back, moving quickly toward the alley.

Doe quietly got out of the passenger seat and followed us. We crept to the end of the neighboring driveway and slipped through some large bushes, stopping next to two big dumpsters filled with old blinds, carpet, and lumber. Parked at the back of the building was a pickup truck with the tailgate down. The bed of the truck was layered in painter's tarps and paint cans.

The Black guy in the bomber jacket was outside the van talking with a slim man dressed in a dark suit who had just come out the back door. Meanwhile, the van driver, a small guy wearing a stocking cap and black jacket, came around the back of the van and opened the doors. Inside, were two ambulance stretchers. He slid one out with a body bag on it, making me clap my hand over my mouth to avoid gasping aloud.

"Is that Ginger?" I whispered in a strangled voice.

"Let's hope not," Blair replied, grasping my hand.

The wheels on the stretcher dropped down, and he was about to push it around the back of the van, when his partner stopped him.

"Forget it," he said in a gruff voice. "They can't take her."

"You're kidding! What are we supposed to do with her?"

"I don't know. Probably take her to Merriman's."

"That'll take another hour at least."

"You want to tell the boss you can't do this?" a voice said from behind them.

They spun around to face the man in the dark suit.

"Listen, man, we have no place to put her," the driver whined. "You gotta take her or go back and find out where we can take her."

The man didn't respond, jingling the keys in his pocket. "We can't take her. We have a painting crew working late."

"Our job is to deliver bodies," the driver said. "So, tell us where to deliver her."

Seconds passed, and then the slim man said, "Give me ten minutes. The boss is with someone. But I'll get you an answer."

He turned on his heel and went back into the building.

"Damn," the driver said. "I'm supposed to be home. My kid has a basketball game tonight."

"Well, not much we can do about it now, Louie. I'm starving," Andre said. "So, I'm gonna walk next door and get a burger. You can stand here in the cold or go with me."

"Hold on. Let's put her back, and I'll go with you."

They pushed the stretcher to the back of the van, folded the wheels up, and slid it inside.

Andre closed the doors, and the two men took off down the parking lot, past the building, and then turned the corner at the street where I could see the golden arches of a McDonald's through the trees next door.

Before I could stop her, Blair dashed out from behind the bushes to the back of the van and opened the doors. My heart climbed into my throat when she jumped inside and pulled out her phone. I couldn't stand it.

"Stay here and watch for anyone coming back," I said to Doe. I left my hiding place and ran up to the back of the van. "What are you doing?" I snapped in a hoarse whisper.

"Seeing if this is Ginger."

She was standing in between two gurneys with body bags on them. She unzipped the bag Andre and Louie had just returned and shined the light from her phone into the opening.

She sucked in a breath and wrinkled her nose. "It's not Ginger. This one's been dead for a while."

She unzipped the other bag, shining her light on the body inside. "Is it her?"

"Yeah," she said. She leaned down until her face was inches from whoever was in the bag.

My skin crawled at the thought of Blair literally face-to-face with a dead woman. But my heart was also pounding because I just knew we were going to get caught.

I was craning my neck to look around the back of the van towards the back door of the building, when Blair exclaimed, "She's alive! We have to get her out of here!"

"What? How? They'll be back any minute."

"Grab the end of this thing," she said, pushing the stretcher toward me.

"Wait!" I turned around and threw my keys to the ground in front of Doe. "Get the car!"

Against my better judgement, I grabbed the foot bar on the stretcher and pulled it out, allowing the wheels to drop to the ground. Blair guided her end out and then jumped down. She immediately unzipped the bag the rest of the way, pulling it away from Ginger's face and shoulders.

"You take her shoulders," she said. "I'll get her feet."

Doe was already backing the Pathfinder into the parking lot. Fortunately, Ginger was small. But, if Blair had a propensity for speed, I have a propensity for mishaps. When we lifted her up and out of the bag, my grip on her right shoulder slipped. Her upper torso rotated to the right, twisting her feet out of Blair's grasp. Poor Ginger landed face down on the pavement. We both just stared at her.

"Seriously, Julia?" Blair shrieked.

Doe had just opened the back of my Pathfinder. "Shhhh! Get a grip, you two."

I erupted in nervous laughter. "Grip. That's a good one."

Doe hurried over. "What can I do?"

"Help me get her off the ground," Blair ordered. "Julia, you put the stretcher back in the van."

Blair and Doe wrangled Ginger off the ground and held her limply between them in a standing position.

"Her nose is bleeding," Doe said.

"Better that than being dead," Blair responded. "C'mon, let's get her into the back of the car."

They dragged her across the pavement, her feet scraping along the ground, while I fumbled with the stretcher. I really hadn't paid attention when the two men put the stretcher back, so I had no idea what I was doing. I proceeded to slam it against the back bumper a couple of times, thinking the wheels would fold up automatically. They didn't. I moved to the back of the van and lifted that end of the stretcher to pull it in. It had two small wheels just under the top bar, and I remembered seeing the driver roll it out on these. I placed those wheels inside the cabin of the van and then ran around to the other end and lifted the other end and began to push.

Bad idea.

The dropped legs of the stretcher just banged against the bumper again. The
stretcher rebounded towards me and bounced out of the van, knocking me to the ground.

"Are you done yet?" Blair said, looming over me with her hands on her hips.

"This isn't as easy as it looks," I said, staring at the sky, winded. "I need to join a gym."

"C'mon, we need to get out of here," Doe said.

"Just help me get the stretcher back inside," Blair said. "Julia, pull the car into the alley."

Doe helped Blair replace the stretcher in the van by physically folding up the wheels. Why hadn't I thought of that? I proceeded to pull the car into the alley and stopped behind the bushes. I glanced back, peering through the leaves, when I saw Louie and Andre coming back from McDonald's. I opened the window and whispered loudly, "They're coming back."

Blair and Doe closed the van doors quietly and hustled back through the bushes to meet me on the other side. Once they were safely inside the car, I slowly pulled back down the alley with the lights off. By the time we reached the cross street, I pulled out of the alley and to the curb, releasing a pent-up breath.

"That was close," I said.

"Why'd you stop?" Blair asked.

"To catch my breath."

"Well, let's at least open a window," Doe said, glancing into the back. "She's a little ripe."

Doe rolled her window down. A minute later, the blue van crossed through the intersection in front of us going east. I pulled up to the light and turned in the opposite direction. As we passed the front of the building, I glanced over, my gaze lingering on a sign at the street that read—Northwest Biomedical Research.

We drove a couple of blocks, until I pulled into the parking lot of a closed veterinary hospital.

"What do we do now?" Doe asked. "I mean, with Ginger."

Blair was leaning over the back seat, looking at our rescue. "They must have drugged her. She's completely out of it. But her breathing seems normal."

"We need David," I said.

I placed the call and put the phone on speaker again. After quickly telling him that we had Ginger, leaving out the rescue itself, of course, I asked what we should do with her.

"Take her to the nearest hospital," he said. "She needs to be checked out. I can meet you there."

"But once they realize she's gone, they'll start looking for her, and the first place they'll probably look are local ERs."

"We'll station an officer there."

"No. I've seen this scenario play out in a million cop shows where the bad guys get past the security guard and kill the witness. This woman may be Rudy's only hope," I argued.

"For heaven's sake, Julia. Don't believe everything you see on TV," he replied with irritation. "She needs medical attention. I'm not going to argue about this. I'm calling Swedish Hospital right now and will meet you in the ER. No arguments. This is now police business."

He hung up. There was a long pause.

"We don't have a choice," I said.

"And, technically, he's right," Doe added.

I started the car. "Okay. Let's get going. We've done as much as we can."

I pulled into Swedish Hospital's ambulance bay ten minutes later. Blair jumped out and went inside, bringing out two nurses and a gurney. They quickly got Ginger onto the gurney and rolled her inside. Blair and Doe went with them, while I parked the car.

By the time I made it inside, David had arrived and immediately checked in with the triage nurse. Then, he came over to talk to us.

"I have an officer on the way, and I'll stay here until he arrives." He glanced at Ginger, who was now in a hospital bed, with nurses fluttering around her, taking her vital signs. When he turned back, he said to me, "You did good. Regardless of what she might be able to provide in the way of information, it sounds like you may have saved her life."

"They had her in a body—"

"I get it," he said, placing his index finger on my lips to hush me. "We'll talk about it later. You'll need to write everything down for the record. And Sean will want to formally interview you." He was staring intently into my eyes. "So, be sure you all know exactly what happened tonight." He glanced at both Doe and Blair.

"Got it," Blair said.

He nodded. "Now… go home. We'll take it from here."

CHAPTER SXTEEN

The next morning, the temperature plummeted to a brisk 35 degrees, making me feel bad for our team in the field as I stood outside with Minnie, making sure she did her business before coming back inside. David had called late the night before to tell us the doctors felt that Ginger wasn't in any danger from the drugs, and that Sean and David would get her to a safe location.

Before I went to the kitchen to help April with breakfast, I did as David had asked and typed up a detailed explanation of our rescue the night before and emailed it to him, at least the one the three of us had agreed upon. Then, I headed for the kitchen to help April. When I returned to the apartment about an hour later, Rudy was up and on her computer.

"I come bearing gifts," I said, carrying in a plate of April's famous cinnamon rolls.

"I'm coming to stay with you more often," she said, jumping up to grab plates.

As we set the table, I filled her in on our adventure from the night before.

"Oh my God, Julia," she exclaimed, grabbing my arm. "Did Ginger say anything?"

"No. She was out of it. In fact, at first we thought she was dead."

Rudy slumped into a chair in front of her plate. "Well, at least she's not dead. But, damn, we really need her to confirm she was at my house that night."

I sat across from her. "It might be a couple of days. At least until they get her stabilized on her medication again."

I noticed Rudy was tapping the heel of her shoe on the floor again. This was something I'd never seen her do before, and yet she'd done it two or three times within the last few days.

"Listen, I have an appointment with Renfroe Security at ten," Rudy said. "But I'll be back later this afternoon. Can you handle any calls coming in from the field?"

"Sure. I have office work to do anyway."

We finished breakfast, and Rudy left for home. I let everyone in the field know that I'd be the contact for the day, and then spent the morning paying bills and doing bookkeeping, while I waited to hear from David. I was anxious to know more about how Ginger was doing and if she was talking yet. It was almost noon by the time he finally called.

"We got Ginger into a safe house. She's awake and functioning, but I use that word lightly. The psychiatrist on duty at the hospital will do an eval, so we can get her back on medication," he said. "We did ID the guy who owns Northwest Biomedical Research, though. Frank Castrano. I have someone doing a deep dive into him and his company. And Nick went down to interview Big Bertha. He said it didn't go well. Apparently, she doesn't like cops."

"Trust me. She doesn't like anyone."

"Well, according to her, you were trespassing last night. The kid who called you was too strung out to know Ginger from Marilyn Monroe. And the guy from the van only brought her an inhaler because she has asthma."

"You've got to be kidding. She's lying."

"You know that, and I know that, but there's no way to prove it. Nick also looked for that guy who tipped you off but was told he'd picked up and left. And, of course, no one else saw anything."

I ran my fingers through my hair. "Damn. Bertha brought them there. I know she did. Couldn't you get her phone to find the last number she called?"

"We'd need a search warrant for that. By the way, the picture you sent me of Patch doesn't show us enough to ID him. And even when we enlarged the picture, we couldn't ID the ring. It'd be nice to know if he has any identifying marks, like tattoos, scars, or moles."

"I can text everyone and have them on the lookout. Will you be over for dinner later?"

"No. I'm sorry. I have to be careful with Rudy staying there. But Sean is switching Nick over to my burglary case, and I'll be working full-time now on this."

"Good. I'm glad to have you back. Talk to you soon."

I texted the group telling them to see if Patch had any identifying marks and then went to the command center to do some research. I did an internet search specifically looking for information on missing homeless people. I found a couple of articles that talked about how the homeless population moves around a lot and another article reporting that over 80,000 people go missing in the U.S. each year. But the two pieces of information were unrelated. There were no statistics on how many of the missing people are also homeless.

I did find how difficult it is to track homeless people through the homeless system, though, because of privacy laws. And a Facebook page called Missing & Homeless, where people can post about missing loved ones. I scrolled through dozens of entries, hoping to find information on any of the five people we were looking for. As I suspected, there was nothing. It seemed that Patch had done his job well. No one was looking for them.

It was almost two o'clock when José texted:

I met Emma's friend who saw Rose Marie abducted. She mumbled a lot about Rose Marie and how she'd been taken by two men, and that one of them was a bald Black guy.

I thanked him and then called David to let him know.

"You realize what this means?" I said, after telling him. "That's got to be the same guy who picked Ginger up at the camp last night. And we heard his name... Andre. The other guy was Louie. He was a medium-height Latino," I said.

"Thanks. I'll let Sean know and get him to talk to Rudy's neighbors again in case anyone remembers seeing either one of them at the house that night. If we can put them at Rudy's house, then it proves the murder and the abductions are connected."

Later that afternoon, Ben texted again to say that Swamp, the head guy at the veteran's camp, was nosing around him, saying that the vets had each other's back. He told Ben to be careful of Patch. When Ben asked why, Swamp said the guy was trying to take advantage of people. I was jotting all of this down when another text came in from Ben.

I've been asking around for a pillow. I was told to check out Jacob's cart under the bridge. When I asked why Jacob didn't want his stuff, the guy told me Jacob left with Patch a couple of weeks ago for a job removing trash and never came back.

I texted Ben back to be on the lookout for a tall Black guy and a blue van. I had just hit 'send' when Rudy came through the door and dropped her purse over the back of a chair.

"Hey, I talked with Gloria, and you're scheduled to do the resume clinic tomorrow. So, how's it going here?" she asked.

I slumped back against my chair, releasing a loud sigh. "It's been busy. Lots of little tidbits of information are coming in. How'd it go with the security company?"

"Huh? Oh, um, they fixed the problem, so I'm not going to upgrade right now," she said plopping into a chair.

"Wait! Rudy, the killers disabled it so easily," I said, interrupting her.

"I know, but I'm just not in the market for an expensive upgrade right now. Is that okay?"

Rudy rarely snapped at me, making me wonder if all the stress was finally getting to be too much. I decided to dial things back.

"Of course. It's your decision, but—"

"Look, Julia," she said, cutting me off. "I might be in prison soon, anyway. And if I go to prison, I'll be forced to sell the house, so what's the difference?"

"Wait. What? You are not going to prison," I said, moving over to sit next to her. "We've found Ginger, remember? She'll be able to tell them what happened that night. It might just take some time before she can give them any information."

"But what if she doesn't remember?" she asked, rubbing the palms of her hands together. "If she was off her medication that night, she might not remember even being there."

I pulled her hands into mine, partly to give her comfort and partly to stop her obsessive movements.

"Let's not be pessimistic. We need to give Ginger time to get her head on straight. Meanwhile, we keep fighting. I've been getting texts from people in the field. We're going to find out who this Patch guy is and what he's doing. Then, we're going to stop the bastard!"

She gazed at me through eyes wet with tears. "It's one thing to prove he's abducting people off the street, but how the heck are we going to prove he's the one who killed Romaine?"

"David's working on that."

"Julia, they have too much evidence against me."

"You didn't have a motive, Rudy. For God's sake, you're as clean as a whistle."

She stared at me for a moment and then dropped her head. "I'm not so clean, Julia."

"What do you mean? You never lie or cheat. I've never even known you to shortchange a server on her tip." When she didn't respond, I said, "Rudy, you're a fighter. Don't give up."

She brought her head up, and there were tears running down her cheeks.

"There's something I haven't told you," she said. "Something you need to know. It could impact everything."

"What is it? You know you can tell me anything."

Count to three.

"I'm addicted to Oxycontin. I have been since before we drove across country last summer."

CHAPTER SEVENTEEN

A bomb going off couldn't have shocked me more. I even thought my ears were ringing. I stared dumbly at my friend, a mixture of emotions fighting for position in my brain.

"What are you talking about?"

My voice shook, which had to be unsettling to Rudy. But she may have just complicated our entire investigation. Looking at the shrunken, vulnerable version of the woman I'd known for over a decade made me question whether to yell at her or throw my arms around her.

"It was after my knee surgery last year," she said, wiping the tears away. "You remember how much pain I was in, especially with the physical therapy. They prescribed Oxycontin. I got through the healing and rehabilitation process okay but was having trouble weaning myself off the pills. And then I started playing fast pitch again."

"Which we all told you not to," I said, immediately cringing at the righteous tone in my voice.

"I know. It's not an excuse. But when I did, my knee began to hurt all over again. I used up what was left of the prescription, and my doctor wouldn't renew it."

"Why didn't you just stop playing fast pitch?" I asked, noticing a touch of reprimand in my voice.

She shook her head and brought her hands together again, squeezing them like she was squeezing an orange.

"I didn't want to. I love being active. And I love fast pitch. And I'm good at it," she said, bringing her head up to look me straight in the eyes. "If you remember, my fastball saved your life in that graveyard a while ago."

She was right. When Clay Finkle held a gun on the rest of us as he was about to bury his wife alive in a freshly dug grave, Rudy hit him between the eyes with a rock that knocked him out, saving all of us. She really was good at fast pitch.

"Look, Julia, I shopped a couple of other doctors for drugs, and then I just couldn't do it anymore. So, I casually asked Romaine if she knew anyone who could provide me with some."

"Why didn't you just say something?"

"Because I… I thought I could handle it. You know me. I never ask for help. It's a curse, but it's who I am. All the way along, I've been trying to gradually reduce the amount I take. But, frankly, it feels impossible."

"That's why they call it addiction."

"I know," she said with a sigh. "Anyway, Romaine knew someone on the street and asked him for me. It's what kept me active and allowed me to keep playing fast pitch for the past few months. The drugs didn't have anything to do with Romaine's murder, but it won't look good."

"No, it won't. I just wish you'd said something. We're trying desperately to keep you out of jail, and now you could go to jail on drug charges."

"I know. I've let you down. I've let everyone down." She dropped her head in defeat.

Rudy was one of my best friends. Someone I'd always looked up to for her strength and resolve. Right now, though, she had shrunk into the chair like a small child, and all I wanted to do was protect her.

"Is this why you had trouble coming up with the bail money?" She shifted uncomfortably and released an exasperated sigh. "I'm sorry," I said, reaching for her hand again. "That was intrusive. But you just dropped a bombshell on me. I'm trying to make sense of all of this."

She sucked in a breath. "It's okay. Look, this has been going on for a while, and I had to pay a premium for the pills. My savings are almost tapped out."

"I'm so sorry, Rudy. You know if you ever need help, you can always come to me."

"I know."

"But do you think there's any chance Romaine was killed over the drugs?"

"No. I didn't owe her any money, and as far as I know she didn't take any drugs herself." She squeezed my hand. "I'm so sorry I never said anything."

"It's okay. But what are you going to do now? I mean, you said yourself that you can't quit."

"I'd already started looking into rehab programs and planned on telling you all before Romaine was killed. There's a promising program in Seattle. I'll have to use my retirement money to pay for it. But I'm okay with that. In fact, I was just about ready to call them when all of this happened." She shook her head. "I thought if I could just get through this, then I'd check myself in. I have enough pills to last a couple of weeks. But I'm spacing them out as much as I can."

"Oh, Rudy, this will probably take longer than that. Have you told Elliott?"

"Not yet."

"He'd support you."

"I know. I did tell Brenda, though. Last night."

"Well, that's good. She'll know what to do." I sat back in my chair, pondering what this would mean for our investigation. "The question now is, what do we do?"

"Do we need to tell everyone else? I mean, right now. I just... I just don't know if I could handle that."

I felt conflicted between my loyalty to Rudy, finding Romaine's killer, and stopping whoever was abducting people off the street.

"Let's leave that up to Brenda. We need everyone focused on finding out what Patch is doing. I won't even say anything to David right now."

"Okay, and I'll call Brenda tonight."

I squeezed her hand again. "You know it doesn't change how I feel about you. You must know that."

She choked up a bit and threw a hand to her chest to catch her breath. "Thanks, Julia."

"But you have some big decisions to make. And soon."

"I know that, too."

I patted her hand, and decided we needed to move on.

"Okay, this will work itself out. But for now, let's you and I focus on something more positive. If you want me to take over your resume clinic tomorrow, I need some practice, along with templates."

"Okay," she said, wiping her nose. "Let's get you up to speed."

We spent the rest of the afternoon going over how to write a resume and cover letter. Rudy's mood improved as she gave me checklists, talked me through the strategies, and printed blank templates for several assorted styles off the internet. Although my mind wandered to Rudy's drug problem more than once, by the time we were done, I felt confident. We were about to leave the command center when Blair walked in.

"I thought I'd find you here. I just wanted to report in."

"You want anything to drink?" I asked her. "I have diet sodas in the refrigerator."

"No. I'm headed home. But I made the rounds today," she said. "I'm scheduled to give makeover clinics at St. Mary's tomorrow, Wings of Hope on Monday, and Everyday Miracles on Wednesday."

"Who did you meet with at Wings of Hope?" Rudy asked.

"A woman named Gloria. She printed out a flyer while I was there and posted it on a bulletin board. She said she'd also put the word out and thought I'd have no trouble getting women to attend."

"What time tomorrow at St. Mary's?" I asked.

"Eleven. My hairstylist will meet me there. She was excited when I asked if she would do it. We're scheduled at Wings of Hope at two o'clock the next day. Gloria is limiting it to four women at a time. Before you ask, I didn't mention either of you. I figured it would be better if I seemed completely independent."

"That was smart thinking," Rudy said.

"I'm scheduled at Wings of Hope tomorrow for the resume clinic at 11:30," I said.

Blair inhaled and released a sigh. "I guess we're back in the game." Blair's gaze drifted to the information Rudy and I had put up on the wall. "I see we're already getting feedback."

"Yeah. And David ID'd the owner of Northwest Biomedical Research."

Her eyebrows arched. "That's good." Her gaze shifted to where Rudy sat staring off into space. "You okay, Rudy? You look pale."

Rudy's head swiveled to her. "I'm tired. That's all."

Blair walked over and gave her a huge hug. "You're our rock star, you know that? Soon you'll be back to playing fast pitch, insulting other people's intelligence, and reading the next book for the book club. Which, by the way," she said turning to me, "should be Colleen Hoover's newest book. She's quite the erotic writer, which would be good for all of us right now."

We all laughed, and Blair gave Rudy one more hug.

"Okay, I've got to run. We're having dinner with someone from the Mariners tonight. Mr. Billings is thinking of investing in one of the minor league ball clubs."

"I didn't know you were into baseball," Rudy said.

"I'm not. It's just another way for Mr. Billings to be connected to people with money. Plus, he likes sports, so there's that. Anyway, good luck tomorrow, Julia. I'll let you know how it goes at St. Mary's."

CHAPTER EIGHTEEN

Sleep didn't come easily that night. I laid awake feeling guilty for not telling David about Rudy. He and I had just been through a difficult patch because I kept getting involved in his investigations. Now, here I was withholding vital information. But I also kept thinking about how hard it must have been for Rudy to keep such a big secret. Mostly, I felt guilty for not having tuned in more to my friend. It was no surprise then, that when I picked Ben up at seven the next morning that I was more than a little bleary-eyed.

"Can you take me directly to campus?" he asked. "I can shower in the gym there. You also won't have to take me back tonight because I checked the bus routes. I don't want you to keep having to shuttle me back and forth."

"But how about tomorrow morning?"

"Like I said, I've gotten someone to take my lecture for me. My next lecture isn't until Wednesday, so I'm good."

"Okay. Anything else you can report?"

"Yeah, something interesting. Yesterday when I followed two guys who were dumpster diving, we ended up a couple miles from the camp. And, lo and behold, I saw Patch across the street in an alley between a bank and a big self-storage building."

"What was he doing?"

"Don't know. But he met up with a woman with big black hair."

"What does that mean?"

"Big black hair," he repeated, as if that was a thing. "I don't know what else to call it. Anyway, she gave him something."

"Cash?"

"I don't know, but he immediately stuffed it into his satchel, turned around and left."

"How old did she look?"

He thought for a moment. "Mid-forties to early fifties. She was tall and big chested."

"Interesting," I said, thinking. "And she didn't look homeless?"

"No. In fact, I saw her get into a black Lincoln sedan that was parked in the alley."

"I'll put it up on the board when I get back," I said, pulling onto I-5 going north. "By the way, do you need anything? I mean, were you okay last night?"

His lips expanded into an impish smile. "Is my little sister worried about me?"

"Why wouldn't I be?"

He let the smile linger and then turned to look out the window. "No, I'm fine. It was biting cold last night; I'll give you that. When I've slept rough, it's always been in a tropical jungle. But I survived. By the way, I did get a chance to see Patch up close. We both ended up huddled over one of the can fires last night. I didn't talk to him, but he wears a gold earring in his left ear and has a tat of an anchor on the back of his left hand. Also, that ring he wears is from Washington State University."

"Good. I'll let David know."

"I also saw him hand a coat to someone," Ben said, still gazing out the window. "I wonder if that's where he gets all this stuff he hands out."

"What do you mean?"

"That storage facility is in an upscale area. That's why seeing Patch there surprised me. What if he has a unit there stocked with stuff he gives out to people he's trying to get cozy with?"

"I wonder how we could find out. You didn't happen to hear his last name, did you?"

"He just goes by Patch, as far as I know. But now that I know where the storage units are, I can keep an eye on the place."

"What's it called?"

"Inland Storage," he said.

"I'll tell David," I said.

I dropped Ben off twenty minutes later at the UW and headed back to the Inn. I called David and caught him just as he was leaving for work. I filled him in on what Ben had reported.

"I'll see if I can get a list of people who rent units there. Maybe we'll get lucky."

"Ben also said that Patch wears a gold earring and has the tattoo of an anchor on the back of one hand. And the ring is from Washington State. The anchor tattoo could mean he was in the Navy."

We hung up a minute later, and I found April in the kitchen getting breakfast ready for the guests.

"How are you feeling?" I asked, heading for the pantry.

"I took it easy yesterday," she said. "No more visions, so I'm good today. How are things going with the investigation?"

"Hold on, let me get the bagels." I hurried into the pantry and grabbed two bags of bagels and brought them back. As I began cutting them in half with a serrated knife, I told April everything we'd gleaned over the last day and a half, leaving out Rudy's addiction. Although I'd told her bits and pieces about our escapade to rescue Ginger the day before, this time I filled in all the humiliating details.

"Did you tell David all of that?" she asked with a chuckle. "Even the dumpster diving? I mean, the whole point of you not going undercover was to let others do the heavy lifting."

"No. I didn't tell him all the details," I said a little sheepishly. "I think he suspects there was more to it, though."

I placed my hand on my chest, feeling as if my guilt for keeping details about Ginger's rescue and Rudy's addiction to myself was giving me heartburn.

"You okay?" April asked, watching me.

"Yeah. Just tired and feel like I could sleep for a week."

"I don't doubt it. You know, I like you having an entire team around you," she said. "You should just rely on them more."

"But we couldn't not have rescued Ginger."

"I know. It's just that once again, you did it alone, and it sounds like it was dangerous."

I began arranging the bagels in a napkin-lined basket. "To be honest, I thought we were only going to pick her up at the camp. I had no idea it would become a rescue attempt."

"Well, don't get me wrong. I'm glad you got her."

"Me, too," I said. "And, so far, things are working well with the team. We don't have any actionable information yet, other than we know one of the guys involved is a bald, Black guy named Andre, and that a woman was in the van at Rudy's home. That might have been Ginger. So, that's good. I just wish that gave Rudy more hope, though."

"She's pretty stressed, isn't she?"

"That's putting it mildly. By the way, I'm filling in for her at the shelter this morning."

"No problem. What time do you have to be there?"

"By 11:30. Rudy will be in the command center."

"Okay. Any chance you could stop at Costco on the way back for supplies?"

"Sure. I'll take the list. Let me know if you need anything else."

We finished putting out the breakfast food and then getting all the dishes into our large dishwasher. Then I stopped at the office to grab bills to put in the mailbox on my way to the shelter.

The Wings of Hope Women's Shelter was originally an old motel in Seattle's Belltown neighborhood near the piers. It had been renovated into a shelter with enough rooms for twenty women, a small recreation room, offices for staff, a meeting room, and even a fenced-in outdoor seating area for women who smoked.

I met Gloria Alvarez in her office. She was an attractive Latino woman in her late thirties, medium height, with brown hair, brown eyes, and a lively smile with dimples.

"So glad to meet you," she said, shaking my hand. "Sit down."

I took a chair across from her desk.

"We were sorry to hear about Romaine's death," she said as she settled back into her chair. "She was well-liked. And I'm so sorry about Rudy, too. It had to be terrible. How is she doing?"

"Um, okay," I replied, thinking not only about the murder but her admission of drug use. "It's been tough. She was really shaken by Romaine's death."

"Did you know her?" Gloria asked.

"Romaine? No. She was just doing yardwork for Rudy. Anyway, the police are handling it. I offered to help here until Rudy can come back, so your residents don't suffer. Rudy can come back, can't she?"

"I'd love to have her back. Listen, since it's Sunday, a few of the women have gone to church, but you'll be meeting with two women who found job openings they'd really like to apply for," she said, standing up.

I patted the big purse I'd brought. "Good. I brought examples with me. Is there a printer we'll have access to?"

She came around her desk. "There's one in the room you'll be in. But most of the job applications our women apply for are online."

"True. But if they can create a couple of versions of the cover letter, they can adapt them for specific job openings."

"That sounds great. Let me show you where you'll be working."

She took me to a room off the main entrance. Inside was a window overlooking the parking lot, a small oval table with six chairs, and a six-foot table against the wall with a laptop computer and printer on top.

"This is where Rudy usually meets with the women." She glanced at her watch. "They should be here any minute."

A tall, heavy-boned woman with hair sticking out at odd angles appeared at the doorway. She wore clean jeans and a sweatshirt.

"Vivian, come in. This is Julia," Gloria said, gesturing towards me.

"Nice to meet you, Vivian."

The woman barely smiled when I shook her hand and then dropped her chin before mumbling something that sounded like, "Nice to meet you."

A young woman with tattoos spread across her neck and forearms appeared in the doorway. She had dark hair and dark eyes, with long dark hair in a long braid. She appeared to be Native American and sauntered up next to Vivian chewing gum loudly. Vivian immediately took a step to the side.

"I'm Isabella," she said to me, popping her gum. "But everyone calls me Izzy."

"Izzy wants to apply for a job at T-Mobile Park," Gloria said. "Where the Mariners play. She has a background in hotel housekeeping."

"That sounds like a great fit," I said.

Gloria put a hand on my shoulder. "I'll be in my office if you need me. There's paper in the printer," she said, pointing to the table. "And Dr. Enzo conducts a Sunday group in here at 12:30, so it'd be good to finish up a few minutes early."

"I can do that. Thanks."

Gloria left, and I pulled out a file folder as we sat down.

"I brought some examples of both resumes and cover letters," I said. "Do either of you have any experience at putting those together?"

"I used to have a resume," Izzy said, snapping her gum. "But that was three years ago."

"Okay, we'll try to recreate that. What about you, Vivian? Have you ever had a resume?"

As tall as she was, it looked like Vivian was doing her best to shrink into the chair. She stared at the table and didn't even look up when she said, "Not really. But I used to work in an insurance office."

"Did you sell insurance?"

"I was the receptionist. I answered phones, made appointments, things like that."

She said all of this to the table, which made me wonder how she ever survived as a receptionist greeting customers.

"When was the last time you had a job?"

She shrugged her broad shoulders. "About a year and a half ago, I guess."

I wondered what had deprived both women of their livelihoods, but I thought I shouldn't get into that. Instead, I grabbed a couple of the resume examples Rudy had given me and placed them on the table.

"Okay, then. Let's get started."

We spent the next forty-five minutes going over the components of a resume and doing our best to fill one in for each of them. Surprisingly, Vivian had been with the insurance company for five years. Before that, she'd worked at an auto parts store and before that as a grocery clerk. Izzy was a good ten years younger than Vivian but had worked for a freelance housecleaning service for several years and then for two different hotels, as well as the Red Wind Casino in Olympia. By the time I glanced at my watch, it was almost 12:30.

"Listen, it's time to finish up for today. Why don't I type these up tonight and bring them back tomorrow? Then we can review them and work on the cover letters."

They agreed, and the three of us moved toward the door.

"Thank you," Vivian said, as I opened the door.

"Yeah, thanks," Izzy added, popping her gum.

"No problem. I hope it helps you get the jobs you—"

My voice caught in my throat as the front door opened and a tall woman with black hair teased into a bubble walked in. She crossed the lobby in three strides and went immediately into Gloria's office.

"Um… sorry, I, uh… anyway, it's been so nice to meet you."

Izzy saw me eyeing the women with black hair. "That was Dr. Enzo. And yes, that hairdo is right out of a retro museum," she said, popping her gum again. "That and her big boobs." She laughed and walked away.

The adrenaline coursed through my veins as the two women disappeared down the hallway. I didn't believe in coincidences, and yet, that had to be the woman Ben had mentioned to me earlier that morning.

I retreated to the parking lot feeling like I'd just sucked down a fifth of Vodka. My hand trembled when I used the key fob to unlock my car, especially when I saw a black Lincoln sedan sitting right next to my Pathfinder. It had to be the same woman. As I climbed behind the wheel of my own car, my phone rang. It was Blair.

"Hey," I said, answering the phone. "You won't believe—"

"Julia! I've got news!" she said, interrupting me. "I'm in the middle of my makeover clinic at St. Mary's, and one of the women just said that Seattle isn't the only place homeless people have gone missing. It's happening in Tacoma, too."

CHAPTER NINETEEN

I called Gloria on my way to Costco to see if I could come back the next day to work on cover letters. We scheduled the meeting for 11:30 again.

I entered Costco on auto pilot, wandering up and down aisles and pulling things off the shelves, thinking about why Dr. Enzo might know Patch and what the two of them were doing when Ben saw them. And then my brain would flick to what Blair had said about Tacoma and more abductions. She'd gone on to tell me that the women had gotten very chatty when they were having their hair done, and one of them said she had come up from Tacoma, where two people she'd known had disappeared without a trace. In fact, the woman said there was a saying among the homeless in Pierce County to stay away from the blue van.

Finally, in the produce aisle, I stopped midstride, realizing I'd filled the cart with double the amount of milk and cheese we needed. With a sigh, I went back to the refrigerated section and returned the excess items. Then I called David and told him what Blair had learned.

"Did she find out who these people were who went missing in Tacoma?" he asked.

"I don't know. She had just started her clinic and said she'd stop by tonight. Can you join us? Just for dinner?"

"No. Sorry. I know it's tough, but there are lines that can't be crossed. And I don't want to screw up Rudy's chances at being absolved of this."

"I get it. By the way, I know who Ben saw outside that storage building with Patch. She's a psychiatrist at the shelter. I'm at Costco, so I'll call you later to fill you in."

It was after two o'clock by the time I returned to the Inn. There was no José to help me take in groceries, so Crystal left the front desk to carry in a box of nectarines and a few other things, while April busied herself with snacks for that afternoon.

"You look distracted," she said as I aimlessly sorted through things to begin putting them away. "How'd the resume clinic go?"

"Um... good," I said, placing items on the table.

"Julia," she said with a clip to her voice. "What's going on?"

I turned to her. "Oh, uh, sorry."

I slumped against the counter and told her about Dr. Enzo and what Blair had said about people disappearing in Tacoma.

"Wow, this is getting a lot bigger than I thought it would."

"I know. I told David, and Blair is going to stop by tonight to tell us more about what she heard."

"Okay, because once again, it could just be people innocently moving around," she said, cutting apricot bars into squares.

"I really hope you're right. If not, there's no way we can cover the homeless camps in Tacoma. But maybe the police down there could look into it if they aren't already. I'd sure like to know if any of our dots connect to Tacoma, though. I mean, like the blue van. I doubt that's a coincidence. Or Dr. Enzo. There's no reason she couldn't work with a shelter in Tacoma. And what the hell was she doing with that Patch guy down by a self-storage place?"

"Slow down," April cautioned me. "You're getting worked up."

"Sorry," I said, slumping into a chair. "There's just so much going on."

"Well, first things first. We have to get snacks out for the guests."

"Right," I said, jumping up again.

Once we had everything laid out in the breakfast room, she helped me put groceries away. Afterwards, on my way to my apartment, I passed Gretchen Engle, the freelance writer, as she was going upstairs.

"How was the wedding?" I asked her.

Her entire face lit up as she stopped at the foot of the stairs. "Wonderful! Everything went perfectly. And the girls looked beautiful."

"I'm so glad. Do you feel better now?"

She paused with her hand on the banister. "My daughter couldn't be happier, and that's all I wanted. How's everything here?

I see you going in and out of the reception hall. Are you planning a big event?"

"Um… no. Some friends and I are doing research. By the way," I said, hoping to change the subject. "I went to a homeless shelter today and taught a couple of women how to write a resume. Writing isn't my forte, but I'm taking over for a friend who took a leave of absence."

"That's terrific. I've done a lot of resumes and cover letters for people."

"We didn't get as far as the cover letters, so I'm going back tomorrow to help them with those. Those are more intimidating, though."

"Would you like some help? I'd be happy to walk you through the particulars."

"My friend Rudy did that. I'm just self-conscious about cover letters because, well, that's actual writing."

"What time do you go? I'm here for a few more days. I'd be happy to go with you."

This was one nice lady, and it took me all of two seconds to think it over.

"I'd love that. One of the two women I'm working with didn't even graduate from high school, so she really struggles. But don't you have plans tomorrow?"

She shook her head. "No. Jennifer and her new wife are spending the day with her wife's parents at their home on Lake Sammamish. I begged off because, frankly, I don't like them very much. I thought I'd just catch up on quiet time. So, I'd love to help you."

My brain was racing, wondering if this was a good idea. But if Gretchen went with me, she could go over things with the two women while I did some sleuthing.

"Great. I'll be leaving about eleven. Does that work for you?"

"Absolutely."

"By the way, the snacks are out in the breakfast room," I said, pointing that way. "April is serving her famous apricot bars."

I gave a wave goodbye as she climbed the stairs. When I returned to my apartment, Minnie assaulted me.

"C'mon, little girl, let's get you outside."

I took her into the backyard and then went to the kitchen to gather things for a taco bar dinner. I texted Rudy to let her know I was back and was taking food to the command center for dinner, where Blair would meet us. She showed up a few minutes later to help carry things over. On the way, I told her all the latest news.

"I'll add all of that to the board," she said when I finished. "Plus, I contacted a friend of mine who wrote an entire series of articles on the homeless about a year ago," she said. "He told me that individuals do often disappear, and that in Florida, there was a big scandal involving a pharmaceutical company that picked people up off the streets and then used experimental drugs on them. Fourteen people died."

"What?" I turned to her. "That's awful. I hope nothing like that is happening."

She shrugged. "They are a vulnerable group of people. I just wish we knew what company was willing to hire someone off the street."

"That might be a ruse. After all, the van that showed up at your house had Johnston Electronics stenciled on the side."

"I know. But I checked, and there's no company by that name in this area."

While we were updating the boards with the current information, my phone pinged. It was a text from Emma telling me that Ileana was talking about what had happened to Rose Marie. Emma was worried about her safety and was going to try and get her into a shelter.

"That can't be good," I said to Rudy. "I mean, Ileana talking about Rose Marie's abduction. That's like putting a target on her back."

"Just like Romaine," Rudy said grimly.

"Could you call Wings of Hope and get Ileana in there?" I asked Rudy.

"You just told me your suspicions about Dr. Enzo."

"Oh, of course," I said, dropping my shoulders in frustration.

"Besides, Emma seems to know her way around. If anyone can get her help, I'd bet on her," Rudy said.

Blair arrived a little before six, just as we were getting dinner ready, and I'd called April to invite her to join us. Soon, the four of us were seated around one of the six-foot tables with tacos and drinks in hand.

I allowed Blair to take a bite and a sip of wine before I said, "Okay, let's hear in more detail what you learned at St. Mary's."

She swallowed and said, "First of all, St. Mary's is a big place, and they take more than just single women. They have a wing for women and children, too. It was actually one of the moms who made the comment."

"What exactly did she say?" April asked.

"I brought up the subject of how hard it must be to be homeless, especially if you had to live on the street. I got them talking about everything from how they find food to how they stay safe. That was what prompted this woman to speak up. She said that when she was married, she lived in Tacoma. Her husband died, leaving her with a mountain of debt. She hadn't worked since she was in her early twenties because she was raising three daughters, and so, within eighteen months, she was homeless."

I noticed April drop her chin to stare at her plate for a moment. The same thing had happened to her when her husband, a successful orthopedic surgeon, died. He'd had a gambling problem and had spent all their savings. If it hadn't been for her job at the Inn and my offering the guest house to her, she might have been homeless, too.

"Anyway," Blair continued, "when she ended up on the street, she found a group of Christian women who regularly prayed together. It was two of those women that just up and disappeared. It was one of the reasons this woman left and came up to Seattle."

"Did she mention Patch?" I asked.

"No. I was careful about asking questions. I mostly wanted to just let the others do it. In fact, one of the other women wondered if the two women she mentioned had just gone home to their extended families."

"Let me guess, they didn't have families," April said.

"Right," Blair said. "No family."

"What did she say about the blue van?" Rudy asked,

"Just that it scares her. The van has been seen driving through one of the parks down there picking up people. And no one sees those people again."

"I wonder if the Tacoma PD would get involved," I said. "Did she mention names?"

"No. But she did say that one of them said she'd gotten a job. When she asked where, the woman only said, 'workin' with dead people.'"

"What?" Rudy and I said in unison.

"I wonder what that means?" I pondered out loud. "Is that all?"

"Yeah, pretty much."

"Well, there's more to report."

I proceeded to relate Ben's story about seeing the woman with big black hair with Patch at the self-storage building and his speculation that Patch might operate out of it.

"That would make sense," Rudy said.

"Yes, but then, I saw her later. She's a psychiatrist that works at Wings of Hope."

"Dr. Enzo?" Rudy asked. "Damn! The women there don't like her."

"What is it, Blair?" April asked, watching her.

"When we were doing the ladies' hair, one of them made a joke about someone named Susan and that she ought to come to our makeover clinic. When I asked why, she said Susan's bouffant hairstyle looked right out of the Sixties."

"That's Dr. Enzo," I said.

"I did some research on her before coming over," Blair said. "I went to her website, and she lists several shelters where she provides services."

"Does she work with any of the shelters in Tacoma?"

"Yes."

"Damn. How would a psychiatrist be connected to all of this, though?" Rudy asked while she fidgeted with the taco that was falling apart in her hands.

"If there's money involved, then she might be the person helping to identify the victims," April said. "After all, a psychiatrist would probably get the most personal information off them."

A text came in from Emma. I raised my hand to get everyone's attention and then read it out loud:

I was able to get Ileana into St. Mary's shelter for the night. Hopefully, she'll be safe there.

"Text her back!" Blair said quickly. "Ileana can't stay at St. Mary's."

"Well, she could stay there," Rudy said. "She just can't be seen by Dr. Enzo."

"Yes, but didn't José say that Ileana keeps talking about Rose Marie being abducted?" Blair asked.

"Which puts her in danger," April said. "What about getting her admitted to a psych unit?"

"You mean somewhere where Dr. Enzo doesn't have privileges," I added.

"Well... yeah."

"How do we find that out without tipping our hand?" Rudy asked.

I pulled out my phone and looked up one of the hospitals in Seattle that I knew had a psych unit and dialed their main number. When a woman answered, I put it on speaker so everyone could hear and asked, "I was wondering if you could tell me if Dr. Susan Enzo is on staff there. She's a psychiatrist."

"I'm sorry," the woman said. "But you'd have to talk to our medical staff office, and they're

closed right now."

"You can't just look it up?"

"No. Physicians have to go through a credentialing process, so you'd have to talk with

medical staffing."

I thanked her and hung up.

"Well, that answers that. If we're going to get Ileana somewhere safe tonight, we'll need someone who can hack into hospital records."

Blair turned abruptly to me. "Do you know a hacker?"

"No," I said, slumping back in my chair.

April stared hard at me.

"What?" I said to her.

"We have a couple of guests who might be helpful."

Count to three.

"Oh! You mean the twins."

CHAPTER TWENTY

"Who are the twins?" Rudy asked.

"They own their own IT company and are in town to do some work for Overlake Hospital."

"Deirdre explained to me yesterday how they started their company," April said. "Apparently, they're wicked smart and were arrested for hacking a drug company to change the price of a prescription drug a friend of theirs needed but couldn't afford. The girls were only nineteen at the time. The company dropped the charges and hired them instead to beef up their security."

"Did the company lower the price?" Blair asked.

"Yes. Not by as much as the twins had, but they didn't do time. After that, Donna said they decided to put their talents to better use."

"And they launched Double D IT," I said.

"Yep. What do you think?" she asked me. "I bet they would help."

"Is the double D because they're twins?" Blair asked, crinkling her brows.

I chuckled. "That and their cup size." I thought about April's idea for a minute. "I mean, I guess we could ask. Hacking is illegal, though."

"Look, they're experts at this sort of stuff," April said. "What if we just talk to them about how we could find the information we need?"

I nodded. "That sounds okay. Do you know if they're here now?"

It was already dark, and April pointed through the front windows of the reception hall.

"That's their room right there," she said, pointing to room 4.

I glanced up to where the light from room 4 shone through the curtains.

I texted Emma back to warn her about Dr. Enzo and St. Mary's and told her we were trying to vet an inpatient psych unit for Ileana. Meanwhile, Rudy had plans to get a drink after dinner with Elliott, and Blair had to drive Mr. Billings to the airport, so they both left. April and I cleaned up the dishes and hauled the dinner things back to my apartment. Then, we went in search of the twins.

They were in our only suite, lounging on the beds watching TV when we knocked. They invited us in, and we sat on the antique sofa under the window.

"What's up?" Deirdre asked.

"We need your help," I said. "You may have noticed several of us going back and forth to our reception hall."

"Yeah, we did," Donna said. "What's going on?"

I couldn't help sharing a glance with April knowing we were going to ask them to consider doing something illegal, but I plunged ahead and proceeded to explain what had happened at Rudy's home and what we believed was happening to homeless people. They both reacted the way you'd expect.

"That's awful," Donna said.

"Why was this Romaine killed?" Deirdre asked.

I took a deep breath and then explained how Romaine had wanted Rudy to write an investigative piece on the missing homeless people.

"Wow," Donna exclaimed. "And someone killed her for that?"

"Yes, we think so. And we believe they killed her in Rudy's home as a warning to Rudy to back off the investigative piece."

I went on to explain how Rose Marie was abducted recently, and that her friend Ileana keeps talking about it, putting her in danger.

"Can't the police protect her?" Donna asked.

"There isn't much to go on. Rudy has been charged with the woman's murder, and we have no actual evidence of anyone else's involvement. The abductions are happening in the Seattle area, so the Mercer Island police department doesn't have authority over there. The Seattle PD did go into the homeless camps to ask questions, but they didn't learn much."

"The homeless are wary of the police," April said.

"That's why we decided to get involved. We have a team of friends who have gone undercover in two homeless camps. And we're tracking everything they learn in the event center. But we've run into roadblocks."

Deirdre was leaning forward with her elbows on her knees, listening intently. "How can we help?"

Her response startled me.

"Are you sure? We're talking about murder here."

"Got it. Tell us how we can help."

"Um… okay. We now know, or at least we think we know, that a psychiatrist that works at a couple of the shelters is involved. We don't want you to do anything illegal, but this Ileana is mentally ill and keeps talking about her friend's abduction. We want to get her into a psych unit, but one where this particular psychiatrist doesn't have privileges."

"Can't you just call hospitals and ask?" Donna asked.

"We tried. They said we'd have to call back during the day and talk to their medical staffing office. We need to get her somewhere safe tonight, but she's scheduled right now to get a bed at one of the shelters where this psychiatrist works. We're worried she might be their next target if they learn she's talking about the abduction."

"Is there anything you can do to help?" April asked. "We don't want you to break any laws, but—"

"Yes, we can help," Donna said, sharing a look with her sister. "This is our world. We have resources that you don't. And of course, we agree that no one should break the law."

A long pause stretched between the four of us.

"How many of your friends are undercover on the street right now putting themselves at risk?" Deirdre asked.

"Um… three," I said. "Plus, another friend and I are working within the shelters trying to get information from some of the residents."

"Got it," Donna said. "So, you want info on Dr. Susan Enzo," she said, writing it down. "And we're looking for inpatient psych units." When I nodded, she said. "We'll see what we can do."

I gave them my cell number.

"Okay, leave it with us," Donna said.

CHAPTER TWENTY-ONE

Rudy was going to be out with Elliott, so David and I planned an evening together. It was after eight o'clock when he got to my apartment. A blustering wind had picked up again, forcing the branches of the large oak outside my window to scrape back and forth across the building again, while rain pummeled my small backyard. It was a perfect night to cuddle up on the sofa and watch one of the Marvel Comics action movies and then see where the evening took us.

As David drizzled butter over a bowl of popcorn, I relayed all the information I'd learned over dinner with Blair.

"I'll talk to Sean and see if we can call the Tacoma PD tomorrow and fill them in on what we know. We also checked and there is no such company as Johnston Electronics registered within the state of Washington."

"That's what Rudy said. They probably just used one of those magnetic signs," I said, pouring the wine. "Because there wasn't any name on the side of the blue van the other night when we rescued Ginger, and yet I bet it was the same van."

"You know, if there really are jobs, even for homeless folks, why would a legitimate company use a homeless person to do the recruiting?" David asked.

"Exactly. I'm convinced there are no jobs, and it's just part of the grift."

We moved to the sofa, and I clicked on the remote to get to Netflix.

"My guess is that Dr. Enzo helps to identify people who don't have family or any other support system," David said, as he settled into his seat. "Then, Patch confirms it and gets into their good graces by providing things they need. And then he gets them to go with him by offering them a job. We just don't know why."

My phone pinged with a text from Deirdre. I read the text to myself.

"Damn," I muttered.

"What is it?" David asked.

"A friend just confirmed that Dr. Enzo has privileges at all the inpatient psych units in the area."

He paused with his glass halfway to his mouth. "And this person knows this... how?"

I raised my eyebrows and shrugged. "I honestly don't know. But I need to tell Emma."

I sent Emma a quick text, and she responded immediately.

That's okay. I just heard from New Life Shelter in Federal Way. They can take her, and Enzo doesn't work there. I checked. But I need someone to pick her up and get her down there.

I texted back. *We'll pick her up. She texted back where to meet them.*

"Emma has solved it," I said. "She found Ileana a shelter but would like us to pick her up."

David put the popcorn bowl onto the coffee table and sighed. "I can't get that close, Julia. You'll have to go alone. But you have to promise me that you're just dropping this Ileana off at the shelter. No rescue attempts. No car chases. Nothing else."

"Okay," I said, standing up. "I'll just pick her up and take her to Federal Way." I groaned. "But I'm sorry about tonight. I was looking forward to—"

He stood and wrapped his arms around me. "Me too, " he whispered in my ear. "You owe me."

After David left, I texted Rudy that I'd be gone for a while and then packed up snacks and extra toiletries we give guests and climbed into my Pathfinder to head downtown.

It rained steadily as I crossed the floating bridge, and then the rain tapered off when I got into Seattle. My appointed meeting place was in front of a busy restaurant on a corner in Belltown. I arrived ten minutes early and circled the block looking for a parking place. The stores along both sides of the street were closed, with the exception of a couple of brew pubs whose windows glowed with neon lights. I finally found a spot and hopped out into the chilly night.

I crossed the street at the corner and approached the restaurant. A few minutes later, two women turned the corner coming from the other direction. It was Emma with a small, disheveled woman next to her. The other woman had her arms folded across her chest as if to ward off the cold and ducked behind Emma when she saw me.

"It's okay," Emma said to the woman.

"I'm parked across the street," I said, pointing to my car.

The three of us crossed to the other side of the street. Ileana stayed close to Emma as if afraid of the world around her.

When we got to the car, Emma said, "Ileana is nervous, so I'm going with you."

"Of course." I unlocked the doors and swung open the back door. "Jump in."

Emma got Ileana into the back seat and then climbed into the passenger seat next to me. Ileana mumbled to herself the entire time. As a brisk wind whipped around the car, I pulled away from the curb.

"Do you know where we're going?" Emma asked.

"I pulled it up on my phone. Will she be okay?"

Looking at Emma, I realized how different she looked now that she was back on the street. Even though she had dressed casually when she'd come to the Inn, she was now wearing dirty, mismatched clothing, and her hair was stringy and tangled. Ileana was in worse shape. She wasn't wearing a coat, and her clothes were streaked with dirt and torn in places. On top of her head was a knot of gray hair. And the rank odor of unwashed flesh and bad breath filled the car.

"She needs medication," Emma said. "The shelter will see that she gets it."

"What's she saying?" I asked.

Emma gave me a cautionary look. "She keeps reliving Rose Marie's abduction, and she's afraid they'll come for her next." She glanced into the back seat. "You know, at one time she was a wife and mother, belonged to the PTA, and volunteered. But the mental illness crept up on her, along with her drinking, and suddenly she was all by herself."

"She wouldn't be a target for these people then, would she? I mean, she has family."

"She would be if she keeps talking," Emma said. "She's a threat to them."

"Well, I'm glad you found a location," I said.

I subtly rolled my window down an inch to flood the car with fresh air as I took side streets to get onto I-5 south. Once we were on the freeway, Ileana grew quiet. The rhythmic movement of the car seemed to settle her down.

"How are you?" I asked Emma over my shoulder.

She sat back and looked out her window. "Okay. I didn't realize going back on the street would impact me so much."

"What do you mean?"

"I'd forgotten how depressing it is. Even though I know I can quit at any time, I still feel trapped. I hope this doesn't last long."

"You don't have to stay," I said. "We've learned a lot already, but it will probably take a few more days."

"I'll be okay. I just keep thinking about Rose Marie, wondering where she is and if she's okay."

"Rose Marie," Ileana mumbled from the back seat.

We drove the rest of the way to the shelter in silence. When we arrived, I got out and joined Emma at the curb as she opened Ileana's door. I reached my hand out to help her out, and the little woman grabbed my forearm in a tight grip and yanked me forward.

"I heard them, you know," she said, staring at me with glazed eyes. "Just before they grabbed Rose Marie, they asked her if she was afraid of dead people, because she'd be joining them soon."

She said this with complete clarity before dropping her head and beginning to mumble again. Emma stepped between us and gently helped her onto the curb.

"I'll get her checked in," she said and led the other woman into the shelter.

"Here, I brought these for her," I said, grabbing the bag of toiletries.

"Thanks, Julia."

The two women entered the shelter, and I got back in the car. Emma emerged ten minutes later. "They're checking her in," she said through the passenger window.

"What do you suppose she meant about not being afraid of dead people?" I asked her.

"I'm not sure. But I've heard her say that before. She says that as they were dragging Rose Marie toward the van, they said her life was going to make a difference and then laughed before saying they hoped she wasn't afraid of dead people.'"

A chill rippled down my spine. "Her life is going to make a difference. That sounds fatal."

Emma heaved a big sigh. "I know. Listen, I'm going to stay with her until they get her settled. I'll get back to camp on my own. You go ahead. And thank you."

It was close to midnight by the time I returned to the Inn. Rudy was waiting for me in the living room eating popcorn.

"How did things go?" she asked.

"Okay," I said, leaning down to greet Minnie. "Has she been out?"

"I let her out when I got back."

I joined Rudy on the sofa, encouraging Minnie to jump up beside me. "There are so many moving parts to this case," I said, stroking Minnie's soft red fur. "Now we have to be worried about Ileana's safety because she can't stop talking about her friend's abduction."

"You took her to a shelter where Dr. Enzo doesn't work, right?"

"Yeah, and Emma said the shelter would get her back on medication, which should stop her from rambling on and on about the abduction."

"That could take a while," Rudy said.

"I know. By the way, April and I talked to two of my guests about finding information on Dr. Enzo's hospital privileges. They're IT professionals."

"And you asked them to hack into hospital records?"

"Those words never left my mouth," I said in mock surprise. "In fact, we stressed that we didn't want them to break the law. But they verified that Enzo has privileges at all the inpatient units in the area. Anyway, how'd it go with Elliott?"

She slumped back against the sofa. "Okay, I guess. I came clean about the drugs."

"Really? How'd he take it?"

"Better than I thought he would. He said he'd noticed a difference in me over the past few months. But he offered to help if I needed it."

"Maybe he could help with rehab."

"I won't ask him for money," she said with a clip to her voice.

"I get it," I said, lifting my hand in surrender.

"Sorry. I just don't want to owe him anything."

"He's obviously angling to get you back, though."

"Yes, but I don't want to owe money to anyone. Including Doe. I plan to pay her back for anything she paid to get me out of jail. I got myself into this mess, and I need to get myself out of it. In fact, I've been thinking about registering with a couple of those online job boards. I could do copywriting to make extra money."

"That's a great idea. But Elliott believes you, doesn't he? About the murder."

"Of course, he does. But he's worried we're not making enough progress with the investigation."

My phone rang, and I swiped it on.

"She's gone!" Emma said in a rush.

"What do you mean?" I asked, sitting forward.

"When Ileana's paperwork was done, I suggested she take a shower. But I never saw her again. I went searching for her, but she was nowhere in the shelter. And then someone said they saw her go out the back door with another woman. I checked the alley behind the shelter, but she's gone, Julia. They've taken her!"

CHAPTER TWENTY-TWO

I asked a few more questions and hung up to call David. After I explained, I said, "We have to help. Now."

"Slow down, hon. Does Emma know who the woman was who went out the back with her?"

"She said it was someone who has stayed at the shelter several times before and came tonight to drop something off for someone. But the staff wouldn't give Emma her name."

"Okay, I'll call the Federal Way police. In the meantime, ask Emma if anyone overheard her when she talked to the shelter earlier or overheard a conversation with Ileana about going to the shelter."

"Okay. I'll do that and wait for you to call me back."

We hung up and I called Emma to ask her those questions.

"No. No one overheard me. I walked off by myself. I was careful, but—"

"But what?"

"I… oh, shit. I told Ileana where we were going and asked her to get her things together. Then I stepped away to text you. When I came back, there was a woman looming over Ileana outside her tent. I asked her what she was doing there, and she screeched at me something about the government trying to kill her and then lurched away. I just figured she was another homeless person struggling with mental illness."

"And you think she may have talked with Ileana about where she was going?" I asked.

"It's the only thing I can think of. God, what if they kill her? Rose Marie and now Ileana."

"What did she look like? This other woman?"

Emma sucked up a breath and said, "Um, heavy-set. She was wearing a blue bathrobe over sweatpants and, uh, a Mickey Mouse sweatshirt. And she had close cropped, bleached, white hair."

"And who was it at the shelter who told you she left with someone else?"

"A Black woman staying in the last room by the back door."

"Okay, stay there. I'm going to call David back and let him know. He's calling the Federal Way police."

I called David and told him exactly what Emma had told me.

"Alright, they're sending an officer to the shelter now. I'll let them know who to ask for. And then you need to tell Emma that she needs to come home."

"You mean quit the undercover work?"

"She's been compromised, Julia. If the woman in the bathrobe is the one who took Ileana, she not only knows Emma heard everything Ileana said but that Emma was trying to protect her. Tell her to stay at the shelter and that I'm on my way down there to pick her up. No arguments."

"Okay, bring her back here," I said.

After we hung up, I called April and explained the situation.

"Of course, she can stay with me," April said. "I'll make up the sofa bed."

My alarm woke me at six-thirty the next morning. I pried my eyes open, and then closed them quickly when a stab of light from my window hit my pupils. At least it wasn't raining, I thought. I got out of bed, pulled out a set of clothes, and slipped into the bathroom to grab a shower and brush my teeth. Once I was dressed, I let Minnie outside and fed her before meeting April in the big kitchen. I took Minnie with me, so she wouldn't wake Rudy and gave her a chew toy, which she took to her bed in the corner.

"How are you doing?" I asked April, stifling a yawn.

She chuckled watching me. "I'll have to catch a nap later, too. I'm not used to welcoming guests in the middle of the night." She was kneading scone dough.

"Yeah, what a night. How's Emma?"

"She was pretty frantic last night and was still asleep when I left this morning."

"Okay. You want sausage or bacon this morning?"

"Sausage."

"I'll get it."

"Can you fill me in?" April asked. "Emma was too emotionally spent. I only got a few details from her."

I told her the entire story as we made breakfast for the guests. At 7:30, the door swung open, and Rudy came in.

"What can I do to help?"

"You might want to check on Emma and let her know to come over here for breakfast," April said.

"Happy to."

Rudy left, as April and I began putting food out on the counter in the breakfast room. We'd just gotten everything situated when Donna appeared at my elbow.

"We have to be out of here in fifteen," she said, grabbing a scone.

"No problem," I replied. "We can create a 'go bag' for you."

Deirdre came up to my other side, sandwiching me in. "Hope we were able to help last night," she said quietly.

"Yes, thanks. Unfortunately, it didn't matter. The woman we were trying to protect was abducted from the shelter last night."

"Oh, shit. I'm sorry," Donna said. "Can we do anything?"

I sighed. "Not at the moment, but thanks."

An older woman visiting from New York reached across Deirdre for a scone, making me wait until we were alone again.

"Can I get your cell phone number just in case?"

Donna programmed it into my phone. "Listen, we'll be tied up all day at the hospital, but we'll help if we can. Just text us."

I returned to the kitchen just as my phone pinged with a text from Ben.

Followed Patch into the storage facility. Hid behind a stack of boxes. His unit, # 34, is filled with coats, tarps, old shoes, and more.

I sighed. So, Patch was buttering people up by giving them things from the storage unit. But that wasn't against the law. Nor did it necessarily point to anything nefarious. I texted Ben back, telling him to be careful. I also texted José and told him Emma had come in from the field, so he was alone at the Magnolia camp. A moment later, Emma and Rudy came into the kitchen.

"Smells heavenly in here," Emma said.

Her eyes were rimmed with gray circles, but her hair was freshly washed, and she was wearing a pair of April's jeans and a blouse.

"Grab yourself a plate from the breakfast room," April said, pointing through the door.

"Yeah, and then come in here where it's private. We need to make a plan," I said. "Since you can't go back on the street, we need to talk about the next steps. Can you grab me a scone?"

"Sure," Rudy said.

The two women returned to the breakfast room and came back with plates of sausage, eggs, and scones. I took one of the scones and added jam before the three of us sat down.

"Can you join us, April?" I asked.

She was scrubbing a fry pan. "I'll listen from here."

I took a bite, swallowed, and then said, "I just heard from Ben. He said he followed Patch to the storage unit and saw that it was filled with old clothing and tarps and things."

"Really?" Emma said. "You know I saw Patch come into camp one day and hand a pair of boots to someone who only had on a pair of tattered tennis shoes."

"Did you ever have a chance to interact with him?" I asked her.

"Not directly. But I caught him watching me a couple of times. And one of the women told me that he asked about me. He thought I knew a lot of people."

"I wonder if that's why he stayed clear of you," Rudy said. "You knew your way around."

She shrugged as she swallowed a piece of sausage. "Maybe. I suppose he could have pegged me as someone suspicious, too."

"Because you showed up after Romaine was killed?" I asked.

"Yeah. And after Rose Marie's abduction. Ileana talked about it a lot."

"Did Patch hear her?"

"I'm not sure," she said. "I always tried to downplay what Ileana was saying, but a few people knew Rose Marie and wondered what happened to her. It kept the story going."

"What do we think the storage unit means?" Rudy asked.

"I think he's buttering people up," I said. "Getting them to lower their guard and trust him. But I'd like to know where he gets everything. Who pays for the storage unit? And is he homeless or just pretending to be?"

"And what does he have to do with Dr. Enzo?" Rudy added.

"I hope to get a better read on her today," I said. "I'm going back to the shelter to work on cover letters, and one of our guests is going with me."

That perked Rudy up. "Who?"

"A gal named Gretchen. She's a freelance writer. With her there, I figured it might give me an opportunity to look around and find out more about the good doctor."

"Yes, but how are you going to do that?" Rudy asked. "I mean, you have to be careful."

"You've been open about covering for Rudy, right?" April asked, turning around, wiping her hands with a towel.

"Yes."

"Then, why couldn't you pull this psychiatrist aside and ask for advice on how you can help your friend deal with the trauma she's been through?"

I felt like a giant lightbulb had just switched on above my head. "April, you're a genius."

CHAPTER TWENTY-THREE

When Gretchen and I arrived at Wings of Hope, we found both Vivian and Izzy waiting for us. I introduced Gretchen, who proceeded to explain how we would approach our time together.

"Julia shared your resumes with me. It's best if your cover letters not only reflect the positions you want, but also the skills and values you bring to the table. I've brought postings for the kinds of jobs you're interested in," she said, holding up several pieces of paper. "How does that sound?"

"That's dope," Izzy said, popping her gum.

"Can… can we also talk about how to interview?" Vivian asked. "I'm not very good in interviews."

Gretchen shot me a glance, and I nodded.

"Absolutely, but let's start with the cover letters."

We spent the next forty minutes creating different versions of the cover letters for each woman. While we worked, I kept glancing into the parking lot, waiting for Dr. Enzo. I was rewarded when the big Lincoln pulled in about 12:15.

Dr. Enzo emerged from her car wrapped in a black wool coat and scarlet scarf. With the black bouffant hairstyle and red lipstick, she reminded me of Cruella De Vil, minus the cute Dalmatian puppies, of course.

She held her phone tightly to one ear and paused next to a Volkswagen bug, deep in conversation. Finally, she shut off the conversation and dropped the phone into the big black bag hanging from her elbow and marched into the shelter.

"I need to run to the restroom," I said to Gretchen. "Can you hold down the fort?"

"Of course."

I hurried into the foyer just as Dr. Enzo disappeared into her office. After taking a cleansing breath, I crossed to her door and knocked. A heavy, modulated voice said, "Come in."

I stepped into a small, bland office. Enzo had her back to me, hanging her coat on a metal coat tree. She turned and sat behind a medium-sized wooden desk facing two straight back chairs before finally looking at me.

"Can I help you?" she asked.

She was an imposing woman with deep-set dark eyes and large hands that immediately began flying over the keyboard of her computer. I stared at that dyed black hair teased into a football helmet wondering what hairdresser in their right mind would agree to do that.

"Yes?" she prompted me.

"Oh, sorry," I said, snapping to attention. "I just need some advice."

"And you are?"

She stopped typing and finally turned to me.

"Oh, my name is Julia. I'm a volunteer, taking over for Rudy Smith until, well, until she gets things sorted out."

"I'm sorry. Do I know Ms. Smith?"

"She comes once a week to help women with resumes and cover letters."

"Oh, yes. Of course. What is it that you want?"

This woman obviously missed the class on bedside manner when she got her medical degree.

"May I sit down?"

"I only have a few minutes," she said, glancing at the clock on the wall behind me.

I ignored the snub and sat in a chair facing her. "I'm sure you know that one of the shelter's former residents was murdered inside Rudy's home last week."

Her thick eyebrows arched. "I heard something about that. Was your friend injured? Is that why she's taking time off?"

"Uh... no. But as you can imagine, it was naturally traumatizing. She had become friends with the woman when she met her here at the shelter."

"Of course. Romaine," she said without emotion. She began tapping the fingers of her right hand on the desk. "I was sad to hear about what happened to Romaine."

A fly buzzed past my ear, and I flicked my hand at it.

"She was one of the fortunate ones," Enzo continued. "When she moved out, we had high hopes for her. It's too bad she got into drugs after she left. Some people have an addictive personality, you know."

"Drugs? Um… I don't think that's how she died."

"Well, I heard drugs were involved. Perhaps it was a drug deal gone bad."

"Did she have a drug problem while she was here?"

"I really can't say. Patient confidentiality and all," she said, tight-lipped.

"Of course," I said. The fly buzzed me again, and I swatted at it. "I just, well, I'm just trying to help Rudy."

"Was she involved in drugs?"

"No. Of course not. But to have someone killed in your own home, well that's hard to accept. And then to be accused of her murder, well…"

The fly landed on the desk in front of Enzo. Enzo ignored it.

"Maybe your friend shouldn't have extended her trust to someone like Romaine. After all, most of the people who come through the shelter struggle with something."

She gave me a condescending smile, as the fly lifted off and headed for the other side of the room. I clenched my jaw, thinking this woman shouldn't be counseling anyone. But I continued.

"Well, I'm only worried about Rudy at this point. She's taking it very badly."

The fly circled around and swooped down between us.

"I'm sure she is…" Snap! Enzo smacked the fly between her big hands and dropped the dead body onto her desk. "Now, if you don't mind, I have a client to see."

I stared at the dead fly stunned. Who was this woman? I drew my gaze away from the dead insect and back to her.

"I was hoping you could give me advice on how I could help her. She's not eating. Not sleeping."

The woman locked eyes with me, flicked the dead insect off the desk and said, "She should probably see a therapist. Not me. I don't take private clients."

"I thought since she volunteered here…"

"As I said, I don't take private clients."

Her tone didn't invite discussion, but I pushed ahead.

"I see. So, you only work with clients here at the shelter."

"No," she said with a slight stiffness to her lip. "I consult with clients at shelters from Seattle to Tacoma, and I see inpatients at most of the hospitals in the area. I'm quite busy."

Tacoma! My heart rate skipped a beat.

"I often thought when I was younger that I might like to be a psychologist," I said, hoping to draw out the conversation.

She leaned forward again with a stony look, resting her generous bosom on the desk. "I'm not a psychologist, Ms. Applegate. I'm a psychiatrist. There is a distinct difference, and the training is much more rigorous. A psychiatrist is a medical doctor and can prescribe drugs. Now if you don't mind..." she said, standing up.

"Of course. Thank you for your time."

There was an uneasy silence before I left the office wondering how she knew my last name when I hadn't given it. I returned to where Gretchen was just finishing up with Izzy and Vivian, feeling the adrenaline thrum through my veins.

"These gals should have no problem finding jobs," Gretchen said with a smile when I walked in.

Vivian beamed at the compliment. "She said that maybe you guys could come back tomorrow so we could practice some mock interviews."

I glanced at Gretchen. "Uh, sure. I'll talk to Gloria on the way out."

The four of us emerged from the small conference room just as a tall, skinny woman went in to see Dr. Enzo. I couldn't help myself and turned to Vivian and Izzy.

"What do you think of having a psychiatrist here?" I asked.

Izzy groaned. "You mean Dr. Death?"

"You call her Dr. Death?"

"Some of us do," Vivian said.

"If you don't feel dead inside before you go in to see her, you will after she drugs you up," Izzy said. Pop. Pop.

I watched the two women amble away, thinking I needed more time. I turned to Gretchen.

"Listen, I need to stop in the restroom, and then I'll talk to Gloria."

Gretchen's eyebrows furrowed in confusion, but she went to the car. I walked over and knocked on Gloria's open door. She waved me in, and I closed the door.

"How'd everything go?"

"Really well."

Gloria smiled. "I heard good things from Vivian after your meeting yesterday. By the way, how's Rudy doing?"

"Um, not great, you know? She's pretty stressed out."

"Well, I have a tough time thinking she had anything to do with it. I admire Rudy, and the clients love her."

"How well did you know Romaine?"

"Pretty well. She stayed here a few times. She was a very sweet woman. An easy keeper if you know what I mean."

"Really? I just spoke to Dr. Enzo hoping she might have some advice on how I could help Rudy deal with the stress. She implied that Romaine was a recovering drug addict."

Gloria flinched at that. "Not at all. Like many of our clients, she was just down on her luck. As far as I know, she'd never used drugs."

"Dr. Enzo seemed to think that since drugs were involved in her death, she had fallen off the wagon, so to speak."

Gloria frowned. "Where did she get that? The police talked to me, but I've been careful not to divulge any of those details to anyone else, including Dr. Enzo. I didn't want rumors to spread… just like that."

I shrugged. "She seemed very sure of herself."

Gloria leaned forward. "Listen, no way did Romaine do drugs. Like most people here, I'm sure she knew people who did and probably even some who sold them, but she didn't drink alcohol and told me she'd never even tried pot. I don't know what happened at Rudy's house. Maybe it was just wrong place at the wrong time, but whatever happened, it wasn't Romaine's fault."

"Thanks. I believe you. Rudy really liked her, too."

"Besides, I'm not sure Dr. Enzo could help you, anyway."

"Why do you say that?"

She heaved a sigh and glanced through the door into the foyer. "Look. I have to be careful, but frankly, she jumps to conclusions, just like she did with Romaine. She only saw Romaine once or twice."

"Hmmm," I mumbled to myself. "Listen, Vivian and Izzy want us to come back tomorrow to practice mock interviews."

Gloria glanced at her calendar. "Um, I'm not sure that will work. Can you give me a call in the morning?"

"Sure." I turned for the door but then stopped and turned back. "And don't worry about Dr. Enzo. She wasn't much help anyway since she doesn't take private clients. She said she only works out of the shelters." I turned for the door again and reached for the knob.

"She also does grief counseling at one of the funeral homes," Gloria said.

My hand froze on the doorknob. I turned back.

"Really? Which funeral home?"

Gloria pursed her lips thinking. "I think it was... Colling or Colar, or something... and Sons." She laughed. "Sorry. I'm not good with names. It was something like that. They're in the Union Lake area."

I left and stopped in the parking lot to quickly Google funeral homes in Seattle. The second one that popped up was Collier and Sons Funeral Home on Phinney Avenue North.

Hope you're not afraid of dead people.

CHAPTER TWENTY-FOUR

When I climbed into my Pathfinder, my mind was a million miles away.

"So?" Gretchen said.

I swiveled to look at her. "Oh, yeah... that was great. Thanks for helping me out." I leaned forward to start the car.

"That's not what I meant. What's going on?"

I stopped and gave her my best imitation of a doe-eyed Shirley Temple. "Huh? I don't know what you mean."

"Either you have a very weak bladder, like many women our age, or you didn't use the restroom earlier when you asked me to hold the fort. What were you doing?"

Damn!

Gretchen waited patiently, while my gaze drifted toward a battered, old pickup pulling into the parking lot. As I tried to decide how to respond, the truck pulled off to the far side of the lot and parked. A heavy-set woman got out and began walking toward the shelter.

"Julia?"

My brain shifted, and I became focused on the heavy-set woman with short, brown hair. There was something about her. She looked more like a client than a service provider, wearing bedroom slippers and a sloppy coat over a sweatshirt. She stopped to toss a cigarette to the ground, turning for a moment in our direction. The breeze whipped open her coat, and my breath caught at the sight of the faded image of Mickey Mouse on the front of her sweatshirt.

"I'll be right back," I said, opening the car door.

Gretchen opened her mouth to say something, but I was out of the car before she could utter a syllable. I re-entered the shelter and stopped in the small lobby, looking up and down the hallways. The woman in the Mickey Mouse sweatshirt had disappeared.

"Hey, Miz Applegate. Forget somethin'?"

I turned to find Izzy at my elbow. "Oh, uh, no. I..."

I looked swiftly around the lobby again and finally saw the woman through the window of Dr. Enzo's closed office door. She was standing in front of Enzo's desk, talking to her.

"Izzy, do you know that woman talking to Dr. Enzo?"

Izzy peered through the window and popped her gum a couple of times before saying, "Oh, yeah, that's Grace. She's wearing one of her many wigs today. Not sure why, she's ugly either way—"

"Wig? What's her real hair look like?"

"White. Close to the head. Ugly."

"But who is she?" I asked, interrupting her.

"Oh, she mostly hangs out at the camp up by the Fremont Bridge. But I see her around a lot. Why?"

"She just… reminds me of someone," I said, still staring.

Dr. Enzo turned and saw me watching them, making my heart skip a beat. While Grace continued to talk, the doctor looked back at her as if to listen, and then back at me as if making a connection.

"Well, she's not someone you want to know," Izzy said.

I pulled Izzy out of Enzo's sightline. "Why do you say that?"

"She's just bad news. She comes to see Dr. Death. And my spidey sense tells me they're up to no good."

"What do you mean?"

"Look, Miz Applegate, no one here was surprised when Romaine was killed. She saw too much and talked too much."

I grabbed Izzy's shoulders. "What do you mean?"

Dr. Enzo's door opened and without a word Izzy pulled away from me and disappeared down the hallway. I hurried outside before Enzo emerged from her office.

When I got into my car again, Gretchen said, "I'm a patient woman, Julia. But what in the world is going on?"

My entire body was a-buzz, and I had to take a deep breath. "Sorry. I'll tell you, but first..."

The front door of the shelter opened and Grace came out. Gretchen sat quietly while I watched Grace return to her truck and pull out of the parking lot.

"Aren't you going to follow her?" Gretchen asked.

I swung around. "That's a great idea."

Within seconds, I was hot on the trail of the woman we believed had abducted Ileana from the Federal Way shelter. As I changed lanes to pass a slow-moving delivery truck, I decided it was time to be honest with Gretchen.

"I'm so sorry, Gretchen. I've been very rude. And you have a right to know. So, here's the Cliffs Notes version of what's going on."

While I followed Grace, I told Gretchen everything. Gretchen only asked a few questions but picked up quickly on what role Dr. Enzo might play in the abductions.

"And you think the psychiatrist is identifying people who then become their targets," she said.

"At least some of them. I think Patch also identifies people."

She was watching the Datsun pickup as we threaded our way through downtown traffic and across the Duwamish River.

"You live an interesting life, Julia. I take it that when you said you were going to the bathroom, you were pumping Dr. Enzo."

"Well, trying to. But I think that's as much as I should tell you. This is murder we're talking about, and I don't want to put you in danger."

She chuckled. "I come from a military family. Grandfather, father, and two brothers. I'm the only girl in the family. I grew up with the concept of 'do whatever it takes.' So, if there's a way I can help, I'd like to. Use me as a sounding board. I have a good mind and can keep everything confidential."

I sighed. "Well, the biggest revelation today was that Gloria told me Dr. Enzo also does grief counseling at a funeral home. That's why I was in such a blur when we first got to the car."

Gretchen drew in a quick breath. "Oh, and you said that when one of the women was abducted, someone overheard them say they hoped she wouldn't be afraid of dead people."

"Right. We still don't know what that means, but funeral homes are filled with dead people."

While we drove, Gretchen toyed with an opal pendant that hung around her neck, obviously contemplating everything I'd told her.

"And Gloria gave me the partial name of the funeral home. I found the address."

"Ah, that's what you were doing before you got in the car. You know, I've always wanted to write a mystery novel, and you're giving me the inspiration to finally do it."

I gave her a wicked smile. "Yeah, well, I think I'm going to check out that funeral home."

"How?"

"I'll make an appointment to talk to them about funeral arrangements for a fictitious friend who just died."

She chuckled. "Man, you are one fearless woman. Walking right into the lion's den. But you realize Dr. Enzo knows who you are now. If she's a part of this, your cover might be blown."

I hit the steering wheel with the palm of my hand. "Damn! You're right. Maybe Blair could go."

We were quiet for a moment, and then she said, "Or I could go."

"What? No. I couldn't let you do that."

"Yes, you could. I have the perfect cover. I could tell them I'm writing a book and need to get an inside look at a funeral home. It could be a murder mystery. Or even a literary novel in which the patriarch of the family dies. I'd come up with a cover story."

"No, Gretchen. It's too dangerous," I said firmly. "You're my guest, and you're here to spend time with your daughter. Not get involved in anything I'm doing."

The Datsun pulled into the parking lot of a small neighborhood park. Although it was the middle of a weekday, several moms were there with small children, and a couple of people were walking dogs.

"I wonder where she's going," Gretchen said, watching the truck.

I pulled to the curb as Grace parked next to the sand pit. She got out and took a cement path around the playground equipment to the other side of the park.

"We need to get a better look," I said.

I pulled into the parking lot and slipped into a slot on the other side of two cars. We watched Grace sit next to a man on a bench. He appeared to be around five foot ten, well-built, but wearing baggy clothes.

"My God, that's Patch," I said, peering through the front window. "I'm sure of it, although he's not wearing the patch over his eye. Damn! I wish I could get a picture of him." I reached into my purse and pulled out my phone. "Stay here."

I opened the door to step out and got my foot caught in the dangling shoulder strap of my purse. With a cry of alarm, I fell, ending up face down on the pavement.

"Julia!" Gretchen yelled, popping her door open.

I stayed there for a moment cursing myself. Before I could push myself up, a small, scraggly dog appeared out of nowhere and stuck his smug little nose in my face.

"Leave me alone," I snapped, feeling once more humiliated by my penchant for pratfalls.

The little dog snorted and then turned sideways, lifting his leg.

"No!" I screamed, scrambling to get up.

Before I could get off the ground, he whizzed all over my leg and then scampered away.

"Damn you," I said, standing up and shaking my leg.

By this time, Gretchen had come around the car and was next to me.

"Are you okay?"

"Just fine," I said dusting off my hands. "I'll just have to have change pants when I get home." I grabbed my purse from the front seat and pulled out a wipe to clean off my hands and another one to clean my pants leg. I glanced over to where Patch and Grace were talking.

"You still want a picture?" Gretchen asked.

"Yes. It's important." I leaned down to get my phone from where I'd dropped it.

"Wait!" Gretchen said. "Grace might have seen you at the shelter. Let me do it."

She grabbed her phone from her pocket and headed for an expanse of lawn where a large group of Canadian geese were resting in the filtered sunlight. Gretchen circled the flock of birds, taking pictures of them. At one point, she got down on one knee and held her phone up to get the shot of a big bird grooming itself. Patch and Grace sat only fifteen feet behind it. When she'd finished, Gretchen got up and came back to the car, where I'd made it safely back inside.

"Okay, done. How are you? Are your hands bruised?" she asked.

"No. Just my ego. But you did great."

She fiddled with her phone for a moment. "There, I've sent them to you at the Inn."

"Thanks."

I was about to start the car when my phone pinged with a text.

"We have to go," I said, after reading it. "That was Emma. Another woman has gone missing."

CHAPTER TWENTY-FIVE

Since Rudy was running errands and would be gone when Gretchen and I got back, I sent David a quick text asking him to meet me back at the command center before we left the park. When we got back inside the Inn, Gretchen stopped at the bottom of the stairs.

"My offer stands, Julia. I'm a very pragmatic and careful woman. And I'm no dummy. I could do this."

She once again began to finger the pendant around her neck.

"I have no doubt you could. This just isn't your fight. Plus, I have no idea if the funeral home is implicated in any of this. But let me talk to the others and see what they think. By the way," I said, nodding to her necklace. "You keep touching your necklace. It's beautiful. Where did you get it?"

She opened her fingers to expose a large fire opal set in gold with a small, gold filigree infinity sign dangling beneath it.

"The opal was my grandmother's, and my husband had the necklace made for me for our 25th wedding anniversary. When he gave it to me, he said, 'it's one of a kind, just like you.'" She smiled sadly, glancing down at the pendant. "That was only four days before he died."

"Oh, dear, I'm so sorry. I had no idea. It's a beautiful reminder of how much he loved you, though."

She smiled, tears glistening. "When I wear it, it feels like he's right here with me. My daughter teases me that I never take it off."

Gretchen asked to be caught up later and then excused herself to call her daughter. I went on to meet David and Emma in the command center.

"So, who's missing?" I asked, stripping my coat off and dropping it over a chair.

"It's someone I know," Emma said, sitting on the edge of a table. "I realized this morning that I hadn't talked to the one person who might have real information about all of this. People call her 'the Madame,' and she's lived on the street for years. In fact, she has a small encampment off Airport Way, close to the intersection of I-90 and I-5."

"What makes you think she knows something?" I asked.

She arched a brow. "Because... there's a reason she's known as the Madame."

"Oh," I said. "I get it."

"She'll entertain pretty much anyone who can pay five dollars, which is a lot of money for a homeless person. Men or women. It doesn't matter. And she has a small RV, so she has more amenities than others. A bed being one of them. The point is that she talks to a lot of people and knows most of what goes on."

"So, what happened?" David asked. "You said someone's missing."

"Yeah... she is."

I plopped into a chair. "How can you be sure?"

"Because I went to see her, but someone else is living in her RV. A man. And the other two women who had tents there are also gone."

"What did the man say?" David asked.

"That he found the camp about a couple of weeks ago. The RV was empty and looked abandoned, so he took it over."

"Did you ask if she ever came back?"

"He hasn't seen her," she said, shaking her head. "Plus, several men have shown up ready to pay for her services and were disappointed when he appeared instead."

"Could she have just moved on?" David asked.

"I don't think so. First of all, I doubt she'd leave the RV and all her stuff behind. This guy said he found a small stash of money, some bank information, an address book, and other personal belongings inside."

"The bank information would give us her name," David said.

"I know her real name. She used to hang out down by the Whole Foods store. I got to talking with her one day when a guy offered only a dollar for her services. When she told him to bugger off, he snapped at her, saying she couldn't be picky. After all, she was no Pollyanna. When he left, she laughed and said, 'Little does he know that I'm actually named after the woman who wrote Pollyanna, Eleanor Porter.'"

"Her name was Eleanor Porter?" I asked.

"No. But close. Eleanor Portman."

"What does she look like?" David asked, taking notes.

"She's an attractive woman. Maybe five foot eight or nine. Probably thirty pounds overweight. Could be in her early forties. Dyed dark red hair. Deep brown eyes. Wore tons of makeup, which is unusual on the street because it's costly."

David wrote it all down. "But again, no family."

"That I don't know," Emma said. "I do know she was from Gainesville, Florida, though."

"I'll do some digging and let the Seattle PD know," David said. "With that much information, we should be able to get her listed in the FBI's National Missing and Unidentified Persons System. And I think it's time we asked for assistance from the FBI. After all, they have more resources. I'll talk to Sean."

"Okay, but wait," I said. "I have something to report, too."

I told them what I'd learned about Dr. Enzo and the funeral home and that she'd known about Romaine being drugged before she was killed.

"She's also known around the shelter as someone who just drugs the clients," I added. "In fact, they call her Dr. Death."

"Are you thinking she's the one who could have gotten the GHB they used on Romaine?" Emma asked.

"I hadn't thought of that, but yeah, maybe."

"You're sure she does grief counseling at Collier and Sons Funeral Home?" David asked.

"Based on the partial name Gloria gave me. But listen, there's something else. The woman who took Ileana in Federal Way showed up as we were leaving."

Emma sat forward. "You're sure?"

"Pretty sure. She was wearing the Mickey Mouse sweatshirt, but she had on a wig, according to one of the residents. But she told me that this woman normally has really short white hair."

"You asked about her?" David's eyes narrowed in concern.

"I asked one of the women from my workshop. The woman with the sweatshirt's name is Grace, and Izzy warned me about both her and Dr. Enzo. She also said no one there was surprised when Romaine was killed."

"What did she mean by that?" Emma asked in a clipped voice.

I shrugged. "She said Romaine saw too much and talked too much. I took it to mean that Romaine let too many people know about her suspicions. But there's something else," I said, pulling out my phone. I thumbed my way to the pictures of Patch and Grace. "You wanted a better picture of Patch. Well, here it is. This is the two of them together."

David's eyebrows lifted as I held the picture up. His phone pinged. "It's Sean. I'll be right back." He stepped away and returned moments later. "They have a lead on the blue van. It was caught by a street camera in downtown Seattle. I'm going to meet Sean to see if we can ID the passengers. Listen, get everything you learned up on the board and send that picture to me. You guys did good," he said, giving me a peck on the cheek. "I'll see you later."

David left, and Emma and I returned to the Inn. Rudy was just pulling into the parking lot and joined us in my apartment. I pulled a pitcher of iced tea out of the refrigerator and offered it to the others. As we added our own sweeteners or lemon, I told Rudy about the funeral home.

"I think we need to check it out," I said.

"How?" she asked.

"I wanted to go pretending someone close to me had just died. But since Dr. Enzo knows me, Gretchen has offered to go in my place. What do you think?"

"It might be a waste of time," Rudy countered. "We don't know if the funeral home is even involved."

"True. But I don't believe in coincidences, either."

My phone pinged with a text from Gretchen.

Having dinner with my daughter tonight. I'll see you tomorrow around 11:00 to go back to the shelter. You can catch me up then.

"So, what's our next step?" Rudy asked.

"Um…" I said, looking up from my phone. "Maybe José or Ben can verify whether there is any talk on the street about the funeral home."

"They'll have to be careful with that," Emma said. "That would be an obvious tip-off."

"You're right. We could just tell them that it's on our radar but we need to know more."

Rudy and Emma helped me word a text to that effect, and I sent it off to the three men.

"Okay," I said with a sigh. "I think that's about all we can do for today."

"Emma and I can go update the wall with all this new information," Rudy said. "You send the picture to David and then take care of Inn business."

They left for the command center, while I sent the picture of Patch to David. Then, I met April in the kitchen.

"Oh, hey," she said. "The twins are back. They said they learned something you need to know. Right now, I guess."

CHAPTER TWENTY-SIX

I quickly filled April in on what I'd learned that day, which frankly, didn't sit well with her.

"I don't like this," she said. "This is much more complicated than what we thought, and you definitely shouldn't be going into that funeral home for any reason."

I released a sigh. "I agree, and I don't plan to. But also, Emma needs to stay here a while longer. You okay with that?"

"Of course. But I don't mind telling you that this is beginning to make me nervous. How many times are you going to put yourself in harm's way?"

"We have a whole team this time, April. I think we'll be okay."

"Why doesn't that give me the peace of mind it does you?"

I smiled and gave her a hug. "I'll go see the twins."

Deirdre answered the door when I knocked.

"Hey. What's up?" I asked, stepping inside.

Donna was on her computer at the small desk under one window and turned. "Listen, we learned something interesting today. Overlake Hospital has an inpatient psych ward."

"Their department was one of the systems that got hacked and why we were hired," Dierdre interjected.

"But that's not why we wanted to see you," Donna said, getting up and sitting on the bed. "As we mentioned earlier, Dr. Enzo had privileges there. Since we spent time with the staff today, we casually asked about her."

"Don't worry. We made up a story," Deirdre said, before I could respond. "We said she was the neighbor of a friend of ours and had a reputation for being a witch."

Donna laughed. "But they did us one better and said the floor staff refer to her as 'Maleficent.'"

Bingo! I finally had the perfect cartoon comparison for the woman who could kill a flying insect midair with her bare hands.

"Except for the hair, I couldn't agree more."

"Well, not only do people dislike her, but she was fired from there recently. Someone snitched on her because she was dispensing drugs to the staff," Donna said.

"Especially ketamine, Rohypnol, and GHB," Dierdre added with a self-satisfied grin.

Time seemed to stop for a moment.

"You mean GHB?"

"Yeah. We thought that would get your attention."

I plopped into a chair.

"You're going to like this next piece of information, too," Donna said. "The woman we spoke with also said that Enzo's husband, Edgar, is a pharmaceutical rep."

"Husband?" I said, my mind whirring.

"Yeah. His company sold psychotropic drugs to the hospital, so when the hospital let her go, they stopped doing business with him, too."

"So, either one of them could have gotten the GHB," Dierdre said with a wink.

"Interesting," I murmured. "I learned today that Dr. Enzo also does grief counseling for a funeral home in Seattle."

Deirdre's eyes lit up. "The dead people!"

"Maybe. They might have just meant they were going to kill her when they said that, though."

Donna pulled out her phone. "What's the name of the funeral home?"

"Collier and Sons."

She nodded. "Okay, we'll check them out. We'll also see what we can find online for both Enzo and her husband."

I left the twins' room, thinking they could probably learn more about the funeral home than I could with my fake visit, which meant neither Gretchen nor I would have to go undercover. That would make April happy.

I was heading to my apartment when José called me on the burner phone.

"Hey, why are you calling instead of texting?" I asked him.

"I just wanted to let you know that Patch approached me today."

I stopped short. "What did he say?"

"He wanted to know about my background. I told him I left LA after my brother was killed down there."

"That's not true, is it?"

"Um, yeah, it is. My brother Julio was only ten when he was shot by mistake in a drive-by."

"I'm so sorry, José."

"Anyway, I figured I'd be honest because it would play better. He asked about my parents, so I told him they disowned me because I was gay, which is also pretty much true."

"But you told him you have close friends here, right?"

"I decided not to. If these guys are looking for people without family, then—"

"No, José," I cut him off. "I don't want anything to happen to you."

"I'll be okay, Miz Applegate. Don't worry about me. I just wanted you to know. I'll text you if anything else happens. But I also told him I really needed money. He didn't offer me a job, but said he'd keep his ears open."

We said goodbye, and I went to my apartment with a nervous twitch in my gut. I let Minnie out and then made myself a sandwich, worrying the whole time about José. I sat down to eat and turned on the news just in time for the local weather report about a second big thunderstorm headed our way. I finished my sandwich and went to the kitchen to clean up after lunch, when the news came back on. A female reporter was reporting from somewhere in Seattle talking about a fire. In the background were a couple of police cars, officers wandering around, and what looked like a burned vehicle.

"Police say the van was torched, and I can smell the gasoline from here," the reporter said. "Officers also say it looks intentional. But that's not all. They're investigating a body found inside the van."

CHAPTER TWENTY-SEVEN

That put me over the top for the day. I was on information overload. When that happens, my mind immediately turns to sweets to reduce my anxiety. Since I carried a few extra pounds, I purposely didn't keep sweets in my apartment, because they wouldn't survive more than a few minutes. So, after finishing my sandwich, I went to the Inn's pantry, where April kept the leftover snacks she made for guests. I found Snickerdoodle cookies and chocolate mint brownies and thought the occasion warranted one of each.

I had just put them on a plate when a cookbook slid out from a line of cookbooks sitting on the counter. It was one of April's favorites, so I reached over and pushed it back, thinking Chloe was just teasing me again. When the smell of rose water wafted around me, I whirled around, expecting to see Elizabeth. Instead, the same cookbook flew off the counter and onto the floor with a slap! I almost dropped my plate.

I glanced up to find the hazy image of Elizabeth in her signature white nightgown flickering in front of the kitchen door that led to the back deck.

"Elizabeth, stop scaring me like that!"

Her partly transparent finger pointed to the book.

I put my plate on the counter and picked up the book. The title was A Friendly Guide to Baking.

"You want me to bake something?"

She appeared to slap the flat of her hand against her forehead, which of course went right through her forehead.

"Did you just face-smack yourself?" I exclaimed.

She threw her flickering hands up in exasperation and disappeared. Excuse me? How was I supposed to know what throwing a cookbook to the floor meant?

I took the cookbook with me when I returned to my apartment. Elizabeth didn't usually appear unless she had a message, but for the life of me I couldn't fathom what baking would have to do with anything we were doing. A call from David snapped me out of my thoughts.

"Did you see the news?"

"Yes. Was it our blue van? They reported there was a body inside."

"Yeah. But we don't know who it is, yet. They think it's a woman, though."

My heart fell. "Oh, God. I hope it's not Ileana."

"The body was burned beyond recognition, so we just don't know, yet. But it was found in the driver's seat. So, maybe it's not Ileana."

"Unless they placed her there," I said.

David took a deep breath. "Yeah, they could have done that. We'll just have to wait and see what the M.E. says. By the way, Sean agrees we should call in the FBI."

"Good. Because José has essentially set himself up as a target for Patch."

"You told him not to do that."

"I know. But he's young and feels invincible. So, the sooner we can shut this thing down the better."

"I agree. Time to let the FBI take over."

We hung up, and I decided to make hot tea to go with my treats. I shoved a mug filled with water into the microwave. While I waited, I thought about José, praying he'd stay safe. The microwave beeped, and I pulled out the mug when a floral scent wafted over me.

Not again!

Rose water had been Elizabeth's favorite perfume because her husband John had given it to her. We often smelled the rose water around the Inn when she was nearby. But she didn't always materialize. I glanced around. For now, at least, it appeared I was on my own. I stirred milk and sweetener into my tea and was just coming around the counter into the living room, when a book from my bookcase flew across the room and landed at my feet, making me jump back. This time, I spilled hot tea all over my hand.

"Elizabeth!" I yelled, putting the mug on the counter, and shaking my stinging hand.

I stomped back into the kitchen to run cold water over my fingers. When the pain subsided, I dried off my hand and went back to pick up the book. It was entitled I'll Be There for You. The author was Kelsey Miller, and the book was a deep dive into the hit TV show Friends. I loved that show and still watched reruns, but wondered why Elizabeth wanted me to acknowledge it.

"What's this supposed to mean?" I said, holding out the book in a scolding manner.

If someone had been watching, they would have thought me crazy since Elizabeth hadn't materialized. I was talking to thin air. She couldn't have answered me, anyway. She usually communicated by either writing in the steam on my bathroom mirror or demonstrating a message somehow, like throwing a book at me.

I placed the book on the counter next to my now half empty mug and the Friendly Guide to Baking.

"Next time, could you please warn me?"

The book on Friends suddenly spun like a top. When it stopped, I glanced down at the title again, feeling slightly dizzy.

"Um, okay, the title is I'll Be There for You: The One about Friends. I still don't know what you're trying to tell me." I tapped my fingers on the counter, thinking about a possible connection between this book and the cookbook. "Okay, I have friends all around me," I said out loud. "I'm supporting Rudy, one of my best friends. I've made new friends in the form of Emma and Gretchen. I'm—"

The book slid off the counter onto the floor. I inhaled a deep breath and narrowed my eyes in thought. *What the heck was she trying to say?*

Although ghosts surrounded me, I often didn't understand them. For instance, when my mother called from the netherworld to warn me of danger, it was never a direct message like, "Julia, don't get in your car." Instead, she would give me some vague notion of danger lurking around the corner. She said she wasn't allowed to directly intervene in people's lives. I wasn't sure who set those rules up, but at times like this, it was frustrating.

"Okay," I said out loud. "I get it… I think. I'm relying too much on my friendships."

The ping from an incoming text from Ben interrupted me, and I glanced at my phone where it sat on the counter.

Opened a conversation about Jacob with someone. Guy said Jacob left one day for a job mopping floors somewhere. No one ever saw him again. And Patch approached me. Said to tell him if I needed anything. He was there for his fellow vets.

An idea came to me, and I texted back.

Me: *Did he say what military service he was in?*

Ben: *Marines.*

So, not the Navy. That was something we didn't know. It could be a lie, but often people used truthful information to sound more credible. Like José, I thought.

After we were finished, my phone rang. This time it was David.

"Hey, what's up?" I asked, forgetting all about Elizabeth and Ben.

"Sean took a picture of Dr. Enzo off her website and showed it to the self-storage place. She pays for a unit there."

My heartrate sped up. "Did you show them the picture of Patch?"

"Yes. And they recognized him, too. But all they knew about him was that he had a key to Enzo's unit. They don't know who he is."

"Well, I just heard from Ben. He said Patch told him to let him know if he needed anything."

"So, he's made contact with him."

"Yes," I said. "And he found out that Patch was in the Marines. Not the Navy, or so he says."

"I wish we had his real name," David said. "Hey, hold on a minute."

There was a muffled sound as he put his hand over the phone. I waited patiently, until he said, "We just got a call from the Seattle PD. They've ID'd the body in the burned-out van."

"And?"

"It's a woman named Grace Cumberland."

I felt relieved. "Thank God. So, not Ileana."

"No. But this woman has a record for prostitution and drugs."

"Oh, wait. Grace," I said. "Remember? That's the woman I followed today. She's the one who was talking to Patch and who we believe took Ileana out of the shelter."

David sighed. "Well, if that's who it is, she's obviously outlived her usefulness to them. I wonder if whatever she told Patch this afternoon at the park sealed her fate. Listen, Sean wants Ben and the others to come in off the street. This is the second confirmed death linked to these guys, and we can't protect them."

I glanced at my watch.

"It's kind of late to bring them in tonight. I'm picking Ben up in the morning. And Rudy could get José at the Magnolia camp."

"That sounds good," he said. "And we'll be meeting with the FBI in Seattle tomorrow. We think it's time to shut everything down, including the workshops you and Blair are conducting."

"But Gretchen and I were hoping to do mock interviews with a couple of women tomorrow. I don't want to disappoint them."

"Okay, but then that's it. Talk soon."

We hung up, and I texted Ben and José, telling them we'd be picking them up in the morning for good. Ben responded affirmatively. When I didn't hear back from José, I texted him again, stressing the importance of a response. Fifteen minutes later, I received a text.

Sorry. I was talking to Patch about a job.

I texted him back, emphasizing the plan. He agreed, allowing me to go to bed feeling secure that my ducklings would soon all be safe and sound.

CHAPTER TWENTY-EIGHT

The next morning, I waited anxiously to pick up Ben near the veterans' camp. Ben arrived a few minutes later pushing his rattling cart with the American flag affixed to the front. When he got to the car, he loaded his cart into the back of the Pathfinder and climbed into the front seat.

"Glad to have you back," I said with relief. "Anything to report?"

"Nothing new," he said.

"You want to go directly to campus?"

"If that's okay," Ben said. "I have some prep work to do for my next lecture."

"No problem. I have news to tell you on the way."

As we headed into the University District, I filled Ben in on the details that led to the FBI taking over.

"I think that's a good call," Ben said. "I went back to that storage unit when I heard you'd be picking me up. A piece of paper was stuck under the door, so I pulled it out. It was a receipt from a thrift store for two sleeping bags and three coats, all purchased by someone named Edgar Collier. Wasn't that the name of the funeral home you mentioned in one of your texts?"

"Yeah," I said, a warm flush flooding my body. "Collier and Sons. But I just learned that Dr. Enzo's husband is named Edgar."

Ben let out a whistle. "Wow, it seems that Enzo may be married to one of the owners of the funeral home. Funny how the puzzle pieces begin to fit together."

"The question now is whether Edgar Collier is also Patch," I said.

Ten minutes later, I dropped Ben off at campus and headed home. When I got back, I went to the kitchen, where I found Emma helping April with breakfast.

"Have you heard from Rudy?" I asked April. "She was supposed to pick up José this morning. Sean wants everyone off the street."

April was at the sink washing our griddle. "Not yet."

Emma was helping out by filling a warming tray with sausages. "How's everything going?" she asked.

"The FBI is taking over. So, I'm glad Ben and José will be home."

"And then all of you will be out of danger," April said from the sink.

"Yep. We'll just be cheering the FBI on from the sidelines."

"Well, I can't say I'm sorry," April said, putting the griddle on a towel to drain.

I glanced at my watch. "I just wish they would get back. José said last night that Patch had offered him a job. Which means he's on Patch's radar."

My phone rang. It was Rudy. When I answered, I said, "Hold on. I'm putting you on speaker. April and Emma are here."

"Julia, I've waited for almost an hour, and José hasn't shown," Rudy said in a strained voice. "And I've texted him four times. I don't have a good feeling about this. What do you want me to do?"

"If he's not answering your texts, I think I should call David."

"I thought David was meeting with the FBI today," April said.

"I think we're going to have to deal with this ourselves," Rudy said.

"No," Emma said, taking off her apron. "Take me back." She draped the apron over a chair and started for the door.

"Wait! Shouldn't we all go down there together?" I asked.

"We don't know what's happened. And there's no room for error here. A bunch of you showing up could just make the situation worse. I'll go back into the camp and see what I can find out. I'm one of them. I'll change." She disappeared through the swinging door.

"She's right," Rudy said, bringing me back to the moment.

"I guess so. You might as well come back, then, too."

We hung up, and April and I stared at each other.

"He'll be okay," I said in a quiet voice.

April didn't say a word but turned back to finish the dishes.

I filled the warming pan with scrambled eggs, and then April and I took everything into the breakfast room. By the time we'd finished, guests had begun arriving, including Brown Eyes and Pug Nose. But I was in no mood and glared at them as if to say, "Just try me."

Emma returned dressed in her homeless garb, carrying an old satchel. A middle-aged couple from Michigan shied away from her as she passed, so I quickly herded her into the kitchen, where April suddenly grabbed her shoulder.

"Just find him. Please."

The trembling in April's voice matched the growing panic I felt.

"I'll do my best," Emma responded. She turned to me. "Let's go."

It took us almost forty-five minutes to get to the Magnolia Bridge area because of morning traffic and an accident. When I dropped Emma off near the homeless camp, I told her I'd find a place close by to grab breakfast in case she needed me quickly. She nodded and marched up the street.

I stopped at a Jack in the Box and ordered a breakfast burrito and coffee because it was easy in and easy out. As I fiddled with the burrito, thinking about José, I realized I wasn't really hungry. My stomach was in knots. I texted David to tell him about Emma going back into the field, emphasizing that it was her decision and that, frankly, we thought she had a better shot at finding José. He sent a text back: *Good decision. Keep me informed.*

I glanced at my watch and saw that it was already after nine o'clock. I was supposed to meet Gretchen in a couple of hours to go to the shelter, so I texted her to let her know an emergency had come up. Then I called Gloria at the shelter to let her know we wouldn't be there, after all. I went back to my sad-looking burrito and was thinking of throwing it away when David called.

"The FBI is in because we're dealing with abductions from at least two jurisdictions, and we don't know whether these people are being taken across state lines," he said. "They're setting up a team and want to talk to everyone as soon as possible. I suggested we meet at the command center. I also told them that Emma is back in the field to find José. They're not happy about it but agreed she's probably in a better position to get information quickly."

"What time do they want to meet? Because I'm still in Seattle."

"Is noon okay?"

"Um, yes. Do you want all of us there? I mean Doe, Rudy, and Blair?" I was afraid we'd be shut out.

"Not Rudy. She's out on bail for a crime related to this meeting. But everyone else."

"Okay, although that's not going to be an easy sell. But I'll see you soon,"

I let Emma know I was returning to the Inn and why. She told me she'd let me know when she learned anything. I called Blair and Doe and then headed home. By the time I got back to the Inn, I found Rudy in the kitchen with April and told them about the meeting.

"I'm sorry you can't attend," I said to Rudy. "It makes sense, though, don't you think?."

She stared at me for a moment, and then her shoulders dropped. "It does. It just doesn't feel good. Listen, I haven't cleaned up the mess the police left at my house after the murder. That's a good role for me, so I'll go do that."

She walked out, and April and I shared a glance.

"You understand how she feels, don't you?" April asked.

"Of course," I replied. "There's just nothing I can do."

"You're doing a lot, Julia. And she knows it."

I sighed. "Do you want to join us for this meeting?"

She was working on brownies for the afternoon snack. "No," she replied, spreading the gooey mixture into a baking pan. "I don't play much of a role in your investigations, but I certainly have a stake now that José is missing. So, keep me updated."

"Hopefully, he's not really missing. Maybe his phone died, or he just lost it."

"You don't believe that any more than I do," she said.

"Yes, but I have to tell myself that to keep from freaking out."

I wasn't lying. I felt as jittery as if I'd drunk a gallon of coffee, or in my case, Pepsi.

"By the way, any chance we have leftovers I could take to the command center for this meeting?"

April sighed. "You know, sometimes your murder investigations interfere with running this inn. But I'll take care of it."

The comment felt like a slap on the hand.

"Sorry, April. You're right. Look, these are police officers. They don't need snacks. Just forget it."

The tension on April's face tugged at my heart. She had always been the one on the outside during our investigations, never really taking part. But now that José might be in danger, it was clearly stressing her out.

"It's fine," she said with a sigh. "I'll take care of it."

I gave her a hug and said, "He'll be okay. He's smart, resilient, and tough." I squeezed her shoulder. "I've got to run up and see Gretchen."

I hurried out of the kitchen and checked in with Crystal at the reception desk.

"Listen, I have a meeting with a bunch of law enforcement personnel out in the event center at noon," I told her. "It has to do with that woman that was killed at Rudy's house. So, if you need anything, can you find April?"

"Sure," she said. "But be on the alert. Chloe is acting up again today."

As soon as she said this, our little silver bell slid to the end of the reception desk and onto the floor with a loud brrring!

"Oh, dear," I said, picking it up. "Chloe, please behave. We have too much to do today."

The brochure rack suddenly spun rapidly in a circle, sending dozens of brochures into the air, left to flutter to the floor.

"Oh, shoot," Crystal said, rushing around the desk to pick them up. "See what I mean? If you ask me, it's because José hasn't been here for the last couple of days. She follows him around like a puppy dog sometimes. I don't think she likes it when he's gone."

I had a thought.

"Hey, Chloe, why don't you see if you can find José? If you can, let me know. Okay?"

"Is José missing?" Crystal asked.

Crystal was aware of our investigations, but usually didn't know any of the details until after the fact. With this case, however, I had told her about José and Ben going undercover in a homeless camp.

"We just haven't heard from him," I said. "But if anyone can find him, I bet CHLOE CAN!" I said loudly.

The front door opened to let a brisk breeze inside and then closed with a bang.

"Ha," I exclaimed. "I think Elvis has left the building." I chuckled. "Have you ever told your friends or family what it's like to work here?"

Crystal laughed, her pretty brown eyes twinkling. "Only my boyfriend. And he doesn't believe me."

I set the bell back onto the counter. "Well, let's see if Chloe has any luck."

I climbed the stairs to Gretchen's room. She answered quickly when I knocked, a brush in her hand.

"Hey, sorry about this morning," I said.

"No problem," she replied. "C'mon in."

I stepped into her room and glanced out the window. Her room looked out on our dock and the lake beyond. The breeze had raised small white caps on the water, and I saw only one brave sailboat skimming along.

"How's everything going?" she asked, sitting on the colorful quilt on her bed.

I inhaled and shook my head. "I don't know. Good and bad. We're definitely making progress. But the FBI is involved now. Everyone was supposed to come in from the field. Unfortunately, we haven't heard from José. That's why I can't go to the shelter. Well... that and the fact the FBI has called a big meeting here at noon."

She frowned. "Wow, a missing person, and the FBI. I hope José is okay. Can I do anything?"

"I don't think so. Emma has gone back to the camp to find him. But after that, the FBI will take over, and we'll all be forced to back off."

She arched her eyebrows. "That doesn't seem fair. You've done all the work."

"But they're the professionals. And they have more resources than our small police force. Plus, things are getting more dangerous now, so I'm happy to let them take the risk."

"What do you mean?"

I told her about finding Grace's burned body in the blue van.

"Oh, dear. Another murder," she murmured.

"We also think that Dr. Enzo is married to one of the Collier brothers. They own that funeral home I told you about. I still wish I knew if the funeral home is involved."

"Seems like it must be, if the two of them are married, and she works at the shelter."

"Well, don't worry about it. I really appreciate you taking the time to help me at the shelter. Just have fun with your family now."

She smiled. "I will. In fact, I'm getting ready to go hang out with the girls."

We said goodbye, and I went to the command center to set up for the meeting, when I got a call from Rudy.

"Brenda has good news," she said, excited.

"What is it? We need good news,"

"She heard from the police. The forensics people found Ginger's fingerprint on the birdhouse at my front door."

"Thank God," I said with a big smile. "That is good news."

"She said it doesn't clear me completely, but it definitely confirms my story if Ginger can tell them she was there and who brought her. God, I still can't believe all this is happening, Julia. I just want it to be over. I'm sorry if I snapped earlier."

"I don't care about that. I only care about you. By the way, how are you? I mean, with the drugs and all."

"I've cut back on the dosage," she said, wringing her hands. "It's hard, I won't lie. But I'm going to beat this thing. Well, both things. The murder rap and the drugs."

"You will. And remember, you're not alone."

CHAPTER TWENTY-NINE

April and Crystal arrived with two trays of cookies and several sixpacks of soda. They put the drinks in the refrigerator, while I continued to update the wall with José's disappearance and the information about Enzo and her husband.

We finished setting up chairs and then organized the snacks on one of the tables. At noon, a line of police officers and FBI agents began filing in. Sean and David arrived with FBI Agent Glass, who helped us with our last investigation. She was a petite, compact woman with dark eyes and mahogany brown hair pulled into a ponytail. She was wearing a navy FBI jacket over black slacks.

"Nice to see you again, Mrs. Applegate," she said. "Sorry it's under these circumstances."

"I'm no longer a missus, but I agree. I'm glad to have you on board again. Let's hope it doesn't get quite so… wonky," I said apologetically.

She smiled at the understatement. Only a few months earlier, she had helped rescue Ben and me from a group of megalomaniacs threatening to kill both of us as they held us captive in a secret room in Seattle.

The door opened, and my daughter walked in, making my eyebrows shoot up in surprise. I introduced Angela to Agent Glass and then pulled Angela to one side.

"What are you doing here?"

"When Sean told me about the meeting, I decided a lawyer wouldn't be a bad addition to the team. The prosecuting attorney agreed. Especially since this involves homeless shelters and homeless camps. She always worries about optics."

I smiled and gave her a hug. "Regardless, I'm glad to have you here."

Blair snuck in. "Doe can't be here," she said.

"No problem. Rudy was told she couldn't attend."

"Oh my. She's not going to like that."

"No. She didn't. But she understands." I glanced around the room. "I must admit that it's a little nerve-racking to have an entire squad of law enforcement on the property."

Besides Angela, Agent Glass was the only woman amongst the law enforcement group. The rest were all men ranging in age from mid-twenties to mid-fifties. It was the most serious looking group of people we'd had in the event center since it opened.

The last to arrive was Ben, who immediately headed for the snack tray. He looked much fresher and more rested than when I'd seen him that morning. I sidled up next to him.

"What about your lecture tomorrow? I thought you had to prepare."

"I got someone to stand in again for me. The topic is 'Human Species: Past and Present.' Anyone can do it."

I bumped his shoulder. "I'm just glad to have you home safe and sound."

In total, there were ten of us. Missing from my group were Doe, Emma, José, Rudy, and April. When everyone was seated, Sean stood up.

"Thank you all for coming. I know it's a bit unusual to meet outside of a law enforcement agency, but you have briefs in front of you, and the rest of the information we have is right there." He pointed to the photos and notes on the wall and the whiteboard.

He proceeded to introduce FBI Special Agent Karla Glass and Sergeant Alan Odell from the Seattle homicide division. Odell was a tall, muscular man in his mid-forties who chose to stand against the front window with his hands clasped in front of him rather than take a chair.

When Sean was done introducing the law enforcement, including Angela, he turned to me. "Julia, why don't you introduce your team?"

My face flushed. *My team?* I wasn't a public speaker by nature and facing a group of professional law enforcement personnel made me queasy. I glanced nervously at David, who gave me a quick nod.

I stood up. "Rudy Smith, who was arrested for Romaine's murder, isn't here for obvious reasons. And José Castillo is still in the field somewhere. He was supposed to come in with everyone else this morning, but we haven't heard from him. Emma Hospers, who was also working in the field, went back to the Magnolia Camp looking for him. We recruited her to help with the undercover operation since she knows some of the people out there. But Blair Wentworth and my brother Ben are here," I said, nodding towards them. "Ben went undercover in the veteran's camp, and Blair and I have been inside a couple of homeless shelters trying to glean information. I think that's it," I said and sat back down.

"Okay," Sean said. "You've been briefed on the basics. We have two murders we believe are connected. The murder of Romaine Garza at Ms. Smith's home, and Grace Cumberland whose body was found yesterday in the burned van. We have three people of interest we're trying to either ID or whose involvement we hope to confirm. One is Dr. Susan Enzo. She's a psychiatrist serving clients at several local homeless shelters in Seattle and two in Tacoma." He pointed to her picture on the wall. "The second is a guy who goes by the name of Patch; he hangs out in the homeless camps. We have two pictures of him," he said, pointing to the board. We had added the photo Gretchen had taken of him in the park, but he was looking at the ground. "We suspect that Dr. Enzo and Patch ID homeless people without family, and then Patch is the one who reels them in by befriending them and offering them jobs."

"The third subject is a tall thin man who walks with a limp. We don't know his name and don't have a picture of him, but he was seen during one of the abductions with a Black man called Andre. We don't have a picture of Andre, either, but he's been spotted three separate times. Once by a neighbor the night of the murder, a second time with the guy with the limp, and a third time when Julia and her friends rescued a homeless woman named Ginger. He and another guy apparently abducted her here on the island a few nights ago. We think they meant to silence her since she's the one Rudy Smith believes came to her house with the killers the night of the murder."

He snuck a glance at me, and I shrunk in my seat. David was more forgiving when it came to our getting involved in the cases, but I was sure Detective Abrams didn't feel the same way.

"The rescue took place behind Northwest Biomedical Research, which is owned by a man named Travis Castrano," he said, continuing. "We don't know yet whether he's involved, but someone from his office was seen talking to the two abductors."

"Has Ginger told you anything, yet?" Blair asked.

"Not yet," David said. "She's being kept at a safe house for now and is under a doctor's care."

"We believe," Sean continued, "that Grace Cumberland was responsible for abducting another homeless woman named Ileana from a shelter in Federal Way. Ileana witnessed one of the prior abductions and put herself in danger by talking about it. Shortly after that, Cumberland's body was found in the burned-out blue van."

"And we have some new information," Agent Glass said.

She nodded to a young Middle Eastern man with large dark eyes and a five o'clock shadow sitting next to her. He pulled out a sheaf of paper.

"We have photos of three more potential players," he said. "We hope someone here knows more about them."

He got up and tacked three 8 x 10 photos onto the wall.

Agent Glass pointed to the photo on the left. It was of a man in his late thirties with short brown hair, dark eyes, and a slender face. "This is Stanley Collier, co-owner of Collier and Sons Funeral Home. Next to him is his brother, Edgar Collier, his brother." She pointed to the picture of a good-looking, clean-shaven man with blue eyes and dark brown hair. "He is also Dr. Enzo's husband and although he's part owner in the funeral home, he works as a pharmaceutical rep."

"No. That's Patch!" Ben exclaimed, standing up. He went to the wall. "I mean, Patch has a deep scar under his lip and deep brown eyes, but I'd swear this is him. Hold on."

Ben grabbed a black marking pen and drew a patch over Edgar's right eye. He then grabbed a brown marking pen to draw a jagged scar beneath the man's lip and colored his blue eyes brown. He turned to the room. "Meet Patch."

Sean joined Ben at the wall and stared back and forth between the two other photos of Patch and the altered one of Edgar Collier. He turned to share a glance with Agent Glass.

"I think it's time we pick up Edgar Collier for questioning," Agent Glass said.

"Wait," David said. "If you do, you'll tip your hand, and their entire operation will go underground."

"Good point," Sean said. "We need to let things play out."

"Okay," Glass said. "At least this is real progress. We'll do a full work-up on these three?"

Ben hadn't left the wall and was staring at the photo of Stanley Collier. "Hold on," he said, lifting his hand. "I've seen this guy, too," he said, pointing to the photo of Stanley Collier. "I saw Patch go into a small grocery store near the VA, so I pretended to rummage through a trash can while I waited for him to come out. A few minutes later a white van pulled up, and this guy went inside the store," he said tapping Collier's photo. "I'd swear it was him, but he was wearing glasses." Ben seemed to think of something. "Oh, shit!" he said. He turned back to the group. "He also walked with a slight limp. I didn't think of it at the time because I was so focused on Patch."

"Did you see Stanley Collier come out?" Angela asked.

It was the first time Angela had said anything, and I perked up.

"No. I followed Patch when he came back out, so I don't know what happened to this guy," Ben said. "Sorry."

"But you think they met inside the store for some reason," Angela said.

"I do. But they didn't come out together, and Patch... or Edgar, came out empty- handed. So, he didn't buy anything, either."

I know my daughter, and I could tell the wheels in her head were turning.

"What are you thinking?" I asked her.

"Well, we know now that they're brothers, but Edgar Collier is posing as someone else. So, I was hoping that if Ben had actually seen them together, whatever he witnessed might be enough to get a search warrant for the funeral home. It would be a stretch, but now, this is just too circumstantial."

"What about cameras in the store?" David asked.

"Sure. Let's see if we have visual evidence," she said.

"I'll check that," David said, making a note.

"Okay, you have a list of all the known missing people so far, and we now have several suspects," Agent Glass said, taking control of the meeting again. "So, let's talk about how we move forward. The FBI will take the lead on the missing homeless people. We need to find out who is taking them and why. However, we'll partner with both Sergeant Odell from the Seattle PD and Detective Abrams from the Mercer Island PD, and possibly the Tacoma PD, if the leads down there turn into anything. The Mercer Island PD will continue taking the lead on the murder of Romaine Garza. And the Seattle PD will now take the lead on Grace Cumberland's murder."

Sean's phone rang, and he stepped away from the group to answer it.

"The good news is that you and your friends can now step aside, Mrs. Applegate," Agent Glass said to me. I opened my mouth to say something, but she stopped me with a raised hand. "There is no investigative role for you to play going forward. But I'm the first one to say that you and your friends have done an outstanding job."

I glanced at Blair, who stared hard at Agent Glass. She wasn't taking this lightly. I felt the same. I knew that while we might bow out for now, we'd bow back in the moment something went wrong.

"Anyway, we'll be taking all of this," Agent Glass said, making a sweeping gesture towards the wall of information.

She nodded to her assistant again. He rose and began taking stuff off the wall and then used his cellphone to take pictures of the whiteboard. Detective Abrams came back to the table and stopped the idle chatter.

"The Seattle PD has cleaned up footage of the blue van the night of the murder. Cumberland, the woman whose body was found in the burned-out van, has now been ID'd as the woman in the passenger seat." He turned to Agent Glass. "Since she has also checked into several of the shelters, we might get lucky in finding out more information about her and who she's been seen with."

Agent Glass turned to Odell. "Can you take care of that?"

He merely nodded without even writing it down.

"Okay," she said, turning back to the group. "We have a lot to do. Detective Abrams, Sergeant Odell, and I have already decided the next big move should be a sting operation."

"You mean like… setting someone up to be abducted?" I asked with a nervous hitch to my voice.

"That's just what we mean," she said.

A whirlwind suddenly kicked up in the middle of the room, spinning every loose piece of paper into the air. People weaved and ducked to avoid getting hit. Many gasped in surprise.

I glanced at Blair. "Chloe," I mouthed.

When things settled down, and people hustled to grab handfuls of paper and return them to the table, a rattled Agent Glass said, "Um, can someone close that back window?"

I got up to close the window behind me that was barely open.

"The sting will begin tomorrow with an FBI agent going undercover in the Magnolia Camp."

"I should go instead," a voice said forcefully from the back of the room.

CHAPTER THIRTY

Everyone turned toward the door where José stood like a bedraggled, wet puppy, holding a dirty backpack. By his side was an actual wet puppy.

I ran over and flung my arms around his neck. "Oh my God, you scared the hell out of me," I said, hugging him fiercely. I stepped back and slapped his shoulder. "And don't ever do that again!"

He gave me an impish smile. "I love you too, Miz Applegate."

I drew him into the room. "Everyone, this is the missing José Castillo."

"Where have you been?" David asked, standing up. "We've been calling your phone."

"And Emma went back to the camp looking for you," I said, before he could answer. "Oh, shoot, let me text her."

I pulled out my phone and shot off a quick text telling Emma that José was okay. As I put my phone back into my pocket, the dog next to him bumped against leg. He was a little Black person, brown, and white Corgi with short legs and big ears that stood straight up.

"Well, aren't you adorable," I said crouching next to him. He gave my hand a tentative lick.

"That's Wilson," José said. "I'm looking after him for a friend."

I grabbed the dog's dirty leash and brought him forward as José's gaze landed on the wall.

"I've seen that man," he said pointing to the row of pictures.

"Which one?" Detective Abrams asked.

"This one," he said, approaching and poking his finger at Stanley Collier. "I saw him try to force my friend off the street and into a white passenger van." His eyes shifted to the picture on the right. "Wow. I don't know who used marking pens, but this one is a younger version of Patch."

"We know," Ben said, moving around the table. "But what did you mean when said you saw Stanley Collier forcing someone into a van?"

José turned and seemed to realize for the first time he was in a room full of police officers and FBI agents. "What's going on here?"

"We've put together a task force with the FBI to solve this," Sean said. "And it sounds like you have actionable intelligence."

José's gaze drifted longingly towards a can of soda. He reached out, but Ben grabbed it and popped the lid.

"Sit down," Ben said to him.

Ben handed him the soda, while I shoved the tray of cookies in front of him. He drank almost half the can in one gulp, wiped his lips and then leaned back, dropping his backpack onto the floor. The dog immediately moved to his side.

"I haven't been in camp much. I've been wandering the streets, meeting a lot of homeless people. And they're nervous."

"Because people have gone missing?" Blair asked.

"Yeah. They don't talk much about it. They're too afraid. But I'd get little snippets about the blue van, to stay away from Patch, and something about dead people. And then there was this guy named Ross." He leaned over and put his hand on the dog's head. "Wilson belongs to Ross. Ross is stuck in a wheelchair because he lost a foot to diabetes. He makes a little money doing pretty decent charcoal drawings down near Pike Place Market. Anyway, he told me that some dude he'd done a drawing for had offered him a job working at an auto parts store. He said he'd just be answering phones and could do it from his wheelchair."

José picked up a cookie and stuffed it into his mouth.

"It made me suspicious," he said, wiping his mouth. "Ross is a nice guy. But I wondered why someone would suddenly offer him a job?"

"And it wasn't Patch who offered it?" David asked.

"No. Ross said it was some guy with a limp. Anyway, he was supposed to meet up with the guy last night and asked if I could roll him down there."

"Why didn't you tell us all of this?" I admonished him.

He hunched his shoulders. "I wasn't sure it was a big deal. Anyway, there's an auto parts store only a few blocks from the camp. That's where he was supposed to meet him. When we got there, the store was closed, and the parking lot was empty. Ross said

I should go and take Wilson with me, because he'd been told to come alone. That made me suspicious, so I hid in some trees at the end of the parking lot. A few minutes later, a white van pulled in from the other end and stopped next to Ross. Two guys got out. A big Black guy and this guy," he said pointing to Stanley Collier. "They were right under a streetlight, so I could see them pretty good. Anyway, the three of them talked for a minute, and then the Black guy walked around behind Ross and stuck him in the neck with something. Ross slumped over almost immediately."

"They drugged him," Sean said.

"That's what I thought."

"Did they take him?" I asked.

"No. I..." He stopped and glanced nervously at David and then at Sean.

"What is it?" David asked.

"You need to tell us," Agent Glass said, staring at him.

"You're among friends," I said, sitting down next to him. "And we need your help."

José gave a little shrug. "I hope so, because I had a firearm with me."

Murmurs erupted around the room, but Detective Abrams raised his hand, and the room grew silent. "Just tell us what happened."

José sucked in a breath. "Like I said, I was hidden at the edge of the parking lot. After they injected Ross, they tried to get him out of the wheelchair and into the van. I don't think they realized how difficult it would be to transfer dead weight. Plus, Ross is a pretty hefty guy. Anyway, I knew they were up to no good, so as they struggled to get him out of the chair, I fired off a couple of rounds to catch them off guard. They got spooked and let him go. Then, they got back in the van and took off."

"And left Ross there?" Angela asked.

"Yeah. I ran down to see if he was okay. He was breathing, but he was out of it. So, I called an ambulance. I didn't want anyone to see me, so I took Wilson and hid in the trees again to make sure the medics found him okay." He turned to me. "When I went back to camp, I passed that same white van in the parking lot of a bar. Wilson and I hung out across the street for a while, watching. But I fell asleep, and they were gone when I woke up." He turned to me. "Sorry Miz Applegate, but I must've dropped my phone and didn't notice it was gone. I didn't even go back to camp. But I didn't have any cash, so it took me all morning to get back here, especially with the dog."

I reached out and put a hand on his arm. "I'm only glad you're okay. We're calling off our involvement now, anyway. You go grab a shower, and I'm sure April will cook you anything you want."

"No way," he said, standing up, his fists clenched in defiance. He looked directly at Detective Abrams. "Look, if you're going after Patch, I'm the logical one to do it since he's already offered me a job. Don't worry about me. I can handle myself. Especially now that I know they're drugging people. I'll be careful."

Agent Glass shared a look with Sean and Sergeant Odell. She got two nods of approval and turned back to José.

"Are you sure they didn't see you last night?" she asked.

"I don't see how they could have," he said.

She held his gaze for a moment, and then said, "Okay. We'll set our plans tonight, and you'll go back tomorrow. Patch could stay off the grid for a while. But it's worth a try. We need proof."

"But José is an eyewitness to an attempted abduction," I said. "Isn't that proof?"

"It wouldn't hold up in court," Angela said. "It was dark. He was too far away. A defense attorney would shoot holes in it."

"What about Ross?" Blair asked. "He must be in a hospital somewhere. You could talk to him. Get a statement."

"Someone should definitely talk to him," Angela said. "But you said yourself that he'd been drugged. Once again, that makes his testimony questionable."

"But he should also be protected," David said. "They might go after him now that he's seen them."

Agent Glass turned once again to Odell and gave him a nod. He immediately made a phone call.

My phone pinged with an incoming text. "Hold on," I said, getting everyone's attention. "It's from Emma." I read the message and then looked up at the group in surprise. "Evergreen, one of the abducted women, has returned to the Magnolia Camp. She's okay."

CHAPTER THIRTY-ONE

There was a flurry of activity as the group broke up. Angela gave me a hug and then left to go back to her office to begin drafting a request for a search warrant for the funeral home. David left to write up notes from the meeting. And José handed me Wilson's leash.

"Any chance you could watch him while I'm gone?"

"Of course," I said, leaning over to pet the dog. "Anything I should know about him?"

José grinned. "He's used to eating scraps, so he'll eat anything. But I doubt he's housetrained, so you'll have to get Mickey's old kennel out of the garage. His dog bed is still in it."

At the mention of Mickey, my throat tightened. "That's a good idea. We'll be fine. So, you be fine, too."

"I'll be careful."

José left to meet with Sean and Agent Glass to plan their sting operation. Meanwhile, Glass' assistant pulled the rest of the information off the walls and packed everything into a briefcase.

I tied Wilson's leash to the leg of a table and then helped Blair fold chairs and put them away.

"How do you feel about being sidelined?" Blair asked me as she folded a chair.

I shrugged. "I don't know. We always knew the police would eventually take the lead on this one. And now that the FBI is involved, well, we're not really needed."

"That never stopped us before," Blair said.

I sighed and moved over to slide the remaining cookies onto one platter and then stacked the two platters on top of each other.

"Look. We've made a significant contribution. Agent Glass even said so. I think we can feel proud. For the first time, they trusted us. I say we let them take it from here. What if we call Rudy and see if she can come have lunch with us?"

"That's a great idea," Blair said.

"I also need to call April and let her know José is back. I'll see if she wants to join us."

Thirty minutes later, the four of us were in April's guest house eating grilled cheese sandwiches.

"Thanks for doing this," I said to her.

"No problem. It's in celebration of José being safe," she said.

"God, I felt terrible when I couldn't be at the meeting earlier. But now that they're taking over, I feel useless," Rudy said, pulling her sandwich apart.

I felt sorry for her. This was not only personal, but she was keeping a big secret from everyone but me, and the stress was evident in the tightness of her muscles, her tapping foot, and her grim expression.

"You have to admit it's hard, Julia," Blair said. "We've always been in the thick of things. They don't even have an obligation to keep us informed."

"Yes, but David will," I said. "I mean, I assume that since the three different agencies are working together, they'll share information with each other. And then… David will tell me."

"You hope he will. They may put him under a gag order," she said with an arched eyebrow.

"Are you going to eat that or just play with it?" I asked Rudy, as I watched her toy with her sandwich.

Her head popped up. "Oh, sorry. I was just thinking that Blair said women at the shelter were wondering about a memorial service for Romaine. Maybe I could do that. Something simple but meaningful. She deserves that. Do you know when they might release the body?"

"I can ask David. And I think that's a wonderful idea."

"What about our workshops?" Blair asked. "I never got a chance to go to Wings of Hope. Couldn't we finish them?"

"It obviously helps the women," April said.

"I'll call Gloria and see what she says," I offered.

My phone pinged with a text from Emma wondering if someone could pick her up. She was at the Seattle police station with Evergreen.

"I can pick her up," Rudy said, dropping her half-eaten sandwich. "By the way, Elliott asked me to stay with him again until all of this dies down. I think you've had enough company for a while. So, when I drop Emma and Evergreen off, I'll go back to his place."

Blair's eyes flashed with mischief. "And then David can come stay with you, Julia. You know… now that we're off the case."

"I'll leave that up to him," I said with a grin.

After we'd finished lunch, Rudy packed her things and went to pick up Emma, and Blair left to get her nails put back on.

"Well," April said, raising her hands above her head to stretch. "No rest for the wicked. It's time for us to get the snacks out. The guests will be waiting."

After helping April with the afternoon snacks, I stopped by Gretchen's room. There was no answer when I knocked, so I left a note on her door saying we were hoping to go back to the shelter in the morning if she'd like to join me. When I got back to my apartment, I called Gloria, but she wasn't in the office.

Rudy texted me forty-five minutes later to say she had dropped Evergreen off at a friend's house and that Emma had gone home. That left me to spend the evening doing normal things like laundry, taking Minnie and Wilson for a walk, and cleaning my kitchen.

David called just after dinner, and we discussed a rerun of our earlier movie night. He didn't get there until 10:30, however, and complained about being tired.

"God, it's been a long couple of days," he said, stretching and cracking his back. He wrapped his arms around me. "But it's nice to finally be alone with you."

We shared a long kiss before I said, "Want a beer?"

"Sounds great. But I'll get it. You sit."

He grabbed a can of beer from the refrigerator and popped the lid.

"By the way, have you heard anything about Evergreen?" I asked.

"Seattle PD questioned her. She told them a story about being drugged and waking up in a small, dark room, chained to the wall. Two people came in to check on her, thinking she was out cold, but she was just pretending. Whatever they drugged her with had worn off. They put her on a gurney and rolled her into another room, talking about moving her to another location. When there was a big commotion outside, both of her captors left her, so she escaped through the back door. She said the second room they took her to looked like some kind of medical facility."

"But why did she go back to the homeless camp?"

"It's probably all she knows," he said with a shrug. "Anyway, I'm sure there's more to the story, but I'll have to wait until I see Sean tomorrow. Also, they had a couple of officers quietly go through the neighborhood adjacent to that funeral home under the guise there had been some break-ins lately. They got people talking about any suspicious activity. The only thing they heard was that people come and go from the funeral home's back parking lot at all hours after dark and that the crematorium sometimes runs all night."

"Wait. They cremate people there?"

"Yeah. Why? A lot of funeral homes do."

My body got cold, and I had trouble catching my breath. "Don't you remember April's vision about a fire and the smell of burning flesh?"

"Um, yeah. But why would they take these people off the street just to cremate them, though?"

"I don't know. Maybe they're holding them for their disability checks, and when they're done with them, they—"

His eyebrows lifted in recognition. "Could be. I called a couple of other crematoriums and asked if it was unusual to run their incinerators all night. They said it was."

I sat quietly with my thoughts for a moment until David finished off the beer and said, "Listen, hon, I think I'll take a quick shower before bed. I'd ask you to join me, but…"

I slapped his arm. "Stop it. We'll have plenty of time for that sort of thing when this is all over."

He grinned and leaned over to kiss me. "I like that thought."

"I'll get you a towel," I said, feeling a warm tide roll over my body.

I was at the bathroom sink brushing my teeth while he was in the shower. The steam shrouded the mirror so I could hardly see myself. I was about to wipe it away when the condensation began to shift and move on its own.

My breath caught. *Elizabeth!*

The faint scent of rose water confirmed my suspicion. Was Elizabeth going to tell me something with David right there? She'd never done that before. I waited with my toothbrush in hand as letters began to form on the mirror.

Two for the road.

The shower curtain whipped open, and David stepped out in all his naked glory. He grabbed the towel and wrapped it around his trim waist and then glanced at me.

"What's wrong?"

I turned my eyes to the mirror.

"What the hell?" he said, coming over. "You didn't write that, did you?"

"Um, no. That would be Elizabeth."

"What does it mean?"

"I have no idea."

With the shower off, the letters began to fade. David and I had never had a formal conversation about our ghosts, although he'd been around when cupboards had opened and closed on their own, or things had moved for no reason. But having words spelled out in the shower mist on your bathroom mirror was hard to ignore. I wasn't sure what he'd say.

"I wonder what she's referring to," he said.

Huh? He didn't even skip a beat.

"Um, well, José is the only one going back to the street," I said. "Emma and Ben have gone home. And Blair and I might be going back to the shelter tomorrow, but I wouldn't think that's 'two for the road.' I don't know what else there is."

Minutes later, as we were climbing into bed, it all became clear when I got a text from Ben.

Just wanted you to know, I'm going to back up José. Better if there's two of us. I'm on my way there now. Sweet dreams.

CHAPTER THIRTY-TWO

There were no sweet dreams for me that night. Terrible scenarios kept running through my head about Ben and José. Fortunately, I figured if my brother got into trouble, I'd hear about it first from my mother, who was somehow deeply connected to both of us from the great beyond. I wondered briefly if the 'friend' Elizabeth was referring to was Ben, acting as a friend toward José.

The next morning, David wolfed down a cup of coffee and a piece of toast slathered with blackberry jam before pulling me into a bear hug.

"I've gotta go," he said into my ear. "I know you're worried about José and Ben, but they'll be okay. We've got this."

"I sure hope so. Besides you, they're my favorite men in the entire world."

"I know. I don't want anything to happen to either one of them." He gave me a lingering kiss. "We'll take care of them." He pressed his forehead against mine as if to emphasize his point, and then left for the office.

I fed the dogs and then met April in the kitchen. I paused when I saw deep circles under her eyes.

"You okay?" I asked, putting my hand on her shoulder. "More dreams?"

"I had a bad night," she replied, rubbing her eyes. "I kept having the same dream over and over again. Someone was being operated on. I couldn't see who, but they kept saying, 'Don't take my legs. Don't take my legs.'" She shook her head. "It was creepy."

"Like someone was amputating their legs?" I asked, as I got two cartons of eggs out of the refrigerator.

"I don't know."

She turned back to the counter where the griddle was filled with sizzling bacon. She used a spatula to flip them over. Meanwhile, I began cracking eggs into a large mixing bowl.

"By the way, David had an opportunity to get up close and personal with Elizabeth last night."

April turned to me with alarm. "She appeared to him?"

"She wrote 'two for the road' in the mist on the bathroom mirror just as he got out of the shower. I didn't know what it meant until Ben texted me and told me he'd decided to back up José at the Magnolia camp."

She took a quick intake of breath. "Oh, dear. But I'm not surprised that Ben would go. It seems he's taken a real liking to José. I've seen them a couple of times talking outside when José was working on something."

"Yes, but now I have them both to worry about."

"Are you going to the shelter today?" she asked, pushing the bacon around.

"I hope so." I glanced at my watch. "I need to call Gloria. I left a note for Gretchen last night to ask if she wanted to go with me."

"Is Blair going, too?"

"She wants to. She really enjoys doing those makeover clinics."

April smiled. "Maybe Blair has found a new calling."

I called Gloria at nine o'clock. Unfortunately, they had an event scheduled that day and couldn't accommodate us until the following week. I thanked her and let Blair know. I ran up the stairs to tell Gretchen and was surprised to find the note from the day before still stuck to her door.

Slumping back down the stairs, I contemplated where Gretchen might be. We routinely recorded people's cell phone numbers, so I looked hers up and gave her a call. It went to voicemail. I left a message.

I returned to the office to follow up on some registrations. Just before noon, the twins showed up at the reception desk.

"Hey, how come you're not at the hospital?" I asked, coming out of the office.

"We need to talk," Donna said, eyeing the two obnoxious girls in the breakfast room arguing over a board game. "Somewhere private."

"Um, sure. Let's go to the dining room."

When we got to the dining room, I closed the door and asked, "What's going on?"

Deirdre leaned against the table. "We spent most of last night researching that funeral home. Stanley and Edger Collier worked for years there with their father, Alan."

"Hence, Collier and Sons," Donna said.

"When he died, however, they took over and changed the business plan," Deirdre said.

"Meaning what? They don't bury people anymore?"

"Oh, no, they do," Donna said. "But when their father died, they inherited a meager revenue producing company. And neither one of them had any money to invest in it. So, they expanded their business model."

The young women glanced at each other with grim looks, creating a knot of apprehension in my stomach.

"C'mon. Out with it. What else do they do?"

"They deal in body parts," Deirdre blurted.

Count to three.

"I'm sorry... what?"

"Well, not hearts and lungs and things," Donna clarified. "They remove bone and tissue and then sell it to big hospital chains and international biomedical companies."

Northwest Biomedical Research.

"How did you find that out?" I said, sitting down hard on one of the chairs.

"That information is online. But once we got an idea of who the key players were, we began to dig deeper into all their online stuff, including social media, and their finances."

"They own the funeral home jointly, although Edgar also works for a pharmaceutical company," Dierdre said. "Like we said, the funeral home and crematorium make a modest amount of money."

"But they make a ton of money off harvesting the bone and tissue," Donna added. "In fact, they've made upwards of two million dollars over the last three years through a company they've set up called Rainier Bone and Tissue Bank."

"That's legal, though, isn't it?" My adrenaline was kicking in again.

"Technically, yes," she said. "In fact, it turns out that tissue-banking is big business."

"Because there isn't enough of it," Deirdre clarified. "Bone and tissue are in short supply because it's used for all sorts of things, including dental implants, burn cases, bone replacement, even research."

"Universities use bone and tissue for educational purposes, too," Donna added.

"You know how you can check the box on your driver's license to agree to become an organ donor?" Deirdre asked. "Well, funeral homes can ask families to give permission for the extraction of certain bone and tissue before their loved ones are buried or cremated."

"But the tissue has to be tested for drugs and disease," Donna said. "So, we don't think that's what's happening to the homeless people who are missing. But Collier and Sons also sell full embalmed bodies for research."

"And that could be what they're doing with the homeless people they take off the street," Dierdre said.

"Damn," I said, leaning back in the chair, my mind whirring. "When we rescued Ginger that night, they were trying to drop off the dead body of another woman to Northwest Biomedical Research."

Once more, it felt like a deafening explosion had gone off nearby, making it difficult for me to react.

"Okay," I finally said with a deep sigh. "But what do we do with this information?"

"Look," Deirdre began. "You can't tell the police all of what we discovered for obvious reasons. But we found a couple of stories on the internet about people who have gone to prison for having done the same thing the Collier brothers are doing."

"What if we walk you through the information that anyone could find on the internet?" Donna suggested. "Starting there, the FBI will have forensic people who can find everything else we found."

"And you can say that when we found out they were tissue banking, which made us research how someone might make money off it illegally," Dierdre said. "Which led us to the two articles."

I was getting dizzy as the two women bounced the conversation back and forth between them.

"It's diabolical," Deirdre added. "But everything that's happened makes sense, don't you think?"

"Perfect sense," I said despondently. "These people are monsters, especially if they're selling the bodies of people off the street to universities or places like Northwest Biomedical Research. I really hoped they were abducting people for their disability checks, because then the people might still be alive. But it sure answers the question as to why they pick people without families to come looking for them."

"And didn't you say that when that one woman was abducted, someone overheard them say she'd be helping others?" Dierdre asked.

I nodded. "Just before they said they hoped she wouldn't be afraid of dead people."

"I hate to say this, but think about it," Donna said. "In their minds, they're getting those annoying homeless people off the street and then selling their bodies to places who use them for the greater good." She shrugged. "Sadly, I think some people would say that's a win-win."

CHAPTER THIRTY-THREE

Before the twins left, we practiced what I would say to David, so I wouldn't implicate them. Then, I called David and carefully laid out their theory. He was intrigued and had me send him the two articles about fraud. He said he'd also dig into the funeral home before turning it over to the FBI. By the time we hung up, it was almost time for me to help April with the afternoon snacks again. After all, the Inn was a business, and I couldn't let that slide.

I quickly went back to my apartment to let the dogs out. I hadn't taken José's idea to put Wilson in a kennel, so I prayed I wouldn't find any little surprises. Fortunately, he'd been a perfect gentleman, and I let the two dogs out in the backyard. When they'd finished, I gave them each a treat and sat down so I could pet them and throw the ball for them a few times. Wilson was a sweet-natured dog and seemed to fit in perfectly.

"We'll get you back to your owner as soon as we can," I told him, scratching him under the chin. He nearly smiled at me with his tongue out. What a happy little guy. "Sorry, but I have to go back to work. You two be good."

I spent the next hour with April putting out the snacks and chatting with guests. Ahab was in a good mood and kept up a constant stream of movie one liners, entertaining everyone. It was then that I noticed how quiet it was. I asked April about it.

"You mean the demon girls. The family left for some sightseeing. But they'll be back tomorrow."

"Maybe we could change the locks," I said with a smile.

I returned to my apartment feeling fatigue roll over me like a wave. I poured myself a cold glass of Diet Pepsi and took a long draw, feeling an immediate rush of energy. Since April was taking a break and wouldn't need me the rest of the afternoon, I kicked off my shoes and sat back in my recliner. I encouraged Minnie to jump up with me. Wilson gazed longingly from the floor.

"Sorry, little guy. But this is Minnie's territory."

He plopped down with a groan and pushed up against my feet. With my fingers entwined in Minnie's fur, I leaned back against the headrest and dozed off.

My phone jingled, waking me a few minutes after four o'clock. The light in the room had shifted with the late afternoon sun. I don't often nap because it makes me groggy, so I stretched my eyes open to wake myself up and then grabbed my phone without checking the caller ID.

"Julia!" my mother barked, making me flinch. "Where's Ben?"

My mother's deep, scratchy voice sometimes made me feel like she was raking her fingernails across a blackboard.

"Hello to you too, Mom," I said a bit churlishly, still trying to get my mind clear.

"I'm your mother. We're past niceties. Where's Ben? Something's wrong."

I sat forward, pushing Minnie to the floor. She fell on top of Wilson, who woke with a start.

"What do you mean?"

"I don't have details. I just feel dark forces around him. Like something bad is approaching."

Since I hadn't talked to my mother since the last time Ben and I were in trouble, she would have no idea about this case, and I was sure she wouldn't be happy if she did. I quickly considered how much to tell her.

"He's in downtown Seattle… uh, helping someone," I said.

"God, you're a terrible liar," she said with a sigh.

That stung.

"Why do you think I'm lying?"

"Because you're my daughter. You get a funny catch in your voice when you're not telling the truth. So, where is he, really?"

"He really is in downtown Seattle helping a friend." I knew that wouldn't appease her and released a sigh. "Okay, we're involved in an investigation again."

"For heaven's sake, Julia. Why can't you just live a normal life?"

"Look, Mom. Homeless people have been disappearing off the streets in Seattle, and we're trying to find out why."

"Maybe that's why I smell feces and vomit. I thought maybe Ben had passed out in a urinal somewhere."

"No… although that was a good guess. But why do you sense danger? Let me rephrase that… what danger do you sense?"

"I'm not sure. It feels like a gathering storm moving in his direction."

"Are you sure you didn't just see the heavy rainstorm that's coming our way? I mean, Ben will be out in it, but he'll be fine."

"Sometimes you're an idiot, you know that?" she snapped. "I'm not talking about the weather."

"Okay, but I don't know what else to tell you, except that now I'm worried all hell is about to break loose with my brother in the middle of it."

"Well, something is headed his way. Can you warn him?"

"I can text him. But this whole thing is a bit complicated. He's with José."

"Okay, good. I like José. But I feel something gathering around you, too. Where are you?"

"Home. I'm fine. The FBI has taken over our part in this case, so I'm out of it."

"Not completely," she said.

"What do you mean?" I asked nervously.

"I don't know. But wherever you go next will be in the right direction. In fact, I never thought I'd say this… but trust your instincts. Anyway, warn Ben."

And then, she was gone, leaving me to stare at my phone. A sharp knock brought me out of my chair. I swung the door open to find April standing there, her hand raised to knock a second time.

"José is in trouble!" she blurted.

"Wait. My mom just called and said that Ben is in trouble."

My burner phone pinged with a text. "God, it feels like an other-worldly telephone switchboard in here." I pulled the burner out of my pocket. It was a text from Ben.

Something is happening down here. Seattle PD is on their way.
I texted back. *What's happening?*
Ben: *Can't talk now. Have to help José.*

"Oh, my God!" I said, showing her Ben's text. "Both of them are in trouble. Do you have your phone?"

"Yes, but… "

"Call David and tell him what's happening to Ben and José down at the camp. I'll call Sergeant Odell."

We both dialed quickly and reported what little we knew. Sergeant Odell said they were already on their way to the Magnolia Camp, because José was wearing a wire. All he knew was that a bunch of gang bangers were coming after him. When April hung up, I realized she had gone completely still, just staring at me.

"April, what's wrong?"

"David said he's on his way to Tacoma. Two of the homeless men you've been looking for—Jacob Nutter and Pepper Long—were found behind the Tacoma Dome. They're dead."

"God, I'd almost forgotten about them." I dropped onto the arm of the sofa, feeling the blood drain from my face.

"David said Sean was going to meet him down there, and that Glass and Odell would take care of whatever is going on with José and Ben," April said.

"Damn. It feels like we've broken open a hornet's nest. And we're not even involved anymore."

April sat on one of the bar stools. "Your part in this isn't finished, Julia. Remember, I heard someone yelling your name. That hasn't happened, yet."

I gave her a guarded look. "My mother basically said the same thing. You must be tuned into the same 5th dimensional wavelength. But there's no point in me going after Ben or José. I don't even know where they are. And Sergeant Odell would get there before I could. Damn! I wish I knew what was going on." I looked over at her. "David said some gang bangers were going after José. And my mother likened it to a gathering storm. So, maybe at this point, it's just a threat."

"But why would those two men who were abducted in Seattle end up dead in Tacoma?" she asked.

"I don't know."

"Well, David said to stay put and wait to hear from Sergeant Odell."

My phone rang this time. It was from an unknown caller. Thinking it was my mother, I answered with a brisk, "Mom, I..."

"Mrs. Applegate? This is Gretchen Engle's daughter. Have you heard from my mother?"

It took me a second to get grounded.

"Um, no. I thought she was with you."

"No. She was supposed to have lunch with us yesterday, but she never showed up. I didn't hear from her last night, either. We've been calling her all day with no luck."

"Wait. Let me check her room."

I put the call on hold. "Gretchen Engle is missing," I said to April.

I headed for the door, grabbing my master keys from a hook next to the door. With April behind me, I ran out of my apartment and up the main staircase. My note was still on Gretchen's door. I knocked and then used the master key to gain access.

"I've called her several times," I said to April as I pushed open the door. "I left that note on her door yesterday."

The room was empty, and it was clear her bed hadn't been slept in. We did a cursory search of the room but there was nothing to indicate anything was wrong. My heart sank, and I pulled out my phone and told her daughter.

"Something's happened," she said. "I'm going to start calling hospitals."

"Okay. Please let me know if you hear anything. And if we see her, I'll tell her to call you right away."

I hung up and called David, who was on his way to Tacoma when he answered.

"What's up?"

"We have a guest missing. Gretchen Engle. The woman who went to the shelter with me the day before yesterday."

"What do you mean missing?"

"She didn't sleep in her room last night. And her daughter called and said she missed meeting with them yesterday, and they've called her several times with no answer."

"She could be anywhere," he said impatiently. "I can't deal with that right now."

I paused to take a breath. "David... she offered to go to the Collier Funeral Home the other day to help gather information. She said she could pose as a writer doing a story she was researching. I told her not to, but what if she went anyway?"

"Julia, you don't know where she is, and unfortunately, we have multiple things going on. Just keep trying to get hold of her. I'll check in with you later."

And with that, the phone went dead.

"Damn! He can't help us."

"Well, maybe she was in an accident," April said.

I glanced around the room again, wondering if I'd find Gretchen's purse. Women didn't leave their purses behind, so I checked on the other side of the bed and in the closet.

"Gretchen's purse is gone. If she were in an accident, she'd have her ID with her, and her daughter would probably have been notified. No, my gut tells me it's something else."

My eyes swept the room a third time, looking for clues. I spied one of our notepads tucked under a book on the nightstand. When the book moved slightly, I ran over and picked it up. After reading the title of the book, I turned to April.

"Sometimes I'm as dense as a rock." I held the book up for April to see. It was entitled "The Book of Lost Friends," by Lisa Wingate.

"Oh, boy," April said. "That's no coincidence."

"No kidding." I dropped my gaze to the notepad, picked it up and read it. I slumped onto the bed, feeling dizzy.

"What is it?" April asked.

With a trembling hand, I handed her the notepad. She glanced at it, and her eyes went wide. On it, Gretchen had scribbled the name and address of the Collier and Sons Funeral Home.

CHAPTER THIRTY-FOUR

I left Gretchen's room with a flush of emotion spreading through my body. On our way back to my apartment, I called Blair to explain the situation.

"And you think she's in trouble?" she asked.

"Don't you? I checked, and her car is also gone. She clearly meant to go to the funeral home, and no one has seen her since yesterday morning. I called David, but apparently some thugs are threatening José down at the Magnolia camp, and Sergeant Odell and Agent Glass are on their way to intercede."

"Slow down, Julia. Let's think this through. Why can't David help?"

"Because two of the men we thought were missing have shown up dead in Tacoma. He and Sean are on their way down there. There's no one but us."

I was speaking so fast that I was gulping air. April forced me to sit down.

"We can't let anything happen to Gretchen," I said, swallowing.

Blair responded with a loud sigh. "Okay, it sounds like we need to step in. I'll call Rudy."

"No!" I said sharply. "Sorry," I added, filling my lungs with a cleansing breath. I proceeded more calmly. "She needs a pass on this one. We don't know what will happen, and she's in enough trouble already."

"But it's her case," Blair said.

"You said yourself that she hasn't been herself lately. Did you see her this afternoon eating that sandwich? Call Doe. Let's meet in my apartment right away."

"Okay," Blair said. "See you soon."

"Do you think it's fair to leave Rudy out of this?" April asked me.

I was leaning over, with my elbows resting on my knees as I tried to calm my nerves.

"To be honest, I'm not sure she can be counted on right now. This is almost too much for me." I straightened up and glanced over at April. "We're not going to do this alone, though. I'm calling the twins."

I called Donna and asked her if they could come to my apartment. When they arrived, I sat them down and explained the situation.

"Whoa, so you think they've kidnapped Gretchen," Deirdre said.

"Yes. Because it looks like she went to the funeral home alone to check it out. And before you ask, our entire law enforcement team is putting out other fires connected to this investigation. So, they're unavailable."

"Couldn't you just call the police?" Donna asked. "I mean there's got to be someone who could help."

"We have no real evidence where she's gone, other than she wrote down the name and address of the funeral home. All they would do is show up at the funeral home and ask about her."

"Which would tip them off," Donna said.

"Right. And I doubt they'd have her tied up in the lobby. They'd have her hidden some place."

"I guess that leaves you," Dierdre said.

"Well, me and my friends. Which includes you guys, I hope."

A smile flickered across Donna's face. "We're part of your team?"

"I hope so because I need to see the floor plans of the funeral home. Do you think you can find those online?"

"Probably," Donna said. "I imagine the City Planning Office has them."

"You're going to try and rescue her, aren't you?" Dierdre said.

"Trust me," April said. "Once Julia gets an idea into her head, there's no stopping her."

"Look. If I'm right, she's there because of me. Enough people have died."

"Okay, we're on it," Donna said, standing up.

"Thanks. You have my phone number. Blair and Doe are on their way here. Once we have a plan in place, I'll let you know, and hopefully, you can walk us through the building."

Dierdre chuckled and shook her head as she stood up. "I like you, Ms. Applegate. You're one badass woman."

After the twins left, I turned to April, who was sitting on the end of the sofa, stroking Wilson's head with long, slow strokes.

"You don't approve, do you?"

She glanced up. "It doesn't matter if I approve. Like I said, you'll do it anyway. I understand. It's just that now, I'll have to worry about you, too."

I reached over and squeezed her hand. "We'll be careful. I promise. Trust me, my stomach is in knots because I'm worried about Ben and José, too. But if anyone can help them, I'd put my faith in Sergeant Odell and Agent Glass. Listen, I have one more phone call to make before the girls get here."

After I made my call, I pulled up a map of Seattle and pinpointed the funeral home and landmarks nearby. Ten minutes later, Blair and Doe had joined us. They had both left their normal attire at home and were instead dressed for business, meaning jeans, tennis shoes, sweaters, and heavy coats.

"I brought two flashlights, just in case," Blair said, holding up two small LED lights.

"Good thinking."

"I'm sorry I've been MIA," Doe said, stripping off her coat. "But I'm here now. What have I missed?"

I filled them both in on Gretchen and how she'd offered twice to do a reconnaissance run to the funeral home.

"She also questioned why the FBI would take over when this was our investigation," I said.

"Sounds like she got invested pretty quickly," Doe said.

"She did. She didn't seem the type to just go off on her own, though. On the other hand, posing as a writer doing a story on funeral homes probably didn't sound dangerous."

"Why would they suspect her, though?" Blair asked.

"I don't know," I said, shaking my head. "Other than she was at the shelter with me. I suppose Enzo could have seen her. And she did take a picture of Grace Cumberland and Patch at the park. They were deep in discussion about something, but that doesn't mean they didn't notice her."

"I think we need to get into that funeral home," Blair said.

"But we have to be sure," Doe said.

"Where else would she be?" April asked, still petting Wilson. "She wrote the address on a notepad right after Julia said the funeral home was the one thread she hadn't been able to pin down before the FBI took over."

"And let's face it," I said. "It's what Elizabeth was trying to say with all the books flying at me. A friend who is in trouble."

"Why can't these ghosts just spell it out exactly like it is?" Blair asked in frustration. "If she had, maybe we could have stopped her."

"It's just the way it works," April murmured, now rubbing her temples. Her eyes were squeezed shut.

"What's wrong?" I said, moving to sit next to her.

"I don't know. I have a splitting headache," she said quietly. "And I keep seeing flashes of something, which is aggravating the headache." She used her free hand to rub her forehead. "I see flames again," she said in a strained voice.

Blair's eyes met mine. "The incinerator," she mouthed.

"And the stench… it's different this time. I smell urine and… God it smells like a dirty bathroom," April continued. "It's making me sick."

"Okay, we've got to get you over to the guest house to lie down," I said, rubbing her back as I talked.

"I'm fine," April said, standing up unsteadily. "You need to find Gretchen."

I turned to Doe. "Can you take care of her? Then, once she's settled, ask Crystal to stay late. Tell her it's an emergency."

"Absolutely. I'll be right back."

She guided April out of the apartment just as there was a knock at my back door. I hurried down the hall to open it and returned with a woman I had called at the last minute. Not a friend exactly. But someone who had come through for us in the past.

"What is she doing here?" Blair asked with a slight lift of her chin.

Aria Stottlemeyer ran the Mercer Island Post Office and was perhaps the busiest gossip on the island. Her pointed nose, bushy eyebrows, and persnickety attitude didn't help her reputation. But we'd learned recently that she'd once worked for the DEA and was now a member of a weekend spy club that practiced covert missions for reasons I couldn't fathom, but which gave her an arsenal of spy equipment we needed.

"I invited her," I said.

Aria answered Blair's question by holding out a box. "Remember these?" she said with a snap. "You guys might really want to invest in some of this stuff."

The box held wireless communication earpieces, like the ones we'd used during our road trip from Hell, when we saved a senator from certain death.

Blair's blue eyes popped open. "Oh! Good idea."

She reached for one, but Aria pulled the box back. "First, fill me in."

Blair's hand stopped mid-air. She turned to me with a perfectly penciled raised eyebrow.

"She has a right to know," I said. "We've relied on her several times in the past. But we have to be quick," I said to Aria.

We explained the entire situation, including the two murders and what we thought might be happening to the people taken off the street."

"So, it's dangerous," Aria said with the hint of a smile.

"Um, yes," I replied.

I finished by telling her our plan to first scope out the funeral home and then hopefully go back in to rescue Gretchen. Aria listened attentively, with one bony hip perched stiffly on one of my barstools.

"You definitely need these then," she said, gesturing to the box. "But there's a major flaw in your plan."

It felt as if someone had magnetized the room because Blair's body stiffened. I put my hand up before she could protest.

"What do you mean?" I asked as calmly as possible.

"Simple," Aria said with her chin up. "I should go in instead."

"No way," Blair blurted, almost coming out of her seat.

"Hear me out," Aria said. "From what you've said, whoever these people are already know Julia. And they might know you, too, Blair, since you've been in the shelters. And they probably know that you are friends with Rudy. So, any story you tell will likely raise suspicions. But they've never seen me. I can say I'm planning a memorial service for a relative."

"But that misses the point," Blair said, raising her chin. "We need eyes on the building to see where they might be hiding Gretchen so we can go in later and get her."

"I have that covered," Aria said, raising her chin another inch to match Blair's.

God, were they having a chin-off?

"I have a tiny hidden camera in the car that's embedded in a pair of glasses," Aria said. "You guys can be somewhere close by and see everything I see on a monitor. And I'll be wearing the comms, so you can guide me wherever you want."

Count to three.

"It's a good plan," I conceded. "Better than ours."

"Julia! You can't be serious," Blair exclaimed.

Blair was usually my comrade-in-arms. We'd lied our way into more tricky situations than I cared to count and then fought our way out. But Aria had a point.

"Listen, Blair. Think about it. One way or the other, we're going to have to do this in two stages. Stage one, we go in and case the joint. Depending on what we find, we go in after they close to save Gretchen."

"They could be keeping her somewhere else," Aria offered.

"I don't think so. I know you don't believe in our ghosts, Aria, but let's just say that one of them warned me that my brother Ben was in trouble and that my part in all of this wasn't finished. I was told to follow my instincts. And my instincts tell me Gretchen is at the funeral home."

"Then the funeral home it is," she said.

I wondered if I was in my right mind including Aria. She wasn't easy to control. I glanced once more at Blair.

"I'm good, Julia," she said grudgingly. "Let's just do this."

We spent the next fifteen minutes clarifying the mission and the story Aria would tell. I had to admit that Aria caught on quickly. Must be those spy weekends.

Doe came back just as we finished.

"April is lying down," she said.

"Then we're ready," I said. "Do you have the waste management contract for the Union Lake area?"

"Yes. Why?"

"We need a truck."

Her eyes grew wide. "I'm not smashing into another building, am I?"

When I was held in the basement of an old church during our first case, and the police didn't have a search warrant, Doe had driven one of her 16-ton garbage trucks into the building to gain access so that I could be rescued.

"No," I said with a smile. "No smashing into buildings."

"Good. Because my board wasn't too happy about that."

"But can you recruit a couple of guys who know the funeral home area? Collier and Sons Funeral Home is on Meridian Avenue North near Union Lake."

She glanced at her watch. "Actually, Robert and Mateo will still be in the field. I can call them."

"Okay, good. Because having your truck there won't seem unusual. First, have them meet us at Gas Works Park with the truck. And ask them if they have an idea of how we can get into the building."

She nodded. "Okay. We'll meet you there."

Doe left, and I turned back to Aria and Blair.

"You guys ready?"

"Yeah," Aria said. "These are new models." She held out the comms again. "Each earpiece connects to this small radio." She pulled out two small black boxes with wide clips on the back. "I've made sure we're all on the same channel. And here is the screen you'll use to see whatever I see through the glasses." She handed me a small tablet. "The sign in information is taped to the back. So, where is this funeral home?"

"Give me your phone," I said.

She handed it over, and I programmed the address into it. "Okay, you'll go into the funeral home to make plans for a memorial service and cremation. Once you're in, you need to ask for a tour so you can look around."

Blair looked down at her phone. "They close at six o'clock. If we hurry, we can get there before 5:30."

"Perfect," I said. "That will at least get you inside."

As we left the apartment, heading for our cars, Blair said, "You know, Julia, you're beginning to think fast on your feet."

"I just wish it were under different circumstances." I turned to Aria. "By the way, how far away can we be from the building to have the picture and the comms work?"

She thought for a moment. "No more than a hundred feet."

"Okay. Good luck. And, Aria," I said, stopping her before she closed her car door, "Don't take any chances. I want you to be safe."

A minute later, Blair and I were following Aria up our sloping driveway. It was unusually quiet in the car as we pulled onto the floating bridge that connects Mercer Island to Seattle. We lost Aria when we got into the city. But when we passed the funeral home ten minutes later, her car was just pulling into the parking lot.

I took a deep breath, thinking, *Please God! Let Gretchen be okay.*

CHAPTER THIRTY-FIVE

The funeral home was set back from the street with expansive, rolling lawns on both sides of a long drive that led to the elegant, minimalist style two-story, wood framed building. Trees and shrubbery functioned as barriers between it and the buildings on either side, while wide planters with flood lights pointed upwards on the building illuminated it in the dark. We drove past it and then pulled into the alley behind it, parking in the lot of a medical supply company next door that had already closed.

"The funeral home looks busy," Blair said. "There were several cars in the lot."

"Let's hope that means they were too busy today to…"

I paused, feeling a sour taste in my mouth at the thought of what they might be doing to Gretchen. Blair put a hand on my arm.

"We're here, Julia. And we'll do whatever we have to do to get her back."

I nodded and swallowed. "Okay, are we within a hundred feet?"

Blair glanced between us and the building. "Yeah, I think so."

My heart raced, and I had to open and close my hands to stop them from trembling.

"Okay, let's get everything set up."

We got out the receiver for the audio comms and turned it on, setting it to the proper channel. Then I pulled out the tablet that connected to the camera and signed in. I set it on the car's dash.

"Aria, are you there?" I whispered.

"Yeah," she said. "Why are you whispering?"

"Um, I don't know."

"Doesn't matter. I'm getting out of the car," she said quietly. "And turning on the camera."

A picture of the funeral home fluttered into view, and the scene swayed back and forth as Aria stepped forward.

"Oh, God, this is going to make me seasick," I said.

"You'll get used to it," Aria responded.

I'd forgotten she could hear us.

"Okay, here we go," she said.

We heard her car door slam and watched the building come closer as she approached. She passed an older couple coming out just as she went in. There was a brief melodic tingling of a bell attached to the front door. Through her eyes, we saw her step into the entryway. Aria's gaze swept the immediate area around them.

"This is nice," she murmured. "Feels like a church."

The interior was quiet except for the gurgling of a cherub fountain in the corner. A highly polished oak reception desk sat to her left with no one behind it. As Aria's gaze moved around the room, we could see framed artwork of pastoral scenes on richly paneled walls, recessed lighting in the ceiling, and upholstered benches strategically placed around the perimeter. Aria turned to an office door that sat behind the reception desk.

"No one's here," she said.

"Move further in," I told her.

She moved forward into a square room with pocket doors to her left labeled the Rainier Chapel. A room to her right was labeled St. Helens Chapel. Console tables hugged the walls around the room. Each had a large vase filled with fresh flowers centered on the table with a lit crystal table lamp on each side. Aria glanced to the end of the room where there was a faux white fireplace mantle set against a red brick wall. An intricately carved oval mirror hung above it. On either side of the fireplace were two upholstered armchairs.

"Looks homey," Blair said.

"I'm sure it's meant to make everyone feel warm and comfortable," I replied.

Voices prompted Aria to turn to the Rainier Chapel on her left. The pocket doors were partially open, revealing three people at the far end of the room in front of a small podium and platform.

"That's Stanley Collier," I said, pointing to the screen.

"He must be talking to someone who's planning a service," Blair said.

My mouth went dry at the sight of him. He glanced toward Aria as if he'd heard me, but merely gave her a vacant smile.

More voices made Aria turn back to the entryway, where a stout woman appeared through the office door with a young couple. The young woman held the hand of a child of three or four as she dabbed at her eyes with a tissue.

"We'll take care of everything, Mrs. Wainwright," the stout woman said. "It will be a beautiful service tomorrow for your father."

The woman gave the couple a Cheshire Cat smile and then showed them to the door. She waited until they had gone and the door closed. Then, she turned to Aria.

"Welcome," she said, coming forward. "How can I help you?"

She wore a matching deep gray skirt and blazer, accented by a pink blouse. Her brown hair was streaked with gray and pulled into a severe bun. As she approached, I cringed at the sight of her eyes, which were close enough to shake hands. I erupted with a staccato bark of laughter.

"Shhh," Blair hissed.

"Sorry," I said, coughing to cover my outburst.

"Um, I'd like to talk to someone about planning a memorial service and cremation," Aria said to the woman. "My uncle was recently killed in a hit-and-run accident."

The woman's beady eyes rested on Aria for a moment. "Of course. My son, Stanley, is busy right now," she said, gesturing into the chapel. "But I'd be happy to talk with you. We're about to close for the day, but we can certainly get started. My name is Lorraine. Let's go into the office."

She gestured to the door behind her, and Aria followed her into a nicely appointed office. As Aria glanced around, we saw an enormous fish tank underneath the window, with three, large rainbow fish swimming lazily around. The lighting in the room was subdued, and we could barely hear the hum from the fish tank motor.

"These comms are good," I said.

"Of course, they are," Aria replied.

"I'm sorry?" the woman asked, turning to Aria.

My heart jumped.

"Oh, nothing," Aria said, sitting in front of a massive oak desk.

As Lorraine sat down, she said, "I didn't catch your name."

"Oh, uh, I'm Stella Madrid," she replied.

Blair choked back a laugh.

Lorraine sat behind the desk and turned to the computer screen. "Well, Ms. Madrid, let me pull up a service form," she said, tapping at the keys. "Here we go. What's the name of the deceased?"

"Uh… his name is… was, Randall Korby," Aria said. "Korby with a K."

Lorraine typed the name into the computer.

"And how soon would you like the service?"

"Well, his body is still with the coroner, but they said they'd release it on Monday or Tuesday. So, sometime next week if that's possible."

"Aria's not doing such a bad job," Blair whispered.

Aria cleared her throat, and I backhanded Blair's shoulder.

Lorraine flipped open a calendar on the desk and studied a couple of pages. I couldn't help but wonder what role this woman might play in all of this, if any.

"We have Friday afternoon available," she said. "Three o'clock. Would that work?"

"That would be fine," Aria replied.

"And you'd like a reception afterward."

"Yes, I think so," Aria said. "How much extra does that cost?"

"Just like Aria to worry about the money," Blair grumbled.

Aria coughed this time in response, and I reached over and slapped Blair's leg.

"If you're on a budget, I'm sure we can work something out. How many people do you expect?"

"Maybe thirty or so," Aria said. "It's hard to tell. He just moved here a year ago, so he didn't know too many people."

"That's fine," she said, typing again. "We can arrange the food. Maybe something simple. We partner with a very reasonable caterer."

"Simple would be good. Uncle Frank wasn't a fancy guy," Aria said.

Lorraine froze. "I thought you said your uncle's name was Randall."

"Sorry. Randall Francis Korby," Aria responded without hesitation. "I always called him Uncle Frank. I was hoping you might have suggestions for a pastor," Aria said with a clip to her voice. "Someone neutral if you know what I mean. My uncle was an agnostic."

"Oh, yes, we can arrange for that," Lorraine said, typing.

"And if you have a good florist, I'd like to order a few sprays," Aria said. "Nothing too fancy, but I want this to be nice."

"Man, she's good," Blair said.

"We work with a local florist who does an excellent job. Do you have a preference in flowers?"

"Lilies," Aria replied. "White lilies."

Lorraine nodded and made a note in the computer. The door opened behind Aria, making her turn. A young woman in her late thirties or early forties stood in the doorway.

"I'm so sorry. I didn't realize you were with someone," she said in a sultry Eastern European accent.

"No problem, honey. This is Pietra, my daughter-in-law," Lorraine said. "This is Ms. Madrid, a new client."

"Nice to meet you," Pietra said, moving up next to the desk.

She turned toward Aria. Pietra was tall and slender, with long brown hair pulled into a loose ponytail at the nape of her neck. She had high cheekbones, large oval eyes framed by light crow's feet, and a wide mouth. She wore a lovely crimson blouse open at the neck showing off an opal pendant with a beautiful gold infinity sign hanging just below it.

I gasped, nearly choking as I slapped my hand over my mouth.

"What is it?" Blair asked.

I had to take a deep breath before speaking. "That necklace. It's Gretchen's. Oh, my God. It's Gretchen's." I felt nauseous and had to lower my head to the steering wheel.

"So nice to meet you," Pietra said to Aria.

"You, too," Aria replied. "That's a beautiful necklace."

My head snapped up. *Dang!*

Pietra's fingers fluttered to the pendant. "Thank you. It was a present from my husband last night at dinner."

"How sweet. Was it a special occasion?"

"Oh, no," Pietra said, almost blushing. "He said he saw it in a window and had to have it for me."

"Even better," Aria said. "You know the shape is actually a mathematical symbol representing the concept of infinity. Marketing people turned it into kind of a sophomoric symbol for undying love."

"Leave it to Aria," Blair whispered.

"Um, that's interesting," Pietra replied awkwardly.

"But it's really quite beautiful," Aria said, standing up. "May I take a picture of it?"

"Careful, Aria," I warned.

"A friend of mine makes jewelry. I'd love to have something similar made for my mother."

"Of course," Pietra said, pulling the collar of her blouse away from the necklace.

Aria's hands appeared holding her phone. She snapped a photo.

"Good job, Aria," I whispered.

"Thank you, so much," Aria said, sitting down again.

"Well, dear, it's late, and we need to finish up here," Lorraine said to Pietra.

"Okay. Do you need anything?" Pietra asked. "I'm going to run to the store before dinner. I'm making holubtsi tonight, and Papa is bringing the wine."

"No, dear. I don't think so. You run ahead. We'll be there soon."

Pietra turned back to Aria. "I'm sorry for your loss, but my mother-in-law will take good care of you."

Aria's gaze followed her out of the room. "She's very pretty," Aria said, turning back.

"Yes, she is. Now, let's continue."

"I'd like a tour," Aria said quickly. "I know it's late, but it would be so helpful. I'm reporting back to my mother tonight. Randall was her younger brother."

The door opened, and Lorraine looked up as a man's voice cut in.

"Mom, I'm sorry to interrupt, but remember we have that thing to take care of tonight."

Aria turned. Stanley Collier stood in the doorway.

"Of course, honey. Pietra had to run to the store. I'll be right there."

He closed the door and Aria turned back to Lorraine.

"I'm sorry," she said. "But we'll have to postpone the tour." She rose from her chair. "Give us a call tomorrow, and we can schedule a time to finish up."

"It's okay. Don't push it, Aria," I said to her.

"I'll give you a call tomorrow," Aria said, also standing. "Thanks for your time."

CHAPTER THIRTY-SIX

Aria left the building, and I sighed with relief as she climbed back into her car.

"That was great, Aria. Meet us at the park," I said.

I turned off the tablet and handed it to Blair.

"What do you think?" she asked as I started the car with trembling hands.

"I think she did really well. I don't know how we're going to find Gretchen, though, since Aria didn't get to see much of the building. But now we know for sure they took her."

Blair placed her hand on my shoulder. "We'll find her, Julia. Don't give up hope."

We pulled up behind the monstrous garbage truck at Gas Works Park. Aria was already there and got out of the car as we parked. Doe got out of her Mercedes, and the four of us walked over to a picnic table, arms wrapped around ourselves for warmth. There was no one in the park. The wind had picked up, and the air was thick with moisture. Although all of us had dressed warmly, the cold still burrowed under my clothes and made me wish I were back at home with a hot cup of tea.

"So, what happened?" Doe asked as we sat down.

I felt, rather than knew, that my friends were all looking at me.

"What is it, Julia?" Doe pressed me.

I expelled a big breath. "We didn't get to see much of the building, since it was closing time. But I'm positive now they've taken Gretchen."

"How?" Doe asked.

"Because Stanley Collier's wife was wearing Gretchen's necklace," Aria said.

"Exactly," I agreed.

Aria pulled the picture up on her phone and showed it to Doe.

"How do you know for sure it's hers?" Doe asked, glancing at the photo.

"Because she told me the other day that her husband had it made for her out of her grandmother's opal. Her husband even used the words 'one-of-a-kind' to describe it. So, yeah, it's hers."

"But we still don't know if she's in there or somewhere else," Blair said.

"I'm sorry I was pushed out," Aria said despondently.

I looked over at her. "It wasn't your fault. I'm just worried that the 'thing' Stanley mentioned is getting rid of Gretchen."

"It could just be a family dinner," Blair said. "Pietra mentioned her father bringing wine."

"I hope you're right," I replied.

"Then, we go back in," Doe said.

I turned to her. Doe was typically the most cautious one in the group, so I was surprised by her eagerness. My phone rang before I could respond. I held up a hand to put everyone on pause as I answered it.

"Hey," Donna said when I answered. "Hope we're not interrupting."

"Perfect timing. Let me put you on speaker." I put the phone on the picnic table. "Okay, we're listening. Did you find anything useful?"

"We're looking at pictures of the funeral home building and a detailed architectural drawing of the entire floor plan."

"What can you tell from the drawings?"

"Nothing much out of the ordinary," Dierdre said. "What did you see inside?"

"It was closing time, so they kicked Aria out before she could see much."

"Well, we found something odd about the floorplan," Dierdre said. "Their embalming room is one big room with a door leading off of it to the crematorium. And there's another small room off the embalming room which could be a closet or a storeroom. What's interesting about that room is that the walls appear to be double the thickness of all the other walls."

"Which means what?" I asked.

"Not sure," Donna said. "But I saw this once on a hospital floor plan. It indicated the lead walls around their MRI machine."

Aria released a sigh. "You can't hear anything through lead walls," she said in a tight voice.

"Shit," Blair murmured.

"That's where they could be keeping Gretchen," I said, feeling a chill blossom throughout my body.

"It's a possibility," Donna said.

"Okay, thanks, Donna. Can you send me the floorplan and then stay tuned?"

"Sure thing."

We hung up, and I turned to Doe. "I guess you're right. We need to go back in. Now."

"It's already after six," Doe said, glancing at her watch. "They should be leaving soon."

"Unless they're going to do something to Gretchen right away," Aria said.

"Pietra mentioned dinner," Blair said. "Maybe they'll do that first."

"Let's hope so," Doe said.

"Okay, but how do we get in?" Blair asked. "Break a window? They probably have an alarm system."

"I talked to Robert and Mateo," Doe said. "Robert says they know the people who run the funeral home since they pick up their trash every week. He's gotten friendly with one of the technicians and the mom. The funeral home is typically in the middle of their run, so both he and Mateo have asked to use their restroom before. He's offered to do it again."

"Is today their trash day, though?" Blair asked.

"No. But he already thought of that," Doe said. "He's going to say they had a pickup at a construction site close by and just finished."

"That would work. And then what?" I asked.

"There's a back door to the embalming room with a bell. He'll ring the bell and ask to use the restroom and then he can block the lock mechanism on the door when he leaves, so we can get in."

"How will he do that?" I asked.

"He chews gum… all the time." She rolled her eyes.

I looked at my comrades. "What do you think?"

"Julia, remember that Evergreen said she woke up chained to a wall and was then rolled into what she called a medical room. That could have been the embalming room," Blair said.

"Which means that Gretchen could still be alive and chained to the same wall," Doe added.

"Okay, let's say we get inside," I said. "How do we get into a locked, lead-encased room?"

"I have my set of lock picks." Aria patted the tote bag she carried over her shoulder.

Doe sighed. "I hope it's that simple. It could be digital."

"Let's figure that out when we get in there," I said. "But we'll need someone to watch the back door. You up for that?" I asked Doe.

"Sure."

"Okay," I said, glancing at each of them. There was palpable tension between us. "Then

I guess we're doing this."

CHAPTER THIRTY-SEVEN

Doe had instructed Robert and Mateo to park the garbage truck at the end of the alley behind the funeral home and wait for her signal. The four of us then climbed into my Pathfinder and drove past the front of the funeral home to make sure the lot was empty. We pulled into the alley and parked behind the medical supply company again. We were blocked by trees and bushes in between the two buildings. A silver Mercedes was parked in the back lot below us, and a white van was just pulling out.

"One car left. I wonder who it belongs to," Blair said, staring out the window.

"Lorraine's, I imagine," I said. "Okay, time for Robert. We don't want whoever owns that car to leave before he blocks the door."

Doe texted Robert. A few moments later, the big truck pulled in behind the funeral home, its massive engine rumbling against the ground. Robert pulled his lanky frame out of the truck and approached the back door and rang the bell. He glanced in our direction, his stocking cap pulled down low on his forehead. He then turned back to face the door. Mateo stayed in the truck with the engine running and the lights on. Thirty seconds later, the door opened. Robert spoke to someone and then disappeared inside.

"You know, since they run the incinerator late," Blair said, "someone might work all night."

"Fingers crossed then that whoever is there now leaves and the night person doesn't come on until later," I said.

I grabbed my phone and pulled up the photo of the floor plan, using my fingers to enlarge the area labeled for the embalming room and crematorium.

"What are you doing?" Blair asked, leaning towards me.

"Just getting my bearings. That back door goes right into the embalming room," I said, showing my phone to Blair.

"Got it," Blair said. "It also looks like the door to the crematorium is off to the right here, " she said, pointing to the floor plan. "And this door next to these counters must be the door to the lead-lined room."

"Okay, so at least we know where we're going once we get in there."

The wind had picked up, and deep shadows had crept into every corner and crevice around us as night began to settle in. The back door opened again and Robert appeared. He paused and then let the door swing shut before he climbed onto the running board of the big truck. Flashing us a thumbs up, he got in and closed his door. The truck backed out and disappeared down the alley.

"Tell them they can go now," I told Doe.

"But—"

"No," I interrupted her. "I don't want them involved more than they have to be. We've got this."

"Okay," she said with a sigh and texted them.

"Now we have to wait until whoever owns the Mercedes leaves," I said to my comrades. "God, I just hope they do their dirty work after business hours. By the way, check to make sure your phones are on vibrate," I said to Blair and Aria. "Then, when we go in, Doe, you should get somewhere where you can see the back door."

We sat in the car until all the lights on the street and in the parking lot had flickered to life, looking like glow bugs in the dark. A light rain covered my windshield, and the wind had picked up, forcing us to huddle deeper into our coats while we waited inside the cold interior of the car.

I was tapping my hand on the steering wheel, anxiously waiting for the opportunity to go in, when the back door opened and Lorraine emerged, carrying a purse in the crook of her elbow. She climbed into the Mercedes, backed out and pulled past the building to the main street. The parking lot was now empty.

"It's time," I said, feeling fear pulse through my veins. "I hope we're in time."

"What do we do if we find more than just Gretchen?" Blair asked.

I turned to her. "Gretchen is our first priority. We need to get her out of there. But if there are others… then we call the police."

The four of us hustled into the alley, coat hoods pulled up to stay dry. As Blair, Aria, and I dropped down into the small parking lot behind the funeral home, Doe hid among the trees to watch the back door. Blair pulled the door open. The chewing gum had worked. I left the gum there and gave a thumbs up to Doe.

We stepped into the shadowed interior of the embalming room. It was lit by two small security lights set into the corners of the ceiling. The room had three walls lined with crisp white counters, cupboards, and two stainless steel sinks. Beneath high-powered overhead scoop lights in the middle of the room were two stainless steel pedestal tables, each with a big drain at one end. A single gurney holding a draped body stood in front of a wall of coolers that obviously held other bodies. A chill snaked its way down my spine as it occurred to me that the body on the stretcher might be Gretchen.

A door in the far-right corner of the room was marked 'crematorium.' The darkened window indicated the lights were off. I hurried over to a door on the opposite side of the room and peeked through. Only a dim glow shone from further down the hallway toward the office.

"Julia," Blair said, coming up behind me. "They wouldn't leave a body out for long. Someone must be coming back to take care of whoever that is," she said, pointing to the gurney.

I expelled a breath. "Okay. Can you guard this door?"

She moved immediately into position, while Aria and I approached the draped body. I silently prayed it wasn't Gretchen.

I took a deep breath despite the smell of chemicals in the air and lifted the drape with a trembling hand. It was an older man with wispy gray hair. I sighed with relief.

"Let's check the coolers," Aria said.

We moved to the other side of the gurney. There were six steel doors on top and six on the bottom. We began opening each one and sliding out the bodies to peek under the drapes. It creeped me out. I've seen my fair share of dead bodies, but to roll them out, look at them, and then roll them back felt too much like we were searching through the crisper drawers in a refrigerator. Fortunately, Gretchen wasn't among the group.

"Thank God," I said with relief as we closed the final one.

"Okay, it's time to get into the lead-lined room," Aria whispered.

We turned to the unmarked door in the middle of the back wall.

"Oh, no," I whined.

The door was secured with a digital lock. The ping of a text alerted me. I pulled my phone out and looked at it.

"Oh, shit. Doe says two cars just pulled into the front lot and are heading back here," I called out.

Blair and Aria froze in place.

"C'mon, we need to hide!" I snapped.

Blair left her post and hid behind a large, rolling laundry cart against the wall. Meanwhile, Aria and I looked at each other in panic.

Where the hell would we hide?

The sound of a car engine under the Porte cochere at the back door had us racing. Aria quickly rolled out one of two empty cooler trays and climbed onto it.

"Push me in and then get into that closet," she said, pointing to her left where a narrow closet stood with one door ajar.

"Are you kidding?"

"Just do it," she snapped.

I rushed over, and with an overwhelming sense of disgust, pushed the drawer back in and closed the door. Then, I hustled over to the closet that held lab coats, pulled open one door, and climbed in, pushing myself behind a group of green coats. Through a slight gap between the two doors, I could see into the embalming room. I had no sooner gotten the closet closed than the door to the back parking lot opened and brothers Stanley and Edgar Collier walked in, letting in a giant gust of wind. A tall Black guy followed and closed the door behind them.

"Man, it's nasty out there," Edgar said, shaking water off his coat.

He hung his coat on a coat tree next to the laundry cart. Stanley also took his coat off but threw it onto a chair.

"Andre, can you check the calendar and tell me what's on deck for tomorrow?"

Andre left through the door to the hallway.

"So, when did Louie leave for Merriman's with our newest recruit?" Stanley asked Edgar.

Edgar was rubbing his hands together to warm them up.

"Maybe five minutes ago. He had to wait until your technician left. You know, sometimes, all the moving parts around here come off like a badly choreographed ballet."

Stanley glanced over at him. "Funny."

"Louie also had to give her another shot because she was coming around."

"That's okay. My pain-in-the-ass father-in-law is coming over for dinner tonight, so I won't get out there until late anyway," Stanley said, limping toward the gurney.

"Shouldn't you be at dinner now?" Edgar asked, glancing at his watch.

"Yes. But I'll use Mr. Robbins here as my excuse for arriving late. I'm sure everyone except Pietra's father will accept my reason. I could be near death from a car accident, and he'd expect me to be on time."

Edgar chuckled. "Maybe Pietra's father should donate to the family business."

Stanley glanced at him. "Don't tempt me."

"So, this old guy is getting an open casket tomorrow?" Edgar asked as Stanley pulled off the drape.

"Yeah. I need to get him dressed."

Stanley was standing in front of the body with his back to me, so I couldn't see most of it. But I thought they were probably talking about the father of the young woman that left just before Lorraine talked with Aria.

When Stanley moved to his left, revealing the full body, I repressed a scream with my hand against my mouth. The poor man's forearms and calf bones had been removed and replaced with white PVC pipe. *Just like in April's dream!* It looked like something from a horror movie. The skin on his abdomen had also been stripped off, leaving behind a large, open wound. I looked away, feeling bile rise in my throat.

When I looked back, Stanley was pulling Styrofoam tubing from a large cannister against the wall. He set about measuring the man's lower legs, and then cutting the tubing. He sliced open the tubing and then fit it over the PVC pipe on the man's calves. As he positioned them just below the knee, he kept talking.

"Don't you need to be back at the homeless camp?" he asked Edgar.

"Soon," Edgar said, sucking on a toothpick. "I want to let Andre's team take care of that Hispanic kid first. He was pretty thick with that guy in the wheelchair you tried to get, and I don't want to take any chances. By the way, we found out what hospital he was taken to, and Andre took care of him right away."

I swallowed my feelings because they were talking about José and Ross.

"But Stan," Edgar continued, "you haven't been listening to me. I'm telling you that we need to take a break. I didn't agree with your decision to kill that Romaine woman just so you could send a message of some kind," he said, using air quotes. "Which by the way doesn't seem to have worked. There are all sorts of people nosing around, and now you've abducted someone who isn't homeless. No doubt she'll have people who will come looking for her."

Gretchen!

Stanley had wrapped the tubing around the PVC pipe on the man's legs and had now taped the tubing, hiding the PVC pipe. He was now measuring the man's forearms, where I could see the pipe was wired to the corpse's hands. I had a difficult time watching him.

"You worry too much," Stanley said. "I agree we need to change things up. What about starting up in a different city? Or going back to Tacoma again?"

As he cut the tubing for the arms, Edgar said, "Jesus, Stan! You don't get it. You dumped two of the people we abducted from Seattle down in Tacoma hoping to throw the police off. But you just brought more attention to what we're doing down there. Let's just focus on the people who come through the funeral home for a time. We still make money on that."

Stanley slammed a fist on the metal table, making his brother jump. "No! You don't get it, Ed! We have contracts to fill. Castrano is hungry for more product. And there's a lot of money at stake. I'm not slowing down."

"You said yourself that you have more bodies coming through here than you can handle. That's why you stash people in that room until we can get them up to Merriman's," Edgar said, nodding to the door behind him. "But don't forget, that girl got away. She could be talking to the police right now."

My muscles flinched. He was talking about Evergreen.

Stanley was taping the tubing to the upper arms of the corpse. "She was drugged the entire time she was here. She won't remember anything."

"But what about that woman you grabbed last night? Hunh? She wasn't homeless."

"We'll be rid of her later tonight. No one will be the wiser."

The heat rose throughout my body. It took everything I had not to burst out of the closet and run at them with my fists flying.

"Look, I'm not slowing down," Stanley said, cutting a large piece of gauze. "I have a big contract with Northwest Bio to provide $100,000 worth of product by the end of the month. If we can make that deadline, then maybe I can rest easy for a few weeks." He proceeded to dress the wound on the man's stomach. "Get that suit over there," he said to Edgar.

Edgar grabbed a sport coat, shirt, and pants hanging on the coat rack and removed the pants from the hanger.

"Here," he said, throwing the pants at his brother. "You know, Dad wouldn't approve of the way you're managing all of this."

Stanley began dressing the deceased man. "Yeah, well, Dad didn't make the kind of money I'm making. He was too worried about being a pillar of the community, letting all sorts of opportunities run right through his fingers. Mom likes her Mercedes, though, don't you? And that bitch of a wife of yours sure does like the summer home you just bought."

"I get it. We all like the money," Edgar growled.

"Help me with this," Stanley said.

Edgar stepped over to help get the man's pants on. Then he lifted the torso up, so Stanley could dress him in a crisp, white shirt, and dark sports coat. Ten minutes later, Stanley stood back to admire his work.

"You'd never know Mr. Robbins just unwillingly donated to the Rainier Bone & Tissue Bank," he said with a wicked laugh. "C'mon, help me get him back into the cooler."

My heart nearly burst. Would they find Aria? But the door to the hallway opened and Andre poked his head in.

"Your wife is here," he said to Edgar. "She wants to see both of you right away."

"Shit," Stanley snarled. "I'm about ready to get rid of her, too."

"Careful," Edgar warned.

"Why'd you marry that nosey bitch, anyway?" He replaced the drape over Mr. Robbins and turned toward the door. "Does she remind you of Mom or something?"

"Don't be disgusting. And you have to admit she's identified good candidates," Edgar said as the two men turned for the door to the hallway.

"Still a pain in the ass," Stanley said.

Edgar grabbed his brother's arm. "Look, I'm telling you that the woman Louie just took out to Merriman's could be real trouble."

Stanley removed his brother's hand from his arm. "If you're so worried about her, go out there yourself and find out what she knows. Your wife's the one who ID'd her as someone who was snooping around the shelter. So, do what you have to do to get her to tell you everything she knows. Then be done with her. I've got this stupid family dinner, and then I'll be out there later tonight." He turned. "Andre, I bought more PVC pipe. It's in the van. Bring it in, and I'll see what the bitch wants." He turned back to Edgar. "You go. I'll tell her you're busy."

Stanley went through the door to the hallway, while Edgar and Andre donned coats.

"I've got something in my car I need help with, too," he said to Andre.

They opened the door to the back parking lot. The wind slammed the door against the building, and he and Edgar had to struggle to close it behind them. As soon as the door clicked shut, I slid out from my hiding place and opened the cooler to pull Aria out. She climbed off the metal slab, wrapping her arms around her.

"I'm free... freezing... to... death," she stuttered.

Blair emerged from behind the laundry basket, and the three of us converged in the middle of the room.

"Did you hear what they said?" I asked them.

"It sounds like Gretchen was taken to another location," Blair said.

"What's Merriman's, though?" Aria asked. "And how are we going to find it?"

"I don't know," I replied. "But, first, we need to get out of here!"

"How? Stanley is out front and Andre is out back," Blair said.

"We could sneak down the hallway," I said.

"Or hide in the crematorium," Aria offered.

"They're liable to see us if we go down the hallway," Blair said.

"Okay, let's go to the crematorium. We just have to move!" I snapped.

The back door opened before we could move, and Andre stumbled back inside, buffeted by the wind. He was carrying a long cardboard box and dropped it before closing the door. When he turned around, we all just stared at each other.

"What the hell are you doing in here?" he snarled.

"We were in the middle of a tour," I said quickly. "We got lost and were just about to leave." I moved toward the back door.

He backed up and pulled out a gun. "Not just yet. I better let Mr. Collier decide if you'll be leaving or not." He reached behind him and pushed a red button on the wall next to the light switch. A short alarm bell rang, making my heart skip.

"We really need to go," Blair said, advancing on him.

"Back up, or I'll shoot that pretty little face off," he ordered.

Blair paused, and I reached out and touched her arm. "It's okay. We can wait and speak to Mr. Collier."

The door to the hallway opened behind us, and Stanley and Dr. Enzo strode in. Their eyes opened wide at the sight of us.

"What the—?" Stanley started to say.

"Well, well, well," Dr. Enzo said, strutting past Stanley. "If it isn't the snoopy friend from the shelter. This is the one I was telling you about. Julia Applegate."

Stanley's demeanor changed, and his lips slid into a sickly smile. "I see we've caught a whole group of little sparrows in our net. You did good, Andre. We don't want them telling anyone about what we're doing here."

"But what do we do with them?" Andre asked.

"Same as always," Stanley said, striding over to the door to the lead lined room.

He punched in a code, and the door clicked open. The light was off, so we couldn't see inside. Stanley stepped over to a locked glass case. Using a key from a small chain around his neck, he unlocked the case and pulled out a vial of liquid and a syringe.

"What are you doing?" I asked. "We were just here on a tour and got lost."

Enzo barked a laugh. "Oh, no, Mrs. Applegate. You weren't here for any little tour."

"We know who you are," Stanley said as he filled a syringe with liquid from one of the vials. "But even your husband the governor, won't save you now."

"Ex-husband," I corrected him.

"Doesn't matter," he said, flicking the syringe to get the bubbles out.

The overhead lights flickered, almost going out, and everyone looked up.

"Damn storm is really creating havoc," he growled.

Or maybe Mom?

My mother had somehow learned how to manipulate electrical currents from the great beyond. I could only hope she'd followed me here instead of going to protect Ben.

"Let's get this done," he said, staring at me. "I'll take you first. You watch the others," he said to Enzo and Andre.

He took a step toward me, when all the lights went out, throwing the room into darkness.

I backed away from Stanley and heard the sound of shuffling feet nearby. There was an "oof!" A loud thump. Some banging and twanging. And then, "You bitch!" and "Stop that!" There was a final cry of pain, which prompted me to start for the back door, when the lights blinked on.

Enzo was on the floor struggling to get away, as Aria sat on top of her. Andre was on the floor next to the laundry cart, which had been knocked over. He was rubbing his jaw. Blair's purse sat near him, but he still held the gun. Blair turned, ready to pounce on him when Stanley yelled, "Stop!" and grabbed me from behind, the needle from the syringe prickling the skin behind my ear.

"If I inject the full amount, she'll die. Fast," he said. "Half that amount only knocks her out. Your choice," he said to Aria and Blair.

Aria gave Enzo a withering glance and kicked her as she got to her feet. She backed up next to Blair, while Andre recovered from what I assumed was a blow to the face from Blair's purse.

"That's better," Stanley said. "Now—"

"Mr. Collier… " Andre said.

Andre stood rigidly against the wall, pointing his finger at something behind us, his eyes wide with fear.

"Just watch them," Stanley snapped. "We need to finish this and get out of here."

"But, Stan," Andre said, his throat catching. His finger was trembling as he stared at something behind us.

I glanced over at Blair and Aria, who had also both frozen in place, staring.

"Uh, Julia…," Blair said, her voice wavering.

I knit my brow and glanced at Enzo, whose face had drained of all color.

"What the hell is it?" Stanley demanded.

He spun me around to face… Mr. Robbins sitting up, his legs swung over the side of the gurney, the drape that had covered him lying on the floor.

I sucked in a gulp of air as the old guy swiveled his pasty white head to stare menacingly at Stanley, his black eyes sunken deep into his skull. He slid off the gurney, the PVC pipe creaking as he stood unsteadily. Would it hold? I wondered. The suit Stanley had dressed him in hung loosely from his gaunt frame, and the pallor of his skin was just this side of a tube of toothpaste.

"Wha… what is this?" Stanley stammered backing up and releasing me.

I hustled over to Blair and Aria, who both stared at the corpse with unadulterated horror. Fortunately, Mr. Robbins' vacant eyes were focused on Stanley. With faltering, creaking steps, he began moving toward him.

Stanley held up the syringe as if to stab the corpse, but Mr. Robbins, dead as he was, was unfazed. He lifted his arm and lurched forward with his hand cupped as if to clutch Stanley's throat. The PVC pipe was only wired to his hand, so I wasn't sure how he could actually grasp anything, but under the circumstances, it didn't really matter. I turned to see Dr. Enzo pressed against the wall, making herself as small and still as possible.

"Shoot him!" Stanley screamed, stumbling backwards and then falling onto the slick, linoleum floor.

Andre fired. Mr. Robbin's shoulder exploded in a puff of smoke. He turned his robotic head to glance down at the injury. Andre fired again, and the bullet hit Mr. Robbins in the chest with a 'thump,' traveling straight through and embedding itself into the far wall.

Mr. Robbins looked at his chest and then swiveled his head so fast toward Andre that we all gasped in fear. If this wasn't enough, the emaciated corpse opened his mouth and released a horrible belch of black, putrid smoke, along with a wretched smell of decay.

The smoke burned my lungs, and everyone began to cough and choke. I didn't believe in zombies, but then what the heck was this? When the smoke cleared, I smelled it: the sweet scent of rose water.

I had to stop myself from laughing out loud. Elizabeth deserved an Academy Award for her ingenuity. But then, Stanley scrambled to his feet and turned to run for the hallway.

"Stop right there!" a female voice yelled.

I whipped around to find Doe standing in the doorway, feet planted wide, hands holding a gun. Stanley skidded to a stop.

Without asking, Andre placed his gun on the floor, right next to a small puddle of liquid I assumed was the urine his bladder had just vacated. He never took his eyes off the corpse.

Fortunately, we blocked Doe's line of sight for the moment, so she remained focused on Stanley and didn't even see Mr. Robbins. Blair moved to grab Andre's gun, and Aria snapped up her bag from where she'd dropped it. She pulled out a handful of zip ties— because why wouldn't she carry zip ties in her bag? She quickly secured Andre's hands behind his back and handed a set to Blair to secure Dr. Enzo.

Once she'd done that, Blair circled around me to come up on the other side of Stanley, her eyes still keeping Mr. Robbins in view. Stanley sat on the floor blubbering about something unintelligible as he continued to stare at the corpse in horror. It hovered above him. Blair skirted carefully around Stanley and pulled the syringe out of his hand and dropped it on the floor. She then secured his hands behind his back.

"Oh!" I heard Doe exclaim.

Doe had finally gotten a clear view of Elizabeth masquerading as a Halloween zombie. She stared open-mouthed at Mr. Robbins with the gun now held limply by her side. I slipped over and lowered the weapon.

"It's okay," I said quietly. "It's only Elizabeth putting on a show."

With Doe's attention diverted, Enzo dashed for the back door with her hands still zip-tied behind her. Aria merely stuck out a bony foot and tripped her, making Enzo take a header into the closed door.

It was then that Mr. Robbins, or what was left of him, slumped to the floor like a rag doll. The old guy's remains lay in a rumpled heap, with part of the tubing Stanley had used to hide the PVC pipe sticking out from under one of his pants legs.

The four of us stared at the crumpled old man.

"Okay, that was kind of gross," Blair said. "Maybe Elizabeth could warn us next time."

"Yeah, that was a new one," I said. "Not sure where the belch of smoke came from, but she's clearly expanding her repertoire." I turned to Doe, who was still staring at the corpse. I slapped my hands. "Doe! We need to go."

She snapped to attention. "Oh, uh, okay. Where's Gretchen?"

"Not here," I said.

I turned to Stanley, who seemed to have mentally snapped. His eyes stared vacantly at Mr. Robbins now, a touch of drool glistening at the corner of his mouth.

"Wow, you'd think after all the dead people he's seen, he'd be made of tougher stuff," Blair said.

The wind outside was still howling, and something smacked against the door, making everyone jump.

"C'mon, we gotta get out of here," I said. I whirled around to face Dr. Enzo. "Where's Merriman's?"

"I'm not helping you," she said with a sneer, a large, red welt rising on her forehead.

"She doesn't know," Andre said weakly. "She's never been there."

He was shaking and breathing heavily, and still staring at the crumpled corpse with a kind of deep-seated fear.

"Tell us where this place is, and we'll put in a good word for you with the police," I said.

He finally pulled his eyes away from Mr. Robbins and glanced at me with a look of relief.

"I never wanted to do any of this, you know. They had something on me--something that would have sent me back to jail. I had to go along with it." He looked back at the corpse. "But I didn't sign up for this."

I leaned over to look him right in the face. "Then tell us."

"All I know is that it's past Sammamish somewhere. Some small town that sounds like ice cream or something. Edgar or Louie always drove, while I guarded the people we'd abducted in the back of the van."

"Okay," I said, turning to Doe. "Doe, see if you can get your guys back here to help guard these thugs."

"Shouldn't I call David? Or the police?"

"None of them are available. Call Angela. Explain the situation. She'll know what to do. And tell her to bring a forensics team to check the bodies in the cooler. I think they'll find more than enough to put these monsters away."

As Doe pulled out her phone, Blair and Aria grabbed their bags. Blair slipped Andre's gun into her purse.

"Now what?" Aria asked.

"We head for Sammamish and call our backup," I said.

"Robert and Mateo will be here in a minute," Doe said, putting her phone down. "Apparently, they didn't leave when I told them to."

I smiled. "They're good guys. Okay, call Angela. We'll be in touch."

We started for the door when I remembered something. "Hold on," I said to my friends. I ran back and picked up the syringe and slipped it into my pocket.

"Just in case," I said.

CHAPTER THIRTY-EIGHT

Stepping out of the funeral home was like stepping into a wind machine. The slanting rain pelted the ground, and the wind howled through the trees, throwing branches and broken twigs around like Dorothy's trip to Oz. I half expected to see Miss Gulch fly by on her bicycle.

I pulled out my phone and called Donna on the way to my car. When she answered, I said, "Hey, we need you to find a place called Merriman's in Sammamish."

"Uh, okay. You all right?"

"So far. But they took Gretchen somewhere else, and all we have is a name and a vague location." I climbed into the Pathfinder and closed the door, shutting out the wind. "We heard them refer to it as Merriman's. Could be a business, a neighborhood, a warehouse, whatever. And it's located somewhere out past Sammamish. My guess is that it's another building they own. We're heading up there now. Let me know when you've got something."

"Will do," she said and hung up.

"We're going to drive all the way out there without knowing where we're going?" Aria asked.

"You have a better idea?" I replied, looking at her in the rearview mirror. "Hopefully, the twins can find the building and give us the address by the time we get there." I started the car and headed for the freeway. "Blair, can you pull up the fastest way to Sammamish?"

"Sure."

She pulled up the map app on her phone. "It's thirty-five minutes to Sammamish," she said. "But wait." She held the phone close to her face. "She must be talking about Carnation. That's only nine miles northeast of Sammamish."

I chuckled. "Yep. Carnation ice cream. Used to be one of my favorites. I'm surprised Andre is old enough to remember it. Okay, do me a favor and text Donna," I said, handing Blair my phone. "Let her know the building may be in Carnation."

We attempted to devise a plan during the drive, but it was difficult since we had no idea what we'd face when we got there, other than Edgar and maybe the guy called Louie.

"Carnation only has a little over 2,000 residents," Blair said. "And it looks like it's surrounded by forest, with rivers on two sides." She looked up from her phone. "No wonder they take people out there to kill them. There's no one out there."

"Remlinger Farms is out there," I said. "I took Angela there for the Harvest Festival when she was young. It was great. I remember it as being a really pretty town."

"We should probably thank Andre when we see him in court for remembering the name," she said.

We were twenty minutes into the drive when my phone rang. "That might be Donna. Can you answer it?"

Blair swiped on the phone. "Go ahead, we're listening," she said, putting it on speaker.

"It's an old mortuary," Donna said. "We had trouble finding it, because it was owned by their maternal grandfather whose name was Herbert Merriman. He's long gone, and the mortuary hasn't been in operation for over twenty years. But the brothers still own it."

"What's the address?" Blair asked.

Donna gave it to her, and Blair typed it into her phone.

"Anything else you can tell us about it?" I asked.

"It looks like an old home that sits alone on a large piece of property. Apparently it's haunted. We found a couple of newspaper articles on it."

"Wait, it's haunted?" Blair asked.

"Yeah. A bunch of kids broke in there years ago to spend the night on a dare. Not only did they see things move, but they also saw the image of an old man in a three-piece suit. But, you know, you're used to that, right?"

"Careful, ghosts don't like to be made fun of," Blair cautioned.

"Well, don't forget they also cremated bodies there," Donna added. "They used an outdoor incinerator located at the back of the property."

"Okay, thanks," I said. "But can you stand by, just in case? We may need you," I said.

"Absolutely."

"And, Donna, find out if Carnation has a police station. We'll let you know when we get there. If you don't hear from one of us within the next forty-five minutes or so after that, call the police or the King County Sheriff."

The weather remained stubbornly antagonistic as we made our way into Carnation. My windshield wipers were running at top speed, and yet the flood of rain made it almost impossible to see. We nearly floated through downtown, peering out the windows at buildings that looked right out of the 1940s.

"Turn here," Blair said, pointing. "The mortuary is out by the cemetery."

"Of course it is," I said.

We took a couple of side streets until we left the Carnation neighborhoods behind and ended up on a long road heading into the country. The car headlights flashed by a sign for Pleasant Hill Cemetery. A half mile farther on, Blair finally told me to turn onto a private drive between two huge trees. As I turned, an old wooden sign for Merriman's Mortuary loomed out of the darkness. The sign's painted lettering was chipped and faded, and two letters were missing. A smaller sign tacked to the bottom said 'closed.'

"They don't want visitors," Aria said from the back seat.

"Turn off your headlights," Blair said.

"I won't be able to see," I countered.

"Just go slow, then. We don't want them to know we're here."

"Got it."

The entry road curved through tall trees and overgrown shrubbery until we got a glimpse of a weathered, two-story Craftsman-style building. I immediately cut the lights and coasted to a stop.

Two outdoor lights illuminated a set of wide steps leading up to a sagging veranda with an equally sagging overhang. Boarded windows flanked the front door, and a single boarded dormer window accented the roofline of the second floor. A white van was parked under the Porte cochere on the right side of the building.

"I imagine that's where they deliver the bodies," Aria said, pointing to the Porte cochere.

Aria's comment made me think about Gretchen being brought here, and I bile rose to my throat. *She just had to be alive.*

We sat silently for a moment staring at the building.

"Why does this make me think of every horror movie I've ever seen, where the audience is screaming not to go in?" I asked.

"We don't have a choice," Blair said.

"Time to let the twins know we're here."

I texted the twins and our forty-five-minute time limit began.

"I'm going to get a little closer."

I rolled the car slowly forward, emerging from the trees into a large empty parking lot pockmarked with broken asphalt and potholes. The car bounced along, making me cringe, hoping they wouldn't hear us. It was the only time I felt thankful for the howling wind.

I pulled to the right of the building and turned the car around so that it faced out again before cutting the engine.

"Good thinking," Aria said. "Perfect for a fast escape. You should also leave the keys on the ground under your door."

I turned to her. "Why?"

"You know, in case you… become incapacitated or something."

She had a point.

"There's a light on inside under the awning," I said, looking toward French doors.

"Put your comms in," Aria said. "We're gonna have to split up. I'll go in through the front, and you two can go in through the French doors. With the comms, we'll be able to hear each other."

Blair and I reinserted the earpieces.

"You sure we need to split up?" I asked. "Safety in numbers and all that."

"It's a two-story house with maybe a basement, and we don't know where either Edgar or Louie are," she said, handing the receiver to me. "So, two men, in a building we're unfamiliar with…"

"I get it," I replied dispiritedly.

"We should also assume they're armed," she added.

"We are, too," Blair said, patting her purse.

"Yes. But leave the purse behind and tuck the gun into your pants so you can get to it faster," Aria told her.

"What if it falls out?" Blair asked, pulling it out of her purse.

Aria frowned. "Seriously? I'm more worried your pants are so tight you'll bend over and unintentionally shoot yourself in the foot."

"Humph," Blair retorted.

"C'mon. Let's go," I said, anxious to get this done. "He could be torturing her right now."

Blair put her hand on my arm. "She could also be dead by now, Julia. You need to prepare yourself for that."

I sucked in air and then nodded.

"Okay. Do you have your lock picks?" I asked Aria.

"Right here," she said, patting a bag she carried over her shoulder.

"I'm sure Gretchen will be drugged, so if you see a gurney, make a mental note where it is. It may be our only way to get her out."

Aria placed her hand on my shoulder. "Also, if you run into either one of them before I do, split up before they see you, if you can. Better if they think there's only one of you to deal with."

"Good idea," Blair said.

I inhaled a deep, ragged breath. "God, I can't believe we're doing this again. But let's go."

We put up the hoods of our jackets and stepped out into the maelstrom. A gust of wind nearly blew me over as I dropped the keys under the driver's side door. Then the three of us leaned into the wind and moved toward the building.

CHAPTER THIRTY-NINE

An outdoor light at the Porte cochere allowed us to successfully navigate the distance between the car and the building without mishap. A Land Rover sat behind the van. A large, gangly oak tree stood to the right of the overhang, its branches swinging back and forth before the outdoor light as if playing hide and seek. There couldn't have been a worse night to rescue a friend. The only good thing was that the storm would cover any sounds we made—at least until we got into the building.

Aria was just about to head toward the front steps when my nose picked up a smell. I gestured for her to stop.

"Do you smell that? Something's burning!"

She glanced up, her little beady eyes searching the area around us. She wiped rain off her face and then peered into the darkness toward the back of the property.

"They've started the incinerator," she said, pointing that way.

Blair and I moved a couple of feet so that we could see around the Land Rover, and my breath caught. A security light at the back of the building illuminated a brick structure that looked like a giant pizza oven. It was probably fifteen feet high and eight feet wide, with a tarnished brick smokestack and an arched metal door that sat a few feet off the ground.

"Shit," Blair murmured. "We have to hurry."

A figure shrouded in a big coat and hood appeared from the other side of the incinerator carrying an armful of wood. We ducked behind the supporting beam of the awning to watch, while he opened the steel door and threw the wood inside. He closed the door and then disappeared again.

"That must be Louie. C'mon, we gotta go now while he's busy," I said.

Aria nodded and evaporated into the shadows, heading for the front door. Blair and I cautiously approached the French doors. We crept up to a small window cut into the wall near the top of the doors and peeked in. Well, Blair peeked in. I was too short. She gave me a thumbs up. I pulled out one of the small flashlights, opened one door, and stepped inside.

Blair followed me into a cold, musty room with a dirty cement floor and a low ceiling. Only a tiny light secured to a crossbeam near a stairway on our left illuminated the room beyond what my flashlight could provide.

We were standing in the old embalming room.

I quickly swept the room with the beam of light. The brick walls, which had once been painted white, were water-stained and peeling, revealing red brick underneath. Rusty surgical instruments and pans had been left on a nearby counter, carefully laid out as they would have been more than a decade ago. To our right, was a medicine cabinet with cracked glass doors. The shelves held long-abandoned jars and cannisters filled with milky liquids that must have once been embalming supplies. A rusted centrifuge sat on the counter. Directly in front of us was an old white enamel pedestal table attached to the brick wall with a drain positioned above what looked like a long planter box. Sitting on a ledge above the table was a dusty, ancient fan, which must have been the only way to circulate air in the old days. Other than the layers of dust, and a few broken bottles, it looked as if Herbert Merriman had just walked out one day, never to return.

Blair bumped my shoulder and nodded to my right. Just inside the door sat a highly polished, new gurney. A chill rippled down my back.

"C'mon," I whispered.

We turned to our left, heading for the flight of stairs. On our way, we passed a timeworn lift with a metal accordion door probably used to transfer bodies between floors. A small light glinted in the upper corner of the lift, indicating it was most likely in perfect working order and used today to transport victims.

We crept up the stairs, emerging onto the dirty threadbare carpet of a long hallway on the main floor. Two flush-mounted dome fixtures in the ceiling cast a feeble light, illuminating empty beer cans and candy wrappers piled up along the sides of the hallway, probably left over from when the local kids had broken inside. To our left, the corridor led to the front of the building and a small foyer where I glimpsed a shadow move, electrifying my body. Aria's sharp features emerged out of the shadows, and she lifted a finger to her lips and then disappeared to the other side of the foyer.

I had to take a breath to calm myself. Blair hovered behind me and bumped my shoulder to keep going. Soft music was coming from our right, along with a shallow light emanating from around the corner at the end of the hall. I turned in that direction, passing a couple of darkened rooms as we went.

As we got closer, I glanced nervously back at Blair, who pulled the gun from her waistband. When a rat scampered across my foot, I released a short cry, clamping my hand over my mouth too late.

The music stopped.

I scrunched my eyes closed, cursing myself. When I opened them, Blair put her finger to her lips and melted into the shadows of the room across the hall from where I stood.

Split up, Aria had said. Great. Now I was alone.

A moment later, the music resumed again. Whether I was safe or not, I couldn't stop. I resumed my approach and inched my way to where the hallway turned left, and the music grew louder. I'm no fan of classical music, but I know Debussy when I hear it. Having classical music playing in this decrepit old building conjured up too many images where the serial killer happily listened to their favorite composer while hovering over their victim with fanatical glee. It was enough to make me turn around and run.

I inwardly chastised myself for getting distracted, took a deep breath to calm my insides, and forged ahead, turning the corner into a shorter hallway. My nose picked up the sharp smell of solvent. An open door in the middle of the hallway led into a large, well-lit room at the back of the building.

I tiptoed forward and flattened myself against the wall, saying a small prayer before I peeked around the door jam. I allowed my eyes to adjust from the dimly lit hallway to the bright, artificial light of the room. My breath caught as my eyes focused. The undraped body of a woman lay atop a metal table in the center of the room. I pulled my head back and closed my eyes.

God... don't let it be Gretchen.

I glanced around the corner again. It was a big, square room with a bank of paned windows across the entire back wall. The music came from what looked like a restored tabletop, cathedral-style radio in the back corner. Two sets of shelving hung on opposite walls above long, laminate counters, each inset with a cast iron sink. The shelves were filled with cannisters and bottles of various colored Liquids, which looked new. A modern refrigeration unit with glass doors sat to my left. It was filled with small jars containing bits of something floating in clear liquid. I presumed it was human bone and flesh. The table with the body took up the center of the room.

The woman's legs and arms had been peeled like a potato in places, leaving behind the raw underlayer of her skin. My throat burned with acid, and I willed myself not to throw up.

There was no one else there, despite the music, so, after taking a cleansing breath, I approached the table, keeping my eyes focused on the woman's face, praying that it wouldn't be Gretchen. It was an older woman, with long dyed-red hair.

"Thank God," I mumbled, dropping my chin to my chest in relief.

"Don't thank God just yet."

I whirled around to find Edgar Collier standing behind me with a very sharp scalpel in his hand and a self-satisfied grin plastered across his face.

"Gotcha," he said with a leering smile.

Seriously? Why didn't I anticipate that?

"And, no, it's not your friend," he said. "She's still coming out of a drug-induced haze, so I thought I'd get a little work done while I wait to interrogate her." He glanced toward the bank of windows behind me. "And as soon as I'm done, Louie will have the fire at just the right temperature to reduce this body to ashes." He leaned into me, forcing me back against the table with his fetid breath. "And the world will be rid of another blemish on society."

"Careful," a new voice said. "I know how to get rid of blemishes." Blair stood behind Edgar with her gun at his back. "Put the scalpel down. Now."

Edgar dropped the scalpel to the floor.

Thank God for Blair.

"You put the gun down," a male voice said.

Blair froze. I leaned sideways to see around her.

Louie stood behind Blair with a gun of his own. Dammit! If Aria showed up, we'd have a Conga line, which would be funny if it weren't so serious.

Instead, Louie reached around Blair, took her gun, and pushed her forward to stand next to me, our backs against the table with the body on it. Louie stuck Blair's gun into his waistband.

"You women don't give up, do you?" Edgar said with frustration.

"Where's Gretchen?" I demanded.

"She's in the next room," he said with a dismissive wave of his hand. "Just where you'll be going. We'll be done with all of you before the night is over. This is getting too risky."

Blair screamed, "Julia... gun!" and yanked me toward her.

Louie's gun went off, and the bullet whizzed past my left arm, embedding itself in the corpse's shoulder with a dull thump—a sound I was sure I'd never get used to.

Louie went rigid and began to vibrate, before collapsing. He whacked his head on the glass doorknob on his way to the floor, the prongs from Aria's taser embedded in his back.

"Really, Aria?" I screamed. "You could have killed me."

Before she could respond, Edgar grabbed me and swung me around to face Aria and Blair with his arm wound tightly around my chest and the scalpel at my throat.

Damn! When did he pick that up?

"I'll slice her neck open," Edgar warned.

This was beginning to feel too much like a comedy routine from an old Carol Burnett show where the Tim Conway character, me, ended up in the same life-threatening position over and over again.

Aria dropped the taser. Good choice. But I swear the grimace on her face scared me, and we were friends. Well, friends might be stretching it. But she was staring at Edgar like a rattlesnake ready to strike. My heart pounded so hard that I felt the vibration all the way to my ears.

"You won't get away with killing all of us," Aria said, her lips drawn tight.

Who was this woman?

She began inching to her right, forcing Edgar to turn his head to the left to follow her. Blair was now behind me.

"Stop moving!" he yelled at Aria.

She stopped.

"How many more innocent people are you going to inject with drugs and then kill?" she asked, glancing at me and then back to Edgar.

Count to three.

Inject! Got it.

"None of your business," Edgar said. "We're cleaning up the streets and helping people who need human tissue."

"You're a monster, and you know it," she said, nearly spitting at him.

Okay, a cobra, not a rattlesnake.

While Aria taunted Edgar, I dropped my right hand to my side, finding my coat pocket where Stanley's syringe was. I reached in and laced my fingers around the tube, careful not to prick myself with the needle. But as I quickly contemplated my next move, I realized I would only be able to stab his thigh. And that wouldn't do the job fast enough to avoid him slitting my throat.

I had to get the syringe to Blair.

A glance to the floor told me Louie was out cold. Edgar's arm was still painfully pressed across my clavicle bones. I looked once more at Aria and purposely shifted my eyes to the left, trying to tell her to move further that way. She hesitated, but then moved a couple more inches, making Edgar turn his head even more to keep her in view.

"Stay where you are," he commanded, twisting to his left.

Aria stopped again. "Don't worry," she said, putting her hands up. "I'm not going anywhere."

While Aria had his attention, I carefully lifted the syringe from my pocket and pushed it behind me into Blair's hand. She grasped it, while I began to pray.

"Get back over there," Edgar ordered, yanking his head to the right "Or your little friend here will die."

I didn't think insulting my size was necessary, but I wasn't in a position to object. As Aria moved back to the right, and Edgar turned to follow her, the soft sounds of Debussy suddenly exploded so loud it hurt my ears.

"What the—?" Edgar exclaimed, the tip of the scalpel still pressing against my neck.

The vintage radio now blared the deafening music loud enough to, well, raise the dead. The radio knob began to spin rapidly, changing stations back and forth from classical, to country, to rock 'n roll in split seconds. Edgar's muscles tightened, making it difficult for me to breathe.

The dial finally stopped on a classical station where the 1812 Overture's grand finale was just beginning to be punctuated by cannon fire. I wasn't sure which ghost had followed us to the mortuary, but thought the music was probably my mother's idea of a joke, since she loved classical music, and I didn't.

But when, one by one, bottles and cannisters began crashing to the floor in perfect rhythm to each burst of the cannons, I thought maybe it was Elizabeth. It was impressive, to say the least. When the fourth bottle hit the floor, Edgar yanked me back toward the door.

"Stop it!" he screamed at the top of his lungs, his voice quivering. "Who's doing that?"

The music abruptly stopped.

The music had elevated the tension in the room, and Edgar was at a breaking point. When a heavy porcelain bottle flew off a shelf and slammed into his shoulder, he jerked around, awkwardly bringing me with him. A second bottle hit the floor and shattered, splashing a thick liquid across the old linoleum tiles. If that wasn't enough, cupboard doors and drawers began opening and slamming shut.

Edgar wheeled around when a tray of instruments scattered across the floor at our feet. Blair jumped to avoid them and hit the gurney. It rolled away, and she landed on the floor, releasing the syringe. It slid under the table.

Edgar saw it and must have known what was in it.

He shoved me away and dove for the syringe, scrambling over Blair trying to get to it. The two of them began a strange sort of wrestling routine, grasping for each other's hands, knocking over a stool as they fought for the syringe. As Edgar bent over trying to get past Blair, I did what any respectable woman in her mid-sixties would do. I leapt onto his back, wrapping my legs around his waist and my arms around his neck.

He grunted loudly and then straightened up and swung me in a circle to dislodge me. The music suddenly came back on with the Flight of the Bumblebee, and I caught flashes of the room pass as he swung me around – Aria going for her taser again – Blair slipping across the floor to get to the syringe – and Louie grabbing Aria's ankle, throwing her into the hallway.

Edgar had finally had enough and slammed me against a counter, knocking the breath out of me. I came off his back and slipped in the gelatinous liquid that covered the floor, doing a cartoonish impersonation of an ice skater, finally going airborne and coming down hard on my bum, with my right hand tucked beneath my hip. I heard a snap and let out a loud cry of pain.

The music stopped, and the room fell eerily silent, until a second roar of pain grabbed everyone's attention.

I whipped my head around to find Aria bent over Louie, her dark eyes filled with a maniacal glee. She had stabbed a cylindrical object through Louie's hand, literally pinning his hand to the floor. When I said before that Aria scared me, I wasn't kidding.

A scuffling sound drew my attention back to Blair. She had finally reached the syringe and was about to grab it, but Edgar had spotted Louie's gun under the cabinet and got to it first. He whipped around and dragged me off the floor, this time by the collar, and wrapped his arm around my neck, banging my wrist with his hand in the process.

I yowled in pain.

"Stop! All of you!" he screamed.

As I hung in front of him, held up only by his arm around my neck, I thought this might finally be it. Aria and Blair had frozen in place, staring at him, and breathing hard. Their hair was askew, coats were torn open, and Blair had some sort of goo spread across her chin and chest.

Edgar used the gun to encourage Aria to move in front of him, while Blair got to her hands and knees and then stood up at the far end of the gurney, holding her right hand slightly behind her hip.

"Get over here," Edgar ordered her.

She moved up next to Aria, while Louie groaned, struggling to get his hand unstuck from the floor. He couldn't. I almost felt sorry for him. No, I didn't.

If I thought the night couldn't get any stranger, a light breeze whispered past my ear drawing out the name, "Edgarrrr."

Edgar jerked, and the hair on my arms stood up because it was a man's voice.

How would Elizabeth achieve that?

Once again, Edgar whipped around, following the sound. Every time he moved, I groaned at the pain in my wrist.

"Edgarrr," the voice whispered again. "There will be consequencezzzzz. There are always consequencezzzzz."

"Who are you?" Edgar yelled, making a full turn.

He paused, his head whipping back and forth trying to pinpoint the source of the voice. We had stopped and were now facing a mirror above one of the sinks. The voice blew through the room again like a summer breeze.

"Mother would be sooooooo disappointed."

"No!" Edgar screamed. "It was all Stan's idea. It's always been Stan."

A deep chuckle emanated from somewhere, which raised the hair on my arms. When the hazy image of a tall, gaunt man with thick, gray hair, dressed in a three-piece suit appeared in the mirror behind us, Edgar sucked in a breath and turned around to face it.

"Grandad," he said, his voice quivering. "It's not what you think."

The image floated about three feet away, its sunken eyes staring intently at Edgar.

"We're only trying to do right by you and dad," he blubbered.

While Edgar was focused on what he thought was his grandfather, Herbert Merriman, Blair's arm appeared suddenly over his left shoulder. She pushed the gun away with a snap of her wrist, and then Edgar gasped. He staggered before collapsing to the floor, releasing me as he fell.

The ghostly image faded immediately.

"Get the other gun," Blair told Aria.

Freed, I stumbled away and turned to see the empty syringe sticking out of Edgar's neck. Blair had depressed the plunger all the way. I swallowed hard. He was dying. As the faint odor of Old Spice aftershave wafted past my nose, I realized the truth.

It hadn't been Elizabeth but Edgar's grandfather.

I gazed into Edgar's eyes as he slowly slipped away, wondering why I didn't feel anything at his passing.

Meanwhile, Aria retrieved the gun from Louie's waistband but left him pinned to the floor. Blair grabbed the one still clutched in Edgar's hand. I watched them, feeling like I was having an out-of-body experience. I just stood there, dumbly shifting my gaze from place to place in the room.

"Julia," Blair said, stepping away from Edgar.

"Huh?" I responded, dimly waiting for my head to clear.

She pointed to my throat. "You're bleeding."

I reached up and ran the fingers of my left hand along my neck, wincing when I encountered something warm and wet. Edgar's scalpel had nicked me during the melee, and I hadn't even felt it.

"Here, let me dab it away," she said, grabbing a cotton pad from one of the counters. She wiped the blood off. "How's your wrist?"

I glanced down to where I balanced my throbbing right wrist on the open palm of my left hand. When my brain re-engaged, I said, "Um, broken, I think. But I'm okay." I inhaled a deep breath, shook my head, and said, "We need to find Gretchen."

She nodded. "Okay. You good here?" she asked Aria, taking control.

Aria nodded, swiped her left hand across her face, leaving a trail of dirt or possibly Louie's blood behind, and then moved in between the two men on the floor. I didn't think Edgar needed guarding, but Louie did.

I led Blair into the hallway, still cradling my arm. We hadn't passed a likely room on our way in, so I turned to my right. At the end of the short hall was another door with a padlock on it.

"This has to be it. Can you get Aria's lock picks?"

Blair disappeared. A moment later, Aria replaced her.

"Here, let me," she said. She knelt down and fished something out of her bag that looked like a dental tool. With a few twists and turns, the padlock dropped to the floor. She pushed open the door, and we stepped into a darkened room with an overwhelming smell of urine and feces. April's vision. Aria flicked on the light.

"Oh, my God," I said, releasing a breath.

The room was empty except for three women chained to the walls, sitting in their own filth. One of them was Gretchen.

CHAPTER FORTY

Before we had time to call the authorities or even release the imprisoned women, red and blue lights flashed across the trees outside. I silently thanked Donna and Dierdre.

"Have we been here forty-five minutes?" Aria asked, glancing out the window. "Guess time flies when you're having fun."

I wasn't sure I'd describe what we'd just gone through as fun, but I had a feeling Aria lived for this stuff. A part of me was glad we'd given her a chance to use her weekend training.

Within a matter of minutes, two county sheriff officers thumped down the hallway. A female officer appeared at the door where Aria and I were, while the other, I assumed, went into the room where Louie and Edgar were being watched over by Blair.

"What's going on here?" the officer asked as she stepped into the room with her gun drawn. Her eyes opened wide at both the sight of three women chained to the wall and the smell. She immediately pulled her radio off her shoulder and called for reinforcements.

The next half hour was a blur of uniformed officers and EMTs taking charge of the scene. With some effort, an officer pulled out whatever Aria had used to pin Louie's hand to the floor, releasing him. The EMTs bandaged his hand before he was taken into custody and then to a hospital.

A second and third ambulance arrived to take care of the abducted women. I tried to speak to Gretchen, but all she could do was grab my hand before she was loaded onto a gurney and whisked away. By the time the deputy sheriff arrived to question us, an EMT insisted I also be taken to the hospital to care for my broken wrist.

There were no more available ambulances, so Aria, Blair, and I climbed into a sheriff's car just as the medical examiner arrived for Edgar.

We were taken to a small, community hospital in Issaquah. Once there, the sheriff separately interviewed Aria and Blair, while I had my wrist X-rayed, the bones set, and put into a cast. When that was done, Sheriff's Deputy Philip Constantine came in to interview me.

He was a short, burly man who I could tell did not suffer fools gladly. His demeanor was all business, and when I mentioned that the FBI was involved in this complex case, he let me know I could name-drop all I wanted, but he was going to do this by the book.

I attempted to tell the entire story, but he kept interrupting me to ask questions, largely focusing on things like how we'd come into possession of two guns, a taser, the thing used to pin Louie to the floor, and a lethal dose of whatever it was that had killed Edgar.

I couldn't speak to Aria's weapon, or what the syringe had held, but explained the rest of it to the best of my ability, leaving out the performances by Mr. Robbins or Herbert Merriman. I didn't think that would add to my credibility; I could only hope that Blair and Aria had done likewise.

Finally, he allowed me to join the others.

My energy had begun to flag, and I had trouble keeping my eyes open. The adrenaline that had helped to keep me alive had worn off, and they'd given me pain medication for my wrist. I was about to say something to that effect when David and Sean walked into the room. Suddenly, I was on my feet, throwing myself into David's arms. Fortunately, he ducked just in time to avoid me hitting him in the face with the cast.

Sean gestured to the deputy sheriff to join him in the hallway, while David squeezed me in a bear hug.

"God, Julia. Are you okay?" he asked, releasing me. Before I could answer, he noticed the Band-Aid on my neck and then my wrist. "Oh, Julia, what happened?" He gently touched the bandage and then cradled my broken wrist in his hand.

"I broke my wrist," I said, my voice quivering slightly. "And Edgar Collier threatened to kill me with a scalpel and then a gun. But Blair took care of him," I said, glancing at her.

Blair was unusually quiet and sat staring at the floor.

"I heard about that," David said. "We were briefed on the drive out here. You killed someone this time, Julia," he said soberly.

"No, I killed someone," Blair said, looking up with teary eyes. "Because he was going to kill Julia. I couldn't let that happen."

Her hands were trembling, and she clasped them in front of her. To my surprise, Aria put her arm around Blair's shoulders.

"That man was a monster," Aria said, coming to Blair's defense. "I'm sure the poor woman on the table in that horrid room would attest to that if she could, along with the three women who were chained to the wall."

David's expression softened as he glanced from Aria and back down to Blair. She was staring at the floor again, sitting tensely in a straight-backed chair. Since Blair would normally be the one jumping in to tell the story with enthusiasm, I was worried about her.

"I get it," David said. "You did what you had to do. They've already identified the women you saved. Besides your friend Gretchen, Ileana Banks and Rose Marie Elmhurst were also in that room. They believe the woman on the table was someone called the Madame. She was another homeless woman."

"Emma told us about her," I said, sadly. "But wait! How are Ben and José?"

He smiled. "They're both fine, although a little worse for wear, from what I hear. They told Sergeant Odell and Agent Glass that a group of gang bangers attacked José, while Ben was diverted to another location. We think that diversion was Andre. Anyway, when Ben figured it out, he hurried back to help José, who was surrounded by about six guys with broken bottles and bats."

"You're kidding?"

"No. But they also told a wild story about exploding streetlamps, spinning trash cans, and small tornadoes in the midst of the fight, which disabled some of the bangers. All of that can be explained by the storm, I suppose, but I guess it was a crazy ride before the cavalry got there."

I smiled, thinking that crazy ride was probably Chloe and maybe my mother, although how she could be in two places at once, I wasn't sure.

When Sean returned, he said, "I've filled Deputy Sheriff Constantine in on the investigation and what brought you to the mortuary. For now, you are free to go. But the Sheriff's Office wants you ladies in their headquarters in Sammamish within the next day or two to go over what happened."

Music to my ears. All I wanted to do was to go home, take a shower, and curl up with my favorite guy. With that thought in my head, I allowed a nurse to put me in a wheelchair and David to wheel me out to his car.

"We'll get your car in the morning," he said. "And I called April to let her know you're okay."

"Thanks. But what about Blair and Aria?"

"They'll ride back with Sean."

When we got back to the Inn, April flew out from behind the reception desk where she'd been waiting and grabbed me in a bear hug. Not the best move.

"April," I squeezed out. "You're pressing against my arm."

"Oh. Oh," she said, releasing me. "I'm so sorry." She patted my cast, which was held up by a sling. "How are you? I heard that monster cut your neck. And how's Gretchen? She's so lucky you went after her, I…"

I put my fingers to her lips. "Shhh. Everything's fine. But I have to sleep now."

"Of course," she said. "Do you need anything? I just finished a batch of…"

"I'll take care of her," David cut in, turning me towards my apartment. "She's exhausted. Let me get her situated, and I'll come back and tell you what else I know."

David steered me to my apartment. Inside, Minnie and Wilson both launched themselves at me, whining and crying. David helped get me into bed, with Minnie tucked in next to me. He kissed my forehead, turned out the light, and closed my door.

My heart swelled. *I was home.*

While our rescue hadn't gone the way I'd anticipated, we'd been successful once again. I was only glad that Gretchen would be okay, although certainly traumatized.

Eventually, sleep overtook me. My dreams were a jumbled mess of corpses walking on legs made out of PVC pipe; Maleficent and her big-ass hat chasing Blair and yelling that she was the fairest of them all; and a group of ghosts converging on Edgar Collier before forcing him into an open grave. When Mr. Robbins' soulless eyes zeroed in on me, I woke up.

CHAPTER FORTY-ONE

The next morning, David was helping me get dressed, when I received a text from Gretchen. I read it out loud.

I'm so sorry to have put you and your friends in such danger, but I never doubted you would rescue me. Just know that if you ever need help from me for anything, I'll be there for you. You have my sincere thanks and are one hell of a woman.

I stared at the text for a moment, feeling overwhelmed.

"I'll get breakfast going," David said, recognizing that I needed a moment.

When I'd calmed my emotions, I sent Gretchen a short reply and finished buttoning my blouse awkwardly on my own. When I joined David in the kitchen, he was flipping pancakes like a chef at Denny's.

"Hungry?" he asked.

"Starving."

"Hand-to-hand combat will do that to you," he said with a little smirk.

I used my good hand to slap his shoulder. "Very funny." I reached around him to grab a piece of bacon. As I munched, I said, "I haven't heard from either Ben or José. I hope they're okay."

As if the gods were listening, my phone rang. Instead of Ben or José, though, it was Angela.

"Hello, honey," I said.

"Hey, Mom. How are you? I heard about last night."

"I'm fine. My wrist throbs, but I'm mostly tired. Have you talked with Sean?"

"Yes. And he told me that the police will be dropping all charges against Rudy."

I flopped into one of the chairs at my small dining table. "Finally. She's free of all of this."

"Yeah. You did good, Mom. Sean also told me that all three women you rescued will be okay, although they're keeping them in the hospital for another day until the drugs are out of their systems. And Louie, the guy who got pinned to the floor, will never have full use of his hand again."

"I doubt Aria will care, but I'll let her know. What about Stanley?"

"I guess he's in some kind of fugue state. I don't know what he saw last night, but he's off in some alternate universe."

"I'll tell you about it sometime," I said quietly, glancing up at David's back.

"Well, Sean said it will take a couple of days to process both the funeral home and the mortuary. Plus, they have a forensic accountant going through the Colliers' books. But he'd like to get you all together in the next day or so to debrief."

"We can do that."

"I'm just glad you're okay, Mom. You know, every time you end up fighting off the bad guys, it shortens your potential lifespan. I kind of wish you'd just do regular senior citizen stuff, you know, like gardening. I'd sort of like to keep you around for a while."

I had a chance to chat with the twins before they checked out around lunch time.

"That was impressive," Dierdre said.

"Ditto," Donna added. "You saved those women's lives."

"Yeah, it felt good," I said. "I hope we'll see you two again someday. Maybe you'll come for a vacation."

"Absolutely," Donna said.

"And you have our card," Dierdre said. "I have a feeling you may need us again."

"Just call us," Donna said. "After all, we're a part of the team now. You said."

"I did. And you are."

"I love it when a plan comes together," Ahab squawked behind us.

The three of us laughed and then hugged before they left.

A short time later, José stopped by the registration desk. I was in the office attempting to work at the computer with one hand.

"Hey, Miz Applegate," he said.

I rushed out of the office and around the corner to throw one arm around him and kiss him on the cheek.

"I'm so glad you're okay. Ben texted me earlier to say he was fine and that you not only can hold your own in a fight but that you're pretty damned good."

He had cuts and bruises on his face, a split lip, and two fingers in a splint.

"He's not so bad, either."

"Well, Wilson's waiting for you in my apartment," I said. "He needs you now, you know."

I had never known José to cry, but tears formed in the corner of those dark, sexy eyes.

"It's just not fair, Miz Applegate. Ross didn't deserve to die. He was just hoping for a job."

"None of those people deserved to die. But you were a good friend to Ross. In fact, it's what put you on the kidnappers' radar, in case you didn't know."

"I figured," he said, wiping his eyes.

"So… can you keep a dog at your apartment?"

"Yeah. But he'd be alone a lot, cuz I'm either here or at school."

I smiled. "You can bring him to the Inn whenever you're here. He's very well behaved, and he's part of the family now."

"Thanks, Miz Applegate."

I squeezed his arm. "Thank you for helping. Really. It's good to know I have more than just dead people I can count on."

He laughed as I handed him the key to my apartment. He left to get Wilson.

The girls and I had made plans for a glass of wine at 5:00 in the breakfast room of the Inn. I'd also invited April and Aria. The Inn was quiet. Most of the guests were out for dinner, including the demon girls. We spent most of the time filling Rudy in on all the particulars about the previous evening and re-living how close we'd come to regretting our adventure. Blair was quiet much of the time. I suspected she was still dealing with the fact she'd taken someone's life.

At one point, April disappeared into the kitchen, and I followed her.

"Hey, I was just wondering what you thought about hiring some extra help," I said to her.

She turned from pulling another bottle of wine from the refrigerator.

"What kind of help?"

"Well, since Libby died, you, me, and Crystal have picked up the extra cleaning and laundry. What if we hired a housekeeper? That way, you could bake things for sale again. And Crystal deserves a promotion. Maybe Desk Manager."

Her eyes grew wide. "She'd love that. And she does deserve it. Can we afford it?"

"Absolutely. We're basically booked for the next year and a half."

She nodded. "I think it's a great idea. Do you have anyone in mind?"

"I do. I met her at the shelter. She might drive you crazy with her gum popping, but I have a feeling she'll be a good addition."

April decided to retire to the guest house, while I swung through the kitchen door with the second bottle of wine. Aria pulled me aside.

"I have something for you." She held out a small, slender box tied with a bow. "Kind of a get well present… for your wrist and all."

"You didn't have to do that," I said.

I took my arm out of the sling to open the box. Inside was a gun metal, cylinder-shaped object with a very sharp tip. My eyes opened wide. It was the same tool she had used to pin Louie's hand to the floor.

"Uh, a nice card would have sufficed," I said.

"But this is made from aircraft aluminum," Aria said with pride. She lifted it out of the box. "It's called an Attack Pen Pro, and it's designed for a strong forward and reverse grip," she said, demonstrating, making me take a step back. "You can do everything from breaking glass with it to actually…"

"Stabbing someone," I said, finishing her sentence. "Yeah, I know."

"Right. Well, I carry one with me at all times," she said, patting a pocket in her shoulder bag. She put the weapon back in the box. "I thought maybe you'd like to carry one, too. Comes in handy, you know?"

I smiled. "Thanks, Aria. That's sweet, and I'll consider it. Listen, we couldn't have done this without you. You were... well, terrific. Thank you."

It was an awkward moment, and she seemed to hang there without saying anything before curtly nodding and saying goodbye. Not one for sentiment, I guess.

I felt a hand on my shoulder and turned to find Rudy. "Are you okay?" she asked, nodding to the cast.

"Yes, I am. They said six weeks tops in the cast. So, that's not so bad. Hey, wait." I went to the reception desk and grabbed a Sharpie. "Want to be the first one to sign it?"

The serious expression on her face lifted, and she smiled. "Sure." She took the marking pen and signed her name, drawing a small heart next to it. "By the way, Brenda told me that she'd hire all of us in a minute at the law firm."

My eyes showed my surprise. "Well, that's a compliment. You know why we didn't take you with us, right?"

She dropped her chin. "Because I couldn't be trusted."

"That's part of it," I said quietly. "But I also didn't want you anywhere near a situation that could put you in more legal jeopardy. But I'm the first to say that we missed you."

"We did miss you," Blair said, as we moved toward the table.

"I know," Rudy said. "But Julia's right. I would have been a liability. Things haven't been right with me lately. And you all know it."

"Well, come sit down again," Blair said.

As we were settled around the table again, Doe asked, "What did Aria give you?"

I held out the pen. "She gave an Attack Pen Pro. Apparently, something every woman should carry with her," I said, laughing.

"Isn't that what she..."

"Yes. It's what she used to pin Louie's hand to the floor," I answered Blair. "She thought I might want one."

"Seems like Julia has acquired a new best friend," Rudy said with a smile.

Doe grabbed Rudy's hand and said, "God, we've missed you."

"Hear, hear," Blair said.

Rudy's mood lifted, and color returned to her cheeks. She snuck a glance at me, and I gave her an encouraging nod. She took a deep breath and said, "Listen, I have something to tell you guys, and I hope you won't be mad at me, but..."

Rudy went on to explain how she'd gotten hooked on Oxycontin, how she'd almost gone broke in the process. If Rudy thought Blair and Doe would be mad or ashamed of her, or even judge her, she was wrong.

"I suspected something like that," Blair said. "I got hooked on diet pills back in the '80s, and I recognized some of the signs."

"You did? I didn't know," Doe said in surprise.

"None of you did. It's not something I talk about. But it can happen to anyone. We have your back, Rudy. You won't have to go through this alone."

Tears formed in Rudy's eyes. "You guys are the best. I don't know what I'd do without you."

"That goes both ways," Doe said, squeezing her hand again. "Don't ever forget that."

"Hey, listen you guys, I've been thinking of volunteering again," I said. "Remember, I volunteered at that domestic violence shelter until all that stuff happened last year with the sex trafficking ring. Doing the resume clinics at Wings of Hope made me realize how much I miss it." I switched my gaze to Blair. "What do you think? Maybe we could do the makeover clinics together."

Her blue eyes flashed, and tears suddenly glistened.

"I'd love that. You know, I may have seemed a bit cold-hearted when we started all of this. I mean, to be honest I was one of those people who would look at the guy holding a sign asking for money at the stoplight thinking, 'Well, yeah, if I give you money, you're just going to go drink it.' I didn't realize—" she stopped and took a deep breath. "Let me rephrase that. I didn't stop to think that these were real people, with real struggles, who just didn't either have the skills or resources to help themselves out. I hate what Stanley and Edgar Collier did to them," she said, wiping her eyes. "The woman on that gurney last night deserved more. Rose Marie deserved more. Ileana and certainly Gretchen deserved more." She paused. "I killed someone," she said, tears flowing freely now down her face. "But I'd do it again in a heartbeat to save you, Julia... or any one of the people those bastards took. So, yeah I'm in for the clinics."

"Okay, but I'll have to come up with something I can do," I said, turning to Rudy. "Won't you take over your resume clinics again?"

"Yes. After I get myself together. But you could work with the women teaching etiquette skills, while Blair does hair and makeup," Rudy said.

"I don't know about that," I replied shyly.

"Sure, you could," Doe spoke up. "These days, etiquette is more than knowing which fork to use when you're out for dinner. It's how to be gracious, how to project self-confidence…"

"How to stand up for yourself without being pushy," Rudy added. "You can do that in spades."

I smiled. "Yes, because we all know how gracefully I stand up for myself after I fall flat on my face."

Doe leaned forward smiling. "Julia, if you didn't occasionally do a pratfall, you wouldn't be you."

I glanced at Doe. "Okay. But how about you? Would you volunteer?"

She put her hand up. "I just don't have the bandwidth. But I've done something else. I was going to save this for maybe a celebratory dinner, but here…" She reached into that big bag of hers and pulled out an envelope and handed it to Rudy.

"What's this?" Rudy asked.

"Just open it, and read it out loud," Doe said.

Rudy opened the envelope, which was addressed to Doe from Wings of Hope. She pulled out a sheet of paper and unfolded it, skimming the beginning silently. Her eyes popped open wide.

"Doe! That's an enormous amount of money. Can you afford it? I mean, I know you're trying to get that new contract."

Doe smiled demurely. "It is a big donation. But since we're sharing all sorts of personal information this afternoon, here's something you don't know about me. While my husband and I built the company together, I came into the marriage with a trust fund."

The three of us responded with a surprise lift to our eyebrows.

"My grandfather," she continued, "was a highly successful dentist here in the Seattle area. In fact, he invented one of the early versions of the dental implant and made a ton of money from it. He set up trust funds for his two grandchildren, namely me and my sister."

"How come you've never said anything?" I asked.

"Because I never wanted it to change the way you saw me. I make a good living through the company and my investments. To be honest, I rarely use the trust fund and then only for donations like this." She nodded to Rudy. "You need to keep reading."

Rudy turned to the letter again and read it out loud. "'Your generous donation will be used to help so many women trying desperately to forge a new path in life. In return for a donation this size, we'd like to name the recreation room in memory of Romaine Garza—'" Rudy stopped, choking on a sob, almost not getting out Romaine's last name.

Blair was sitting next to her and put a hand on her shoulder. "Just suck it up and keep going."

Rudy took a deep breath, wiped her face, and kept reading. "'Romaine loved that room,'" Rudy read in a shaky voice. "That's because it looks out on our garden, where we would often find her putzing around, weeding or fertilizing our flowers when she was here. She would be very proud of this donation and naming the room after her. Thank you from the bottom of my heart. It's signed by Gloria." Rudy looked up at Doe. "Thank you, Doe. I can't tell you how much I appreciate this."

"Well, Gloria said they'll have a nice plaque up by the end of the week. Maybe we could hold Romaine's memorial service there and celebrate the naming of the room at the same time.'

"Brilliant," Blair said with a beaming smile.

"So, we all played a part," I said, wistfully. "Remember what Emma said... it was Romaine's death that got the rest of us involved to stop what was happening." I turned to Rudy. "We couldn't have done it without her, you know?"

"I know," Rudy said, still teary-eyed. "And now she'll get the recognition she deserves."

I put out my hand. "One for all?"

"And all for one," they said simultaneously, slapping their hands over mine.

"No matter what," Rudy said.

CHAPTER FORTY-TWO

After they left, I grabbed a brownie from April's stash and went back to my living room and plopped into my recliner with a glass of Pepsi feeling exhausted but with a tremendous sense of pride for having saved Gretchen, Ileana, and Rose Marie. What grated on me most was that the Colliers had so little respect for life itself. To them, the homeless population represented nothing more than a resource to be mined. Like gold, oil, or water, human flesh and bone had become a commodity to buy and sell.

When I stifled a yawn, I realized I needed to stop ruminating on things and just rest. I was still on pain medication and began to doze off when my phone rang. Because the screen read 'unknown caller,' I immediately felt the acid in my stomach sour and sat forward.

I thumbed on the phone. Before I could even say hello, my mother barked, "Julia! What's going on?"

I sighed. "Nothing, Mom. It's all over. We've solved the murder, and the bad guys are in jail. In fact, one of them is dead. I thought you'd know that."

"It's not like I'm notified every time someone crosses over. But good. I'm glad things turned out okay. I'm telling you, though, I still see something big coming your way."

"What?"

I was too tired to figure out any ghost puzzles at the moment.

"I got the distinct impression that your life is about to change in some big way."

My mother had always been right, so I thought I probably shouldn't dismiss her. I sucked it up and asked, "Okay, but in what way?"

"I don't know. I saw a tornado or something and then a sunrise. I have no idea what that means..."

"We just had a big storm, and Chloe already did her whirlwind thing to help save José. But it's all over now. I was just talking about it earlier to Angie. Maybe that's what you were sensing."

"Maybe. But you're okay?"

"I did break my wrist," I said, glancing at the cast.

"Oh, did you fall on your face again?"

I sighed. "No, Mom. A serial killer slammed me into a wall, thank you very much."

"Sorry. You have to admit you've always been a bit clumsy."

"You don't have to remind me."

"All right, then. I'd better go."

"You could stay and talk, you know. I do like hearing from you."

"It's not like that. I'm not supposed to be calling you to chat about things. Actually, I'm not supposed to be calling you at all."

"I know. I just thought… it's just good to hear from you. Even if it's only to warn me."

"I miss you, too, Button. Take care. And I'm sorry about your wrist."

She hung up, and once again, I felt a pang of deep sadness that she was gone. In life, she'd been a challenge. Obstinate. Opinionated. Sometimes rude. And yet, I felt a fierce gratitude for the life she'd given me. I patted Minnie on the butt.

"It's just you and me tonight, little girl. David said he has to work late tying up loose ends. I sure miss Mickey, though. He'd be spinning in circles about now," I said with a smile. "You know, since we're surrounded by ghosts, maybe Mickey will come back to visit us sometime. I'd like that."

After an hour's nap, I was in my kitchen searching through the freezer to find something quick for dinner, when I got a text from David saying he was at the front desk. I marched into the hallway with Minnie close behind.

"What are you doing here? I thought I wouldn't see you until late."

He was in the foyer with April by his side. She was grinning like a drunken sailor.

"Okay, what's going on?"

David was carrying a box and set it on the floor. "We have a present for you."

"We?"

He glanced at April. "We conferred about it."

"We think it's something you need," she added.

"Like a new toaster? Cuz mine is pretty old."

"No," she replied. "Not a toaster."

I crinkled my brows. "It's not my birthday, and Christmas is still weeks away."

The two bratty girls suddenly burst through the front door and raced into our breakfast room, giggling, and screaming. I had grown very tired of them. But watching them made me wonder if my mother had been talking about them. Every time I saw them, it felt like a tornado had just blown through the room.

"Darn it," April said, frowning. "Those girls drive me nuts," she said.

"What were you saying about a present?" I asked, my gaze drifting to the box on the floor.

David put his hands on my shoulders and gazed deep into my eyes. "I know how much you miss Mickey. After all, you had him for almost fifteen years. So, I got you something soft and cuddly to take his place."

"You got me a stuffed animal?" I said with a laugh.

The box at my feet moved, and I stepped back, staring at it.

"Well, not exactly a stuffed animal," April said.

The corners of the box suddenly burst open, and a fuzzy, black-and-cream face with a long snout and fluffy ears popped out.

"Oh, my God!" I exclaimed, throwing my free hand to my mouth. I looked at David. "You didn't."

His grin widened. "I guess I did."

I leaned down to try and pick up the puppy when it wiggled its way out of the box wearing a giant pink bow.

"Oh, my God, it's a miniature Dachshund!"

"Long-haired," April said with a stupid grin.

"She's six months old," David said. "I got her from a shelter; they'd gotten her from a breeder who couldn't sell her because she has a slight deformity in her left back leg. But she gets around fine."

Minnie took one look at the puppy and started barking at it. Instead of being afraid, the puppy barked right back.

The three of us laughed.

"She's just adorable," I said, my heart swelling.

"Aaaargh!" the two girls screamed, racing past us again, down the hallway and into the library.

The puppy whipped around and ran after them on her short, little legs, letting out high-pitched yaps. Minnie took off after her, barking loudly.

"Oh, dear," I said, hurrying after them.

When the two girls realized there were two dogs chasing them, they made a U-turn and barreled out of the library again, nearly knocking me over as they headed back down the hallway and up the stairs. The dogs did a 180 to chase after them, but David scooped up the puppy as she raced past. Minnie chased the girls halfway up the stairs and then stopped, looking back at me.

"She's a handful," I said, as the puppy squirmed in David's arms.

"Yes, she is," he said, as she wiggled to get free.

April said, "Excuse me, while I have a word with those two girls." She turned and headed up the stairs.

I stopped her. "Thank you so very much, April. Actually, for everything."

She smiled. "No need for thanks. Besides, it was mostly David. He just asked for my opinion."

We took the dogs to my apartment, where we could let them get to know each other. As David set the puppy onto the living room carpet, she cowered until Minnie came over and began licking her face. She had a fat belly and short, squat legs with big feet. She was mostly black, with cream-colored paws, a lion's mane of cream-colored fur on her chest, and two matching cream eyebrows. She made me think of Mickey. I leaned over to pet her with my good hand.

"I can see that she favors that back leg a little," I said, watching her begin to play with Minnie. "Are you sure she's sound?"

"I took her to a vet. That's actually where I was this afternoon. Apparently, her leg got twisted in the womb, but the vet says she's not in any pain, and she's not hampered by it in any way."

As I watched the two dogs begin to wrestle with each other, growling and biting at each other, a knot grew in my throat at the thought of losing Mickey.

"Oh, David, she's just perfect," I said. "You don't know what this means to me."

"What will you name her?"

I glanced over to where the two dogs had begun to play. The puppy was rolling on her back, punching Minnie in the chin, while Minnie pretended to attack her by pinning her down with a front paw and warning her with a velociraptor-sounding growl.

"I don't know. I'd like it to be meaningful. I named Mickey and Minnie because of an especially memorable trip to Disneyland that Graham and I took one year when Angela was little."

"Well, your favorite movie is Wizard of Oz," David said, glancing over to one of my movie posters. "How about a character from that?"

I studied the poster. In it, Dorothy, the Tin Man, the Cowardly Lion, and the Scarecrow, were dancing down the yellow brick road, while the witch in her black hat hovered in the background. Toto was Dorothy's constant companion, but I couldn't bring myself to name one of my dogs Toto.

"I'm just not sure any of those would fit. My all-time favorite character has always been the Wicked Witch of the West. Margaret Hamilton played her in the movie. She was brilliant, by the way. But I can't call her Margaret. I mean, that would just be, oh, wait… what about Maggie?" I turned to David; my eyes opened wide. "What about Minnie and Maggie?"

He grinned. "I think it's perfect. By the way, there's something else tied around her neck. You should check her bow."

My brows furrowed. "I didn't see anything else."

He got up and grabbed the puppy before it scooted away and put her into my lap.

"Pull the bow off," he said, a smile picking up the corners of his mouth.

I pulled one end of the big bow to unravel it. Tied to her collar was a strand of curling ribbon the same color. At the end of that was a beautiful gold ring with two diamonds on either side of a fire opal.

My mouth dropped open in shock as I gazed up at him. Before we could say anything, Minnie barked and lunged at the newly named Maggie, and the puppy scrambled off my lap to begin chasing Minnie around the living room.

"Wait a minute," I yelled. "Bring back that ring!"

David tried to catch her, but the two dogs got going faster and faster, zooming around the furniture, in and out of the kitchen, down the hallway at top speed, and back into the living room doing turbo-charged U-turns to do it all over again.

David kept trying to catch Maggie but kept missing her. I was laughing so hard I had tears in my eyes... until... crash, bang!

"Oh, no," I screamed, jumping up.

They'd smashed into a plant stand in the corner of the living room, sending the plant to the floor. The ceramic pot broke into pieces, causing the dirt to spill out onto the carpet.

The dogs stopped short, and Minnie looked at me as if she knew she was in trouble. She immediately went to her bed and lay down. Maggie, on the other hand, just sat down panting as if she'd just had the best time of her life.

David chuckled. "Sorry. I guess Chloe's not the only tornado around here anymore. I'll get the vacuum."

"Wait a minute, Mister," I said, standing up and grabbing him. I pulled him toward me. "Don't you have something to say to me first?"

He grinned. "I suppose I do." He dropped down to one knee on the dirty carpet as my heart soared. He grabbed my good hand and said, "Julia Applegate, I know you're mine. But now... will you be my wife?"

Tears blurred my eyes as I pulled him back to a standing position and said, "In a heartbeat."

We shared a lingering kiss before I released him to get the vacuum. But his comment about the tornado rang in my ears as he left the room.

"Tornado," I said under my breath. I smiled and shook my head. "God, Mom. When you're right, you're right. A little tornado did just blow into my life."

Maggie suddenly flopped down on her side, her fat belly huffing and puffing from the exertion. I leaned down and untied the ring from her collar. Then, I glanced toward the ceiling, as if I could see through it to heaven.

"You called it, Mom, when you said something big was coming my way." I glanced at the puppy and then at the engagement ring in my hand. "It was a little whirlwind named Maggie, and the man of my dreams. I think it's a perfect combination."

THE END

YOUR REVIEW IS IMPORTANT

Thank you for reading *No Place Like Home for a Murder*. It was a joy to write. If you enjoyed it, please honor me with an honest review. Go back to Amazon and scroll down to the review bars on the lefthand side of the page and click on 'Write a customer review.' Self-published authors live and die on the number of reviews our books receive – good or bad.

ACKNOWLEDGEMENTS

If anyone believes that authoring multiple books in a series gets easier with each book, it doesn't. It seems I need a growing list of people with expertise and skills I don't have to help me flesh out these stories. I am eternally grateful for all the help I receive and the true spirit of cooperation as I craft these storylines.

The first group I present the stories to is my critique group, who I have been with for over ten years. They methodically read each book two chapters at a time over a period of ten months (sometimes more) and help to clarify the storyline and characters, challenge me on specific details, eliminate things that just don't work, and highlight internal 'gems' I didn't even know I had. As always, I give special thanks to Tim McDaniel, Michael Manzer, Gary Larson, and Irma Fritz.

This time around, I needed to research funeral homes and crematoriums. I'm grateful for my friend Dawn Crowley for information on funeral homes and her friend Bonnie Chance who shared her experience about being homeless and the 'white van' who people feared in San Francisco.

I also rely on a group of advanced readers to give me honest feedback. They volunteer to read the book from cover-to-cover to not only catch mistakes but identify inconsistencies in the storyline or things that just don't make sense. This time around my thanks go to Karen Gilb, Rex Caldwell, Chris Spahn, Ann Joyce, Deborah Caldwell, Sophie Lechner, Melissa Gehrig, and my daughter, Jaynee Bohart. I have a special shoutout for Rex Caldwell, who is my go-to expert on all things related to police matters, and Melissa Gehrig, Executive Director of Vision House. I mention Vision House in the book, and Melissa graciously agreed to read the entire book to give me feedback on how to portray honestly and carefully.

A shout out goes to both my daughter, as well as my close friend Dakoda Mondragon for listening to me brainstorm endlessly about the storylines for these books. And lastly, I would be lost without my friend and colleague, Liz Stewart, who edits my books. She is also very patient with me because she is forced to listen to more of my endless brainstorming whenever we have lunch.

I would also like to extend my sincere appreciation to Dakoda Mondragon for writing the music to the book trailer. He is an exceptionally talented music producer/composer. You can listen to his music on Spotify and Band Camp: *Crystalskin, Lidocaine Lounge, Android Visions, and 23 Inch Wings.*

And while Mia Bradshaw designed the book covers for the first five Old Maids books, she was unavailable this time. Thanks to Dijartsy who worked from the original art to create the new cover.

Finally, thanks to my 'street team' who help get the word out when the books launch. I'm proud to thank Karen Gilb, Jaynee Bohart, Cindy Warden LaSance, Susy Gaffney, Christie Kathleen Michael Dimon, Venetia Vango, Terri Zura, Jenny Cabuag, Ann Nordquist, Charles Seil, Barb Horton, Becky Nickels, and Anne Harbove.

MY INSPIRATION FOR THIS BOOK

The crime for this book was sparked by a Netflix true crime docuseries where a couple of guys who owned a funeral home did exactly what the Collier brothers do in my book, minus abducting people off the street and killing them. In the Netflix show, they illegally extracted skin and bone from the deceased who came through their funeral home, never telling the families. And they really did use PVC pipe to be able to still have open coffins during the services. When outed, the families were outraged, and they went to prison.

I chose to expand on their crimes by drawing attention to the fact that the homeless population across this country is vulnerable to a variety of predators, not the least of which are people who want to make money off them. The sad truth is that homelessness isn't going away anytime soon. In fact, fluctuations in the economy and global events like the pandemic bring each of us closer and closer to its doors.

Homelessness is a complex issue that requires more than empty platitudes or single solution ideas from our politicians. And I don't expect that anyone reading this post will solve the homeless crisis on their own. There are, however, a myriad of ways you could help. Donate to a homeless organization in your community. Volunteer to write their newsletter, help them run a fundraising event, or volunteer to work in their office. Here's a great idea—instead of asking friends or family for another toaster for your birthday, ask them to donate in your name to a local homeless charity.

It's the character Brenda Valentine, Rudy's attorney, in the book who says "What do they say? Seven out of ten people are one paycheck away from being homeless." Scary, but true.

As a side note: I remember interviewing the CEO of the local Salvation Army back in 2008 (during the recession), asking him if they required people who used their food bank to provide proof of their income or living situation. He said, no. And then he told me that I'd be surprised by the number of people who drove into the food bank in nice cars. Many of these people, he said, had lost jobs and/or their homes and maybe only had their car left. His staff felt the loss of dignity that one feels when they're forced to go to a food bank in order to eat was enough to eliminate the need for proof.

You might remember that the next time you see a homeless person on the corner with a sign that says, "Anything will help." These are real people. Not cartoons or caricatures. They need food, water, housing, safety, and compassion. I keep one-dollar bills in the console of my car just for that purpose and hand them out whenever I can. It's not much, but anything will help.

If you'd like to help an organization that's doing wonderful work to lift up the homeless, consider one of these in the Seattle area. I've worked closely with them both, and they are excellent.

Vision House: https://rb.gy/qmq53u
Birthday Dreams: https://birthdaydreams.org/

ABOUT THE AUTHOR

Ms. Bohart spent 35+ years as a nonprofit executive for three different hospital foundations and finally a regional community foundation. She holds a master's degree in theater, has published in Woman's World, and has a story in *Dead on Demand*, an anthology of ghost stories that remained on the Library Journals bestseller list for six months. She has taught writing through the Continuing Education Program at Green River College for 10+ years and has written for *Patch.com* and the *Renton Reporter*.

No Place Like Home for a Murder is her tenth full-length novel and the sixth in the Old Maids of Mercer Island series. *Inn Keeping with Murder*, the first book in this series, remained in the top 100 ghost stories on Amazon for ten months.

You can check out her other books, including the Detective Giorgio Salvatori mysteries, on Amazon.com. The third book in that series, *The Essence of Murder,* takes Giorgio and Grosvenor, his faithful Basset hound, into the dark worlds of vampirism and dog-fighting rings.

If you would like more information about the author or would like to join Ms. Bohart's mailing list, please visit her website at: www.lynnbohart-author.com. When you join her mailing list you'll be notified of upcoming publications or events. You may also join her author page on Facebook.

ON A PERSONAL NOTE: I bought a tactical pen years ago like the one Aria uses to pin Louie's hand to the floor. I held onto it for some time and finally gave it to my daughter to carry for protection. So, they do exist. I couldn't resist adding it to this story. Especially, as another odd tool for Aria to own.

DO YOU LIKE SCARY STORIES?

Read on for a short story based on the concept that when you dream you are falling, you always wake up before you land, because otherwise you would die. This is the first story in my collection of speculative fiction *Your Worst Nightmare*, available on Amazon.com.

If I Should Die Before I Wake
By Lynn Bohart

A noise from somewhere in the bowels of the old house woke her. It wasn't a thud. Or the house settling on its foundation. The noise was more like a low growl, and it chilled her to the bone.

She sat up in bed, shivering, but not from the cold. The thing was here, and it would come for her tonight.

And, so, she had to run.

In a flash, she was out of bed and heading for the door. No time to get dressed. No time for shoes. No time to wake anyone else in the house. She had to get away from the thing that stalked her.

Scrambling into the hallway, she heard the noise again and slid to a halt. It was closer this time – a raspy, wheezing sound now coming from the basement. Quickly, she turned and ran for the back staircase, hoping to escape through the kitchen.

She hurried to the first floor, bursting into the kitchen, gulping for air. The kitchen was cool and dark, with the faintest odor of fried chicken still hanging in the air from dinner. She glanced down the hallway to where a shadow shifted, as if something large was coming upstairs. Her body flinched, fear oozing like sweat from every pore.

Could the thing hear her? See her?

She didn't think so. It never had before. But surely it could smell her. How could she escape?

She glanced through the kitchen windows. Outside there was nothing. No lights anywhere. There was nowhere to go. She was isolated in upstate New York, in a farmhouse surrounded by open fields, miles from another building or help of any kind. She had only one option.

She had to run.

Without another thought, she dashed for the back door, throwing it open and slamming through the rickety screen door. A moment later, she was down the back steps, heading for the fence that partitioned the yard from the fields beyond. She had just swung the garden gate open when something grabbed her foot, twisting it like a pretzel. She lurched forward in agony before falling and landing on the damp grass. A few feet away, a tangled root grinned at her from a blackened hole. *How could she be so careless?* She pulled up her left pants leg, wincing from the screaming pain in her ankle.

Tears wet her cheeks, filling the corners of her mouth with a salty reminder of how human she was. *Animals didn't cry*, she thought. *Neither would whatever it was that was chasing her.* With a strength that surprised her, she hefted herself off the ground and turned to limp away.

Damn! She had to run. But how could she?

Perhaps, if she could make it into the forest at the south end of the property, she could hide. Still sobbing from the pain, she hurried toward the first few trees, gasping every time she put weight on her injured ankle. She grabbed an old hoe leaning up against a shed and used it as a crutch, hobbling into the relative safety of the grove of evergreens.

Stones and twigs dug into her bare feet, while branches grabbed her night dress and snagged her hair. Anxious to escape, she rebounded from one prickly bush to another, ripping clumps of hair out by the follicles as she hurried past. She stumbled further and further into the dense underbrush, finally toppling over a short fence that encircled the family graveyard and landing face down.

Her ankle throbbed with pain, and she turned over to lay on her back. She was surrounded by decrepit wooden crosses and ivy-covered headstones that tilted at haphazard angles out of the leaf-strewn ground. The moon above seemed to smolder in the night sky, like the dying embers of a campfire.

With a hefty grunt, she struggled to her knees and gazed around. The air was warm, and yet a chill raised goose bumps across her skin. She was surrounded by death. In fact, the Angel of Death sat atop a stone monument at the center of the small graveyard with a provocative grin spread across its granite face.

Dazed, she slumped forward and began to sob. Blood from a deep gash on her cheek ran into her mouth, blotting out for a moment the pain in her ankle with its metallic taste. She dabbed the blood away, feeling grit and dirt between her fingers as she did. She wiped it away on the thin fabric of her night dress.

A minute went by. Then another.

She began to hope she'd lost the thing, but a moment later the sound of the screen door creaking open caused her to suck up a sob and go silent. In the distance, the back stairs of the house groaned under the weight of something big. Squelching a scream, she pulled herself up again.

She had to run.

Her hands and feet stung from the bleeding cuts and bruises, and her night dress was torn and now smeared with blood. Grit and dirt filled her mouth. And she could hardly breathe.

Like a zombie, she stumbled and lurched to the back of the graveyard, pushing through a wooden gate into the underbrush, where shadows from the dark underbelly of the forest enveloped her. She found a narrow path barely visible in the dark and moved further and further away from the house. Finally, she paused, her senses reaching out for sounds she might recognize. The rustle of leaves in the trees above her. The chirp of a cricket.

The snap of a twig.

She froze.

Another snap, but lower this time, as bushes were pushed aside. A heavy footfall.

Her heart nearly burst from her chest. The thing was close—too close. How could it move so quickly?

She had to run.

With a deep breath, she turned and hobbled as fast as she could around a thicket of blackberry bushes, barely catching herself before she went over the edge of a deep ravine. With a gasp, she stopped, her toes hanging over the edge of the cliff, her hand stopping her free fall by grasping the branch of a nearby tree.

This was as far as she could go. *God, why was always like this?* Why did it always have to be like this? With adrenalin buzzing in her ears, the anxiety began to build into a full-blown panic attack.

This was the end.

A shuffling behind her made her body go rigid, as a putrid odor swirled around her, burning her eyes and nose. She began to shake,

---

her muscles twitching uncontrollably. The ground beneath her moved as the thing inched its way towards her, sniffing as it came. When she felt its fetid breath upon her neck, she turned, knowing what she would find.

A hulking, stinking shadow loomed behind her. The thing grabbed for her in the darkness, forcing her to step back. When her foot came off the ledge, her mouth opened in a yawning scream. She grasped for support, and her fingers snagged a tuft of the thing's hair just before both feet slipped off the ledge. As she dropped into empty space, the image of burning red eyes and teeth the size of scissors were indelibly imprinted on her brain.

"Is she dead?" Andrew whispered.

Emily stood over her friend, tears running down her cheeks.

"Yes," she replied. "For several hours, I think."

"What in the world happened to her? Why did she go outside?" Andrew pointed to the scrapes and cuts on her arms and feet. "I mean, it looks like someone beat her up."

"I think she must have run through the forest," Emily replied, looking through the window towards a large pine tree at the edge of the property.

"But why?"

Emily turned her brown eyes toward her husband. "Perhaps something was chasing her."

"You don't believe that."

Emily wrapped her arms around herself for warmth and then turned back to the battered and bruised body of her best friend.

"I'm not sure what I believe."

"But how did she end up back here looking like this? Why wouldn't she have come to us? I mean, we didn't hear anything."

"I don't know. She was troubled. That's why I suggested she visit. I thought getting her out in the country would be a good thing. I never thought something like this would happen."

Andrew picked up a prescription bottle that sat on the nightstand. It had Maddie Renfrew's name on it.

"You said the doctor put her on medication. Maybe she didn't take it tonight," he said, shaking the bottle.

"Perhaps," Emily replied, pushing an errant wisp of hair away from her face. "We may never know what really happened."

Andrew leaned down to touch a large bruise on the side of the young woman's head and pointed to other injuries on the young woman's body.

"Emily, she didn't die of natural causes. Look at this. She's been attacked. Or maybe she fell down the stairs or something. But this isn't normal."

Emily turned toward her husband. "What did you say?"

"I said she must have been attacked."

"No, the other thing."

Andrew's eyes betrayed his confusion. "That she fell? I mean, look at those bruises."

"Fell," Emily murmured. She shivered and hugged her arms more closely around her. "I wonder."

"What?"

"Maddie's mother was diagnosed with schizophrenia and killed herself by jumping from a fourth-floor window when we were in junior high. Maddie started having the dreams shortly after that. They were always the same. Something horrible would chase her to the edge of a cliff, and then she'd fall."

"Then what happened?"

"She'd wake up. My brother used to tease her about it. He said you always wake up before you hit bottom, unless…"

"Unless what?"

Emily looked at her husband again, feeling a knot in her stomach. "He said that if you don't wake up before you hit bottom…you die."

"That's ridiculous."

"Maybe," Emily said, keeping her thoughts to herself. "But I think it's time we call someone."

She reached out and pulled something from between Maddie's tightened fingers before the couple retreated to the hallway, where Emily paused at the door. She glanced at the substance in her hand, and then back at the once lovely young girl who had been her friend. The lifeless body was sprawled across the bed, her nightdress torn and bloody, eyes staring wide, and her mouth drawn open as if suspended in a horrifying scream.

"What's in your hand?" her husband asked.

He had stopped. Emily glanced down at her fingers and then turned to him feeling cautious.

"Fur," she whispered. "Dirty fur. Maddie had it between her fingers."

The couple stared at each other for an awkward moment before a low groan from somewhere in the house startled them both. They froze.

"It's just the house settling," Andrew finally said with a laugh. "Don't go getting spooked on me."

Emily looked down again at the filthy brown hair between her fingers and then back at the body on the bed.

"Yeah...maybe it's just the house," she said quietly.

She stepped away from the door, but her shoe got caught on the carpet runner. She looked down to where her foot had smeared a string of muddy saliva across the hardwood floor and onto the carpet where it got lost amongst the fibers.

""But—maybe not."

The End

OTHER BOOKS BY LYNN BOHART

OLD MAIDS OF MERCER ISLAND SERIES

Inn Keeping with Murder

A Candidate for Murder

A History of Murder

All Roads Lead to Murder

The Key to Murder

DETECTIVE GIORGIO SALVATORI SERIES

Mass Murder

Murder in the Past Tense

The Essence of Murder

STAND ALONE & SHORT STORY BOOKS

Grave Doubts (a novel)

Your Worst Nightmare (anthology of short stories)

Something Wicked (short story)

NONFICTION BOOKS

When Hope is Not Enough

The Little Book of Unconventional Marketing Ideas for Self-published Authors

Made in United States
Troutdale, OR
01/22/2024

17039206R00156